Incident

at the
Bruce Mine
Shaft

Stephen M. Ivancic

Monarch Tree
PUBLISHING

Eau Claire, Wisconsin

Published by Monarch Tree Publishing, P. O. Box 387,
Eau Claire, Wisconsin 54702-0387. (888) 895-7166.
First printing 2014.

ISBN 978-0-9843170-6-6

Library of Congress Control Number: 2014952751

Edited by Elizabeth K. Fischer and Sharon R. Lowry
Layout by Elizabeth K. Fischer

Attention organizations and educational institutions:
Quantity discounts are available on bulk purchases of this book for
educational purposes or fund raising. For information, please contact
Monarch Tree Publishing,
P. O. Box 387, Eau Claire, Wisconsin 54702-0387.
(888) 895-7166.
Fax: (715) 874-6766.
www.monarchtreepublishing.com

Dedication

This story is dedicated to the notion that people and animals matter to the economic, educational, and cultural systems we create in our communities. After all, these systems were intended to support us in a fair and equitable manner as we go about our lives in the pursuit of personal happiness and fulfillment.

Table of Contents

Characters (Partial List)

Joe's Family

Dad Gustav

Mother Irene

Brother Jon

Sister Becky

Uncle Launo

Cousin Niilo

Sara's Family

Dad Martin

Mother Elizabeth

Brother Tommy

Sister Hannah

Uncle Unlucky Andy

Uncle Karl

Cousin Karla

Grandmother Grace

Grandfather Mattai

Friend Arvi

Arvi's Dad Impi

Arvi's Mom Eileen

Arvi's Sister Irene

Friend Elaine

1   Naked Family Sauna

"Where do I put my clothes?" I asked.

"See the nails over there?" Arvi replied.

"Where?"

"On the wall by the mirror."

"Yeah?"

"Hang your clothes there."

"Okay."

Arvi Eskola stripped off his clothes, threw them in a pile, and grabbed a cedar bough by the door. Standing naked, he opened the door between the well-lit breezeway and the dimly lit sauna and, using the cedar bough, motioned me into the sauna while he held the door. I entered naked. I smelled cedar. I felt the hot, moist air. Then I saw two larger figures and a shorter one silhouetted in the low light.

Oh, no!

Arvi hadn't told me his dad, mom, and sister were in the sauna. I had assumed the rest of his family would come after the two of us had finished sweating, rinsed, and dressed. Arvi and I were good friends, but, between school and duties at home, we seldom got a chance to talk. We hadn't talked since summer camp ended at Mesaba Park. Dad's sudden meeting at Taisto Rantala's had given me an opportunity to go to Arvi's after school and catch a ride home with Dad. Arvi had suggested I join him in his family sauna. I had thought a sauna would be refreshing after a long day at school.

Through the steam, the two larger rectangular-shaped folk looked identical: square heads atop three unequal rolls of flesh. Chest, belly, and thighs rose like loaves of bread on the kitchen stove. I assumed they were Impi and Eileen, Arvi's dad and mom. Below the bottom loaf of each shape hung a couple of sausages. Flattened against the sauna bench, they were about two feet above the sauna floor, hanging like they were being smoked. They didn't look appetizing. With Halloween a month away, my imagination transformed their shapes into bales of hay, topped with pumpkins.

I wanted to be polite and say hello, but in the semi-darkness of the sauna I could not see any identifying physical attributes – not even obvious genitalia – to help me decide who was Dad or Mom. I directed my attention to the shorter one on the far right, who I assumed was Irene Eskola, Arvi's sister. I hoped that Irene would have some defining female characteristics I could recognize.

I panicked. *Where should I stare? What if I looked at Irene's crotch while I tried to make up my mind, and I took too long? What if she was as young as I thought she was? Damn! She might not even have pubic hair.* My heart beat accelerated, and my anxiety mounted. My head moved back and forth, back and forth, my eyes scanning. Everyone's legs were close together. I didn't recognize shapes. No one was talking. I was glad we are all sweating, making my trauma less noticeable. *How had I gotten here?*

Sensing my inability to communicate, Arvi announced, "Joe's Dad is in town to meet with Taisto. Joe's riding home with his dad. I asked him to sauna with us while he waits."

Grunts were uttered; no shapes moved. Impi spat on the floor. "Gustav's meeting with Taisto? Good! Come on in, Joe."

The middle pumpkin-headed hay bale slid to the left, creating an opening. Steam rose. Arvi stepped up, turned, and sat down. The shorter one slid over to give Arvi more space. Now there were four. Halloween seemed closer than I had thought. I was haunted.

I realized that there was no room for me with the family on the top bench. I was relieved. After slowly settling down on the lower bench, I leaned back to rest my head against the top bench. *Uh, oh.* I felt something warm and wet against the back of my head. What was that? I didn't know what piece of anatomy rested near me.

Quaking, I mumbled that I was going to the bathroom. I stood up awkwardly and walked as normally as I could muster to the door, opened it, and left. As the door closed behind me, Arvi's dad said something about a coffee can or bucket next to the wood stove. Impi probably wanted to gather some water and throw it on top of the rocks to create steam. Quickly, I put on my clothes and headed out into the cold.

I knew some Finnish families sauna naked together and had done it that way for generations, but that was my first experience of nakedness with another family. Since my dad worked long hours and Mom didn't feel well sometimes, my family did not sauna together. We did not have a family sauna tradition.

After a sauna, the participants ran out steaming hot and plunged into a lake. This action applied dramatic temperature change on all their dearest body parts. As I stepped outside the breezeway, I noticed a garden hose hooked up to the outside faucet, turned on with cold water running out. I guessed that was Impi's improvisation for the missing lake with an icy plunge.

Since I had not been in the sauna very long, I didn't need to cool down with water from the hose. Before Impi or Arvi came out to fill the bucket, I hurried away from their house. Dad had said that he would pick me up at Arvi's, but, since I left the sauna early, I started walking. I remembered hearing Dad say Taisto Rantala lived at 317 Third Street North.

That might have sounded easy to find, but it wasn't for me. I could tell where I was in the country, but I wasn't in the country now. I was in town, in Arvi's neighborhood. I felt lost. Finding my way around the area where I lived, east of Hibbing, was easy. Each home or farm had different types of trees and sizes of fields and farming areas. I knew what each family's location looked like, and no two families' homes were the same. The way a home looked was its address. My cousin Niilo had three large maple trees at the entrance of the road to his place. In my mind, Niilo's home address was my mental picture of the three maple trees. Andy Ronala, Sara Niemi's uncle, had built a stone wall along the old cow path behind his place. It ended at a half-burnt cow barn not too far from the house. On the other side of the barn was a group of seven Norway pines. I thought of Andy's address as group of pine trees with a dilapidated barn.

I preferred to visualize addresses as natural objects in landscapes with each address being a picture rather than a number. Each picture had trees, stones, and arrangements of buildings and nature. Those were interesting ways of remembering where someone lived rather than numbers painted on signs.

317 Third Street North. A number like 317 and words *Third Street*

North made city people feel comfortable, like things were under control. But I didn't. This number, or any number, was too exact. There was no room for interpretation. There was no poetry or symbolism or imagination involved.

These thoughts brought me back to one winter morning in the woods when my father tried to connect the words north, south, east, and west to the world around me. In fourth grade geography class, I had been learning about north, south, east, and west on a map of the United States. But Dad wanted me to connect those four words to where I lived and walked every day. I hadn't forgotten that lesson.

We had just walked into the woods when Dad stopped and picked up a stick. He drew a vertical line and then crossed it with a horizontal line in the snow. Together, they had looked like a giant plus sign. I had thought, *Maybe we're going to add something.*

I looked closer.

On the top of the vertical line he scratched an N and on the bottom an S. "Joe, the N is north, and the S is south."

Though I had first thought we were going to add, I then realized we were going to do something different. I said nothing. With my dad, if I didn't respond to a point he made, he would wait and say it again in a different way. After the second explanation, I would tell him I understood.

Actually, I was hoping he would lapse into a Civil War story. We were studying Yankees and Confederates in school so I knew Yankees were from the north. Minnesota had been a Yankee state. This wasn't about the North and the South from Civil War history, though. As I expected, my silence prompted him to continue the geography lesson in a different way. Instead of making another statement or asking me a question, on the right of the horizontal line he drew the letter E and on the left the letter W. Now I saw a large addition sign in the snow with N, S, W, and E surrounding it. I was confused. I didn't say anything. Dad broke the silence. "I am going to connect the picture I drew in the snow with the woods we are standing in."

I remained quiet.

My silence urged him to explain further. "If you look at the drawing in the snow, the sun rises in the morning by the letter E." He placed the stick on the E. "In the evening it sets down on the letter W." He pointed the stick at the W.

"What you drew is like directions on a map of the United States. We are studying the Civil War right now in school. I know this stuff," I replied.

Dad was silent. He didn't like me telling him I knew something, especially when he had been trying to teach me. To him, learning was serious. He didn't like my saying something in the wrong way or giving an answer that wasn't correct. I let my smile fade and remained quiet. His anger began to rise.

"We're talking about getting lost, Joe."

I didn't respond. I looked down. His anger increased.

"Someday you will need to know how to find your way back home when you are out in the woods … alone ... without me. You don't know when that might happen. What if I get hurt? Cut my leg with an axe? Or you wander off chasing after a rabbit and get lost … "

Dad paused a few seconds.

"Now, Joe, look at the sun in the sky. Come on, look up."

I did.

"The sun is right above us now 'cause it is lunchtime."

"Dad, I thought I was going to find out where I am in the woods so I will not be lost, not when lunch time is." I knew that wasn't the right response.

"Damn it! Why are you such a wise ass?"

Dad tightened his grip on the stick. He hit the snow. Snow scattered. My father's face bunched up. He swallowed air, held it, and exhaled slowly. "Why don't you just listen for a minute before you start asking questions?"

I waited a little longer and then replied in a slow, steady voice, "Okay. The sun is above us when we are eating lunch."

"Yes. When we finish eating our lunch and look back up into the sky, the sun will have moved. It will have moved west."

Dad then pointed to the W in the snow. I waited for him to connect lunch with how I was to find my way out of the woods when I was lost or he was hurt. He didn't continue so I decided to say something. I knew that a question could put me in a place where I would be in trouble quickly, and I might have gotten hit, but… "Okay," I bit my lip. "So if we are sitting eating lunch in the middle of the plus sign where the line that connects the E and W crosses with the line that is the N and the S, Dad, where are we?"

Dad stared at me for a few seconds, and then he shifted his gaze to one of the large balsam trees next to the frozen swamp. I was sure his foot was tapping up and down inside his large boot. He spit.

"I'm sorry. I was just making a joke, Dad."

"You are a joke."

I'd heard him say that before. The sting was long gone. I knew better than to ask stupid questions, but I was bored and tired. I didn't know why he couldn't have had some fun. He was serious all the time.

"Joe, the sun is a marker that marks the time of day, but it also marks where we are located in the woods."

"Thanks," I said politely.

"If we are in the woods after lunch and you and I get separated, look up in the sky and locate the sun. It will be lower in the sky because it is getting ready to set. The direction it sets is west." He took his stick and pointed at the W marked off in the snow.

My thoughts went back to school and the map of the United States. America was settled on the East coast, to the right of the plus sign, where Dad had drawn the E. California was in the West, where the sun set. We lived in the North where the N was. The Confederates were by the S. Dad coughed. He was ready for more of the lesson.

"You are by yourself in the woods. The sun is setting, and you want to go east to get home. What do you do?"

This was the test. I knew I better not fail.

"I would turn around, have my back to the setting sun, and walk toward where the sun had come up 'cause that is east."

Dad smiled. I had passed the test.

I never forgot that explanation. Since then I connected lunchtime to the sun above my head and west as where the sun moved after I had eaten lunch. The plus sign in the snow popped into my mind whenever I was in the woods and had to figure out which way I had to go to get home. But now it was late afternoon; the sun was setting in the west; and I had to find Rantala's house. With the sun to my left, I knew I was headed north.

I wondered, *Can the plus sign idea work here? How will I find 317 Third Street North? If I do, how will I know it is Taisto Rantala's house? I had never been there and did not know any distinguishing trees, buildings, or landscape features to help me recognize it.*

I was glad it was Friday night, and I didn't have to go to school the next day. I wouldn't have to talk to Arvi about why I didn't stay to sauna. I wouldn't have to say "Hi" to his sister Irene, either, especially after seeing her naked. Then it occurred to me. I had been so worried about seeing them naked I had forgotten they were staring at my nakedness. I remembered that I had been standing in the light from the breezeway. They saw more of me than I did of them. That thought made me even more grateful tomorrow was Saturday.

How will I find 317 Third Street North?

I took a deep breath and remembered Arvi's explanation of streets and avenues. He had told me to imagine Main Street in downtown Hibbing as a line connecting east and west, like the second line Dad had drawn in the snow. By that time, I had walked from Arvi's house to Main Street. When I stood on Main Street with east to my right and west to my left, I was facing north. From that position, I figured out what streets were north and south. If I walked one block forward from Main Street, toward the N on the plus sign, I would find First Street North. If I walked backward one block south of Main Street, I would come across First Street South.

I figured Dad must be three blocks north of Main Street because Taisto's house was on Third Street North. I headed north from Main Street.

Arvi had told me houses had numbers and that they were part of a system. First, they were always in hundreds or thousands, like 317 or

126 or 4508. The higher the number, the further away I was from Main Street or downtown. I guessed there was some rule about what side of the street determined whether the house had an odd and even number. I didn't remember rules well, but I liked the idea that streets, avenues, and house numbers had logical patterns.

As I walked, my thoughts drifted from streets and avenues to animal trails in the woods. They were more interesting than streets and avenues. Animal trails weren't in straight lines. They followed the shape of the forest floor, trees, and other objects like large rocks or low-lying creeks. They were connected to nature, not cut into or paved over the forest floor. Animal trails were the most obvious in the winter, so that season was the best for tracking wild animals on the trails they made. Rabbit trails were the easiest to identify.

The snow preserved the footprints of rabbits in a unique way. As they hopped through the forest, their two large rear feet landed first, followed by their two small round front feet. Together the four footprints made a face in the snow. The rear feet were the eyes. In back of their side-by-side rear footprints were two smaller ones, one on top of the other. The front feet became the nose and mouth for the snow face. Arvi thought of their print as a sling shot. The large feet were the uprights, and the two front feet were the handle.

I thought my father was teasing me when he described his method of looking for the snow face as a way for finding rabbit sign in the woods, but it worked. What also assured me I was on a rabbit trail were small marble-shaped droppings in between or sometimes on the faces. These were rabbit poop or smart pills, as my dad jokingly called them. Dad said when he was a kid his brother Launo talked Impi into eating these frozen rabbit turds. I didn't believe that.

Once I was able to recognize, follow, and trail rabbits, Dad taught me about snaring them. Rabbits were an important food source for us. Winter was the best time to snare them. A snare was a piece of wire I hung like a noose from a branch or stick over a rabbit trail. The rabbit could not see the wire and unknowingly jumped through the hoop. Typically, its shoulders caught in the wire hoop. This movement closed the noose around the rabbit's neck. Once snared, the animal's body froze. A frozen rabbit body didn't spoil or rot. This meant I could wait until the weekend to check my snares and harvest the caught rabbits. On an average winter weekend I snared four rabbits.

The first time I took a frozen rabbit carcass from a snare, I was surprised by the animal's transformation from a soft, furry, warm creature to a stiff, hard, chunk of meat. I carried a gunny sack into the woods with me when I checked my snares. After several frozen carcasses were in the sack, they made clinking sounds when the bodies rattled against each other. I had thought that odd. Arriving at home, I left the bunnies outside by the back door until Mom was ready to clean and prep them for a meal. Rabbit stew was my favorite.

One winter day I was walking past the barn toward the house with four rabbits, and Dad was just coming out of the barn. The miners had recently had a run-in with the mine owners. That was on Dad's mind. He heard the rabbits clinking in my sack. "Humph!" Dad sneered. "Those rabbits are just like miners. They were minding their own business and got trapped in your snare. The miners work hard and get caught up in the greed of the mine owners!"

Dad often found comparisons in everyday situations to the struggle of the miners with the mine owners.

Pulling my focus back to my surroundings, I looked up and saw that I was at Third Street. I peered at the nearest house number and saw 303. *Okay,* I thought, *I am close to 317. I have almost found Dad.*

About five houses down, I saw Dad's truck. Parked behind it was the Hibbing police car. *What were the police doing there?* I wondered.

I hesitated, uncertain what to do. Before I made my decision, the front door of the house opened. Sheriff McFarland stepped out, stomped to the police car, slammed the car door, and sped off. Was Dad in trouble? Dad and Taisto followed closely behind. Dad cupped his hands around his mouth and yelled at the disappearing squad car. Taisto stood in the front doorway. Suddenly, he hit the door frame with his fist. I thought he might have split the jamb. I froze. What was going on?

I crossed the street to Dad. He and Taisto were talking. Dad glanced over and gave me a stay-out-of-my-way look. Skirting around them, I climbed into the truck cab. I sat there, watched them, and speculated about their conversation. As if to keep their conversation private, he and Rantala moved further from the truck and continued talking.

What imaginary conspiracy was Dad concerned about now?

2   Orchestra Pit

Being Sara Niemi, the daughter of the local opera star, is double-edged, I thought. *I'm so proud of Mom and love to hear her sing in the hall, but I miss her when she is rehearsing and performing. Mom's been gone more and more as her fame has grown. I don't mind helping Dad, Grandma, and Grandpa with my sister Hannah and brother Tommy. Getting to see her perform tonight is a special treat, though. Grandma's taking me for my sixteenth birthday.*

I was anxious. "Mummo Grace, let's go."

She responded positively. "I'll see if Isoisa (Grandpa) is okay with Hannah and Tommy. We will go out the back door Storeen ja kujalla saliin. (and down the alley to the hall.)"

I watched Grandma climbed the stairs to check on Grandpa Mattai and tried to wait patiently.

When I was younger, I had leaned against the painted wood railing at the bottom of the stairs and waited. Pressing my face against the spindles, I made shadows on the wall. Sometimes I took my left hand, raised it up next to my head, and wiggled my fingers as I moved my hand away from me. I imagined the flickering shadows as a grouse flying by flapping her wings. Once I put my right hand next to my left hand and placed both on top of my head. When I wiggled all ten fingers, I imagined worms were crawling all over my head. I laughed.

I was startled out of my reminiscing when Grandma's shadow covered mine. She was done checking on Mattai. "Menkaamme." (Let's go.)

I got my sweater and Grandma's scarf. Grandma Grace took her scarf from my hand and threw it around her neck, letting the longer end cascade into place against her blouse. She smiled. We left through the back screen door. The hall was two blocks away. From our backyard, I already heard the music and singing. Grandma Grace and I walked down the alley toward the music.

We passed a large dog. His shadow was huge! I was quiet. Dad had told me never to panic. When I was younger, he had said that a dog had three positions for his lips and mouth. "When a dog's lips are pulled back so we see all his teeth, we are the most afraid," he had begun. "But remember, it takes energy for the dog to hold this position. He won't hold it long; he's just threatening."

The second position was also safe. "That is when a dog is relaxed; his lips are partially open. Sometimes you will see the dog's tongue and hear causal breathing." Dad had explained that the third position signaled caution. "If a dog's lips are straight, like a line, and you hear a low persistent growl, not a bark or a yip, but a low gurgling sound, you are in danger. This dog is neither relaxed nor exerting energy. It has decided to strike. He is pumping up and storing strength for the attack." Dad had added, "This is the same for a wolf."

My father had said no one knew the trigger which caused a dog or wolf to lunge, bite down, and break open skin. Was it a smell we had? A motion we made? A sound we emitted? Since we didn't know what mechanism triggered the attack, we needed to be careful.

Joe Koivu said it more simply. "Dogs can smell your fear."

Grandma and I watched as the dark beast looked toward the open door at the backside of the bar. Loud voices were yelling; other dogs were barking; and smells like a cow barn early in the morning after a hot summer night hung in the air. The alley here never smelled fresh. Even by the Work People's Co-op Store where we left the trash for the garbage pickers, the smell was not rotten like this. At the Mesaba Park Festival and Campgrounds, we burned our garbage, but that smelled sweet, not like this alley's stench. Maybe there was more fresh air in the forest.

My thoughts were interrupted by Grandma Grace, "You are special, Sara. So is your mother. She has a beautiful voice."

"Did you sing with your mother, Grandma?" I wondered.

"Hiljeta, hiljeta, (Hush, Hush) Sara. I have told you before – my mother Maria did not sing. We didn't have halls in Finland. We sang in our houses with our friends. Everyone brought their own instruments."

"How did you get all those people in your house?"

"Se oli erilainen siella. (It is different there.)"

"Grandma Grace, nobody at school goes to halls to sing, dance, and play. They do it anywhere they want."

Grandma didn't want to respond to my questions. "Olemme siella. (We are there)," she announced.

Light, happy sounds and sweet smells brightened the alley from the hall as Grandma Grace pulled open the door to the back stage area. My ears filled with lyrics from *H.M.S. Pinafore*:

> *Hardly ever will I be untrue to thee.*
> *Then give three cheers, and one cheer more*
> *For the former Captain of the Pinafore.*
> *For he loves Little Buttercup, dear Little Buttercup,*
> *Though I could never tell why;*
> *But still he loves Buttercup, poor Little Buttercup,*
> *Sweet Little Buttercup, aye!*

Dad was standing beside the door. Seeing us in the doorway, he reached over and held the door open for Grandma Grace and me. "Happy Birthday, Sara."

I flashed Dad a big smile.

As we entered, we received all kinds of greetings and hugs.

"Hyvää iltaa, Sara. (Good evening, Sara)"

"Hauska nähdä taas. (Nice to see you again.)"

"Meillä oli ikävä sinua! (We missed you.)"

Amid this commotion, I heard my cousin, "Sara. Missä olet? (Where are you?) Sara. Missä olet? (Where are you?)"

That was what I wanted to hear. I yelled back, "Karla, I am over here!"

Karla Ronala responded, "Sara, hurry, they are almost done! You will miss my crash."

I ran to my cousin.

When I attended a performance Grandma and Dad let me sit in the orchestra pit with my cousin Karla. She got to crash the cymbals in the finale, *Oh Joy, Oh Rapture Unforeseen*.

Viola Turpeinen directed the musicians. He looked like a drunk vigorously waving a fly swatter. While standing on his toes trying to hit an imaginary fly high above his head, Viola weaved left and bobbed right, going back and forth like a marionette dancing. His hair was wet, and, as the musical had progressed, he had exposed more and more of his forehead by pushing back his sweaty hair. The top of his head looked like a triangular hair piece.

Grace stayed behind the stage next to my father. "Rakastan sinua laatuaan Isoäiti. (Love you, kind Grandmother.) You are a little late, Grace," Dad noted.

"Hush poikani! (Hush my son.) I didn't know how comfortable Mattai was about being left with the children," she admitted.

"He was glad to give Sara a chance to hear her mother as a birthday present. You worry too much." Martin took a deep breath before bringing up the next subject. "Well, Jacque has his son Ian here tonight. Elizabeth is hoping Sara can meet him."

"Jacque!" Grace replied. "Look! Sara's found Karla already. They are sitting together in the musician's pit!"

I noticed Grandma point in my direction and assumed she and Dad were discussing me. I slumped in my seat. If they wanted me to do something, I wasn't moving until Karla crashed the cymbals.

Neither Grandma nor Grandpa worked. Sometimes they helped out in the store, but mostly, they watched me, my brother, and sister. I liked having them with us. We were a little crowded, but someone was always around, and Grandma cooked all the time.

Martin and Elizabeth Niemi, my father and mother, were part of the Finnish peoples who immigrated to the United States in the late 1800's. Both were active in the Hibbing, Minnesota, Work People's Theater and Hall and the Work People's Co-op Store. The buildings were a few blocks apart on Main Street.

Just like other Finnish immigrants, the Finns in Hibbing had built halls in town. These halls hosted music, lectures, and social study discussions. If the Finnish population was large like ours, orchestras and brass bands were added, and plays and musicals were developed.

In addition to the hall, our Mesaba Range Co-op Federation had purchased 120 acres around North Star Lake about five miles outside of Hibbing. The Federation named this plot the Mesaba Park Festival and Campground. The park was chartered for the elevation of the cultural, educational, and economic position of the wage worker and working farmer. Normally, only Finns gathered at the park.

I met and got to know Joe Koivu at the park.

Before Grandpa and Grandma Levanieman lived with us above the Work People's Co-op Store, they had their own land and house just outside town. When Dad was busy at the co-op and Mother was practicing at the opera hall, I had stayed with them.

Grandma's kitchen at her house was lit with kerosene lamps; their flues were soiled black. A sour yeasty smell muddied with fish oil hung in the air. Large pots, lots of pans, and two black iron skillets were stacked on the white chipped metal table to the right of the sink. Among these were spatulas, soup scoopers, and knives. As a young girl, I had wondered why Grandma didn't keep all her cooking gear in her cabinets instead of leaving them all piled up. Mom always had us put the dishes away right after we washed and dried them. *Didn't Grandma care about how her kitchen looked? Why didn't Grandpa tell her to put things away?*

I wondered what this pile had looked like to visitors. Most visitors came in the back door and had to pass through the kitchen on their way to the living and dining rooms. I felt bad for the mess people saw in her kitchen as they walked through.

Had Grandma put things away, I would have lost my favorite hiding place when I was younger, the laundry tub. Two feet high and three feet long with rounded ends and worn wood handles, the tub sat on the floor further into the house. Being out of the way and in the corner, I liked to sneak over and peer into the tub. Sometimes I crawled in. The smell of Ivory Soap Flakes calmed me as I curled up and appreciated the quiet.

The wall behind the tub had no photographs or paintings, and I made it my movie screen. Curled in my tub, I watched the black images of Grandpa, Grandma, and the neighbors flicker back and forth against the dark mountain of kitchen utensils. Kaveri, the German shepherd, was not tall enough to cast a shadow, and I never knew where he was. When I least expected it, Kaveri stuck his head into the tub and licked my face. I always smiled at him. Once I had held a wooden spoon and swung at Viola Turpeinen's shadow. The spoon had flown out of my hand and hit his pants leg. Without hesitation, he had kept on walking.

As I watched Viola conduct the orchestra, I remembered how I had held my breath in anticipation of being discovered in my hiding place. He reminded me of a praying mantis: tall, slight build, and glasses sitting on the end of an oversized, elongated nose. His looks bugged me. He had attended music school in Vienna with Johan Julius Christian Sibelius and loved to brag about it. In 1899 under his new French-influenced name, Jean, Sibelius had finished the composition *Finlandia*. Although Finland was still under Russian rule, *Finlandia* became the song of Finnish nationalism. Viola talked about *Finlandia* like he had a part in its creation just because he went to school with Sibelius. He mistakenly thought this fictional association prompted respect from us.

Tonight, though, he was focused on *HMS Pinafore*.

3   Baby Chicks

Josephine. When love is alive and hope is dead!

My mother's soprano voice singing this chorus line from *Sorry Her Lot Who Loves Too Well* stirred emotions deep inside me. I wiped a tear from my eye. I didn't know how to explain the feelings I had during this scene. They were near that place in me where I had the stomach flu and had to bend over and curl up. They were like honey settled at the bottom of the pores in a slice of Grandma's warm homemade bread. Tasting and eating this sweetness was messy.

Captain. My child, I grieve to see that you are a prey to melancholy. You should look your best today, for Sir Joseph Porter, K.C.B., will be here this afternoon to claim your promised hand.

Josephine. Ah, father, your words cut me to the quick. I can esteem – reverence - venerate Sir Joseph, for he is a great and good man; but, oh, I cannot love him! My heart is already given.

Captain. (aside) It is then as I feared. (aloud) Given? And to whom? Not to some gilded lordling?

Josephine. No, father - the object of my love is no lordling. Oh, pity me, for he is but a humble sailor on board your own ship!

Captain. Impossible!

Josephine. Yes, it is true - too true.

Captain. A common sailor? Oh fie!

Josephine. I blush for the weakness that allows me to cherish such a passion. I hate myself when I think of the depth to which I have stooped in permitting myself to think tenderly of one so ignobly born, but I love him! I love him! I love him! (weeps)

Genuine! I thought.

My mother's face glowed as she said these lines. I saw the same aura around her face when she looked at my father at home. Mom brightened even more when they held each other and danced on the porch. I had these loving images buried in the hope chest of my heart for my love. I couldn't wait to lift the lid and let the love orbs float out, surrounding Joe and me.

My Uncle Andy Ronala played in the orchestra with my Uncle Karl. Andy's smile reflected the twinkles in his eyes. He was the middle child in his family: quiet, helpful, unnoticeable, with no idiosyncrasies or obvious rough edges. He seemed content with himself and his place in life. Since Andy had lost his job in the Oliver Mining Strike of 1906 and two years later lost his wife Lillian during the birth of their daughter Karla, I called him Unlucky.

Unlucky had been a fuser in the underground mines. He lit the fuse for the blast charges in Soudan. After lighting, he raced through long, round red-orange tunnels of iron ore veins yelling, "Vaara! Vaara! (Danger, Danger!)" I wondered if Karla had ever worried about her dad's dangerous job but didn't dare ask her.

After losing his job, Unlucky lived outside Hibbing and traveled to the Alango area to help Finnish farmers and perform odd jobs. A tall figure and full of good will, Unlucky looked out for others. Joe thought of Unlucky as a kind of Robin Hood. He roamed the range, providing for the common good and avoiding the bad sheriff of Nottingham.

My thoughts about Unlucky were interrupted as I noticed Viola wink at Karla. She raised the cymbals. Steadily and slowly Viola raised his arms upward. At the height of his reach, he stopped moving his arms and winked again. Karla crashed the cymbals together. Cheers and applause ripped the air as the audience jumped to their feet. *Oh Joy, Oh Rapture Unforeseen* ended the performance.

I watched Jacque Trompeure', our producer and director, and Viola head to the front lobby. After every performance, they did this in order to meet and greet the people in attendance. This interaction was an important part of the role that theater played in our Finnish community. The lobby was always a buzz of conversations mixed with clouds of cigarette smoke. Mom said that we sold more concessions after a performance than all that were sold before and during the intermissions. The Work People's Theater and Hall was a public setting where we Finns felt safe to be ourselves and not worry about harassment from the townspeople.

Every night of a play or a meeting, Sheriff McFarland stood in the lobby. He watched everyone.

I noticed Viola associated with the new immigrants and Jacque with any non-Finnish attendees. This month was the first time we had larger groups of non-Finnish attendees in our opera hall. It was also the first non-Finnish play Jacque had directed.

After the musical ended, Karla and I climbed further into the pit and played the different instruments. My fingers were short, which made the violin's neck hard for me to hold and play the strings at the same time. The first time I tried, I got the bow caught in my hair. I preferred the trumpet. The trombone was too long and the tuba too big. Buzzing my lips in the trumpet's mouthpiece was easy for my strong lungs.

Sometimes I wondered if Dad ever wanted to play in the orchestra. Seeing him play the upright bass as mother's soprano voice reached out to the back of the auditorium would have been romantic! Watching them working together under stage lights would have caused my love orbs to spin frantically out of control.

My mother interrupted our play. "Sara. Come on, Sara, let's go."

I said a quick goodbye to Karla, climbed out of the pit, and caught up with Mom who had started down the aisle toward the exit.

"We need to hurry tonight. Dad is not coming home until late, and we have to box up the chicks for tomorrow. Members will be picking them up after church."

We left the hall and headed down the alley to the store to sort and box baby chicks. I loved working with my mother after a performance. She was always in a good mood with songs and jokes. As we entered the store, I heard the chicks' cacophony.

"Sara, the order list is on the front counter. Would you get it please? I am going to the back of the store and start unloading."

"Yes, Mom."

I pushed around sheets of paper scattered on the counter. Gosh! What a mess! I wondered, *How does anything ever get done right? Items must be forgotten and lost!*

I rustled through another pile, but I still didn't find the list. I heard mother yell impatiently, "Forget the list, Sara. I know the Johnsons need two dozen, the Rantala's always get four dozen, and Grandma needs a half. Why don't you start by packing Grandma's? She doesn't mind if we give her the smaller ones."

Hurrying to the back of the store, I found Mom had opened the shipping crate of baby chickens. I looked into it and saw hundreds of yellow cotton balls packed together. They reminded me of a meadow in the spring covered with yellow dandelion blossoms. My sister Hannah liked to pick dandelion blossoms and rub their centers onto her cheeks. Sometimes she smeared the color up to her forehead and around her ears. When Hannah was done, she looked just like a clown! At times she pressed too hard, and the green leaves made thin streaks across her face like the whiskers on a cat. If Halloween had been in the spring, her costume would have been all set!

Chicks were not like dandelions, however. When I touched their yellow feathers, the color stayed on their warm bodies. Their wings were like small pancakes or ping pong paddles. They stuck to each of their round sides. Their baby fluff didn't feel like the feathers in my pillows. As the chicks grew older, their feathers' quills would harden, especially after they started laying eggs.

We picked up our chicks north of Duluth at the Twig Hatchery. From there it was a short ride home. When we received a chick shipment, one or two or three might have been dead or dying. This wasn't because they were sick. Some chicks just weren't hardy. They were stressed from being shipped and bounced around in the cold temperatures of early spring. Usually, we didn't lose many chicks.

Mom wanted me to care for the weak birds as best as I could. If they died, I was to bury them, just like I would any other pet.

Although Mother had asked me to leave the umbilical cords alone, I liked to pick them off if they were still attached. These thin, black strings were stuck on their feathers near their rears, like loose threads on a dress or blouse. Mother maintained they would fall off before the chicks were sold.

Baby chicks were big poopers. Sometimes droppings caked up and plugged a chick's rear end so she couldn't poop. When I spotted this situation, I took a warm wet rag, placed it on the chick's butt, and softened the poop. Then I used the end of a matchstick to knock off the softened blockage. If this didn't work, I gave her a bath. Dipping and holding her bottom in warm water for a while softened the droppings so they floated away. Then I dried the chick and returned her to the other chicks. If a chick was always poopy, one of us checked her every couple of hours and wiped her butt while the poop was fresh.

Because chicks pooped so much, we lined the bottom of the pick-up boxes with newspapers. This prevented slippery surfaces from building up. If a chick slipped, she could hurt her legs and have permanent deformities. An injured chick was like a runt to the rest of her sisters. The other chicks would turn on her and peck her to death.

I had learned from experience that baby chicks were easy to catch and didn't bite. I reached into the box, took three from the back corner, and carefully set them in a shoebox with the other three. I placed the cover on, wrapped a red shoe lace around the box, and tied the ends into a bow. That's how Grandma wanted her chicks packed.

Then I thought about how Grandma handled these chicks after they grew up.

My mind wandered back to Grandma's kitchen at her house. Against the far wall was a refrigerator. To its right was a large, flat surface for food preparation. Only she worked there. Since she prepared more than one dish at a time, I wondered how she saw things in the dim light. On the afternoon I was remembering, she had egg noodle dough stretched out to dry on top of the board. A white-speckled blue colander full of baby lettuce leaves sat next to a small bowl of scissor-cut chive tips. Beside them was a chicken lying atop green onions.

Grandma blanched the chicken in hot water in order to pluck the feathers. I guess that's why chickens didn't swim; their feathers might have fallen off. While the water boiled, she grabbed the chicken by its feet with her left hand, immersed it in the hot water, and used the long wooden spoon to hold the chicken's body under water. She didn't want it float to the top.

She pushed the carcass around the pan to soak all the feathers thoroughly. After a short while, she removed the chicken from the water and set it on the counter. I jumped onto a nearby chair, and both of us grabbed handfuls of feathers and pulled them out. It stunk. We usually took thirty minutes to pluck a chicken. If there were a lot of pinfeathers, we took longer.

Grandpa didn't like pin feathers floating in the chicken noodle soup so we had to be sure to remove the pin feathers that our fingers didn't grasp. Grandma lit a stick match and handed it to me to hold. I took it in my right hand. Grabbing my hand firmly in hers, she steadily moved my hand up and down the fowl's breast, close to the skin. Wisps of smoke appeared and vanished with a spitting noise. These were the tiny down feathers burning away. I liked it when they turned black. Using our hands, we brushed all the ashes off the chicken corpse and wiped our hands on our aprons. I had thought everyone did this with chickens.

I found out that wasn't true when I wrote in English class about plucking chickens with Grandma. My teacher Mrs. Kohler got upset. The idea of raising chickens so that Grandpa could chop their heads off and let them flop around the yard for a while was disturbing to her. When I added the part about taking the hen and placing her into boiling water to scald the skin, the activity became sadistic. I hadn't yet mentioned burning the pin feathers off. "This is not what young ladies should be doing!" Mrs. Kohler admonished.

Elaine Schwartz told me not to listen to what the teacher said. Her Rabbi Morris Greenberg was a holy man in her church, and he killed chickens. Instead of chopping the head off, he used a special knife to cut the throat open quickly so the blood gushed out. *Shochet kashrut* or *Shechita* was the word Elaine said he used for this. Elaine hadn't seen Rabbi Morris do it, but I believed her.

I tried to picture these chicks all grown up. "Mom, how come chicks don't look like chickens?"

"What, Sara?"

"I said how come chicks don't look like chickens?"

"Don't be silly. They do, dear. They have two legs, feathers, a beak, and cheep."

"Well, they could be baby geese or ducks…"

"No, Sara, then they would quack up."

"Funny mother. Ha, ha. Is the reason we sell chicks because they are cheap?"

"Not quite as funny, Sara."

We finished sorting and packing and washed our hands.

Chicken poop could be dangerous, more poisonous than other animals' poop. I knew that if I stepped in a cow pie with my bare feet, nobody got upset. No one made me rush into the house and wash my feet. But after we were done packing chicks or when I came out of the chicken coop from picking eggs, I had to wash my hands and the eggs right away. I guessed not all poop was the same.

4   Duluth Opportunity

As we dried our hands, Mom took time for a conversation. "Did you enjoy the play tonight, Sara?"

I was surprised Mom would ask. "I always do, Mom. Your voice is pretty."

"Thanks, Sara. I'm glad you could come for your birthday!"

"Hearing you sing made my day special." I paused and then mentioned a subject that had been bothering me. "Dad said you might be going to Duluth and singing there."

"Oh, he did. Well, I haven't decided yet. That would mean you would have to miss more school to take care of the house while I am gone."

"You know I can do that. I do it already for you… and still get good grades."

"Yes, Sara, but now I am here to help and check on you. Duluth is almost two hours away."

I protested, "Dad said you still won't get paid money."

"Sara..."

"Well, that's what he said."

"So, what do you think? Do you think you can be me if I am gone?"

"I won't sing at the opera hall for you!"

"I was hoping you would be Josephine."

"I'm not tall enough, and I don't look like you."

"But you sing well." Mom smiled at my reaction. "Sara, I meant, do you think you can spend more time caring for Hannah and Tommy if I start singing in Duluth?"

Mom made me nervous. I thought all this talk about moving to Duluth was just talk. If she moved without Dad that would…I didn't know what it would mean.

"Sara, let me tell you something.   Jacque asked me if I can work as his assistant."

"Aren't you already his assistant? You make sure everybody has costumes; you make up the rehearsal schedules; you're always collecting and counting the music sheets …   Why can't Mr. Viola Turpeinen do that stuff? He's the pit orchestra conductor. Let Viola do it; his name sounds like an instrument. He should do it!"

"Sara, Viola was the director of the Finnish National Metropolitan Symphony back in Finland, so he didn't have to take care of responsibilities like that."

Confused, I asked, "Mom, are you saying Viola doesn't know how to help out?"

"No. I'm saying he had assistants who helped him. Musicians who wanted to be in the symphony would work for him for nothing. They would do anything to get close to him in hopes of getting a chance to sit."

"I think he's creepy."

"Sara, listen to me. When I become Jacque's assistant, I'll be paid to do the same things as those who worked for free for Viola."

"Mother, that's great! Wait till Dad hears. He'll be so proud!"

"Sara, don't tell Dad! This will be our little secret. I plan on buying extra Christmas gifts with the money I earn. If you keep our secret, I'll wake you up early Christmas morning, and you can help me sneak in the gifts and place them under the tree."

"I can't wait, Mom!"

"When Dad, Hannah, and Tommy wake up and see all the presents, we can both yell, 'Surprise!' Can you imagine the looks on their faces?"

We smiled at our secret and took one last check on the chicks before leaving. Thinking to play a joke on Dad, I picked up one chick and tucked it in my pocket. We headed upstairs to our apartment. As we climbed the stairs, I thought about how I loved the co-op during Christmas season. Dad set up a huge blue spruce tree in the front of the store, and our family decorated it with ornaments made by children of the co-op's members. When the toys started arriving at the store in November, Karla and I handled them. Dad gave us the responsibilities of placing them under the tree, setting-up doll houses, wrapping certain special requests, and storing others until members were ready to pay for and pick them up. These activities allowed us to see all the toys before anyone else.

Late Sunday afternoons after the Sunday studies and federation and co-op member meetings were over and everyone had left, Karla and I would spend time in the store with the toys. Karla was skilled at opening and closing the toy boxes in such a way that no one could tell which toys we had touched. Dad didn't know Karla and I did this, only mother did, which made me love Mom even more. Dolls were my favorite. I liked their shiny faces, fixed smiles, and stylish clothes. I was puzzled, though, that I had never seen any of the clothes on the dolls worn by anyone. I never saw dolls that looked like us.

When Mom left the theater to head home Sunday evenings in late November and early December, she stopped downstairs first. She knew I might be there with Karla. If she found us at the store, she took time to tell us stories from her childhood when her parents had managed a co-op back in Finland. She, too, had played with the Christmas toys when the store was closed. She had had fun back in Finland because the toys weren't in packages.

Mother's Christmas stories were full of hope. They helped Karla and me look forward to the holiday. Joseph Koivu had a sad holiday story that stayed with me. Some of his relatives working in the copper mines on the Upper Peninsula of Michigan had attended a Christmas party arranged by the community for all the children of the striking miners' families. Suddenly, someone had yelled, "Fire! Fire!" and then disappeared. The city fire horn sounded. Everyone was panic-stricken. They ran for the doors.

Since everyone rushed to the exit, opening the doors had been impossible. The narrow halls and stairways leading to the front doors became filled with hysterical people. Fifty-six children and eighteen women and men were trampled to death in the hall. Eight more died later at the hospital. Three of Joe's cousins died.

The mining company offered to bury the eighty-one victims, but the strikers turned them down. The *Tyomies* newspaper reported the person who yelled "Fire, fire!" and the one who sounded the false fire siren during the party were members of the Citizens Public Safety Committee commissioned by the governor.   Later in December, the *Tyomies* newspaper's office in Superior, Wisconsin, was raided. Oscar Corgan, the newspaper's editor, told my father the reason police gave for the raid was "sedition." Mr. Corgan and the journalists had been suspected of being unpatriotic because they felt sorry for the dead children, women, and men who were strikers or related to the miners.

Joe had said his father and mother told that story to him and his cousins every Christmas Eve.

The story made me sad. When Joe first told me the story, I wanted to reach out and include him in my family's Christmas. I invited him over, but he didn't come. I asked him why. He said he was needed at home. I wished he would have come.

When we got upstairs, the apartment was dark. Mom flicked on the hall light.

We paused. Mom whispered, "I don't hear anything . . ."

"Neither do I . . ."

"Grandma must have gotten Hannah and Tommy to fall asleep. Sara, get to bed. Remember, we'll have to get up early to hand out those chicks."

"Rakastan sinua. (Love you!)"

"Rakastan sinua myos. (Love you, too!)"

On the way to my room, I stopped at my parents' bedroom door. Predictably, Dad's Sunday slippers were sitting there. On late Saturday nights, Dad left his slippers in the hallway so that they were easier for him to find on Sunday mornings. Once a month, Viola, Jacque, and Dad stayed out late after the play to discuss business. He was still out. I placed a chick in Dad's right slipper. Gently, I pushed a sock back into the slipper to hold the chick in and quiet its cheeping. I chuckled to myself. Dad loved practical jokes. He'd love this one.

If Mom went to sing in Duluth, I knew I would miss her. Right now, I didn't mind helping Grandma babysit my brother and sister and take care of the house, but that was because Mom let me watch her on stage sometimes. If she sang in Duluth, I feared I wouldn't be able to see her. *Hmmm, I thought. There was another theater in our town, the Lyric, which was owned and run by the richer people. Maybe Mom could sing for them. Her voice was as beautiful as their sopranos, if not better, and she would gather a larger crowd.*

There were Finns who didn't believe musicals were a serious lifestyle activity. A few had told Mom she was a capitalist and more interested in entertaining than devoting her time to the common good. I didn't think they knew how much time she practiced her singing. If they did, they would have realized how hard Mom worked, even harder than many of the other mothers I knew who didn't go to the opera hall.

I didn't think of my mom as a person who had to do housework, help out at the co-op, and teach classes at summer camp. My mother was my mother. I thought of her as the person who loved me and spent time with me. I loved my mother because she talked to me like a friend. In fact, we talked with each other every day, more than other Finnish girls I knew talked with their mothers.

The *HMS Pinafore* was the first non-Finnish play performed at our theater. Jacque Trompeure' thought it would be good to direct a theater production which was not Finnish or had political ideas aimed at organizing the workers in the lumber and mining operations of the area. My father and Jacque were becoming concerned with how many Finnish people were going down the street to the Lyric Theater for their entertainment instead of coming to our Finnish hall. Not only were all the plays at the Lyric performed in English, but comedians and vaudeville acts were also offered. Dad and Jacque were not against this type of entertainment, and they did not believe the use of English on stage was immoral.

Dad believed attending the Lyric Theater was morally wrong for other reasons. For him, purchasing Lyric tickets was a public statement that you agreed with the blacklisting done by Oliver Mining to Finnish workers who had gone on strike to promote unionization of the mines. Half of the theater's profits from the ticket sales went to the mine owners. Dad believed this revenue provided more capital for the steel men to hire their anti-union thugs and mercenaries. The Finnish people attending the Lyric either didn't make this connection or didn't care; they were simply looking for entertainment. Because of their lack of political backbone and willingness to accept the status quo, they were called White Finns.

White Finns also didn't like Bill Haywood's increased use of opera halls' facilities in several cities for strike organizing. Dad understood Haywood caused trouble. He also knew Haywood had been arrested more than once for trying to organize workers here and in other states. However, my father believed we shouldn't be ashamed of Bill Haywood. He was helping to make a better world that was fair. Sometimes this was a messy process. Haywood's organizing activities were in opposition to what the mine owners were attempting to do. They mistreated their workers, were not ashamed of the unsafe working conditions, and provided poor equipment for the men.

What bothered me the most about the mine owners was that they took the ore from the land and weren't concerned about what happened to the land afterward. When my dad cut down a tree, I planted a baby tree near the stump. Dad had taught me always to replace what I took from nature.

Jacque disagreed with Dad on these issues. Jacque believed good theater attracted more White Finns. He wanted to offer and produce more plays which entertained and attracted even larger audiences, Finnish or not. Jacque preferred to have the theater used as a theater and not shared with the Red Finns who used it as a stage for organizing activities.

I crawled into bed with my head full of theater, mine owners, and, most of all, my mother. How would my life be affected if she went to Duluth? I pondered the scenarios for what seemed like a long time. Finally, I drifted into an uneasy sleep.

5   English Class

"Joseph, would you please stand?"

I didn't want to; I had a sinking feeling in my stomach. Mrs. Schultz stared at me in that hard way of hers. I could tell she didn't like me even though she tried not to let the class know. I was a Finn, and she didn't like Finns. I didn't know why. She looked like a weasel: short and no shape to her body with tiny arms and legs. Her hair was pulled back tight. In the pale classroom light, her eyes were beady. I imagined her on four legs, low to the ground, and sauntering towards the chicken coop. I picked up my imaginary shotgun, looked down the barrel, sighted her head, and squeezed off a shot. *Pop goes the weasel!*

"Joseph, please, begin the passage. We are waiting."

I thought of what my father said about being strong and rose from my seat. All eyes were on me, but I was brave. Holding the book in front of me, I read from William Blake's *Love and Harmony*. My voice sounded strange.

> *Love and harmony combine,*
> *And round our souls entwine*
> *While thy branches mix with mine,*
> *And our roots together join.*
>
> *Joys upon our branches sit,*
> *Chirping loud and singing sweet;*
> *Like gentle streams beneath our feet*
> *Innocence and virtue meet.*

I heard snickers. No one liked the way I said my "o"s in roots. My face was red. I wanted to sit down, but I couldn't because Mrs. Schultz had to give me permission first. I looked at her. I was helpless and shamed. *Forgive me, I didn't mean to pop your weasel!*

"Joseph Koivu, you must work harder on your pronunciation," Mrs. Schultz corrected. She paused and then added, "How do you expect to be a citizen when you sound like a foreigner? You must work harder to blend in. Think of your classmates; you can do the same."

Everyone was quiet. The other students didn't want her attention shifted to them. "Yes, Mrs. Schultz," I obediently agreed.

"Good!" she replied, sounding like goot. "You may be seated, Joe."

I sat. Mrs. Schultz moved on to the next boy. She spent the rest of the class going from student to student, having each read a piece, and giving corrections. I didn't want to listen and knew I would be bored. I leaned back and looked behind me. Tammy Browersfield smiled. I smiled back at her. I leaned forward. *How I could get more of Tammy's attention even though she was the principal's daughter? I wondered. Could I ever have a chance to go out with her?*

I turned my head and stared out the classroom door. I allowed my mind to wander out the door and down the hall from our room to the Hibbing High School auditorium where all the school programs were staged. At last year's Christmas program, Sara Niemi played St Lucia. She wore a crown of lighted candles and sang *Santa Lucia, Ljusklara Hägring Saint Lucy, (Bright Mirage.)* Sara was angelic in a white gown singing on the stage.

When I thought about how Sara had looked that night, my earlier thoughts of Tammy faded.

My dad hadn't been at the program. He said St Lucia was a Swedish, not Finnish, Christmas tradition. He always became upset when Finnish people were thought of as Scandinavian. Although Sweden controlled parts of northern Finland at one time, the Finns hadn't become Swedish as a result.

Designed after the old Capitol Theater of New York, the auditorium had 1800 seats. This was more capacity than the People's or the Lyric Theaters downtown. Above the seats four $15,000 chandeliers were perched. Each fixture was made with cut custom glass from Belgium and Czechoslovakia. Dad estimated the cost of one chandelier was equal to the cost of three to four houses. Hmmm... The idea of twelve to sixteen houses hanging from the ceiling instead of chandeliers made me smile. I knew that was not what Dad wanted me to imagine with his "house" metaphor; he preferred I realized the injustice. I tried to lighten his thoughts with my imagination. One small white house loosened, slipped a few inches down from the ceiling, creaked, and dropped.

The auditorium ceiling was handmolded with the majority of the work done by Irish craftsmen. Dad didn't like Irishmen. They drank too much and were Catholic. Dad believed Irish priests were pedophiles who had found an easy paycheck here in America. This caused him to dislike Catholics even more. With this attitude and since he didn't know how to calculate the price of piece labor, he couldn't put a value on the Irish craftsmen's work. He wasn't certain how many houses the handmolded ceiling would buy.

Stage right was a 1900 Barton Company vaudeville pipe organ, one of two in the country. Her pipes filled the auditorium with sounds of every instrument in the orchestra. Dad thought the organ represented fifty to seventy houses. That brought the house count around sixty-two to eighty-six homes, plus a few more for the Irishmen's handiwork.

Our high school was built in 1923. The four million dollars required to build it were donated by the mine owners to make room for the expanding Hull-Rust-Mahoning Mine operation. If my math was right, the four million represented approximately 1,000 houses hanging from the auditorium ceiling. My dad thought the new high school was a bribe from the mine owners as insurance to do whatever they wanted as they continued to mine their ore.

In the library, Dad had found another injustice. A large historical oil painting covered the back wall. Depicting the journey iron ore made to becoming steel, Diego Rivera, a Mexican Marxist, used this piece as part of a study to develop his ideas for the four massive murals he painted on the walls of the Detroit Institute of Arts. I guessed Edsel Ford had given Rivera $30,000 for the project. Dad didn't like the mural because no Finnish workers were present anywhere. I didn't know how he could tell the nationality of the men in the mural. I could hardly tell who the figures were and what they were doing. All their bodies looked similar: wide, brown, and round. Maybe he objected to the obesity of the shapes.

Suddenly, I heard the roof creak. Was that real or in my head? *Hmm...* The hanging houses made me think of bats. I turned my imagination to visualizing a cave, full of bats hanging upside down. As I entered the cave, I accidently kicked a rock, which crashed against the cavern wall. The bats, disrupted from sleep and scared into swarming, began to dive bomb my head and got tangled in my hair. The weight of hundreds of skin-winged fur bodies forced me down to the cold cavern floor on top of a marbled stalagmite. I mentally yelled, *Ughhhh! I've been impaled!*

I was brought back to reality by Mrs. Schultz giving the next day's assignment. We all wrote it down, and Mrs. Schultz dismissed us.

6 Fish Slime

Yesterday had been rainy, and the road home was muddy. One large puddle was right outside the Lincoln Elementary School's main door. Children were playing in and around the water-filled hole, splashing each other, laughing, and yelling. I moved away, not wanting to get muddy slop on my pants. My shoes sank into the mud.

Sikojen likaista vähän! (Dirty little pigs), I thought.

The day was overcast, and the air was chilled. I breathed the air in deeply, humming.

Vuonna menee hyvä ilma, ulos tulee huono ilma (In goes the good air, out comes the bad air;)

Vuonna menee hyvä ilma, ulos tulee huono ilma (In goes the good air, out comes the bad air;)

I heard footsteps behind me. Sara Niemi caught up and walked next to me.

"Hi, Joe."

I smiled. "Hi, Sara."

Taking my arm, Sara said, "Tammy told me Mrs. Schultz has been picking on you. Who needs all that poetry, anyway?"

A little caught off guard, I responded, "I like poetry. It is good for the soul."

Laughing, she replied, "Oh Joe... You are so sensitive. I like that." She stopped and gazed into my eyes for what seemed like a long time. As if to break a spell, she shook her head and continued, "The Bolsheviks are the main movement in Russia now. We are making uniforms and shoes for them with all the spare materials we can find at the co-op. Do you want to help tonight? You can play a part in changing the world –"

I interrupted her. "I have to be concerned about my family before changing the world, Sara. I worry about Dad in the woods alone. Mother's ill, and Becky and Jon need my help, too."

Sara nodded politely and kept her head down. Her eyes were shy, but she found her voice. "I know, Joe. You work hard." Pausing, Sara lifted her head and blinked once. After we walked ten more feet, with a firm squeeze on my arm and a soft, steady voice, she whispered, "You are a good man, Joe."

Sara held my arm until we reached the end of the street. "See you, Joe." She threw a look over her left shoulder at me, turned right, and headed toward the co-op store.

"See you in school tomorrow, Sara."

I faded into the trees. They shaded me as I walked.

Sara Niemi was a friend. I had met Sara at Mesaba Park, a co-op campground east of Hibbing. Both of our families were members. She worked in the kitchen, and I was responsible for the beach area.

She had invited me for Christmas with her family after we met. I didn't go. Dad had wanted me home because Mother was sicker than normal that season.

Sara's father Martin managed the Work People's Co-op Store on the north end of town. Her mother's parents Mattai and Grace lived with Sara's family. Sara's mother Elizabeth had been thinking about temporarily moving to Duluth to work with Jacque Trompeure', who directed and managed the productions of the socialist opera halls in Hibbing, Virginia, and Duluth. Her family members were good people; all the Finns said so.

Most Finnish girls were task-orientated and serious about everything they did compared to the non-Finnish town girls who appeared more relaxed. The town girls also seemed to have more time to spend away from their families and homes. They had fewer ethnic-based responsibilities. However, having a non-Finnish girlfriend was not a reality for a Finnish boy like me. Being smart and the captain of the baseball team had not been enough to shed my stigma of being an undesirable immigrant. I thought that was why I was attracted to Sara. I didn't just think it was her accessibility. She was different from the other Finnish girls I knew. One of the differences was her sense of humor. I have never forgotten the first practical joke I tried playing on her.

The previous winter, North Star Lake's level had been lower than normal. When the lake froze over, so many fish had crowded in the deep end of the lake that the smaller fish or runts were forced to stay in the more shallow areas on the east end where the lake ice was harvested for camp. I laughed out loud when one of the blocks of ice we cut out of the lake had a small northern pike or jack frozen in the middle of the chunk. A taxidermist couldn't have mounted the three pound fish better. I hid this dead jack ice block in the back corner of the ice shed, saving it for a special occasion.

After the April work bee, I moved the block from where I had hidden it during the winter and carried it to the kitchen ice box cooler. I did this the night before Sara's kitchen shift at Camp Mesaba.

Sara was responsible for keeping the box stocked with ice. When the ice melted during our Mayday celebration, the dead jack stunk up the kitchen. The kitchen worker bees had thought it was a dead mouse or mole left over from winter and ignored it. They assumed a cat would eat it. However, Sara recognized the smell and knew its origin. She opened the ice chest, picked up the dead jack in her hands, carried it down to the beach, and threw it at me where I sat in the row boat. "Jack lupasi! (Jack, Back!)" she screamed.

Ugh! Fish slime was always unpleasant, but long-dead fish slime was a curse! As she ran back to the hall's kitchen laughing, I started to laugh, too. I didn't know of any town girl who would have touched a dead fish or carried a fish corpse in her arms to throw at someone as a practical joke. I was glad she had left right away. Knowing Sara, she would have wiped her hands on my shirt, too, had she stayed.

Sara was not a bad looker, either. She was shorter than me with blue eyes that sparkled when she laughed. Blonde hair cascaded onto her shoulders and over her breasts. Slender hips set atop long legs separated her from looking peasant-ish. Sara wore nice clothes, nicer than mine, and cleaner. She carried herself well with a welcoming expression on her face. With a deeper tan and the right swimming suit, Sara would have been one of the better lookers in northern Minnesota – even better than Tammy.

I laughed as I remembered the stinking jack lupasi. I was reminded of another story about Sara using slimy things for a practical joke.

In the spring, green caterpillars made white silk-like tents. These sticky canopies hung down from the trees. Some even stretched over ten feet from the higher branches of a tree to the ground. On the way to school I saw nothing, but on the way home I noticed their tents had been built. One nickname for them was tent worms, another army worms. Walking into their tents was creepy, especially when I wasn't watching where I was going. They were sticky like a spider web and much thicker. I saw and touched the caterpillars crawling up and down the white sheets. They didn't have dead flies or beetle bodies in their silk like spiders' webs did, but I still didn't want to touch them. There was so much of the white silky stuff that it was impossible to get it off my hands or out of my hair without warm soapy water. The girls always screamed when they saw the tents. Sara didn't. I'd known her to take a stick, poke at the worm tent with it, and then chase boys while flailing the stick with worm webs whipping the air!

My thoughts about Sara were interrupted when I saw my house. I heard Dad in the woods logging. When I got inside, I found my mother Irene taking her medicinal nap and checked on my sister and brother. Then I put Rudolph, our horse, in the barn. After that, I threw a few logs into the sauna's fire box, lit them to begin heating up the sauna, and headed into the woods to help Dad.

My father Gustav and his brother Launo came from the Lapua region in Finland and had worked in the underground iron ore mines near Hibbing when they arrived in Minnesota. My dad said Lapua was like northern Minnesota, heavily forested and scattered with mining operations. Their parents, Jonathan and Lena Koivu, accompanied them to Minnesota. All of them were forced to lumber for a living when the mine workers went on strike in 1906 and they subsequently lost their jobs at the Oliver Mining Company.

After my uncle Danny was hurt in a lumber mill accident back in Finland, my grandparents returned to help care for him. He was barely able walk or talk. Uncle Danny had to move in with his younger brother Farley who lived in an area north of Lake Ladoga. My Uncle Irv was a constable there.

Dad didn't say so, but he seemed happy when he was working. He and Uncle Launo had their own lumber company. They had purchased large trucks and motorized saws for cutting and hauling timber. Rudolph was the last horse they used.

They had promised the Mesaba Co-op Federation they would help expand the pavilion on North Star Lake for the festival and campgrounds there. With their lumbering equipment, they were able to extend the main hall quickly. They believed their ownership of a company and willingness to help out the Finnish community with building projects modeled the way industrialization should be run – by the hands of the people who did the work. They had built town halls, barns, co-ops, and houses in rural areas. But they avoided doing projects in larger towns and cities such as Duluth. They said they didn't like working in front of the townspeople. I didn't think that was the reason. I thought they felt bad about losing their jobs trying to organize those mining iron ore and didn't want to run into any mining officials.

I heard Dad's axe chopping. He sounded close. Dad worked alone on Friday nights. His brother Launo did, too. That was the only time they did. They never told me why. I thought it was because of their Saturday morning discussions with the others about organizing workers, getting reports on the success of the Bolshevik Revolution in Russia, and sometimes reviewing personal issues. Working by themselves cleared their minds, I guessed. When Dad came back to sauna after a Friday alone, he seemed more settled and determined. Often he'd tell a joke or laugh during our sauna.

Sara's dad Martin worked alone on Saturday nights. She said he wrapped up the week's business from the co-op that night. The blue laws prohibited stores from opening on Sundays, so the co-op store was closed. On Sundays, he held membership meetings for the co-op and the federation. Sometimes Martin also attended Sunday studies.

On Sunday afternoons, Mr. Ivanovich, a teacher from the high school, held Sunday studies. These were formal political forums held at the theater or Mesaba Park. Socialism was discussed. Often, speakers from around the country stopped by and shared their perspectives on Marxism and the Russian Revolution. Bill Haywood, the leader of the Industrial Workers of the World, was a regular. When Ivanovich didn't have speakers, he would read to the men. Chapters from Marx or Milton were favorites. Other times he read articles from the local newspapers or the *Tyomies*, the Finnish Socialist newspaper. He also gave short speeches on socialism and reports of the progress made by the Bolsheviks over in Russia.

The Niemis didn't go to church on Sundays. Instead, Sara's family had Sunday lunch together with Mattai and Grace in their apartment above the store. Sara's dad always invited special speakers for the Sunday study sessions to join the family for lunch. I was amazed at some of the people she got to meet.

I never had a common time with my family, even to eat. Since my mother's health was unpredictable, she wasn't able to make meals on a regular basis. My dad tried to help her, but he often had interruptions. Either my uncle wanted help, or the lumbering equipment needed repairs. Before my grandparents went to Finland, they gave us a hand running the household. Since they left, my only regularity was from the sounds and smells outside the house and in the woods.

As I followed the sound of Dad's axe chopping, I smelled the sauna's smoke drifting past me. Even as a young boy, I had liked the sauna stove smell better than cigarette smoke. When Dad lit a cigarette, the fresh smell excited me, but it staled quickly. Sauna smoke didn't. Arvi said the *Kiuss* became seasoned from its constant use. This seasoning created a blend of burnt sap and wood ash which became a comforting potpourri under the sky on a Friday night.

As I neared Dad, I noticed he was brushing the trees they had felled earlier in the day and piling the limbed branches together on the south side of the trail. After a week or two, the branches would be dry, and my little sister and brother would join Dad and me for a small bonfire. Mom was always asleep by then. After the fire was out, we'd head home to sweat the smells off.

"Dad!" I called. "Dad!"

He ignored me. That was normal. He preferred not to talk until he was done and came to sauna. I called out one more time, "Dad!"

"I'll be done in about fifteen minutes. You make sure the sauna is ready and Jon and Becky have their chores done. We're going right to bed after we sweat."

When he used my brother's and sister's names, I knew he was more worried than normal. That made me curious about what would be discussed tomorrow morning in the woods.

7   Spies

A few hours later, I found out what had been on Dad's mind the night before. I didn't want Dad to know I attended that Saturday morning session. That's why I huddled in the bushes on the edge of the clearing and listened intently.

"Figlio di una femmina! (Son of a bitch!)"

"Sin Rich Bitch! (Son of a bitch!)"

The mixture of dialects and languages between the men was hilarious. The Finnish picked up words from the Italians, the Serbians from the Norwegians, and the Irish from the Croatians. Cussing words were especially mobile among the lumberjacks as they worked in the woods. Most had been miners until the 1906 strike failed.

"Sønn av en tispe, drittsekk! (Son of a bitch!)"

"Kurvin sin. (Son of a bitch.)"

I liked hearing them because it was the opposite of each day at school. School was quiet and had no laughing. The workers told jokes. I imagined the jack pines shaking their branches as they echoed the lumberjacks' laughter.

"Prasec! (Son of a bitch!)"

"Sin Bitchste!"

Some of the Finnish miners had joined the lumberjacks for the meeting. While some did not speak English well, they were bright men. A few had been doctors and lawyers in Finland. My father wanted me to hear what was discussed in the Saturday morning sessions. Often I joined them openly. That day I wanted to remain hidden and find out what had upset Dad so much.

I knew George Ivanovich would be at the meeting that morning. His presence heightened the political talk. Sometimes the tensions created by their political conversations bothered me. I was afraid if I didn't talk about politics in just the right way or ask a question using the right words, they would yell at me. At those times, they became like grumpy old men,

Miesten Lisä, looking for their false teeth while they complained about how poor they were.

That's another reason I didn't show myself.

At last night's sauna I had become more concerned about Dad. Later I lay in bed wondering what was bothering him. To answer my questions, I decided to go to the meeting without him knowing and hide in the brush. My father was the first person I heard talking. "Everybody believes Oliver Mining cares about us. They gave us a beautiful high school so when they moved our houses across town, broke up our neighborhoods, and had us work long shifts, we were supposed to be grateful."

Dad stopped speaking and lit a cigarette. His left eye squinted when the smoke from the Lucky Strike crawled out of the corner of his mouth and floated up that side of his face. He shook the match out, threw it on the ground, and ground it out with his boot. The first hit off a lit cigarette always gave him a perk of energy.

Matthew Wirtannen continued with his observations. "Oliver Mining really intends to break up our solidarity and slow down the organizing so they can have a better life off our backs."

"You're right," my father agreed. "If they say there is ore underneath our houses, what are we going to do? We only have one choice. Let them move our houses so we can dig out the ore for them so we have our jobs and can keep our families together. No one wants to question Oliver Mining publicly."

"We have to trust them," Impi stated, "not because we believe in them, not because we like them, not because they are our neighbors, but because they have the money to buy the equipment, make the maps, and pretend they know the location of the ore. Don't you think if they knew the ore's location for sure that all the other capitalists would also know its location and want to get at it, too?"

Rantala affirmed Impi's thoughts. "I guess that's right, Impi. If the ore was that sure of a bet, wouldn't Germany or England want to come here and invest money to get the ore out of the ground?"

"I never thought about it that way," Elder Metsa added. "Does anyone know how to map out the location of the iron ore?"

"Damn, Elder, we don't even have the money to buy the equipment that is needed to take the ore out of the ground!" Impi exclaimed.

"I agree," Matthew Wirtannen inserted. "Why are we afraid of them? Those barons did not find the ore. They do not mine or mill the ore, but by some weird alchemy they believe all the iron ore we mine for them belongs to them."

There was silence. Impi spat. Niilo Koivu, my cousin, switched the topic. "George, Impi says there are spies at the Bruce Mine."

With a wry smile, George teased Impi, "Don't believe Impi, Niilo. He is so afraid of spies that he can't even sauna naked by himself."

Herman Bjorkland sensed the mood for humor, so he tried to provoke some laughter. "I agree, George. Not only does Impi imagine there are spies in his sauna, he thinks they might go downtown and tell everyone what he looks like!"

A smattering of laughter rippled through the assembled men.

Impi grinned and spat on the ground. For good measure, Herman Bjorkland added, "Or what he doesn't look like!"

"Or doesn't have!" someone yelled boisterously.

That was followed by more laughter. George stood up and held both hands in a gesture of Stop! The snorts subsided into sporadic chuckles around the group like popcorn scattering all over the stove from a black ironcast skillet without its lid. Once everyone quieted, George sat down.

Niilo persisted, "I am serious about spies watching us. Impi's wife Eileen said she saw one new miner mail four to six letters all at one time, on three different days. . . Nobody does that."

A hush ensued. The men looked around at each other. Impi spat.

My dad asked, "So, what's the mail got to do with spying, George?"

George didn't immediately reply. The look on his face was sober. As he waited, seriousness filled the air. "Each letter goes to a different post office box number in Duluth. In the letters is information on different people who are considered suspicious to Oliver Mining. There are no names used in the letters, but there are number codes."

"How do you know that?" Taisto quipped.

"Eileen asked Wayne, who hauls the mail to Duluth each day. Wayne is her second cousin. Wayne says there's more than one person mailing letters without names to post office box numbers in Duluth. Some days he has over fifty letters by the end of the day."

"Nessuna merda!" interjected a couple of shocked men.

George continued, "And this has been going on for a while."

The men leaned forward as the interest intensified. Impi spat again.

"What happens then?" Launo Koivu wondered.

"A group of decoders at Oliver Mining headquarters opens the letters and puts them together based on the number codes they are given," George replied.

"Secret codes, Dodjavola, I don't believe that!" shouted Helmer Valamaki.

Taisto looked over at Gustav. "Nels Soumi has never been hired. He stops by Niemi's co-op regularly and talks about his socialist relatives back in Finland."

Niilo sneezed.

"Terveydeksi!"

"Dopo uno starnuto!"

"Bog vas blagoslovi!"

George stepped up on a stump and continued, "Eileen watched the mustached guy mailing letters. She also saw him in the co-op store on some of the days Nels was talking about unions. She didn't think anything of it. After Wayne told her there were lots of letters getting mailed, she started putting the pieces together."

Helmer Valamaki tried to lighten the conversation. "So, George, you're seeing Impi's wife now. What's she like?"

A few chuckles rippled through the crowd. No one added more jokes. They all noticed Impi was spitting on the ground every thirty seconds while he tapped his left foot up and down.

Taisto tried to alleviate the fear he sensed building in some of the men. "Come on, George. Don't you think we'd be able to tell if someone was a spy?"

Frank Vainionpaa thoughtfully suggested, "I like to think everyone I know is honest."

Most of the men nodded and quietly agreed. Frank leaned back. My father asked, "George, where are the Oliver Mining offices in Duluth?"

Taisto quickly answered. "They are downtown, above the Lyceum Theater. You know, where Jacque brings Elizabeth Niemi sometimes to sing."

Taisto's answer caught me off guard. I hadn't known the theater where Sara's mother sang in Duluth was in the same building as the Oliver Mining Company's headquarters. Hmm. I guess Sara had no need to tell me this information. Maybe she didn't know. I hadn't said anything to Sara, but I knew some of my father's friends thought Jacque and her mother seemed to be a little too close at times.

George Ivanovich turned to his left and questioned Niilo. "Do you think the owners are spying?"

"I know somebody is," Niilo replied.

"Why are they spying?" George asked.

"Remember the bastard that fell out of the tree in Alango next to Sturgeon Hall?" Helmer Valamaki interjected.

"Yes I do," said Elder Metsa. "That's a great story. Tell it for George."

Before Helmer began to tell the story, Niilo's father Launo cut into the conversation. "Toivo saw this skinny mustached guy lying on a large branch in a tree next to where we eat lunch. He sneaked up on the bastard and pulled him down, but Toivo accidently removed the spy's pants!"

Everyone began hootin' and hollerin'. Launo stepped into the middle of the circle with Toivo Soumi, and they acted out how Toivo pulled the spy's pants off. Launo yanked Toivo's trousers to his knees and pushed his head down. Crouched over, buttocks bare, Toivo slowly turned a circle showing his full moon to everyone in the group. Toivo was a heavy man, and his ass was monstrous!

As Toivo rotated, Launo continued the story. "That mustached man was a spy – a spy working for the Pinkertons and Rainey Lake Lumber Company. We didn't hurt him, but we sure embarrassed him! Once the weasel was on the ground, Toivo held him there, slapped the spy on his ass, and said, 'If you are gonna spy on us, we're gonna spy on you!' Then Toivo rolled the guy over and added, 'I spy on you. Gee, your dick is too small to see so you must be a prick!'

"Toivo cupped his large hands together and shouted to all the jacks, 'Hey, come over here so you can see this little prick!' We were laughing so hard, I thought Toivo might be encouraged to pull the spy's dick. When the foreman saw what was going on, he came over real quick and apologized to the spy. He let the spy get up and walk away. The foreman told us we were mistaken and the mustached guy was a hunter, not a spy.

"Yeah! We thought. We didn't believe the foreman for a minute. The spy didn't have a shotgun or a knife on him. He was a spy. He even smelled like perfume!"

The hooting and hollering peaked. It took a while to get quiet. Even George had tears in his eyes from laughing so hard. I remembered my dad telling me this story once, but watching Toivo and my Uncle Launo act it out was hilarious.

Toivo pulled up his pants and zipped them. As he stretched the suspenders over his shoulders, he finished, "We never saw that spy again, but I had to see that foreman every day. I don't trust him no more. I don't trust any foreman. They don't trust me. I like it that way."

Unlucky commented, "No foreman is ever going to share his food with you or invite you over to eat with him, Toivo."

"If one does, he'll probably invite you over to watch him and his family eat!" said Launo.

"Then he will ask you to do the dishes while he has a smoke and a shot of brandy!" quipped Helmer Valamaki.

Frank added, "And that's what those foreman think is spying!"

"Funny pieni poikaa (little boy)," said Unlucky.

George looked around at the group and redirected the talk. "Those were some good laughs and acting. Now let's discuss what's happening in Europe."

Herman Bjorklund muttered, "Kuulostaa aivan kuten Stalin minulle (Sounds just like Stalin to me)."

George looked at him. "Bjorkland, why did you say, 'Just like Stalin'?"

"Stalin thinks we need strong leadership to be faithful. He wants a central party to make plans for everyone. Also, Lenin writes there should be leaders who make sure the plans are followed for the common good."

Someone yelled out, "Toisaalta!"

"Tolstoy and the rest think they must plan for us. Shit! We can plan for ourselves," said Impi. Then he spat.

George stepped down as Launo Koivu stood up on a stump. "Socialism is about living with a cooperate spirit… sharing within the community for the common good... and that includes the leadership, too! Ja cu se složiti! Socialism is meant to be democratic. We all share!"

Launo reached down and helped Helmer Valamaki onto the stump next to his. Helmer raised his arms and spoke out, "Yes! We, the workers, should decide together what to do, how we should work, what we should change."

"What the hell do you know, Valamaki?" said Metsa.

Toivo yelled back, "You'll never lead a revolution, Elder."

"Vaffunculo!" Metsa responded.

A scuffle started. Four or five guys wrestled on the ground. Other voices drifted back into the perpetual search for the best version of Marx's theories of socialism. Like waves on North Star Lake's shore at Mesaba Park lapping over and over again, pounding the lake's shore sand into ridges, these conversations carried on and on every Saturday and Sunday and sounded the same.

Feeling stiff, I shifted where I was seated. I thought about spies. Up until now, I had assumed force – law enforcement, thugs, and Pinkertons - was the method used for busting worker solidarity. Today I had heard a new twist, spies. I decided to ask Yrkki about today's conversations.

Yrkki had told me about spies in Finland during the Winter War. The Czar used them to monitor Finland. I had never thought of spies being used in the US, especially during non-war times. I had always associated spies with wars. Using spies seemed sneaky, like cheating and looking at somebody else's cards during a card game. Spying seemed contrary to the way freedom of speech was described in our social studies and Americanization classes.

The more I thought about spying, the more I wondered about the Oliver Mining Company. I didn't think of the common good as having secrets which needed to be ferreted out. I wondered if Oliver Mining management should try to talk with the miners. My dad said in Finland you couldn't talk with the Czar. He just told you what to do. Besides, he lived in Russia and didn't care. Here, freedom of speech was the American way. We were supposed to talk things out, maybe figure out a way that everyone could be helped. Only czars and evil kings needed spies sneaking around like weasels spying on the chickens in the coops. If spies from Oliver Mining were penetrating the co-ops to listen for conversations about organizing, other spies could have been at church services or Sunday afternoon study sessions at the co-op.

I wondered how someone became a spy. I thought it must be hard to pretend to be one person when you were another person. I wasn't able keep my own thoughts organized. I didn't know what I would do if I were two people and had to keep track of two separate trains of thought, two identities, and even two different names. I would have been confused; I'd forget when I was acting like spy and when I was not.

Out of the corner of my eye, I caught a movement on the road. Turning, I saw Sheriff Robert McFarland get out of his police car and head toward the session in the woods. As he passed me, he noticed me hiding in the brush and said, "Hi."

Startled, I smiled nervously at him. *Did he know me,* I wondered, *or was he just being friendly?* Maybe the sheriff recognized me from the Finnish festivals and dances he attended. Some of the men at the study sessions were prone to fighting when they drank in public. The sheriff had started showing up at the festivals and dances to keep a lid on the "incidents." Everyone liked having him around, especially since he never arrested anyone. I knew his son from school. He was named Robert, just like his dad. He was the quarterback of our football team. He had set the record for the most touchdown passes last year. My dad said the sheriff had a Finnish wife. Marian was her name. That didn't sound Finnish to me.

As the sheriff got within sight of the men sitting in the woods, I heard them hollering,

"Watch what you say. Here comes a spy!"

"Don't let him handcuff you. He'll take you for a ride in his car."

"No telling what will happen then!"

Robert appeared to enjoy the banter. He straightened up, pulled his hat down slightly over his eyes, and yelled jokingly, "If you don't shut up, I will arrest every one of you!"

Toivo stood and boxed at the air. "Just try!"

I was hoping his pants would fall down and show off his big ass again.

"Okay, guys, let's give the sheriff a little respect," said George. "Good to see you. What do you have for us today?"

"I wanted to make an announcement to you guys first, before you read it in the newspapers. I don't even know if the *Tyomies* will cover it. You'll be seeing much more of me in the next year."

"So the word's gotten out that all of us are communists?" said Rantala.

"Even better, Taisto. I've joined the party," McFarland answered.

"Let's see your red diapers then," Rantala answered.

"Oh, no, we have a bed wetter," teased Toivo with smile.

"Well, I didn't want to take too much of your time today and spoil all your fun, but I just got a call from the governor. He is putting me on special assignment," McFarland explained.

"Sorry to hear you're leaving us," said Helmer.

"Yeah, let me kick your ass on the way out," added Frank Vainionpaa.

"Not so quick, men. I haven't told you what I'm doing," McFarland responded.

McFarland walked toward the center where most of the men were gathered. He looked rather calm and happy with himself. His hand wasn't resting on his gun. "As I just said, the governor has put me on special assignment. I will still be the sheriff, but I'll spend most of my time with you Finnish people."

"I don't know if I want you eating at my house," said Unlucky.

"Or mine, either," agreed Helmer.

Impi pointed a finger at McFarland. "Are you sure you talked to the governor? Maybe it was your wife Marian. She knows we are good people. You should listen to her."

"She is the reason why I spend so much time with you in the first place," answered the sheriff. "It wasn't because I thought you were too rowdy or dangerous socialists. Because of her, I think I understand you guys better. So does the governor, now. So I just wanted to stop by and let you know you'll be seeing more of me."

McFarland tipped his hat, turned, and walked back to his car.

When McFarland climbed into the car, I saw another man in the car, too. He was young, tall, and dark-skinned. Behind McFarland's back, some of the men at the session were making faces and imitating McFarland's walk. I heard them laughing. My dad and George got them to stop. My father trusted McFarland. Dad said you have to trust somebody, even if you thought they worked for the mine owners. I guessed you didn't know who really worked for the owners, anyway.

I didn't know why we shouldn't trust McFarland. He'd stopped by our house several times to say "Hi." He'd also stopped by the co-op to say "Hi" to Sara's dad. As the sheriff and his passenger drove off, they scared up a covey of grouse. The flying birds got me thinking about hunting with Arvi tomorrow. I always looked forward to being in the woods with Arvi. I thought back to the sauna I didn't take at his house. For Arvi's family, saunas were more than a place to clean up. They contained traditions.

One sauna tradition Arvi's family maintained was to place stones which were reminders of sentimental and fond events in the rock box. Then as they relaxed in the humid heat, they thought back to those memories and shared them with their guests. Arvi had sauna rocks he had picked from Lake Superior, Finnish festivals, and other sentimental places. Impi had told my father, "In my sauna, there is a rock from the camping spot the night Eileen and I created Arvi after a case of beer."

I had heard old man Taisto Rantala was waiting for a stone from Europe that was from a road in front of Karl Marx's house. Another old timer had told me that Industrial Workers of the World (IWW) families had rocks from each of the mines where they had organized strikes.

What had Dad said about that? I couldn't recall. From others I had heard many stories about different rocks in the sauna at Mesaba Park. One unusually large brown stone with black bituminous and false gold flecks was from the last Finnish governor of Finland. Viola Turpeinen's father took a sauna with Nikolai Bobrikov after a symphony performance one evening, and Bobrikov let Viola's dad take one rock as a gift. My father said Turpeinen made that story up. "I heated the rock up, scraped the dark spots, and found the black flecks were just paint," Dad had pointed out. "I didn't have the heart to tell Viola or his father and embarrass them."

The use of rocks in a sauna box as mementos from or symbols for other events in life was how my father and his friends interpreted all of life, especially politics. My father was good at pointing out the symbolism between capitalism and socialism in everything. These two political ideas were his foundations for interpreting reality. He saw these two ideas enmeshed in every event around him, even in stories from the Bible like the story of the first two brothers Cain and Abel making sacrifices to God. Dad told me Cain didn't like that his brother Abel had pleased God and he hadn't. So in order to have his sacrifice accepted the next time, Cain murdered his brother Abel. By killing his brother, Cain demonstrated that it was more important for him to do better than his brother than to cooperate. The most telling part of the story came when he was questioned by God as to the whereabouts of Abel. Cain answered God, "Am I my brother's keeper?" For my dad, the question Cain asked proved his relationship to his brother wasn't a primary priority. His lack of family loyalty and the drive to have his sacrifice accepted despite the cost was at the core of capitalism.

I thought my Dad jumped to conclusions in interpreting the story. I have often thought I needed to find out what Abel was thinking and doing before he was killed and then decide who was right or wrong. I had many ideas. Maybe Abel was secretly gloating over God's rejection of Cain's offering. Maybe Abel didn't care if his gift had been accepted. Or maybe Abel was thinking about how to help his brother Cain do a better job the next time. I liked the last interpretation the best.

The sheriff's announcement seemed to perplex those at the meeting and deflate the discussion. George wound the meeting down and suggested they further discuss spies next Saturday. I used that as my cue to exit my hiding place and head home before the others left.

8 Unfamiliar Hunters

The next morning I watched Arvi kick some rocks past the trees. "Joe, you never did tell me why you didn't stay for the sauna."

I looked at the red maple leaves above Arvi's head. "I didn't know your sister was going to be in there with us. Gosh, Arvi, that was embarrassing."

"I don't know why, Joe. Irene knew you were coming." Arvi found a few more rocks to his liking – white quartz. He kicked them. They hit the large birch to the right of the maples. I think he imagined himself a place kicker on the football team.

"What?" I still didn't look at him.

"Joe, I told Irene you would be coming. You didn't have to be shy or anything. You are a nice guy. Besides, this isn't the first time our family has saunaed with someone from another family."

The red leaves above Arvi's head seemed to be getting redder. I turned and looked at Arvi directly. When I talked with Sara she always looked at me. It was the only way I knew she was listening. "You know our family doesn't sauna together naked."

His blonde eyebrows squeezed together and then relaxed. "I would have said something, if she would have objected."

"It's more than that. It's also about your dad and mom being there naked, and you didn't tell me."

"Come on, Joe. You are making a mountain out of a mole hill. Your dad has saunaed with us before. He never said anything."

"When was that?" I quipped.

"Last year, after the Fall Festival at the park," Arvi answered.

He sounded matter of fact like that's the way it was. Frustrated with my inability to know what to say next, I looked up at the maple trees again. I noticed some yellow leaves mixed in with the red. I hadn't seen those splotches before today. Some leaves looked orangish. They were toward the bottom of the tree.

Arvi interrupted my thoughts. "Come on, Joe, does your dad have to check us out first and approve before you'll sauna with us?"

"That's not what I meant. I thought it was going to be just you and me. And I wanted to be polite. I don't like embarrassing people, especially friends of the family."

Arvi looked at me. "Well, how about the night you ran out naked and jumped into the lake at Mesaba Camp?"

"What!" I was caught off guard. "I am not sure which night you are talking about, Arvi." I thought if I gave him more than one choice maybe I could distract him.

Once again Arvi spoke in his straightforward manner. "Don't you remember, after the dance … the last weekend in August? You were yelling like a banshee! A madman! Then you took your clothes off and jumped into the lake."

He was more focused than I thought. "Yikes, I almost forgot that one. But it was just us guys running to the beach …"

"Think for a moment, Joe. Girls were staying at the women's cabin. Remember? Irene was one of them. So was Sara."

Actually I had forgotten there were girls in the women's cabin that night. "So you are saying Irene and Sara have seen me naked?"

"With the ruckus you made running through the bushes to the beach and then yelling for everybody else to follow you, I think the whole campground knew what was up! I suppose you are going to tell me you forgot that the women's cabin sits right above the beach next to the birch tree grove." Arvi sometimes sounded like the teachers at school, focused on just the one thing they wanted to communicate. They didn't let go, like a dog with a new bone. Nobody could take it away.

I didn't know how we had gotten to that point. I did remember Arvi started the conversation. Boy, I'd rather talk to Sara any day than have this kind of a conversation. I didn't even know how to get off this merry-go-round. I didn't want to have any more conversations today. I thought I would be better off with a short walk in the woods to look for grouse instead.

"I just wanna say I'm sorry, Arvi. Let's hunt."

We entered the woods a little west of Chisholm. We began on a trail that branched off from the one I took to school. We had heard some coveys there last weekend. With all the drumming we had heard on the way to school and back each day this week, I thought we would be able to scare up a few grouse and shoot them.

I liked fall weather. Even though the temperature sometimes got down to freezing or below at night, some days the temperature rose to 60° or 70° when the sun came up. That was one of those days. Maple trees were screaming red. They were the first trees to color their leaves. Next were the birches; they would shout out bright yellows. Against the blue sky, the yellows and reds seemed brighter that sunny fall day. We were lucky.

Although we were out in the morning, the best time to hunt grouse was in the evening. They liked to warm themselves in the late afternoon sun. You could find them in coveys of four to eight birds sitting together near sandy areas such as a road's edge. While sunning, they bit off fresh clover leaves and tender green grass blades near the edge of the road. As they pecked at the grass, they swallowed gravel. The small rocks ended up in what Arvi's dad called the gizzard. Their gizzards were like our stomachs but not exactly the same. A grouse's digestive system had two parts: gizzard and crop.

The crop was the first part; it was before the gizzard. When a bird bit off a shoot, it traveled down the bird's throat into a skin sack called the crop. The crop looked like a soap bubble, kind of thin and cloudy. It tore open easily. By examining the contents, we knew what the bird had eaten that day. Impi taught us to dress the first grouse right after we had killed it and examine the crop's contents. By observing what the bird had eaten, we got a clue as to what other grouse might be eating. Then we prioritized our hunting to areas which had the same kind of feed. Hopefully, other birds were eating in the same place as the first one we had shot.

The gizzard was after the crop. This was where the chewing and digesting were done. The bird's muscles moving the gizzard walls back and forth manipulated the swallowed rocks. As they were pushed around, the pebbles acted like teeth, grinding the food to be digested. I guessed their gizzards were like my mouth. When Impi had told us this, I had wondered why we didn't learn that in biology class. We had been taught the only animal that ate differently than we did was a cow. If I remembered right, we'd learned cows had four stomachs and chewed on cuds. They coughed or threw up the cuds to eat them again and again.

Taisto Rantala thought a grouse's digestive system was like underground mining. The grouse's beak was the large metal sculpture everyone saw above ground. This was where miners climbed into the cable car which lowered them down into an open area underground. There the foreman checked in the miners. Then the men picked up any special tools needed for the shift in addition to the ones they had brought from home. From this staging area or "crop," miners walked down a narrow tunnel to the iron ore vein or gizzard. They used picks, pinas (long metal bars), and shovels to chip the ore into smaller chunks much like the rock granules in the gizzard tore apart the green foliage.

Taisto, my father, and Uncle Launo saw reminders of their work and socialism in everything, all the time. They were obsessed. I was concerned about Arvi and his disappointment in me, but that was more understandable than Dad's or Uncle's obsession. Mentally shaking myself out of my comparison, I knew Arvi wasn't going to talk about anything other than grouse hunting and realized I needed to give my attention to the hunt.

"What do you think our luck is going to be today?" I asked.

"I had been excited walking here because I was thinking about all the birds we saw the last three days. This morning seems too quiet, though. I don't even hear the smaller birds chirping carelessly. That's not a good sign," Arvi answered.

"Let's stop for a few minutes. Maybe we were talking too loud and spooked them," I suggested.

We stopped. Arvi was right; there was not much bird chatter. Even the squirrels weren't running back and forth, scurrying and gathering. I signaled Arvi, and we started the hunt. We walked slow and steady, looking for game, for about one hundred yards. Suddenly we noticed two men in the shade of a tall tamarack tree. Both were smoking. One of the men called to us, "Hey boys, grouse hunting today?" He was the taller of the two with a dark mustache.

"Yes, sir. We saw some coveys here going to and from school this week. We thought we'd see if we could find them and bring a few home for supper," I replied.

"If this will help you, we saw a few coveys this morning. We were right past the jack pines over there." The mustached man pointed east with his cigarette.

"That's the place! That's where we saw them, too! Were they still there?" Arvi asked, excited.

"I got three. Cleaned them right over there." The short man pointed west and back of where the mustached fellow had had us look. His tone was friendly.

"Ahhhhh! I knew we should have started earlier," Arvi sighed.

As if to stem Arvi's disappointment, the short guy added quickly, "But we saw a covey of at least ten ... just west of the jacks... by the cedars." After he spoke he turned his head to the mustached one.

I thanked them. "Okay, that's where we will go then. See you!"

"Whoa . . . Wait boys . . . Could you help us?" yelled the mustached man.

"What?" I responded, grabbing Arvi's shirt sleeve to slow him down and make him stop.

"We need some help. You see, we have some friends who were hunting over by the Bruce Mine shaft. Do you know where that is?"

"Yes, sir," I replied. "Bruce is north of the Dunwoody Mine, about a football field's length from here."

"Well, we haven't seen them since this morning." He paused to blow out some cigarette smoke. "Can you go there fast and come back to let us know if they are still hunting in that area?" the mustached one instructed.

The short guy winked at us.

I shouted back, "Do you want us to tell them anything before we come back?"

The tall, mustached man waved us on. "No. Just ask them if they have seen any grouse anywhere else and then come right back. Tell them you are hunting, too."

"Sure," I said.

Arvi and I turned back to the trail and started walking toward the underground mine location called Bruce. After we had taken a few steps, I glanced back at the two men and thought I saw the mustached one aiming his gun in our direction. I looked at Arvi who was moving forward. I was tempted to grab Arvi's arm, but instead I turned my head slightly so that I could see the men again. The two men were just like we had found them, causally smoking with their guns resting against a tree. I shook my head. I must have imagined it.

I still felt uneasy, though, and reached to take the safety off my gun, just in case we flushed up a grouse. That was when I realized we had forgotten to load our shotguns. I guessed the conversation about the sauna and then meeting two men had distracted us. But I thought that loading our guns might be dangerous since we weren't hunting, and my shotgun had a hair trigger. I decided not to say anything. We didn't need any guns going off prematurely before we helped those guys out. We could load up once we were by ourselves again and hunting.

As we walked to the Bruce Mine shaft, Arvi was the first to speak. "Joe, did you know those two?"

"No."

"Didn't they look different? Like they aren't from here? Those haircuts, shiny hair like they had oil in it … Their clothes ain't dirty."

"I didn't notice." My thoughts had drifted back to Arvi's description of my running naked through the campgrounds at Mesaba Park. I was preoccupied with trying to imagine what I looked like naked to Irene and Sara that night. I wondered if I had looked good. What did they think was attractive? I had heard they liked muscles, large biceps. I knew the football players liked to brag about how large their muscles were and how the girls liked muscles. My father said the larger your muscles were, the more weight you had to carry around with you. He thought being strong was nice, but being quick on your feet was better. You never knew when you would have to run away from something or someone.

Arvi persisted in calling my attention to his observations of the two men. "Do you really think they were hunting, Joe?"

"I do. They sounded sincere. I guess I didn't think about how they looked ... What are you worried about, Arvi?" Arvi seemed more worried about two men with clothes on who we didn't know than about his family naked with a friend.

Arvi seemed determined there was something suspicious going on. "Joe, do you think they cleaned their birds looking like that? That doesn't make sense. There weren't burrs stuck to their clothes or socks... I would like to see you looking that good after hunting. They looked more like they were going to a meeting or church."

I thought I would agree with him. This seemed a better approach than the one I had used earlier in talking about the sauna. Besides, he had me thinking now. "Come to think of it, Arvi, they didn't even smell like they had been hunting."

Arvi was focused. "I knew you would agree with me, Joe. Okay, let's get to the shaft as quick as we can, see if their friends are hunting, and then go back and let them know."

The Bruce Mine shaft was further away than we thought. Arvi and I stayed on the trail and didn't talk. I thought about yesterday's study session. Arvi's mom said the guy she saw putting letters into the mail every day for Duluth had a mustache. Maybe Arvi was onto something here. Before we got in too deep, maybe we should just turn around and go back. We could tell those two guys we didn't see anybody... Who cared?

Then I began to wonder why we were looking for their friends, anyway. Those two guys had legs. What did we owe them? But that wouldn't have been polite or right ... I decided not to change what we promised. Finally, we saw the tall iron structure with cables running up through the center of the small building to the top of the head railings. The cables weren't moving; there wasn't any noise. I thought maybe the mine was shut down for the day.

"Do you see anyone, Joe?" Arvi asked.

"No..." I replied. "I don't get it. There's always somebody here."

"Come to think of it, Joe, I didn't see guys working here when I was walking over to meet you earlier."

"I don't remember seeing anyone, either, Arvi ..." We both stopped to think for a moment. I heard a grouse drumming. When they drummed, my heart picked up speed. "Maybe they went into Chisholm and are fixing something at the shops," I said.

"That must be it," agreed Arvi.

As we neared the mine shaft's cable hoist shed, we still didn't see anybody moving about or hear any noises. Curious as to whether anyone was around or not, I stepped up on a wood crate underneath the window near the back of the shop and looked in. It was dark inside. I couldn't see anything. I called back to Arvi. "Arvi, go around and try the side door. I'll watch from the window and see if anything moves inside."

"Oh, no, Joe, I'm not doing that ... The last time we did that, old man Rantala scared the shit out of me!"

"Arvi, that was Halloween, it was nighttime, and Taisto had a pumpkin under his arm with a carved face. This is broad daylight."

I laughed to myself. I remembered when Rantala had scared Arvi last Halloween. At the maintenance shops outside Chisholm, Arvi's dad and Mr. Rantala had taken some pumpkins, carved them, and placed them in scrapped-out cable cars lying around the north side of the building. Then they had scattered candles around the metal carcasses, even setting some on the ground. In the middle of the junked machinery sat an operator's chair with all the controls, floor pedals, and brake levers. That was where Mr. Rantala had been hiding.

The men had told us there were bags of treats hidden in the mess of pumpkins and candles. They had told us to grope around in the dark and find them. The lit candles hadn't been bright enough to overpower the dark shadows. In our minds, the scene was haunted, like a cemetery. Creeping through the shadowy darkness, we concentrated on reaching and touching rather than looking and watching where we were going.

Mr. Rantala had crouched behind the door in front of the operator's chair. Arvi had been so focused on reaching for candy in the corners of the operator platform that he hadn't noticed Mr. Rantala. When Arvi accidently touched Mr. Rantala's leg, Mr. Rantala yelled "Boo" right into Arvi's face. Arvi fell backwards and hit his head. He screamed so loudly I stopped my search and ran in the direction of his shriek. Arvi cut his head and had some blood on his face. I think Mr. Rantala wiped Arvi's face off.

Putting Halloween out of his mind, Arvi walked around to the side door. He pulled it open and stepped in. "Nobody is in here, Joe," he hollered through the walls. "I don't even see lunch buckets or jackets."

"Where are the hunters?" I wondered. I didn't like this. I remembered the discussion of spies yesterday. I felt Arvi and I were dealing with something our dads would want to know. "Okay, let's head back," I said out loud.

It was warmer now. The fall sun could be as hot as a summer day by late afternoon, but it wasn't even noon yet. Maybe the warmth I felt was from within. I touched the back of my neck and felt moisture. Then I placed my hand on my forehead and felt moisture there, too. I didn't know what was making me damp, the sun or my nervousness.

As we approached the tamarack tree, we saw the mustached man and his friend standing by the road. They hadn't moved. They were still smoking cigarettes. The mustached guy looked at his watch and then at us as he ground his cigarette into the tree's bark. "Hey boys ... How did it go? Did you see anyone hunting?" he said.

"No, sir," replied Arvi.

The short guy asked, "Are you sure? Did you look inside the cable hoist shed, too?"

"Yes, we did," I answered.

"Good boys, good boys! Here's a dollar for your time." The mustached man leaned over and placed a dollar bill in each of our pants pockets. Arvi took his out and looked at it. "A dollar?" he questioned.

"Yes, a dollar." The mustached man nodded. "I hope we see you boys again. You are real nice kids, real nice kids." The corners of his mouth turned up for a slight moment and then returned to flatness.

The short guy didn't say or do anything. He just watched.

"Thanks!" I said.

"Bye," said Arvi.

The two men walked off. We stood for a while and stared as they left our sight. Even out of sight, I still heard the two walking away from us.

Noises in the woods sounded crisper in the fall. If I listened closely, I heard the click-clack noises made by leaves swinging in the breeze. My dad thought fall tree leaves had less water in them, so when they bumped each other they rustled louder than in the summer. Their stems were drier in the fall. When they moved in the wind, they snapped off their branches and fell to the ground. That was why Dad taught me to move slowly and watch my step when hunting small game. Any snap of a twig from a hunter's weight was a loud sound like the crack of a .22 rifle to the rabbits and grouse. Crushing a large branch resembled a shot gun blast. That scattered the game further.

Arvi was right. Those two were noisy. They weren't hunting. . .

9   Maintenance Shop Scuffle

"Arvi," I said.

"Joe?"

"Let's go back to the mine shaft. I think we missed something." I motioned for him to follow me.

Arvi just stood there. He fondled the dollar bill in his hand and then looked up. "We already got our dollar. Why would you want to go back?"

I did not want to get caught in a long conversation with him again, but I wanted to find out why we got dollars. I knew my dad was going to question where I got all the money and why. I had never heard of strangers giving money to kids…especially this much money. Something wasn't right. We had to figure this out by ourselves, just Arvi and me.

"Arvi, I think you're right; those men weren't hunters. I don't think they've ever hunted in their lives. Something else must be going on here. Maybe we can find out what it is. This might help us figure out who those men are," I suggested.

Arvi was still holding the dollar. Finally, he moved to follow me.

Maple reds and birch yellows colored the scene as we walked back to the mine shaft. Both Arvi and I examined the sides of the trail on the way back. There weren't signs of bird entrails or empty shotgun shells. There wasn't any smell of spent gunpowder or grouse guts. Nothing was trampled. The trail brush and long grass were in place. It sure looked like nobody had been down this path before Arvi and me. I began getting warm again. This time I felt a drop of sweat roll down the back of my neck. It soaked into my flannel shirt.

When we hunted with our fathers, they lectured us. Hunting was more than shooting a gun and killing a feathered creature. In order to make this point clear, they only allowed us to carry and shoot single shot 410s, one shot, one bird. If we missed with the first shot, the partridge would be out of range and sight by the time we reloaded. I thought this unfair and told my father. My dad's shotgun held two shells. I had heard some boys at school talking about some shotguns which held four in the stock and one in the firing chamber. Why did I only have one shell? I had heard the "one shot lecture" so many times that I had it memorized.

Joseph, you have the advantage with a shotgun. The grouse has only luck. To be fair for the bird, you need to shoot and take the grouse down with one shot. If you can't take the bird down with one shot, then you don't have the privilege to hunt.

When you do take her, make sure you look at her closely. Appreciate her beauty. Kneel beside her on the forest floor. Admire the camouflage her feathers create. Feel the warmth of her body. Thank your dead feathered friend for her sacrificed life.

Shooting a bird for supper isn't about killing; it is about how and why you shoot the bird. She has a right to life just like we do. She is not hunting you. She only has luck. You must take only what you need because you have the power to decide.

I knew I shouldn't be wasteful. One bird was enough for me to eat. I needed to save game for the others who hunted, too, but I still thought it was unfair that I only got one shot per bird. Not one of my friends had this damn rule. Why did we have it? What if I was a poor shot? How fair was that? I was just as hungry as the other person who was a good shot.

"Over here, Joe," Arvi yelled, breaking up my thoughts.

"Should we go in the shed?" I wondered.

Arvi motioned for me to walk over to him. "Let's scout around first."

Before we entered the cable car's machinery shed, we circled the area. I didn't know what we were looking for, but we kept looking. We didn't see extra boot prints in the soil. No new windows were broken. Everything seemed to be in place, except no one was working. I opened the main door, and we both went inside.

I walked over to the large cable spool and noticed there wasn't much cable spooled. This meant the cable was extended. The other end of this particular cable was attached to the cab in which the miners were lowered down and pulled up from the underground mine shaft. The ore they blasted and dug out was also carried up in the cab. Sometimes the ore and miners shared the same ride to the surface. As I looked at the spool,

Arvi climbed over the railing. He stomped up the steel grate steps and then headed to the back platform where the operator's "cage" was located.

The nervousness I had felt last Halloween during the candy hunt in the Chisholm maintenance shop yard crept into me. I swallowed. *There was nothing to be afraid of,* I thought. We had been in the machinery shed other times. Impi had even let Arvi and me sit in the chair and play with the pedals and levers … and this wasn't Halloween.

I watched Arvi climb into the operator's chair. He looked at me. "Watch this, Joe. I'm going to start the cable winch."

"Be careful!" I shouted.

Like a madman, Arvi started to pull levers, twist knobs, and step on floor pedals while he spun the seat back and forth. As quickly as he started, he stopped. The grin on his face froze. "Whoa! Joe, come up here!"

I walked toward him. "What is it, Arvi?"

"Just come up here! Right now!"

I could see Arvi was bent over, pulling on something below the operator's chair. He was grunting, and his back was arched. When I got there he had both his hands around what looked like a metal broomstick, and he was wiggling the metal pole back and forth. Three other poles were next to him.

"The brake levers, Joe, they aren't locked."

"Let me see that..." I hurdled over the railing and entered the cage. At the top of each broomstick was a small lever. They were about five inches long. When you gripped one and held it against the larger metal stick, the smaller lever locked into place. The levers Arvi was playing with wouldn't lock up.

"You are right, Arvi, the drum isn't locked. Damn! That's why there isn't any cable on the spool. The cable car must still be at the bottom of the shaft." I slammed my closed fist on the lever closest to me.

"We'd better tell somebody, Joe. Maybe some miners are still down in the mine shaft." Arvi sounded nervous, even scared.

"If there are guys down there, why isn't there somebody here in the shed? I don't like this, Arvi. There are always two or three men atop. You never know when a load needs to be brought up and supplies sent down. What should we do?"

I didn't know why I asked Arvi what to do. This day was getting darker and darker. Arvi's instincts were right about those two guys. "Arvi," I said. "Let's go over to the maintenance shops. There has to be someone there who works on these cable shaft cars."

"Let's hurry, Joe! They will be there if we hurry!" Arvi took off running down what looked like a cow trail toward the repair shop which was just over the mine dumps.

Mine dumps were hills made from the earth and lower grade ore excavated from strip mining. This earth covering was piled up on the ground away from the ore veins in open pit mining. These dumps stood forty to sixty feet high. We had given nicknames to each of the different dumps like Big Red, Devil's Hill, and the Fat One. Older dumps had trees and grass growing on them. The only way you knew they were a dump was by their shapes. Dumps were flat on top, and their sides were all at the same angle. They looked man-made compared to nature-made hills.

I followed Arvi through a shortcut across the top of the largest one, Big Red. We ran so hard our sweat collected the red iron ore dust we kicked up. My forearms and forehead were red. Arvi and I stopped at the end of the dump and looked down at the Chisholm shops. At one time, there had been trees all over this area, but they had been removed. A large work yard and open storage areas for mining equipment had replaced the trees.

At either end of the two large buildings were doors that swung open for mining equipment to be taken in and out. On hot days, the repair guys kept the doors open. This cooled down the inside work areas and allowed daylight to lighten up the work benches. These buildings had few windows or doors since glass was expensive and broke easily.

"Look, Arvi, there are your dad and six other guys from the Sunday study session. They must have gotten done early." I was huffing so hard from running that I couldn't keep my finger steady as I pointed to the men.

Arvi wasn't even looking at where I was pointing.

"Let's go down and let them know there is no one in the cable car shack and the cable is out," I urged.

Arvi didn't seem to hear me. He continued to stare down at the repair area. "Wait. Joe, see those guys over there? I think they are the men who met us in the woods and gave us the dollar bills."

"I see them, Arvi."

"I don't know if we should go down there, Joe."

"Okay. Let's just lie down on the ground here and watch for a while."

Both of us lay down, our bellies flat and our heads up. We saw one group of about thirteen men located near the west end of the largest building. They were huddled close to each other and out of view. Most of them didn't seem to have guns or weapons of any sort, except some had holstered batons. They all were dressed the same. Their clothes matched, like a group of ants.

Unlike the hidden group, the mustached man and his hunting partner were in full view of the study session men. Gesturing behind his back with his arm, the mustached man motioned for the hidden group of men to stay.

Frank Vainionpaa, Toivo, and Matthew Wirtannen led the miners' group of seven which included Arvi's dad Impi. They walked toward the two men who had given us the dollars and formed a semi-circle around them. Mika was the miner furthest away from the two would-be hunters we had met earlier. Addressing Frank, Mr. Mustache was doing most of the talking. We didn't hear what they said, but their exchange didn't look friendly.

Slowly, Frank kicked dirt back and forth with his right foot. Toivo Soumi had crossed his arms. He squinted from behind his thick glasses. When he was nervous, Impi spat. He was spitting after each chew and then wiping his mouth obsessively. Yrkki moved in closer, trying to calm Impi down. Impi shrugged Yrkki away, but Yrkki stood firm. Mr. Mustache's partner stared at Impi.

Some of Mr. Mustache's hidden men who could see the confrontation began mimicking Impi's spitting. Their antics caused the other hidden men to move forward, and they bunched up at the building's edge. Mr. Mustache started to push Frank back. Using the palms of his hands, he leaned into Frank, relaxed, and then leaned in again. I'd often heard that Frank could explode and thought this might be the time I would get to see it. My father had told a story once about Frank losing it when a Federal person asked him about his role in the 1906 strike. Dad said Frank had started throwing whatever was nearby, including shovels, railroad spikes, and rail plates. He had even knocked out a couple of windows in the maintenance shop, but he hadn't hit the Fed with any of the objects. He had just scared the guy. Frank would have lost his job if he had touched or hit the Fed.

Suddenly, a black car stopped on the road at the south side of first building, and a small group of men wearing police uniforms got out. They walked toward the two strangers from the woods. As the police approached, the men huddled out of view slowly began to move around the corner of the shop into a position behind the miners. Impi and the rest were so fixated on Mr. Mustache and what was being said that they didn't notice the thirteen.

The distances played games with my eyes. From a distance, everyone kind of looked the same. They reminded me of ants next to a picnic table. Unless the ants were different colors, like red or brown, it was hard to tell one ant from another. If a small chunk of potato salad fell off the picnic table onto the ground, before I counted to ten the dressing-covered piece was swarmed. Antennae touched other antennae; the chunk was walked over by two or three sets of ant legs. When the ants pushed the sweet bite back to their hill home, six pushed one way, one the other way, and two circled. That was what seemed to be happening below us. Guys were milling around, looking at each other, ready to push. Now the black ants were joining the potato salad fiasco.

"Arvi, that's Robert McFarland, the sheriff, walking toward both groups."

Mr. Mustache and his friend had turned ninety degrees away from the miners' group. They were now positioned between the miners and the law enforcement.

"Look, Joe, Mr. Mustache is saying something to Sheriff McFarland. Oh, oh, McFarland is shaking his head and stomping his foot now."

"Do you think McFarland can see those other guys coming around the corner?"

"Joe, did you see that? McFarland got pushed hard."

"Yeah! Arvi, look. McFarland just got pushed again! Now he's grabbing some dirt and throwing it into Mr. Mustache's face."

"Mustache is trying to kick McFarland in the crotch."

The sheriff's men moved around Mustache toward the miners' group. The miners gathered close to them. The men who had been behind the shed moved up on both the miners and the officers. Suddenly, they sprinted through both groups, pushing them aside. Three of them tackled McFarland.

"Joe! McFarland's on the ground! They are kicking him!"

"Oh, my God, Arvi we've got to tell someone! I have got to let Dad know what is happening."

"Wait, Joe. Shit, Frank just jumped Mustache. He has Mustache on the ground."

"Boy, did he hit Mustache in the face! Go, Frank, go!"

Mustache's hunting partner pulled a whistle from his pocket and blew three short shrills. As if on command, the men from behind the shed took out wooden batons and brass knuckles and started hitting Impi, the miners, and McFarland. Mustache was kneeling next to McFarland. His boot buckle had gotten caught in the sheriff's shirt. In yanking his boot to free the buckle, he shredded McFarland's shirt, and the Sheriff's badge dropped to the ground. Quickly, Mustache covered the shiny metal star with his hand. As he stood, he slipped the badge deep into his pocket. Then he joined the assault on the miners' group.

Arvi closed his wet eyes, turned, and buried his face in the grass. When the hunting partner blew one long shrill whistle, Arvi's head bobbed up. Abruptly, the men from behind the shed stopped fighting. They ran back around the west side of the building and down the orange ore road to the back dumps. McFarland's men helped McFarland and Frank up, brushing both off.

"Dad! Dad!" Arvi yelled as he ran down from where we had been hiding and watching the fight.

I ran after him. No one seemed to hear Arvi's yelling. We both ran faster. When we got to the maintenance shop, McFarland was in the back side of the police car lying down. Impi had gone into the shop to help clean up Frank. Arvi headed toward his dad in the shop, but the youngest-looking deputy stopped Arvi. The deputy noticed me and waved me over. He introduced himself as Stephan Steblibovich.

Looking at Arvi, Steblibovich asked, "So, where did you two come from?"

Arvi didn't answer, struggling to leave to see his father.

"Ted and Scott," Steblibovich ordered, "come here and hold this kid. I am going to talk to the other one."

The officers came over and stood on either side of Arvi. Each grabbed one of Arvi's arms. Arvi calmed down and looked at me.

"What's your name?" Deputy Steblibovich asked me.

"Joe," I replied.

"Joe who?"

I didn't know what to say.

"What's your last name, Joe?"

"Koivu."

"What's your friend's name?"

"Arvi. Arvi Eskola."

"Impi's son?"

"Yep," I responded.

"So what happened here, Joe?"

"Well, Arvi and I were hunting grouse over there," I pointed over to the dump Arvi and I had walked over. "We heard this ruckus, so we stopped hunting and came over here to see what was going on."

"Okay. So what did you see?"

"It was kind of hard to tell," I answered. "There was dirt in the air, I mean red orange dust. Some guys that were behind the shop came around here and then jumped the miner guys."

"Okay. So who started the fight?"

"I don't know. It was going on when we got close enough to see everyone. We did see the sheriff get punched."

I didn't know why it was hard for me to tell the truth. Arvi didn't say a thing or help. He looked at me. I realized that I was too shook up to tell a good story. Satisfied that I was telling the truth, Steblibovich told both Arvi and me to go home. He said he knew our fathers and would get in touch with us next week. The officers holding Arvi released him. Arvi and I began to walk back to where we had been earlier that morning.

"Why didn't you tell them the truth, Joe?"

"Leave me alone."

"Joe, what is it with you?"

"What do you mean?" I snapped.

"You didn't figure out Mustache and his friend weren't hunters. Then you couldn't tell the deputy what really happened."

"I know my dad will get mad at me if I get into trouble with the police. He always told me if I ever have to talk to an officer, never say too -much and act dumb. He doesn't trust them."

"Well, my dad says Robert McFarland is a good guy."

"That's what your dad thinks, Arvi. He still works for the mines. My dad didn't get to come back after the last strike." I stopped, grabbed Arvi's arm, and looked him straight in the eyes. "You know what? I don't think you should tell your Dad that you were here and saw what you saw."

"I don't know, Joe."

"What if we meet Mustache in the woods again, and he recognizes us? He might do something to us," I cautioned.

"Like he did to those miners?"

"Yeah, he might beat us up like he did to your dad. If you are wondering about who was down in the mine shaft, we don't know what happened down there. We don't know if anyone was down there. We never got the chance to tell anyone about seeing the extended cable. There could be miners hurt or dead down there, but we don't know that. Let's keep it that way until someone says something about a mining accident or dead miners, okay?"

Arvi looked back at me, uncertain. "You don't want me to tell Dad?"

"Not now. It might get him into more trouble."

The image of Impi getting beat up by those guys with brass knuckles made Arvi shudder. "What do I say if the deputy comes around?"

"Maybe he'll forget," I said, hoping that he would.

Arvi gave me a doubting look, turned, and headed back the way we had come. When we got back to the woods where we had started the day, we parted.

I didn't want to tell Arvi that my father was afraid that his membership in the IWW might get him into trouble with the cops. My Uncle Launo and cousin Niilo were afraid, too. People who lived in town in a nice house like Arvi's had an easier time getting along with the cops. Arvi didn't get that.

I didn't know what I would say if the deputy came to our house next week.

10   Dissection

"Mr. Keestir?"

Mr. Kaiser walked toward the student. He noticed that the student's hair didn't lie down. Here and there a tuft pointed up and out in an odd way. *At least his shirt is buttoned right,* Mr. Kaiser thought before he addressed the student. "Jerry. My name is Mr. Kaiser not Mr. Keestir."

"Mr. Keestir, my name is Jeremiah, not Jerry."

Jeremiah wasn't being disrespectful, but he wasn't being helpful, either. He just stared back at Mr. Kaiser and waited for a response. He wondered why some of these Finnish children had such strong dispositions. They were like dwarf King Lears yelling into the Tempest.

The first hour was always the hardest because those students who were not focused usually made their presence known. To them the classroom was not a formal place, one in which levity was to be minimized so principles of science could be grasped.

"Sorry, Jeremiah Rantala," Mr. Kaiser responded.

Jeremiah understood Mr. Kaiser's response not as apology but as another contribution to the conversation they were going to have. Jeremiah continued, "Mr. Keestir, do we get to piss on frogs?" His question was sincere.

Giggles broke into laughter. Mr. Kaiser had to reply quickly. He didn't want to set any bad precedents. With immigrant children and their lack of formal education, he knew this could be difficult. They didn't have examples of normal conversations in their homes. Besides, Mr. Kaiser been tipped off to Jeremiah's behaviors in the classroom by the other teachers. He thought it best to take Jeremiah's remarks at face value.

"We won't be pissing on frogs, Jeremiah. We will be pithing frogs. Please notice I used the word 'pithing'."

"Oh, I thought you said pissing," Jeremiah smiled.

Mr. Kaiser dreaded that he even used the word pissing to answer

Jeremiah, but his word choice seemed to quiet everyone down. He knew immigrant children's parents never reported incidents to the principal, so he was safe using inappropriate language today.

A girl with braided raven-black hair raised her hand.

"Yes," said Mr. Kaiser.

"Mr. Kaiser?" she questioned.

He turned toward the front of the class where she sat and took three steps in her direction.

"Yes, Elaine Schwartz?"

Elaine turned her head slightly toward him and continued, "I don't know why we have to cut animals open to learn about life. Can't somebody else do it and then tell us?"

Mr. Kaiser was pleased with her question. He had heard the other teachers mention Elaine. She asked sincere questions which were more than operational. Rather than remain silent and listen, Elaine probed for the "real" reason if she was afraid or threatened.

"That's a good question, Elaine."

Now Mr. Kaiser had a chance to use Elaine's question as a way to communicate more about why the school required biology.

"Elaine and the rest of you listen to me for a moment. *Bio* means life in Greek; *ology* means the study of. We will be studying life. Now I'm sure you've heard all kinds of stories about what happens in this class. For example, Elaine has mentioned we will cut open some animals –"

Before he could launch into his prepared rationale for dissecting, Jeremiah had another question. Of course, Jeremiah asked his question without raising his hand or thinking about the timing of his thoughts.

"Mr. Keestir, do we have to bring our own animals?"

Mr. Kaiser had never heard that question before. Was it a joke? It didn't matter. It was a practical concern, and it demonstrated Jeremiah was focused – at least for now. Looking at Jeremiah in the back of the classroom, Mr. Kaiser responded, "Quiet, Jerry – Jeremiah. The school will supply the animals. Most of them will be dead – deceased."

Ouch! Mr. Kaiser realized what might be on Jeremiah's mind. The boy was nervous about his or someone else's pets.

"So we'll have to kill some animals?"

This was a difficult issue in his biology class. Most students didn't comprehend the importance of dissecting. Their parents had never taken biology, so they weren't able to pass on the necessity of this type of scientific study. Mr. Kaiser walked to the center of the classroom and stopped. He had his pat answer for the nervousness that students have about biology lab.

"Class, how many of your parents hunt deer? Please raise your hands."

Most raised their hands.

"Okay, thanks. How many of you are in families who hunt or snare rabbits?"

Not as many hands were raised.

"All right. Thanks. Grouse?"

Half the students raised their hands.

"Do you fish?"

All hands went up.

"That's what I thought. Most of you do, and I bet most of you eat fish."

All the students nodded in agreement.

"That's what I thought. How many of you eat chicken? Beef? …"

Mr. Kaiser paused. After naming off at least six different meat sources, the brighter students began to make the connection that what they were doing in biology lab wasn't that different than what happened in their homes.

After a short pause to let the idea sink in, Mr. Kaiser continued, "So, if we kill animals to eat them, I think we can kill animals to study them. Killing animals just to eat them is more selfish - don't you think? It only helps the people eating them. Killing animals to study them helps everyone."

Mr. Kaiser liked this logic. In fact, he had learned how to use this approach when he moved here from New York. He had not hunted or fished before coming here. His father had worked in a bank. When he moved to northern Minnesota, he had observed the lifestyles of people who were much more self-sufficient than the urban people back home.

Once again, Jeremiah couldn't contain himself. He popped off another question without raising his hand. "Mr. Keestir. Will we eat them?"

Mr. Kaiser wasn't ready for Jeremiah's persistent curiosity and reacted, "Jeremiah! Stop with the questions!"

Mr. Kaiser paused and looked around the class. They were innocent, he consoled himself.

"I know some of you may be nervous about studying what's inside an animal's body. I was the first time I took a biology class. However, we won't be doing those activities until the second part of the course, which is after Christmas. So we have plenty of time to get ready for this type of study."

Elaine poked me in the back with her shoe. I leaned my head back and held it there. I wanted to hear what she had to say but look like I was stretching while I listened.

"I feel sick, Sara. How about you?"

Her words surprised me. Elaine was always happy and never got sick, especially in school. I wondered what was bothering her.

"I guess I feel okay. What's bothering you?" I replied.

Elaine lowered her voice and said the same thing over again. "I feel sick, Sara. How about you? Aren't you worried?"

"Elaine, I'm not sure. What are you worried about?" I asked.

"In my religion, there are animals we cannot touch or eat. I don't think I can cut them open to study, either," Elaine explained.

"I'm not sure what you mean," I responded.

We had never talked much about religion. I guess there hadn't been a need.

Elaine elaborated. "We have a word kosher in our religion. Kosher means God has said a certain animal is okay to eat and touch. For instance, I can eat goat meat because it is kosher, but I cannot eat pig meat – like bacon or ham."

"You mean you don't have bacon with your eggs in the morning for breakfast?" I wondered.

"No," Elaine replied quickly.

Her response sounded definite. I didn't get what she was trying to say to me. I knew her religion was different. She wasn't like the other friends I had who went to church. They ate just like I did.

Elaine was always good at trying to explain things to me when it came to her religion, and I liked her ideas.

I continued, "Have you ever tasted bacon? It's good."

"No."

Elaine had me a little irritated now. I wasn't accustomed to a short answer from her, and she had made two in a row. She liked words. Why wouldn't she use them? I felt like she was either mad at me or hiding something from me. A little unsettled, I inquired, "Then how do you know you don't like bacon?"

Elaine's face looked like she had just sucked a sour lemon. I'd never seen her do that with her face before. Just as I was going to ask her another question, she said, "Sara, I said, 'I can't eat bacon.' I didn't say I don't like bacon."

Her logic was eluding me. I couldn't understand why a person wouldn't eat something she liked. I thought everyone ate food because they liked it. They thought it tasted good. I realized I would get distracted talking to Elaine, but I didn't care. I was determined to understand what was on Elaine's mind. "Don't you have ham at Easter?"

"No," Elaine replied, attempting patience. "That is bacon, too."

I knew ham was bacon. Bacon and ham weren't the same size or shape, but they came from the same animal. It was kind of like chicken which had white meat and dark meat. Some people liked white; some people liked dark; and some people ate both.

Hoping to get a better idea of what she was trying to tell me, I asked, "How can you not like something if you haven't eaten or tasted it?"

Elaine wasted no time replying. "Because it's not kosher."

"What?"

"I told you, Sara, Kosher means God has said it's okay to eat. As a Jew, I am not to eat pig meat. It is not okay to eat. It is not kosher."

"So the only reason you don't eat bacon or ham is because the Rabbi said God told you not to?"

"Yes."

That was the first time I understood a part of Elaine's religion. Some parts of her faith were just rules. They were followed whether they made sense or not. I guessed those rules were like traditions. You did them all the time because people before you did them all the time. Nobody seemed to mind. I knew Elaine was smart, but not eating food because God said not to eat food, even though the food tasted good, didn't make sense to me. When everyone else ate the food, I thought that you should, too.

Elaine was different than the other girls. She had darker skin and black hair, and she dressed nicely all the time. She wore glasses. I thought that was why the boys didn't like her. I got to know her because her father's clothing store wasn't too far from our co-op.

Sometimes I saw Elaine in her parents' store and stopped by to talk. They sold clothing, shoes, and undergarments, much nicer than the ones we had at the co-op. They had what were called Sunday-go-to-church clothes. You didn't work or play in those clothes. They were kind of like the costumes my mother wore when she sang on the stage. I guessed those clothes would be called fancy. They were the type of clothes you bought in order to look good. I wondered what I might look like in fancy clothes. Would I like what I saw? Would I want to wear them in front of people? One evening when I was with her, I hoped Mother would let me try on some of the costumes kept in the back of the theater. Then I would have seen how I looked in fancy clothes.

The entire time I was thinking about Elaine, Mr. Kaiser was telling us about our class. A great deal of class time, I daydreamed or thought about other things. I didn't think that was wrong. How could I pay attention all the time, anyway?

11   Co-op Mouse

"Sara," Mr. Kaiser called my name.

"Yes, Mr. Kaiser," I responded.

"Can you tell me who Charles Darwin is?" Mr. Kaiser asked.

"I'm not sure what you mean Mr. Kaiser..." I decided to stop there and not say anything more.

"That's what I thought, Sara."

His voice sounded like he knew me or was disappointed in what I had said. For a moment, he didn't say anything. I waited.

As he continued to look at me, he said, "We are going around the room and reading from the first chapter of our textbook. Kalle just finished her passage. Now it is your turn to read."

He didn't tell me the page or paragraph. He was testing me.

Lucky for me, Elaine kicked me in the back and whispered, "In the middle of page ten, Sara, the second paragraph."

I lifted the book up in front of my face and read loudly,

Darwin used the term natural selection to describe the process by which organisms with favorable variations survive and reproduce at a higher rate. An inherited variation that increases an organism's chance of survival in a particular environment is called an adaptation. Over many generations, an adaptation could spread throughout the entire species. In this way, evolution by natural selection would occur.

As an example Darwin noted that the ptarmigan turns white in winter. This color change helped protect it from predators, which would have a hard time spotting the bird in snow. Ptarmigans that didn't change color in winter would be spotted easily and eaten. In this way, Darwin implied, ptarmigans that turned white in winter would be more likely to survive, reproduce, and pass this adaptation to future generations.

As I heard my voice, I liked the way I sounded. I didn't stumble over the words. I said all of them, and I thought there was a nice rhythm to my reading. I thought of Mrs. Schultz, our English teacher. She also directed the school plays and read poetry at public meetings, even at ones that weren't school-related. During the Fourth of July, the mayor had her read the Gettysburg Address. I thought I sounded as good.

"Excuse me, Mr. Kaiser, what's a ptarmigan?" Eino Vainionpaa asked. Eino didn't ask questions unless he thought it was important to know the answer.

Mr. Kaiser was polite and smiled when he talked to the class. "Eino Vainionpaa, Sara is reading. Please raise your hand if you have a question."

This wasn't really true. I was done with my passage. *Mr. Kaiser just doesn't want to deal with more questions,* I thought.

Sometimes teachers got like that. They wanted a class to be about information, reading, and taking notes. Questions slowed the class down. I didn't know if I agreed with that. When I worked in the co-op with my dad, he always told me to ask questions to make sure I really knew what I was supposed to be doing and why. He said that whatever I did I should do it well. That was important to him. When he was happy, I was happy, and our members were happy. The Work People's Co-op Store was about making life better for everyone.

Eino raised his hand this time.

"Yes, Eino," acknowledged Mr. Kaiser.

"Mr. Kaiser, what's a ptarmigan?" Eino lowered his hand and crossed it over his other arm on the desktop. Was it a protective barrier?

Mr. Kaiser cleared his throat and directed me, "Sara, please stop reading. I want to answer the question."

I had already stopped. Mr. Kaiser stood up from his desk, went to the chalkboard, and picked up a piece of chalk. On the board, he wrote two words next to each other: ptarmigan and partridge. Then he placed the chalk in the tray, brushed his hands, and answered Eino. "A ptarmigan is another word for partridge."

"Then why doesn't the book say partridge, Mr. Kaiser?"

Mr. Kaiser didn't hesitate. Eino was bright, and Mr. Kaiser wanted to avoid nurturing another Jeremiah. "Ptarmigan or partridge are both grouse, but there are eighteen varieties of grouse. You might want to think of a family, Eino. You all have the same last name, but you have different first names. When you have been hunting, I am sure you heard someone say he shot a Hungarian partridge, a ruffed grouse, or spruce hen –"

Before Mr. Kaiser could finish his answer, Jeremiah blurted out, "My grandfather says spruce hens are real dumb. They just sit there. You can walk right up to one and grab her. My grandfather says they use gunny sacks when they hunt them. They club them on the head with a baseball bat and throw them in the sack."

Jeremiah's comments got quite a few different responses and laughs. I guessed everyone needed a break from all the reading and no talking.

"Quiet!" Mr. Kaiser yelled. "The original question was 'What is a ptarmigan?' So I am going to answer that question for Eino. The type of grouse living in Newfoundland is called a ptarmigan. This grouse turns white in winter. The grouse we hunt here keeps the same color year round. Newfoundland is one of the areas where Darwin studied evolution. I don't know if Darwin ever used the word partridge. Grouse is the family or species name."

Mr. Kaiser picked up the chalk and wrote species on the board. Then he turned and faced the class. He looked at Eino. "Thanks, Eino."

Eino smiled.

"Does anyone else have something to add?"

Elaine raised her hand, which made me happy. Maybe she had gotten over her kosher thing.

"Mr. Kaiser, you mean the ptarmigan is like a rabbit. Rabbits change from brown to white in the winter. You can't see them in the snow until they start to move."

I didn't know Elaine knew anything about animals. I was surprised. She had given a good example to help explain what Mr. Kaiser was trying to teach us. I felt proud of her. Mr. Kaiser must have, too. "That's correct, Elaine."

Eino raised his hand. He was pleased that Mr. Kaiser had thanked him earlier and wanted to contribute more.

Mr. Kaiser recognized him. "Yes, Eino? Do you have something more to add?"

"I know what Elaine is talking about when she said a rabbit's fur changes colors, but she forgot what happens when we get an early snow and it melts."

Everyone could hear the self-confidence in Eino's voice.

"I am not sure what you mean, Eino?" replied Mr. Kaiser. He sat on the top of his desk and appeared to expect a longer answer or perhaps a discussion.

Eino started his response a little louder. "When it snows, a rabbit's fur color begins to change from brown to white. Some rabbits change faster than others. What that means is that if the first snow melts, then the rabbits that started to turn white are easy to see. They have a hard time hiding. Their white color shows up against the darker forest floor."

The bell rang. It was the end of class. Everyone began putting their books away but remained seated. Mr. Kaiser gave his closing comments, "Sorry, class is done. I will see you all tomorrow. Remember to find an example of an adaptation from nature for class tomorrow. You may leave."

As the classroom emptied, I glanced at Elaine. She had that look on her face that she needed something. Elaine reached out, touched me, and got my attention. "Sara, can you eat lunch with me?"

I hesitated. I had eaten lunch with her every day last year, but this year I was hoping to make some new friends. "Sure. Where would you like to sit?"

"Let's go to the other side of the building, Sara. I have something I want to talk about."

"You do? What is it?" I wondered.

"Wait until we get away from everyone."

Elaine and I found a spot for lunch underneath an elm tree. The school grounds had lots of trees with sprawling canopies under which we loved to sit. I liked eating outside; it was relaxing, especially since my little brother and sister weren't around to make trouble. Most of the other kids went home for lunch, but a few of us whose parents both worked stayed at school and ate.

As we unrolled our lunch bags and removed our food, Elaine began talking. Whenever she spoke first, I knew she wanted to share something important to her. When nothing was pressing, she usually let me talk about the Work People's Co-op, and then she talked about her parents' store.

"Our rabbi told me that I mustn't believe all the science ideas that we will hear in biology." She stopped for a moment and looked at her sandwich, trying to find the edge of the wax paper so that she could unwrap her lunch. As soon as her fingers were pulling on the wax paper, she continued, "The ideas from Charles Darwin in our biology book are not good. He thought we came from apes." Elaine relaxed. "This is a step that may lead me away from God. I am not going to think about it."

I liked that Elaine was talking to me about religion. We never talked about it at my house, even when Uncle Karl was over. Grandpa and Grandma didn't say much, and I didn't know much about what being Jewish meant. The few Jewish people who lived around here stayed with each other. Joe had said they didn't play sports, either.

"I don't get it, Elaine. Isn't evolution just an idea?"

"Yes, Sara, it is an idea. But we are to be careful of all we think about. The wrong idea can lead us to make bad choices."

"I understand that, Elaine, but I don't think science is just made up. People have studied and done experiments, and our teachers have gone to college. I don't know if I would say evolution is wrong. Besides, I'm not sure why you would think learning about evolution would lead you to make wrong choices."

She had already eaten all of her sandwich. "Sara, if you believed you came from monkeys, would you care about people?"

"I don't know."

That's a strange question, I thought. Elaine was linking ideas together. I wondered about how her rabbi explained these ideas in church.

The few times that I had gone to church, the person up front had talked about the Bible and used stories from the book. The stories had messages that taught us how to live, like stories told around a campfire.

Elaine interrupted my thoughts. "Aren't monkeys animals we can hunt and kill and eat like grouse or fish?"

"Well, I don't know of anyone who has eaten a monkey, Elaine."

The joke flew right by her. She was focused.

"Sara, why wouldn't we think of people as animals to hunt and kill if we are from animals? Why couldn't people be like the frogs we cut up and study in biology class?"

The conversation had jumped from animals to cannibalism, and I was unsettled. I hadn't eaten a thing yet and didn't know if I wanted to talk about this. I didn't even know what evolution was. In fact, I had never thought about where I came from. I had to say something. "Elaine, let's pretend I came from a monkey." I paused and then started again. "No, not a monkey. Let's pretend I came from a chicken. If I had come from a chicken, would you cook me and eat me?"

Elaine stopped and thought. Her pause gave me a chance to unwrap my sandwich. I had made it this morning with bacon and raspberry jam, salty and sweet. I also had an apple and some carrots.

Elaine looked at me. "Sara, do you like the idea of having a monkey as your great-great-grandparent?"

"Well, that's too far back for me, Elaine. I don't know who my great grandparents were. I think they were from Finland, but I don't really know. Now that I think about it, for all I know, maybe one could be."

I tried that joke to see if Elaine was still stuck in her mind.

"The idea makes me cry, Sara."

"Cry?"

"Yes, I feel dirty, unimportant. I always thought Ha Shem made us."

A tear rolled down her cheek. I hoped this lunch wasn't setting a tone for the way things were going to go this year at school. I knew that I had to have lunch with other people.

"I'm sorry, Elaine. I didn't realize how upsetting this is to you." That seemed to work. She wiped her cheek. I continued, "I'd like to get to meet this rabbi guy of yours."

"That's all right, Sara. He's always busy. You now, you are the only person I can tell these things. You listen."

"That's nice of you to say to me, Elaine."

"Please keep this entirely secret. I don't want you telling anyone."

"I promise."

We finished eating and didn't talk the rest of the lunch time. As I sat in classes that afternoon, I thought about our conversation and Elaine. Elaine was different, but I hadn't expected that an idea from science class would make her so upset. After all, it was just school. Heck, we never used a lot of things we got taught in school. Many things we did outside of school were important, too. My mom said, "Käytä maalaisjärkeä (Use your common sense), Sara. Niin kauan kuin voit selvittää asioita, voit olla kunnossa. (As long as you can figure things out, you'll be all right.)"

I guessed if humans came from animals – evolved – that sounded pretty interesting to me. It made me want to get to know my grandparents' German shepherd Kaveri a little more. Maybe he was smarter than I thought. Maybe he could talk? A talking dog...

I wondered what my dad and mom thought about evolution or Elaine's kosher ideas. I hadn't heard them talk about animals in socialism. I had no idea of how many pets a socialist could have or not have. I knew capitalists had pets. In the pictures from my school books, kings and queens had pets such as cats and dogs. I even saw a monkey in a painting with Marco Polo. Marco must have had fun! I remembered that Napoleon had used elephants to fight wars and animal mummies had been found in the pyramids of the pharaohs. When I thought about the United States, I didn't remember a picture of George Washington or Benjamin Franklin with pets. Come to think of it, nobody had talked about Karl Marx's having a dog.

I did know people had always lived on farms and worked with animals. In Finland some people had goats and sheep in their houses and even gave them names. I didn't think people would keep animals in a house only for enjoyment. The first pets probably were working animals. Animals had been expected to work for a living to pay for their food, but certain animals got special treatment like a bed or shelter from the rain.

My grandparents' dog Kaveri roamed the store freely. He had a bowl of water by the front door. Customers sometimes gave him treats. He was like a pet to everybody. Kaveri was more than a pet to Grandpa Mattai. He was also Grandpa's messenger. Grandpa had created a small two-part container that he fastened to Kaveri's collar. He had trained Kaveri to take messages to our family at the co-op, Dad at Mesaba Park, and a hunting friend. When Kaveri showed up with a message, the receiver knew to check the container, tell Kaveri he was a good dog, and pat him on the head three times. That was Kaveri's signal to return to Grandpa Mattai.

I don't know how my grandparents got Kaveri. I had never heard of pets being sold in a co-op.

Our co-op was like a general store. We sold hardware, groceries, clothing, some furniture, and crockery along with feed for livestock such as chicks, horses, and cows. We didn't sell dog food. Kaveri ate from the kitchen table. Most of what we sold was groceries and hardware.

When the store first opened, Mother worked with Dad at the store. She took care of the clothing, furniture, and stuff for the kitchen. When the opera hall was built and she became involved with the musicals, Dad and Mom decided to let me handle the clothing, including the clothing pricing. I got the job because I was the oldest and had always helped Mother. I liked pricing. I even thought of a system for doing it.

When new clothes arrived, I unpacked them, shook them out, and examined them. First, I looked for loose threads. When I found one, I pulled it, first gently, then harder. Most threads weren't a part of the garment; they were leftover pieces that stuck to the fabric as it was sewn. Dad called what held them in place static electricity. Picking these threads off the clothing did not cause the piece to change in any way. When I found a thread that was attached, I pulled. If the material tightened, I stopped pulling. Then I reversed the direction of my tension to see if the piece of clothing relaxed to its previous position. I cut off any length that remained. If no threads were visible, I tugged at the seams next.

One beautiful red velvet Christmas dress had shredded when I tested the seams. I was shocked. The fabric seemed to be rotten; the seams had no strength. When I looked at the cloth closely, I noticed lightly faded areas that stretched across the surface of the material. They were water stains. My mother said the rain had been intense one weekend during the unloading and transferring of the goods on the docks in Duluth. Since many pallets had sat in the rain, Dad and Mom were able to purchase all the products for a good discount. They had known this was risky, but they had hoped most of the product would be salvageable. The red dress wasn't.

After I checked the quality of a garment, I had the job of attaching the price tags on the clothes. I had a miniature printing press located on top the desk in the basement of the co-op. On the top of this machine was a 1" by 1" by 1" box-like container. I selected individual pieces of lead type from a cigar box and placed them into the little box on my press. My cigar box was divided into ten sub boxes with each sub box containing one of the digits from 0 – 9 stamped on the end of the lead silver. I also had lead blanks which were the same size and shape as the lead letters. I used them to take up the space where there weren't numbers. After I had the lead type set to indicate the price of a garment, I secured it in the box. Picking up a roller, first I rolled it across an ink drenched pad and then across the lead type. I grabbed a strip of twelve price labels, inserted them into the printing press, turned the press handle, and printed the price tags. After that, I laid the dozen tags on the sill of the open window next to my desk. The ink had to dry before I could attach the price tags to the clothes.

Each price tag had a wire attached across its top. The wire looked like a needle set in a piece of fabric lying flat. I tore off one price tag at a time, bent the wires so they stuck out away from the tag, and inserted the two wire prongs into the garment. They pierced through the clothing and penetrated to the underside of the material. Then I bent back the two wire prongs in opposite directions. This attached the tag to the garment.

I liked doing that.

When I sat at my desk, the co-op's basement window where my price tags dried was to my right. I watched the legs of people as they walked by. I often wondered why nobody stopped, bent over, looked through the window, and saw me. No one realized how much influence I had over the price of the clothes they bought. They didn't even know I worked in the basement of the store. The people who bought their clothes assumed my parents were in charge and directly supervised the pricing of the clothes.

I imagined I was living in the Renaissance working with Gutenberg. Instead of printing books, I helped the merchants market their goods. I was accepted and respected as I provided for the common good and commerce of the city.

I also imagined myself as an aristocrat. Since I was the first to see the store goods, I was able to acquire the better-looking clothes before other members of the co-op or community. I dreamed of being one step ahead of the local fashions. I entertained the thought of changing the price tags on certain Christmas clothes so they were out of the price range of the girls in town. Then I would have all the newest fashions for myself.

In reality, I was treated like a country mouse no matter how I dressed. The city mice looked down on me, the co-op mouse. No matter what I wore, I was labeled as out of touch with what was current and contemporary in clothing and, in fact, anything else in the culture. I didn't feel I'd get any additional dates or looks from the boys if I had a stylish wardrobe. I also didn't think that the boys would drool over this Finnish girl.

When Joe walked by my window to go into the co-op, he tapped his shoe three times against the glass. After his signal, I always got a little love shiver – the kind that happened quick and left me a little warm. On the shelf below my desk, I kept three to four gifts ready to give to him for his mother or sister Becky. When I sprinted up the stairs to bring one to him, I always imagined him giving me a gift in return, a small ring-sized box. In my mind's eye, I saw myself screaming and giving him a hug. I had tears in my eyes. Everyone in the store stopped shopping, turned, looked at us, and smiled. My father announced to everyone in the store that we were engaged to be married.

12   The "Fight"

"Don't swear at me or anyone else again, Marvin!"

Lying on the ground was a worn-looking, dark-skinned male. I didn't recognize him. On top of him sat a white person. Moving in closer, I saw the white guy was Robert McFarland. 'Little Rob' was his nickname because his father's name was Robert. 'Little Rob' took a swing with his right arm and punched Marvin in the face again. Marvin's face rolled to the side.

"You don't belong here, Marvin. You had your chance, you stupid Indian!" Robert yelled and glared.

Marvin blubbered. Red blood mixed with clear mucus hung from Marvin's nose and mouth. A puddle flowed downhill toward Robert's left shoe. Robert leaned over and looked into Marvin's face. I knew I didn't want to get that close to anyone's face, especially Marvin's. He wasn't good looking. His pot-marked face propped up a purple nose. From where I stood, the Indian looked like a turtle. His obese belly mounded into the air.

'Little Rob' delivered a left-handed fist to the turtle's head. The turtle couldn't pull his head back into his shell and protect himself. I shuddered at the blow. One-sided fights weren't fair. Robert could have let Marvin lay there. I wondered why the teachers standing with us didn't stop the beating.

I turned to Arvi. "How did this start?"

Arvi kept staring at the fight. "That Indian came walking up to the school and reached for the door. At the same time, Robert swung the door open from the inside. He knocked Marvin down the concrete steps to the ground."

"Did Robert apologize to Marvin for knocking him down?" I wondered.

"No," answered Arvi.

"How did the fight start, then?"

"Marvin cussed at Robert, Joe."

"Marvin cussed Robert?"

"Yeah."

"Arvi, why didn't Robert tell a teacher? Or the principal?"

"Joe, everyone knows you shouldn't swear in school. You don't need to ask somebody about that."

"Come on, Arvi. That's no reason to start a fight. Every Finlander would be black and blue."

"Robert knows it is wrong to swear. He jumped on top of Marvin before he could get up. Then Robert told Marvin never to swear again, especially in front of girls. That's when the fight started."

"The fight?"

"Yeah."

"Arvi, you didn't say there were girls around when Robert knocked Marvin down with the school door."

The school bell rang.

Arvi didn't answer me. He and the others headed for the front door. I waited. I wanted to see how this fight was going to end. After most of the crowd was in, Robert stood up. Marvin opened one eye and mumbled something. Robert gave him a kick in the ribs. I winced. Marvin's chest heaved and collapsed.

As he lay there, I took note of the amount of blood on his face. Dad said bare-knuckled fighting was the worst type of a fight for both boxers. Nothing protected your hands when you slugged the other person. The force of your punch pushed your skin-covered knuckle bones into the other person's cheek. Your opponent's cheek flesh slammed against his skull. Your knuckles contacted his skull bones. Something had to win. Skin and flesh lost. Bones won and turned one's face into human hamburger, tearing the skin from the slugger's fist.

I looked up. No one was around. Thoughts raced through my mind. *Should I tell someone? What happens now? Do the police come? Where was the principal?*

No one answered my thoughts.

I walked into classroom 5A on the first floor, late. First hour classes were called homeroom. Mr. Charles Marolt was our first hour instructor. He took attendance, made announcements, and asked if anyone had any questions. No one spoke. I felt sick and squirmed.

Come on, I thought, *someone please ask about what happened outside today and who were the two people fighting! Will I have to look at Marvin during lunch?*

After some silence, Tammy Browersfield raised her hand.

"Yes, Tammy. What is your question?" asked Mr. Marolt.

"Mr. Marolt, did Robert get hurt?"

"I am not sure what you are asking, Tammy."

"Nyrkkejään kylän (Village Idiot), didn't you see the ruckus outside, Mr. Marolt?" said Alvin Metsa.

"Mr. Alvin Metsa, watch how you talk to me! I can't speak Finnish but I do know a few words. You come with me to the principal's office. Class, take some time for yourselves and be quiet. I will also see if we can find an answer to Miss Browersfield question."

Every morning in homeroom we had time to finish our homework, talk quietly, and read. My second hour class teacher was Mr. Brad Van Hellion, third Mrs. Schultz, and fourth study hall. Arvi was in all my morning classes. Right after lunch I had Miss Walker, and then shop classes filled the rest of my afternoon. These were in the building across the street called the Manual Training Building. I liked the afternoon walk there. The fresh air woke me up.

Mr. Marolt came back from the principal's office, but Alvin did not.

"I talked with Mr. Browersfield. He informed me Robert is fine. He will be able to play quarterback Friday night for the homecoming game," Mr. Marolt informed the class.

"Mr. Marolt?"

"What's on your mind, Mark?"

"Who was that guy outside on the sidewalk this morning, the one McFarland was fighting with?"

"Mr. Valamaki, that 'guy' is a young man named Mr. Marvin Shamebone."

"What does he do, Mr. Marolt?"

"Marvin happens to be one of our townspeople."

"He doesn't look like anybody I have seen around town. He'd scare my little sister without a mask on Halloween." Mark Valamaki looked around the room to see how many laughs he got. Snickers and giggles rolled across the classroom, and Mark seemed satisfied.

Mr. Marolt admonished us, "Back to work, everybody. Remember to remain quiet. Homeroom time is almost up."

From listening to the classroom chatter, I found out Marvin lived outside of town in a small house not too far from the municipal slaughterhouse or abattoir. His family had lived there since the Civil War. Apparently, Indians were allowed to have pieces of land outside of communities if there wasn't a reservation nearby. President Lincoln had guaranteed that. Tammy said Mr. Shamebone hadn't been able to pass eighth grade. Tammy's friend Suzanne said he had tried sixteen times, but she always exaggerated. Her father Mr. Swanson taught social studies. Robert was his star student and also captain of the declamation club coached by Mrs. Schultz.

When I walked over to my shop classes after lunch, I saw our principal Mr. Browersfield outside talking with Sheriff Robert McFarland. I thought, *Little Robert's in trouble now.*

Mr. Browersfield wasn't known to be a friendly man. Who knew how he was explaining what had happened this morning. As I watched, their conversation seemed more than business-like. There was a lot of head nodding. They were even using their hands as they talked. The sheriff was not taking notes. I didn't want to stare long. My father had told me never to stare at important people. It made them nervous. They got suspicious. Then they suspected you of wrong doing.

As I walked by the site of the earlier "fight," I noticed Marvin was gone. Some of his blood and mucus was still there, though. I stopped. I wondered why someone hadn't cleaned up the goo. At least they could have thrown a bucket of water on the area to wash the matter away. Wasn't it unsanitary? I dipped the tip of my right shoe in the goo. The stuff had the chemistry of fish guts. I dragged my shoe's sole through the middle of the puddle. The goo grouped itself. A quick kick of my shoe against the pavement shook the remaining clump off. That seemed better than wiping off the mixture with my hands. I didn't want blood and snot on my hands. Besides, the only thing I had to use was my handkerchief, and that didn't seem right.

Teachers had cleaning materials. Why didn't a teacher clean it up? My father said people who become teachers couldn't do anything for themselves; they lacked common sense. He called them *Jacks of All, Masters of None*. He also said school teachers didn't like to get dirty or work with their hands. If that was true, I didn't think they would know how to clean up after a fight.

Shamebone's bloody leftovers reminded me of the times I helped my father and my uncles make sausage at the town's slaughterhouse. The Hibbing Abattoir was built in 1917 and owned by the city. For a small fee, anyone could use it. My family butchered on Sunday morning. The place usually was available then. I had two jobs on sausage-making morning. The first job was to wash the hog heads after the decapitations. The pork heads were lined up on the concrete slab near the large back door by the railroad tracks. Dad never let me see how the heads got placed on the slab or who lined them up. He thought I didn't need to know.

There was lots of goo, like the stuff from Marvin's face, all over the pork faces. When I washed the heads, I placed my left foot on the top of each head, held it steady, and doused water all over with the slaughterhouse's water bucket. Then I took a floor scrub brush, bent over, and scrubbed the goo off. I got the brushes from Mom. They were the worn-out ones she had used to scrub our house floors, but, due to their condition, they were no longer wanted.

My second job was easier. I had to stir two five-gallon metal containers full of pigs' blood every ten to fifteen minutes to prevent coagulation. I also wasn't told how the pigs' blood had been collected and stored. Both jobs took about forty-five minutes to an hour to do.

My cousin Niilo and I experimented once by pouring some water into the blood so that it wasn't as thick. The water thinned out the blood so it was like soup rather than stew. Niilo, who secretly dreamed of being a world-famous scientist, thought the concoction might stay liquefied longer. If it had, I wouldn't have had to stir so much. Niilo wasn't concerned that dilution of the blood was a variable. When the new sausage was sampled at the end of the day, everyone said the batch of blood sausage made with the thinned-out blood didn't taste as good as the sausage from the past years. Niilo and I didn't mention what we had done.

Taisto Rantala had an idea of what had happened. He was convinced the farmer we bought the hogs from had sloshed the pigs full of water the night before. After drinking all the water the previous evening, the boars and sows weighed more when we picked them up the next morning to bring them to the slaughterhouse. Because of their water weight, the farmer gained more pounds per pig, which translated into more money for each one he sold us.

As Rantala told the story over and over, the plot evolved. The farmer who sold us the pigs married the sister of Peter Armstrong, one of the foremen at the Mahoney mine. Then the plot thickened. Peter's father was Kenneth Armstrong, the Oliver's Mine director and owner. This twist gave the story an opportunity to develop into a capitalistic conspiracy concocted by the mine owners to oppress the socialist Finlander immigrant in yet another way. The story had evolved to such a degree that Nillo and I had almost forgotten the truth.

I didn't forget Marvin Shamebone, though. I was reminded of him every school day of my senior year. To get to my shop classes I walked by the spot where Marvin's goo had pooled. Arvi didn't. The high school started an honors advanced student track, and Arvi was selected to participate. I wasn't. He had to stay in the main building for more book learning. He lost the time to work with his hands or move around during the school day. I still had it.

Sometimes I think back to the day I naively pushed my way into the center of the circle where Robert was "fighting" with Marvin. I was curious; I wanted to see the excitement that day. I knew I was going against my father's advice. He had told me fights were common in high school and I was to stay away from anybody who was fighting. My curiosity had won out. I had to see for myself. I saw something, and I lost something that day.

13 Worlds Collide

"Another good performance tonight, Elizabeth!"

"Thanks, Jacque. Did you have something you wanted to discuss with me?"

"Why, yes, I did. How did you know?"

"Usually you are at the side curtain at the end of the performance. You kiss me on the cheek as I come off the stage and then race to the theater lobby to greet those leaving. Tonight you haven't kissed me, and you are still here."

Whether Elizabeth saw him before, during, or after a performance, Jacque signaled his level of tenseness with his right hand. The more tense he was, the deeper he drove his hand into his right trouser pocket. Elizabeth thought he was touching his knee that night. In his extreme moods, Jacque also was not direct with his speech and what he wanted.

"What's on your mind?" Elizabeth asked calmly.

"First, I want to thank you for agreeing to continue as my assistant and spend most of your time in Duluth settling the productions there. You have a real talent."

"You're welcome, Jacque. I'm excited. I know I will be in Duluth for just a short time. I believe you know I have friends in Duluth and some relatives in Superior. I'm looking forward to having extra time with them."

Jacque was having a hard time making direct eye contact. Elizabeth moved closer to him.

"That's what I thought... And... Elizabeth … It's the second thing I would like to talk to you about."

"I don't understand, Jacque."

Jacque lifted his eyes. They were restless and tired. Elizabeth wasn't surprised. He had the marks of being very unsettled. Often she had wondered if he ever slept.

"All this is difficult for me to explain, Elizabeth."

"Jacque, you have always been able to talk to me."

"Things have changed since the last time we discussed this idea. The people I work with are proposing a series of productions that would start in Milwaukee and then head to Minneapolis, Duluth, Virginia, Hibbing, and Winnipeg."

"I didn't know there was a theater in Winnipeg."

"Well, there is, but it's not up to the standards that the business company would like. They have asked me to spend some time in Winnipeg with their Canadian financier. Together we will decide if we should work on remodeling the current theater or look for another hall."

"I'm excited for you, Jacque! I know you have a relative in Winnipeg you rarely get to see, and I'm sure, money-wise, this will be better for you."

"You are right, Elizabeth. Initially, my interest was and still is to work closer with you and the theaters here in Minnesota. With the added work in Canada, I am hoping you and my son Ian will get to know each other better in Duluth."

Jacque did not have to say anything more. Elizabeth had guessed correctly. There had been more on his mind. Jacque was a taker. If you gave him one thing, he asked for another until he had everything and you had nothing.

"Jacque that is kind, but I have a family of my own."

"I know, Elizabeth, I know. But only me and my son are in Duluth... I've watched your daughter Sara as she has come to the theater. I'm impressed."

"I'm not sure what you mean, Jacque?"

"She is well-mannered and intelligent. Her presence has made me think about Ian's needs for a mother."

Jacque appeared to get choked up a bit. Elizabeth let him continue. He never spoke about his wife. Never had he used her name in conversations. Even his son Ian never talked about or mentioned her. This was the first hint there were things in Jacque's past that Elizabeth didn't want to know.

"I had hoped when you came to work in Duluth, you would spend more time with Ian… Influence him. Now with this opportunity to go to Winnipeg, I am not interested in bringing him along. I'm also not interested in leaving him alone."

"Jacque, Ian is a fine young man. You have done well with him. I am sure you will do well in the future, even if it means taking him to Winnipeg with you."

"Elizabeth..."

Jacque was glancing toward the lobby in the theater and getting more pensive. His conversation with Elizabeth had gone longer than he had expected. He was torn and appeared to be evaluating whether Elizabeth was in his way. Was there something Elizabeth could do for him, or did he need to find another deal maker?

"Jacque, I know some good people who would be more than willing to take your son while you're gone. They are hardworking Finnish immigrants like me."

Jacque's eyes dropped immediately to the floor, and he held them there for a few seconds. Then he looked to the lobby for the umpteenth time.

"Elizabeth, you have a good heart. You are very kind and devoted to my work, but I only know you. I don't know your friends or relatives."

"If you can trust me, you can trust them. We all had hurdles to get over coming to the United States, finding work, and growing our families. There still are obstacles."

"I was hoping you could live in my place while I'm gone and take care of my son. I won't charge you rent. I'd leave additional money for the both of you. You can even have your daughter and your relatives from Duluth and Superior stay with you to help out. I have a large place on the hill above downtown."

"I don't know what to say, Jacque."

"All I ask is that you think about it."

"When would you want a decision?"

"As soon as possible, Elizabeth."

"I'll do what I can, but I won't be able to come to Duluth any sooner than we had already planned."

Elizabeth gave Jacque a quick embrace, and he headed toward the lobby. She doubted if many people were left. She knew that she would have been uncomfortable if he had stayed by her side for an answer to his request. If there weren't any people left, Jacque could talk with Sheriff McFarland. The sheriff never left until it was time to lock the doors.

Elizabeth had not expected to supervise Jacque's son Ian, and she wondered what else he had in mind. She didn't know what to think. God! She hadn't told her husband Martin the dates she and Jacque had discussed, the best time for her to move to Duluth, or how long she would stay. Martin assumed she would be helping out for just a few weeks.

This opportunity to work in Duluth had been difficult for Elizabeth to navigate. She loved Martin and her children, but at the same time she loved the excitement of performing. Both worlds clashed and collided inside of her. In the same way that she practiced her lines and sang the songs for the musicals Jacque picked out and directed, she had her own script for a short three-scene play she had rehearsed over and over in her mind:

The first scene began with her getting the children up in the morning. The stage was the same every morning; she spoke the same lines to all three:

Good morning. Did you have a good night's sleep?
We are having oatmeal with raisins and cinnamon for breakfast.
Would you like some milk?

There was no applause. She didn't feel a connection.

She knew there should be one. She knew she would like to have one. She believed the other actors and actresses with her felt the same. They wanted a connection, too, but there was none.

The second scene was in the morning, too. It was the morning after the Saturday sauna. She approached Martin as he headed toward the breakfast table.

"Honey, I need to talk to you."

"What is it, love?"

"I think it's time for me to leave."

His eyebrows twisted into a frown. "What for?"

"Well, maybe I should just stay in Duluth, instead of traveling back and forth …"

"That's odd."

"What is?"

"Jacque told me the same thing last week ..."

"He did?

"Yes. I don't understand why all of a sudden both of you are trying to leave me here by myself."

"No, that's not what I'm doing."

"Independence, then?" he responded. "You'll have a lot of that once I'm dead."

"Don't say that, dear! You have plenty of years to go."

"You don't know that, honey."

"Why not?"

"We still have Tommy and Hannah to raise."

"Look, Martin, I need to do this. Don't get melodramatic on me. I need you telling me things like: Okay. If this is what you want, then I'm all for it – if it'll make you happy. I'll always be here for you when you want to come back."

This second scene ended when she kissed him on the cheek and began making breakfast. He sat down and petted Kaveri lying on the floor by the kitchen table.

The third scene took place on the landing outside the kitchen door. She had her suitcase in one hand and a shoulder bag in the other. She took the first step off the landing onto the steps heading down to the sidewalk alongside the co-op.

Martin asked, "Who'll take care of me when you're gone?"

"Maybe it's time to find you a girlfriend."

They both laughed. Nothing more was said. Then he watched her descend.

This was as far as Elizabeth could imagine the scene. She had to stop there. Never in a million years could Elizabeth imagine life without Martin. She also didn't know of a director who could draw sentiment out of her to change this imaginary three-scene play. Now the lights had dimmed. She was still in the dressing room, and no one was in the audience.

After what Jacque had said tonight, Elizabeth thought about taking the children, her mom, and her dad out to Mesaba Park tomorrow afternoon for a picnic. There she would discuss the situation with her parents while the children played. Her parents had had to make hard decisions. The biggest had been leaving their community in Finland, separating from the co-op that they had managed for twenty years, and coming here to Minnesota. Their decision had been hastened by political circumstances in Finland.

When they arrived here, her dad had gotten blacklisted in 1906. Shortly thereafter, Elizabeth's mother had lost her sister and parents who lived in Finland. Her mother and dad hadn't had enough money for her mother to attend the funerals. Now with the Russians trying to force Finland not to be Finnish and Lenin and Trotsky continuing to gain support for overthrowing the czarist empire, Elizabeth knew that her mother might never be able to go back to Finland again.

Elizabeth was sure the issues she had to share weren't as complex or long term. Hopefully, her parents had guidance to offer her. She turned her focus back to the present. Sara had come to the theater tonight specifically to meet Ian. Where were they?

14   Sneak Visit

"Sara, have you ever been in that place?" Ian pointed at the Lyric Theater about three blocks away on the opposite side of Main Street.

"No, Ian," I replied.

He looked mischievous enough to interest me in going. "Is there some way we can sneak in?" Ian wondered.

"They have an entrance in the alley just for the musicians, actors, and actresses like our theater does. We can go around to the back alley and pretend we belong," I suggested.

"I'd like that, Sara. If anyone has a question, I'll use a heavy accent. They will be so shocked at how I sound they won't ask more questions, thinking they might offend me. "

Every time Ian came to Hibbing, his father brought him to the opera hall. Ian hadn't had a chance to walk around town and see what the people were like. I felt guilty leaving our hall, but I had seen the musical many times and wanted to please him, especially since my mother might be taking care of him. In my mind, we were already almost brother and sister.

We headed downtown to the Lyric Theater. We didn't talk much. Ian smiled a lot. I was hoping he would ask about our Work People's Co-op Store and want to see it, too, but his attention was captured by the lights of the larger opera hall on Main Street.

We stopped, took deep breaths, and walked to the back entrance. Ian opened the door, and I walked in. The musical *Florodora* had just started. Since this was the first night for the musical, no one was near the door. Everyone was watching the opening lines. We found the stage door and looked out at the audience. I couldn't believe how much larger their hall was than ours. The balcony alone looked the same size as our main floor.

Most of the men were dressed the same as the guys at our place, but the women were dressed in fancier clothes. They wore many more pieces of clothing. Most of their garments I'd never seen in our inventory at the co-op. They looked beautiful. Elaine had told me her parents sold clothes to people attending plays at the Lyric. At our theater such clothes were only for the actors, but here women in the audience were wearing multiple-layered, dressy clothes. I thought many layers would be uncomfortable, but these women seemed at ease.

I felt uncomfortable. "We'd better leave. We got to see what it was like. Let's go back before anyone notices we're here, Ian."

"Thanks, Sara. I'm glad you did this with me."

I smiled.

I liked Ian's accent and his courtesy. Mother said not to let that fool me. All French children seemed nice whether they had been to school or were just hooligans. Ian had green eyes and a thin build. I thought I was stronger than him. His eyelashes were long, and his hands were smooth and soft. His face was long, and his hair was thin. He moved his hands around when he talked. He was much more animated than the boys I knew, Finnish or non-Finnish. The first time I saw him on stage, he looked like he had acted longer than my mother.

"What's the opera hall in Duluth like, Ian?" I wondered.

"Well, it's larger than the one we were just in."

"Which one do you like better?"

"I wouldn't be able to say until I watched a whole musical. I would want to know how all the voices sounded all the way to the end of the performance," he assessed.

I didn't know why Ian or anyone would take that long to decide if one play was better than another play. I listened to some singing, looked at the costumes, and knew whether I liked one play better than another one. Watching two plays from beginning to end to decide which one I liked better took too much time.

"What do you do when the play is done, Sara?"

"I go into the orchestra pit and try all the instruments," I replied.

"Doesn't the orchestra director get mad?"

"No, my uncle Andy who is in the orchestra and plays in the director's dance band loves to see me. Viola leaves the pit right after the show is done. He doesn't seem to care if we play with the instruments."

"Viola? You mean a person, right? "

"Viola Turpeinen. He directs our orchestra."

"Is he a tall, skinny guy? Looks like a bug with his glasses on?" Ian described Viola perfectly.

"Yes," I agreed.

"Sometimes he comes by and visits my dad in Duluth. Viola doesn't say anything to me. He picks my dad up, and they go out. They never talk at home."

"I don't think that's Viola. He always talks to me. He used to visit my grandpa, too."

Ian didn't seem to care if we had the same Viola. That was one thing I noticed about Ian. He was courteous and all that, but if someone didn't pay attention to him, he didn't pay attention back, either, even to his father's friends.

"Sara, would be it okay if I come with you to the orchestra pit?" Ian asked.

"Sure –" Ian cut me off before I could say anything further. He was not usually abrupt. I wondered what was so important he couldn't let me finish my sentence.

"My dad and the musical director in Duluth won't let me get near the instruments or the musicians. They think musicians can be bad people. They call some of them 'Gypsies'."

"Gypsies?"

"You never heard of Gypsies? They are people who wander around Europe. They don't have homes or a country. They play music all the time and dance around fires at night," Ian explained.

"If they are bad, why does your dad hire them to play music?"

"They are good musicians. My dad says most of them are the best at what they do. Since they don't have homes or real jobs, they will play for food or a place to stay. They are also cheaper to hire. Dad says he doesn't want me breaking their instruments. That's all these people have."

"That sounds stupid to me, Ian. All the musicians at our opera hall are the same ones who play at our festivals and campground dances at Mesaba Park. Everybody knows everybody else. We don't use Gypsies."

"Dad says you do," Ian stated.

Gypsies! Sometimes I wondered where Ian got his ideas. I had never heard of people roaming around without homes. Everyone wanted a home, a place to live. Those who found it too hard to have a house of their own moved in with relatives. My family lived in an apartment with my grandparents. People did it all the time.

"Let's talk about something else, Ian. Have you been to Mesaba Park? I can ask my parents if you could come with us."

"My father says I am to stay away from there. He says people from the People's Labor College run the campground and park."

"Who told your father that?" I wondered.

"That's what my father says."

"Does he know my mother, father, and grandparents are members of Mesaba Park and work there?" I asked.

"I don't think so. If he knew your mother was a member, I don't think he would trust her or even want her to take care of me when he starts to travel to Canada."

"I have a hard time believing my mother didn't tell your dad. I'm going to ask her tonight," I replied.

"My dad says those Finns from the college and at the campground are anarchists."

"Antichrists?" I repeated.

"No anarchists."

"I don't know what that means," I confessed.

"They are mean people who want to change things, and they don't care how they change them. In fact, they just want to destroy everything. They even blow things up with dynamite."

"But –"

"Dad says most Finnish people are anarchists. That's why he likes your mother so much. She's Finnish but not like the rest of them. Dad never liked coming to Hibbing to do productions. He was glad when your mother joined. She is such a good singer and leader that he doesn't have to spend so much time up here."

"I don't believe you, Ian," I responded.

"I have heard him say the Hibbing opera hall won't last that long."

"Well, I don't think Duluth is any safer."

"My dad isn't going to stay in Duluth. He told me we are moving to Winnipeg. He's going to get a large theater there, bigger than the one in Duluth."

There Ian went again. He always sounded like he knew what he was talking about and that everything he said was true.

We arrived back at our theater. Since the performance had ended, I brought Ian over to the orchestra pit. We had just sat down to choose the instrument he wanted to play when we heard Jacque calling him, "Ian. Ian!"

"I'm here, Dad!" Ian answered.

Jacque walked over to where we were. He was always dressed in gray dress clothes with white shirts and black ties, and he never moved very fast. Tonight he had a little spunk in his approach. Every time I saw Jacque in the theater, he greeted me like he had never met me. That seemed odd. Mother thought he was naturally forgetful. After what Ian had told me tonight, I thought Jacque might have had other reasons.

Maybe Jacque didn't want people to know that he knew me or my mother, especially if he thought we were antichrists. When he and my father got together, they never met in our apartment above the co-op store. That had made me suspicious. I knew Grandpa Mattai did not care much for Jacque, neither did Grandma Grace. Neither greeted Jacque when he stopped by to pick up Dad.

"Hi, Sara, I am Ian's father Jacque Trompeure'."

"Hello Mr. Trompeure'," I greeted him.

"Your mother said that you wanted to spend time with Ian this evening."

I didn't think I wanted to spend time with Ian. I thought it was the right thing to do. I had to remember not to take what Jacque said seriously. I kept forgetting he was prone to telling stories or acting rather than relating to people.

Jacque continued, "I want to thank you for helping. I'm sure you both enjoyed your time together. There will be additional times in the future when you can do this again. Let's go, Ian."

Ian had that my-father's-a-pain-in-the-butt look. He wiped it off quickly and turned to me, "Thanks, Sara."

"You're welcome, Ian," I replied.

"Good night."

"Good night."

I watched both of them leave through the front lobby and entrance. Often I wished Ian could stop by and visit during the day. In the evening when a play or a musical was being performed, we were always so busy.

I wondered what mother thought about Ian telling me the theaters were going to close. I hadn't heard anyone talking about the musicals stopping. Mother had never mentioned anything about Jacque living in Canada. I was sure she would have told me if she knew. I was certain Ian had lied. Dad had told me Jacque lied. Ian probably learned to lie from his father.

Mother startled me out of my thoughts. "Sara, did Jacque come by and pick up Ian?"

"They just left, Mother."

"Good. I get a little worried. Sometimes Jacque is forgetful. I imagine he might drive back to Duluth and forget Ian."

"Are we stopping at the co-op tonight?"

"No. I promised your father we'd come home right away. He said he has a surprise."

Being with Ian tonight had been fun. Although I think Karla would have liked to see the Lyric Theater, she would never have gone with me. Her father Unlucky thought going to the Lyric Theater was immoral because the mine owners were part owners. Since Unlucky hadn't been rehired by the Oliver Mining Company after the 1906 strike, he viewed attending the Lyric as supporting the industries that were making life hard for his family. Since the strike, he had held odd jobs but never found full-time work.

Grandma would never go, either. She didn't even go to our theater, except to walk me there so that I could watch Mom. My father was opposed to attending operas at the Lyric, too. Thinking about it, I guessed that I shouldn't have gone there. Mother had only asked me to take care of Ian, and she had said to do that at our theater and hall. But I had been curious about the Lyric.

In one way, I was glad that I had gone. I got to see how the women who attended the Lyric were dressed. I wondered where they got their clothes. I had been told people formed opinions about you from the way you dressed. When you worked in the mines or woods for a living, you didn't have a lot of variety in clothing. Most of the people who attended the Lyric didn't do dirty, hard work like us Finnish, so they dressed differently.

When mother stays in Duluth to sing and direct, will she dress differently? I wondered. If she buys new clothes, where will she buy them? In Duluth, she won't be working at the co-op, and I don't think she will get another job. When I find out where she buys her clothes, I would like to go there. Maybe I'll get some ideas for our co-op in Hibbing.

"Sara!" Joe's voice broke my self-absorption.

I was surprised to see him. "Joe! What are you doing here? Didn't you have to put Jon and Becky to bed?"

Why would he be in a hurry to see me this late at night? I wondered.

"When Dad came in, he said he'd put them down. He suggested I stop by the theater and catch you before you went home."

"Well, that was thoughtful."

Hmmm. Joe's Dad had encouraged Joe to see me tonight ... This must be important. I imagined Joe pulling out the little ring box. I moved next to him. When I got closer, I noticed he was panting, as if he had been running. I thought that was odd.

"Are you moving to Duluth?" Joe blurted.

His question caught me off guard. I felt his tension. Joe rarely got tense. *Was something wrong?*

"Duluth?" I quizzed.

"Yes, Duluth." Joe replied.

I took Joe's hand in mine. He didn't relax. I tried to piece together what could be going on in his head, but I didn't have enough pieces. This was out-of-the-ordinary behavior for Joe. I realized I didn't know how to ask the right question.

Joe took a deep breath. "Dad said he saw you go into the Lyric Theater with Ian tonight."

I relaxed my grip on his hand. His shoulders dropped. Our eyes connected. I smiled.

"Joe," I whispered. "Joe." I wrapped my arms around his waist and leaned my head against his chest, hugging him. He didn't push me away. I noticed my mother walking toward us. She stopped and winked at me. Her eyes glistened with permission for me to finish my conversation with Joe and come home late. I knew she'd tell Dad.

15   Powers That Be, First Meeting

"I can't imagine coming here to dig for gold," noted Jacque Trompeure' as he looked out the window.

"Especially before railroads," added Charles Finnegan, shaking his head.

"Imagine riding your horse up from Duluth through the woods to here," responded Armstrong.

"I can. Gold is money," answered Finnegan. "In fact, it's better than money. You can spend gold anywhere in the world you want. Being from Europe, you should know that, Jacque."

"Just because you are from the big Island off the continent, Charles, doesn't mean you know everything. We Frenchmen do more than make love," Jacque replied. He grinned and lifted his snifter for a sip.

Armstrong swirled his brandy around the sides of his glass. He loved its bouquet. Sweeter than Scotch, he thought to himself. He was hoping the meeting tonight wouldn't be long. He wanted to get a good night's sleep because he was looking forward to fishing tomorrow morning. Armstrong had heard northern pike or "jack" fishing in Vermillion was the nastiest in northern Minnesota. Stories of men being pulled out of fishing boats while they tried to land large ones floated around the company office. *Sure they were exaggerations, but there had to be something to the stories because there were so many of them,* he thought.

Even if he weren't pulled from his boat, a tough man vs. animal struggle would be a distraction from his thoughts about the IWW and all the organizing. Armstrong just didn't understand the Finnish radicals and their demands.

Lake Vermilion was about thirty minutes from Soudan where the first underground iron ore mine had been dug in northern Minnesota. Located on a ridge on the south shore of Lake Vermilion, the Vermilion Grand Lodge's vista was staggering. The upland area was covered with stands of white and Norway pine mixed with balsam, aspen, and birch. Rugged rock outcroppings added to the view. Staring out the Grand Lodge's windows, Armstrong imagined Oliver Mining as the largest outcropping. He was proud to be the leader of such a striking hunk of stone towering over the area. Lower down were white cedars interspersed with balsam, tamarack, black spruce, ash, and muskeg. *What a combination of beauty and money the company has made,* he thought. *How lucky he was!*

"We are here because of the red gold, iron ore gold," said Armstrong. "If it hadn't been for the gold rush fifty years ago, no one would have discovered the mother lode of iron ore here."

"When the towns of Tower and Soudan were established in the 1880's, there was so much ore lying about that a special barge was built to pick it up and convert it to nails for the first houses in the communities. Some of these houses still stand," Edward Browersfield added.

Jacque chuckled to himself. He wanted to mine the imaginations of the immigrants, not the red ore in the ground. By capturing their imaginations, he sold theater tickets.

"Who else did you invite?" asked Finnegan.

"Samuel Snively, our mayor of Duluth, my cousin Thomas Armstrong, and Hibbing's Sheriff Robert McFarland," answered Armstrong.

"Then it looks like everyone is here. Let's start the meeting," stated Finnegan.

Armstrong had met with each of these men on a one-to-one basis when he needed a favor. This was his first attempt at uniting the community members around the goals of the Oliver Mining Company. He chose to sit in the middle of the conference table rather than at the end. Armstrong welcomed everyone. Then he began with the first introduction, "Jacque Trompeure' this is Thomas Armstrong."

"Pleased to meet you, Jacque," said Thomas, not making eye contact with Trompeure'. Thomas did not like Jacque. He had heard Jacque was pretentious and more focused on his interest in women than accomplishing the steel trust's business goals. Thomas looked at Jacque and remarked, "I think we have met before."

Jacque leaned back, looked Thomas square in the eyes, and answered, "Yes, Thomas, we have. It was backstage in Milwaukee after Charlie Chaplin performed. Mayor Daniel Webster Hogan sat with us.

We were joined by Charles Finnegan, one of my financiers, who is with us again tonight."

Thomas turned his head toward Armstrong and responded in a soft, sarcastic undertone. "Hogan. There's another shithead socialist mayor like that Thomas Van Lear in Minneapolis. I am glad Sheriff Long Gun —"

Armstrong interrupted, correcting Thomas, "Sheriff Langum, the sheriff of Minneapolis."

"Okay. Sheriff Long Gun... I am glad he informed the public that Mayor 'Tommy-boy' Van Lear loved the Germans. The sheriff twisted the knife in Tommy Boy's back by reporting that the mayor wanted Germany to win the war. Tommy Boy wasn't re-elected after that one." Thomas sat back in his chair, his posture presuming he had accomplished something with his statement.

The others were surprised Armstrong allowed Thomas to comment candidly before everyone was introduced. Armstrong sensed this but continued with the introductions. Turning to his left and raising his left hand slightly as if pointing, he announced, "I doubt if many of you know Robert McFarland, except for Principal Edward Browersfield. This is Robert's first time with us. He is the sheriff on the Mesaba Range from Hibbing. McFarland has worked closely for a long time with the Finnish immigrants."

Polite nods of recognition went around the table.

Duluth's Mayor Samuel Snively greeted the sheriff politely, "Good to meet you, Officer McFarland."

Robert looked around the table and cleared his throat. He was determined to say something after his introduction as a way for the others to get to know him. Before he could begin, Thomas interjected, "Is it okay if we call you Wyatt Earp, Robert?"

Baffled, McFarland responded, "I don't understand, Thomas."

Robert's surprised tone was sincere.

Unabashed, Thomas continued, "Why did you try to arrest me in Chisholm at the mining equipment sheds?"

Looking surprised, Robert replied, "I thought that was what Armstrong wanted..."

Armstrong felt stymied. The introductions weren't completed, and already there was conflict. Armstrong did not want to be made a fool at this meeting before it began, especially by his cousin. He looked directly at McFarland and said, "I understood the plan was for Thomas to pick a fight with Frank Vainionpaa. Then you were to arrest Vainionpaa for harassing Thomas."

Either McFarland lacked fear or misunderstood his role in the group because, without hesitation, he turned and stared at Armstrong. "That's not what I was told, Mr. Armstrong."

Armstrong was taken aback by McFarland's quick and direct response. He sat up straight. "God, Robert!" Armstrong adjusted his tie and continued, "My orders to you and Thomas were to stage the event so you, as the sheriff, were seen as supportive of Thomas, not those Finnish communist instigators. I needn't say any more."

McFarland snapped, "Well, having Thomas knock me down and kick me in the groin didn't present that picture!"

Thomas angled his eyes down and to the right. He held them there, daring Armstrong to get his attention and accuse him of doing wrong.

Armstrong's face softened. "I'm sorry, Robert. I didn't know that had happened. I was misinformed."

Then Armstrong looked at Thomas. "If that is what happened, Thomas, you just made your group look like a group of union busting thugs with no respect for the Finnish or the law."

"I haven't forgotten my role," Thomas replied. "I roughed Robert up a bit so those damn Finnish Wobblies would trust him more and want to defend him, despite his stupidity."

Thomas pushed his chair further out from the table.

"We'll not have more bantering about the past event, Thomas and Robert," Armstrong commanded.

Armstrong adjusted his tie for the second time and hand-pressed his shirt, smoothing the creases out with his palms. He cleared his thoughts and decided to move ahead with the business at hand.

"Tonight, I wanted to use our time to give everyone an overview of where we see the economy going, especially the changes that we know will be coming. After those words, I hope you will have an idea of the mine owners' vision. My desire is that you will want to join us in building a future here."

Charles Finnegan, the financier, spoke. "The mine owners agreed early on that script rather than cash was the best way to pay the workers. Script doesn't end up in the offering baskets in churches, saloons, or co-ops. In fact, it doesn't end up anywhere. It finds its way back to us when miners spend it in the company stores we have sponsored and the ones we own."

"However, the people's co-op movement grew fast. The co-op store takes away revenues from our store," Armstrong added. "We did not expect this and that means we over-estimated what we could make in this area."

Armstrong stopped. He lit a cigarette and then nodded to Finnegan to speak.

Charles continued, "We have had discussions among the owners about what might happen if a time came when we would have to pay the workers in cash. This prompted us to focus our attention on company stores and paying closer attention to the small store owners. We initially controlled the majority of the wet and dry goods being sold in the mining towns. However, as Armstrong mentioned, we didn't think the co-ops would grow here like they did in Europe. We missed that one."

Armstrong looked across the table. "But despite the growth of the labor store co-ops and our losses as a result, Jacque has found a new part of the economy. That will help us maintain our investments even when script, our major bartering chip, fades. Jacque?"

"I have worked hard to create a captive audience by getting the workers into the theaters to hear and see their propaganda through plays and musicals. I know gathering the Finnish contingent in socialist halls has caused trouble, too. As the organizing increased, even Bill Haywood got involved. I apologize for that nuisance. I, too, was naïve to the depths of the Finnish reticence. But, being a good director and producer, I went ahead and built loyal audiences here on the Mesaba Range, in Milwaukee, Duluth, and soon in Winnipeg."

"And you did that well, Jacque," said Finnegan. "What Jacque has done I humorously liken to the ants and aphids … Continue."

"My backers have made a recent investment on the East Coast in the new technology of moving pictures. We are working on a timetable by which we can begin to convert each of the socialist halls we now own into moving picture theaters. Milwaukee is scheduled to open first, then Duluth. After those two cities, we will look at the Mesaba Range and Canada. With the theaters full to capacity for socialist trash, introducing movies in the same theaters will be easy. We will begin by playing a moving picture between live shows and socialist tirades."

Finnegan elaborated, "When all mine owners move away from script and pay in cash, the workers and their children will have money to spend. As Jacque's investors convert the opera halls into screens with moving images, tickets will be available. They'll be cheaper than the live shows. Hopefully, the younger generation will like this option."

"We have seen this already on the East Coast among the urban second and third generation American immigrants," Armstrong said. "This won't stop the local live 'theater' here immediately. In northern Minnesota, there is still the attraction of the Finnish motherland. Mesaba is rural and much like Finland, but Jacque has informed us that the younger children aren't as interested in memories of the motherland as our current radicals. Many of the children speak English, even if their parents don't."

"Hopefully, the moving pictures will distract them from realizing that their entertainment is propaganda-based," said Armstrong. "What Rockefeller wants is for the younger generation to let go of these crazy ideas about work being shared or equal, which their parents rehearse in the theater and discuss at their organizing meetings."

Finnegan emphasized, "We want the younger generation mesmerized by the actors and actresses on the screens. The young eyes will see urban settings and different lifestyles rather than stories about the plight of the worker."

"Think about the business side of this change," Jacque added. "Props and equipment are expensive and need upkeep and storage. Working with actors and actresses is difficult, even if they are local talent."

Finnegan turned to Jacque and winked. "And good directors who will work for reasonable pay are also hard to find."

Everyone smiled. With his elbow, McFarland gave Jacque a soft poke and laughed the loudest.

McFarland grabbed the opening to ridicule Jacque since everyone's attention was focused on him. "But don't forget that when the actresses are gone, it will be harder to find ladies who will put out for Trompeure'! He might lose his motivation to convert all those theaters to movie houses."

Armstrong cleared his throat loudly. "Let me take Jacque's and Finnegan's information, summarize it, and expand on it further." He looked around the table to make sure everyone had refocused. "With the elimination of all the trappings for theater and live productions, we'll have a much better take at the gate. Also, we won't have to worry about competition from different plays at other theaters in other towns. Every theater will be playing the same movies. There will be no need for our workers to go where there are better actors and actresses."

Finnegan added, "Once we get the theaters set up under one business structure, we'll get more of our money back through increased attendance. We believe the majority of workers really don't care about culture or organizing. They're just like us. They want be able to have some money to please themselves with some entertainment."

Duluth's Mayor Samuel Snively spoke for the first time. "I like what I am hearing. It sounds like moving pictures are a way to grow the local economy down at the port. My wife and I have enjoyed our trips to New York to watch the moving pictures."

McFarland's eyebrows perked. He hadn't thought about taking occasional trips with these men. Even if the travel was for business, he wanted to have his wife Marian along. They hadn't had a chance to travel.

"Every town, even a remote location like International Falls up by the Canadian border, can have a theater because there is no need for all the trappings which come with live productions," said Finnegan. "Now there's the common good."

Browersfield added, "When the depression hit us rather hard, I was surprised that so many people came out to see the live shows in town."

"That provides a little entertainment for the radicals now and then, and there is some money to be made," commented Mayor Snively.

"Now that the economy is picking up, I bet we can really get moving pictures booming," Browersfield continued.

Jacque lifted a finger to interrupt the principal, who then stopped to acknowledge Jacque. "Excuse me, Mr. Browersfield, I have heard that on the East Coast they include projectionists as guest speakers in the lyceum series in the public schools."

Principal Browersfield agreed. "That's right, Jacque. In order to take the younger generation's minds off organizing, we are going to call attention to the new workers that the moving picture industry needs. Being a projectionist will become a sought-after job."

"Jacque, we will need to make sure the projectionists in each theater and hall are from the community," Mayor Snively strongly suggested.

"And they need to make good money," Jacque stated.

"I would like to suggest some additional funding for projectors to be placed in the auditoriums in all the schools. I would like to see moving pictures there, too," Principal Browersfield added.

"That is something we can look into," replied Armstrong. "And you can help me with making sure the school boards understand this need."

"Will do," answered Principal Browersfield. "I am in contact with administrators on the coast who have projectionists go around and speak to the different schools. The projectionists give speeches on what they do. The ones I have heard are impressive. In fact, most of the projectionists are local actors."

Armstrong stood and interrupted Browersfield. He announced they would take a break, freshen up, and eat.

The group broke up. Armstrong had food and beverages brought in and set on the table in front of the windows. The staff placed cigars and brandy decanters nearby. Members of the group took a quick view of the lake as they filled their plates and took the food back to the conference table.

McFarland decided to engage Jacque in a one-on-one as they walked back. Curious about the topic of their conversation, Armstrong followed closely to hear their exchange. "Jacque, did you put on those plays in Duluth, Virginia, and Hibbing knowing that they would be eliminated eventually?"

Jacque took McFarland's question as a compliment. He began to think McFarland may have some respect for his acumen. "Well, I was looking at more than just that, sheriff. By promoting the plays with union and socialist slants in the Finnish halls, I have been perceived as one who holds those values. This has allowed me to make very strong contacts in the communities with the Finnish immigrants who are the most volatile against free enterprise, and –"

"And?"

"Elizabeth Niemi is more closely tied to the anarchists than I ever imagined. Her husband Martin has even had Haywood stay at their place when he was in town."

"Above the co-op store?" McFarland asked.

"Yes," Jacque agreed. "One of our goals is to eliminate Haywood. I think that I could use my association with Elizabeth to track his movements and set up an assassination."

"You mean murder Haywood when he stays with the Niemis?" McFarland questioned.

By this time, McFarland and Jacque had sat down next to each other at the conference table. Finnegan and Browersfield pulled up chairs next to them. Armstrong took a seat nearby to hear the rest of the conversation.

"If Bill Haywood passed away, I would repeat a Croatian Catholic immigrants' saying 'May he rest in peace, now and forever, Amen,'" Browersfield added. "Can any of you say that in Latin?"

No one responded.

McFarland thought about what Jacque had said. He became suspicious. *Why was Jacque talking about assassinating Haywood?*

Martin had always assured him that Jacque could be trusted. McFarland began to wonder what Martin really knew about Jacque's connections with Armstrong and Finnegan.

Finnegan tried to get a laugh. "I am glad Finnish organizers are not Catholic. Imagine having to battle and share our wealth with people who are going to give it to the Pope in Italy."

Everyone remained quiet.

Armstrong quipped, "I am sure if the Pope finds out how much ore is here and what it is worth, he will want his share."

Some laughter ensued.

McFarland added to the anti-Catholic sentiment. "But at least the Pope won't be chasing Jacque's women."

Chuckles ripped through the group.

McFarland continued his joke, "You know the Pope only has a few good looking nuns!"

Finnegan smirked. He turned his attention to Jacque. "The Pope isn't as lucky as you with that Finnish bombshell of yours."

"Does Elizabeth have any sisters, cousins?" asked Thomas sarcastically. He had taken a seat across from Jacque.

"How about the other towns you are in? Are there women in those towns available for us, too? They don't have to be blondes," Finnegan joked.

Armstrong cleared his throat loudly to gain everyone's attention. "Thanks for participating in our meeting. Before today, I had had interactions with you as needed for the good of Oliver Mining and the communities you represent, but we had never all sat around the table together."

"Thank you for having this meeting, Armstrong," said Browersfield. "Thank you, too, for the beautiful high school you have built for our community in Hibbing."

"You are welcome. The high school is a good example of what happens when we work together," acknowledged Armstrong. "For this reason we will continue to meet. We need to look out for the economic good of our communities."

"As Jacque outlined for us today, moving pictures will bring a major economic change to our local communities. This new form of entertainment will provide more exciting options than the socialist theaters and their radical ideas," added Finnegan.

"I am excited Jacque has helped us understand that the moving picture circuit will travel between Milwaukee, Minneapolis, Duluth,

Virginia, Hibbing, and now Winnipeg," inserted Armstrong. "He has a goal of establishing one theater in each city by the end of next year. I have assured him of our support."

"As Jacque changes the theaters to moving pictures, I hope we can meet to discuss other ideas. I agree with our early discussions today on providing some type of alternative stores to compete with the co-ops. Many co-ops are politically radical," suggested Mayor Snively.

"My expectations are you will use any opportunities to create interest among people you know. Remember, we are working as a team. Expect a meeting within a year," Armstrong concluded. He pushed back his chair, stood, and gathered his papers. The meeting was done.

16   Special Assignment

Back in his room, Armstrong picked up the newspaper and noticed this story:

When gold mining operations began on the Vermilion Range in 1882, the small crew led by Stone settled down to work what later became known as the Lee Mine. Lee Mine Hill was apparently 'nothing but iron ore.' Stone and his men stripped a breast of ore at the north Lee sixty feet wide and eighty feet long. It was rich iron ore running about 67 percent iron content, covered by only a few feet of overburden. Work was proceeding concurrently at other prospects, including the Breitung, and several were operating before the railroad reached Soudan.

The exact year in which the Lee Mine was opened has not been ascertained, but one report says that soon after the Lee Mine was opened, it was abandoned on account of the low grade of ore, and operations were transferred to Soudan Hill. There they found a large outcrop of hematite iron, and thousands of tons were mined from an open pit before shaft sinking was commenced. Another report infers that the quality of the ore was not the true reason for closing the Lee Mine.

At that time, the Minnesota Iron Mining Company operated both the north and the south Lee Mines, employed about three hundred men in them, and had two mining plants and railway tracks to both mines. Yet, in one night, all disappeared. All trace of surface property was blotted out.

The miners who 'dropped their tools' at 6:00 p.m. and were back at the mine at 7:00 a.m. the next morning had to do some 'hard blinking' to be sure that they were awake. All visible mining company property had disappeared and not a vestige of anything but the hill itself was in sight. Even the railway tracks had been torn up and carried away.

Litigation followed the closing. The Astor Estate of New York filed a claim to the Lee Mine Hill. Astor had acquired rights under a grant given by the general government to an Indian for treaty services. Eventually the Minnesota Iron Mining Company was confirmed as a part of the Astor estate's holdings.

After reading the Lee Mine Hill article, Armstrong thought about how remote he was from the East Coast. As a college student he had been in the northern part of New York State. The Finger Lakes were like northern Minnesota lakes; the lakes even froze over during the winter season. As rough as upstate New York may have seemed to him as a young man, civilization was still close; literacy was accessible; and people followed common business practices. By contrast, Duluth, the largest city in this area, wasn't a city of any significant size. It had a port that wasn't even a sea port.

Armstrong's thoughts drifted back to his room at the lodge on Lake Vermillion close to where the Lee Mine Hill was located. *How could a mine disappear overnight?* He had difficulty imagining it.

Was a missing mine a good or bad investment? Armstrong couldn't decide. The most striking part of the story was the fact there was still mystery about what took place.

This didn't happen that long ago, he reminded himself. Once again he reflected on the remoteness of this part of the nation. His reflection strengthened his belief that this story's relevance was in the mine owners' favor. A soft smile appeared on Armstrong's face as he continued his thoughts.

The stars in the night sky seemed to twinkle for him and his work. He felt reassured from the missing Lee Mine Hill incident. The possibility of any mayor of one of these towns or, for that matter, anyone else understanding the economics of what was going to take place diminished and became more remote. He was confident Oliver Mining and the steel industry were positioning for the future – unions or no unions. They had the "big" picture under control despite the periodic interruptions by the Finnish radicals. In time, the radicals, including Bill Haywood, would be eliminated.

Maintaining his smile, Armstrong opened the door to his room. Grabbing the Lee Mine story in his left hand, he headed toward the large stone fireplace in the lodge's main area. With ice, brandy, and a dash of water in his glass, he found Finnegan and struck up a conversation. Afterward he returned to his room, retired to bed, and looked forward to go fishing for monstrous "jacks" in the morning.

Driving his car back to the police station, McFarland felt a chill, not from the night air but from the meeting he had just left. His special assignment from the governor as liaison to the Finnish seemed manipulative. McFarland had felt honored with the assignment. He had first interpreted the governor's action as recognition of the good work he had done. After the meeting with Armstrong, he began to see the action differently. Now he realized the assignment pushed him to be on the government's side. McFarland wasn't sure what the government's side was, but it wasn't the side of the laborer. The direct invite from the president of Oliver Mining Company to tonight's meeting extended the special assignment into a willingness to participate in what's best for the economy of northern Minnesota. From this meeting, he could tell that this group's best didn't consider the people he was now on special assignment to cover.

McFarland had willingly agreed to stage the scuffle with Thomas and his union-busting Pinkertons at the maintenance shops. This was the first time he had played a charade like that. When he had become sheriff, he had been surprised at how his uniform affected people's perception of him. When he wore his uniform to any public gathering, the number of incidents which went wrong or not according to plan seemed to stay at a minimum. This was different than when he was in a bar having a beer without wearing his uniform. Then if a fight took place between some men on the stools next to him, the men fighting often pushed him out of the way to make room for their sparring. Sometimes one of the men asked him to hold the other guy so he could punch out that guy's daylights. McFarland had discovered his uniform meant something to the people he met every day.

After sitting around the table with the president of Oliver Mining and others, McFarland realized he had expanded his influence beyond that of a local law enforcement officer. He was now part of a group of people determined to reach their goals, whatever the cost. He was no longer keeping order in the town but imposing an order on it. He first sensed that the day he had to meet Edward Browersfield at the high school to pick up Marvin Shamebone. Robert had felt bad about what his son had done to that Indian at school. When he expressed his regret for his son's actions to Browersfield, the principal didn't acknowledge the apology. In fact, Browersfield thought the incident preserved what little bit of democracy and social structure there was in the community. In Browersfield's words, *The Indians had their chance and lost it. They needed to let go and make way for industrialization. Teepees and peace pipes don't make a nation.*

McFarland thought about talking pictures replacing musicals and plays. He enjoyed meeting and being with the Finnish people during those events. He hadn't seen any of the talking shows. He thought watching pictures on the wall instead of people on a stage seemed funny. Why would people come if the entertainment was by people you didn't know? It didn't seem community-like. He also did not like the way Thomas had roughed him up in front of the shops and then made it sound so casual during the meeting. Armstrong had no idea the pain Thomas's kicks had caused him. *I hadn't known the special assignment to the Finnish meant that I would be a convenient punching bag for Oliver Mining,* McFarland thought.

17   Out-of-Control Bonfire

"Joseph, in recognition of the job you have been doing as captain of the baseball team, the faculty and I have decided that we want you to light the homecoming bonfire tonight."

"I don't know what to say. . . Thanks, Mr. Browersfield."

"By the way, Joseph, Tammy said she enjoys having you in her English class this year. She likes when you read out loud in class, especially poetry."

Principal Browerfield's words floated in my ears. I didn't know that anyone from the baseball team ever got recognition for anything. Typically, football, hockey, or basketball players received that recognition. I was also surprised he mentioned that his daughter Tammy talked about me. *This is a good day*, I thought.

The fall homecoming and football game were huge celebrations for our high school and the town. I looked forward to the homecoming festivities every fall. This was one of the few times I could attend school functions. Most of the time, I was busy lumbering with Dad or helping out at Mesaba Park.

For the fall homecoming, an effigy of the Chisholm Tigers (Tiikerit Chisholm), the opponent in the game, sat atop the unlit bonfire and snarled at the pre-game crowd. Orange crepe paper strips taped to the tiger's body waved in the wind. The spectacle reminded me of the opening lines from *The Tiger* by William Blake.

Tiger, Tiger.
Burning bright,
In the forests of the night;
What immortal hand or eye
Could frame thy fearful symmetry?

When the pep band began the school song, homecoming King Leonard Campbell and Queen Angela Armstrong emerged from the high school to the whistling and clapping of the student body. Following the royal couple was the rest of the week's student-elected royalty. King Leonard and Queen Angela were the first to enter the fenced-off area. The royalty stopped next to the pep band musicians. Everyone cheered. Along with the high school students, children from the neighborhood, parents, and interested townspeople applauded the crowned seniors.

The pep band members' antics increased. The bass drummer moved the drum left and right, bumping the band members on either side. A trombone player exaggerated his slides, leaning into the faces of some of the people waiting for the bonfire. The tuba player moved around, jostling anyone he got near.

This was one of the rare times I loved being in a crowd. The loud singing and clapping of the crowd and improvisation of the pep band energized me. The pep band was composed of those who didn't make the marching band – for whatever reason. They used the leftover instruments the band and orchestra didn't want. They never staged concerts. Mr. Browersfield referred to them as "clowns," but they entertained the townspeople. I think that was why Mr. Browersfield allowed them to play despite their sound. He kept them to amuse the townspeople at outdoor festivities held at the school.

King Leonard raised his scepter high into the air to signal it was time to light the bonfire. Then he struck a stick match down the metal fly of his pants. The match flared to life. I walked over to the king holding a kerosene soaked rag on top of a broomstick. Keeping the broom straight, I stopped and bowed. King Leonard immediately touched the match to the torch. Seeing the fire catch strongly, I raised my head, turned, and headed toward the south side of the bonfire. Black-streaked smoke trailed behind me. The crowd cheered, and the drums rolled.

Bending over, I ignited the crumpled Sunday *Industrialisti* stuffed between the boxes and pallets as a starter. Flames erupted. Boxes ignited. Burning wood pallets smelled like charcoal. The fire became hot. Heat roared. The intensity slapped our faces. We all watched bright yellow-orange flames dance and flicker. The bonfire roared higher and spit ash into the air. Shooting up over ten feet, flames touched the painted tiger. Leonard, Angela, and the royal crowd began the cheer, "Burn the Tigers! Burn the Tigers!"

When the Chisholm Tiger became engulfed in flames, the crowd joined the chanting, "Burn the Tigers! Burn the Tigers!"

High above the flames, black clouds billowed. People watched the menacing fire. High in spirits, they continued chanting. The intensity of the fire created updraft currents which ripped off chunks of cardboard and hurled them into the night sky. Laced with orange embers, the streaming sparks thrown by the fire were clearly visible. Spinning like flat rocks skipping across a smooth lake's surface, they shot into the midnight blue.

The two firemen assigned to watch the bonfire fixed their gazes on the larger cardboard pieces. They watched to see where the pieces would land. Roofs of houses near the school were vulnerable to the larger pieces that climbed the current. Last year, a few had fallen on the Dragnettis' roof. Their shingles had caught fire. That had stunk!

The royalty began their march to the football field to watch the game. Behind them, the pillar of fire towered. As they promenaded up the sidewalk, their shadows loomed large. Underclassmen closely followed carrying homecoming banners. The Hibbing Blue Devil's marching band waited on the football field. When the band leader saw the procession's approach, he lifted his baton for the band to play *God Bless America*. Cheerleaders shook their golden crepe paper pom-poms, and the field lights sprang to life. Family, friends, and visitors rose to their feet clapping, shouting, and stomping. The stands shook. Everyone loved the spectacle.

Back at the bonfire, Walter Rosina and Jim Stark, the firemen, were ready to hose the fire out. Suddenly, Boris and Bill Dragnetti, two young boys from the neighborhood, dashed out from behind the fire truck, snatched pieces of burning cardboard, and ran. Dropping the burning pieces of cardboard, the boys stomped on them and caused smoke, sparks, and ash to squirt all over. Smaller shadows came alive and reflected the chaos.

When the pressurized water from the firemen's hoses hit the bonfire, the pile collapsed. Fiery boxes hit the dirt and bounced off the ground, scattering more ash and hot chunks into the air. One large box accelerated ten feet into the air, tumbled, and slammed into the ground near Boris and Bill. The box shredded, showering the boys with debris. Boris screamed. His hair had caught fire. Boris's flailing arms hit Bill in the face, knocking his glasses to the pavement. The glasses skidded away.

Mr. Stark grabbed Bill and dragged him over to the fire truck. On the way, he stepped on Bill's glasses, which snapped under his weight. I stopped picking up litter and ran to help the boys. I tackled Boris with both arms and rolled across the dirt, clutching the boy while smothering the flames. Our rolling stopped right in front of Mr. Rosina. Mr. Rosina took Boris from me, carried the boy over to the grassier area, and laid him down.

While the two firemen attended to the boys, I went in search of Bill's glasses. The fire hose dropped earlier by Rosina had pooled water onto the grounds. One lens floated on the surface and flashed rays of light. I saw it and scooped it up. I walked back to where I had heard the first crunching sound made by Mr. Stark's feet. I saw wire frame glasses further back, looking like they had been kicked. I grabbed the bow. Then I noticed the other lens partially covered with dirt close to where the boys had been playing. I picked up the second lens and walked back to the firemen and the boys.

Mr. Rosina was still attending to Boris. He looked up. "We need to take these boys home. Would you like to come with us?"

I nodded.

The three of us took the boys home. When we arrived, Mrs. Dragnetti was making a spaghetti sauce. Mister was drinking red wine and eating white cheese at the kitchen table while reading a paper. It wasn't the *Tyomies*. It was the local *Mining News*. Mario and Maria were William and Boris's grandparents. They never left the house except for Mass early Sunday mornings. I didn't know where the boys' parents were. I hadn't seen them at the bonfire, and they never attended high school sporting events.

"William! Boris! Mary, Mother of Jesus! What have you done?" Maria greeted us, eyes wide.

"Buona Sera, Maria," said Mr. Stark. William and Boris stood next to him in the doorway.

"I'm so sorry. What did the boys do?" said Maria, looking down at the two. "You know I'm a gonna tell your parents when they come back." She said some things in Italian – very fast. Mario didn't look up from the table.

"Maria," Mr. Stark repeated, pushing the boys into the kitchen. They ran thorough the kitchen and into the next room.

"The two were down at the bonfire," continued Mr. Stark. "William's glasses broke. Boris is quite dirty. Joe rolled him on the ground to put out the fire on his jacket."

Mario looked at me. He smiled. I liked the twinkle in his eyes. Maria lapsed into Italian again. She wrung her hands in her apron and said, "Sono davvero dispiaciuto. (I'm so sorry.) Che cosa hanno fatto i ragazzi? (What did the boys do?)"

Mr. Stark tried to explain to her what had happened. He even tried to let her know I had saved Boris from some major burns. Maria didn't understand a word, and Mario wasn't going to get involved. Maria kept repeating, "Sono davvero dispiaciuto. Che cosa hanno fatto i ragazzi?"

As I stood there and watched, my mind wandered.

The aromas of cheese, wine, oregano, thyme, anise, and garlic made Italian houses smell delicious. I thought the scents soaked into the walls in the same way that grease from your hair seeped into the wall if you rested your head against it too long in one spot. When my brother sat up in bed at night, he sat with his back against the wall. Each night he added to an old grease spot or created a new one. Eventually, he ended up with a row of spots two feet above his mattress. They made a border across the wall on his side of the room. As he got older, I had thought the spots might climb higher and higher, but he slouched more. That way, he inadvertently kept the line even.

My cousin Niilo said there were oils in garlic, sausages, and cheeses. These oils held the smells of the foods. He said that every time you cooked the steam from what you prepared rose with an oily scent from the pan. This vapor added oil to the oil that was already in the air of the house. The smelly oil floated in the air, soaking into things. That's why Italian houses always had spicy aromas.

Niilo liked science and had theories on all types of things and how they worked. I never learned any of those in school. I thought he was right about the oil. When Mom burned something, she opened the door, and the smell was gone before the next meal. She boiled more food than she fried so she didn't have as much oil in the air as the Italians did.

Mr. Stark put his hand on my shoulder and led me out into the yard. "Joe, I thought you did a good thing tonight. How did you know to roll the fire out?" he asked.

"My father taught me that," I answered.

"You got a good dad then," Mr. Stark responded.

When we walked back to where the bonfire had been, we heard cheers resounding from the stadium crowd. The Blue Devils had scored on their first possession! I wanted to be in the stadium watching Tammy shaking her pom-poms during the celebration.

Mr. Stark noticed my yearning. "Joe, come with me back to the high school. I'll open the door to the boys' locker room so you can get in and clean up. Then you can head to the game. I'll help Mr. Rosina finish cleaning up the leftovers from the fire."

"Are you sure, Mr. Stark? I can brush myself off here and go to the game right now," I answered.

Mr. Stark smiled. "Joe, get in the locker room! Wash up a bit! You never know what the night might bring!"

I felt like he knew something about me and what might happen tonight. I didn't think too many people even knew I liked Tammy. Everyone knew I was friends with Sara. After all, we were both Finnish.

I followed Mr. Stark over to the high school, and he unlocked one of the large gray doors. Glancing to the side of the door, I saw Dave O' Malley. I was surprised.

"Dave, what are you doing here? Shouldn't you be suited up and playing in the game?" I asked.

"Mr. Stark! Am I glad to see you!" Dave exclaimed, ignoring my question. "I need to get into the building!"

"What for, Dave?" asked Mr. Stark.

"Coach wants me to suit up and play."

"Why didn't you suit up with the team?"

"I had to finish some things at home. Coach said he'd tell you I'd be coming late and you could let me in after the bonfire."

Mr. Stark stared at Dave for a second, shook his head, and then stuck his key into the door lock. "Okay. Get in, guys. Now, I'm locking both of you in. Mr. Varastadt Narayan's on duty tonight. Be nice to him. He can let you out. Good luck, Dave! Thanks, Joe!"

After we walked in, Mr. Stark closed and locked the door. I stared through the door window at Mr. Stark as he walked away into the night. It was the first time I'd noticed his steel key ring and its size. It must have been a foot in diameter! I had never seen so many keys in one place before. I was surprised they didn't pull his pants down when he attached them to his belt. His wide suspenders must have held his pants firm. I imagined Mr. Stark had keys to every padlock in town. He was able to unlock any building or business. I thought of Jacob Marley in the Christmas Carol and compared Mr. Stark to Marley. Jacob didn't like keys and padlocks, but Mr. Stark seemed fine with them.

I turned and bumped into Dave who was standing right behind me. I had never liked Dave. He was a smart ass. He thought he knew everything. He didn't fool me, and I planned to let him know. "You lied to Mr. Stark. You –"

"Joe. Listen to me," Dave interrupted. "I know Tammy Browersfield has her eyes on you. She told my sister Lee Ann."

"Yeah, yeah, Dave. Now you are going to help my love life. Stick it up your dark hole."

"No, I mean it, Joe. If you listen to me, I'll let you know how you can meet her tonight."

I didn't trust Dave for a minute, and he knew that. Now he was going to help me. Why? What for? I wished Mr. Stark hadn't let us into the locker room. I was angry. I began to wonder why Dave was really here. He had never intended to suit up for the game.

Come to think of it, I had felt strange when Mr. Stark locked the door on us. But I forgot about that when over Dave's shoulder I saw Mr. Narayan mopping in the hall. I decided to give Dave an opportunity to explain our "chance" meeting.

"There's a party tonight after the game. Tammy said if I can get you there, she'll come outside and talk with you. Maybe even take a walk with you."

"Bullshit, Dave. If you can get me to the party and she wants to talk to me, both of you can get me inside the house with the rest, and I can talk to her there."

"Joe, listen to me. If she doesn't come out and talk to you, you can do anything you want to me."

I thought Dave was the strangest dealmaker. I could do anything I wanted to him? I never had had such an offer before. I liked the idea of a chance to be with Tammy. Maybe this might increase my odds of getting a real female's attention.

I was still shaking from what had happened to the Dragnetti boys. I was also feeling bad that I had missed the first touchdown. Niilo always said that the team who scores first usually wins the game.

"But I want to see the game –"

Dave dismissed my interest. "You just want to see Tammy shake those pom-poms. By the time you get cleaned up, the game will be almost over, anyway. Come on down to my house. I'll give you one of my shirts to wear. Then you'll look good for Tammy tonight. The one you have on is a little ripped up. I'll even give you some of my cologne to splash on."

"What you mean, Dave, is that I won't look or smell so much like a Finlander." I let that sink in.

Dave didn't reply. He looked down at his feet.

If I was going with him, I wasn't going to be easy. I wanted him to know that. I thought, *What if I did meet her? What did I have to lose?*

"Are your parents home?"

"No, Joe, that's what will make this so sweet!" Dave replied enthusiastically.

"Makes this so sweet? I don't get it."

"You'll see."

I stopped talking and headed toward the locker room with Dave in tow. I thought he was searching for another way to convince me to go to his house.

The locker room was edgy at night. Lights were dim. Most of the players never put their clothes away. Their clothes were piled on benches along with their shoes. Nothing was organized. Paint chips from the walls were scattered around. One of the benches was no longer bolted to the floor and wobbled when you sat on it. With the players gone, every step Dave and I took sounded like a metallic echo reverberating down a tunnel.

By this time, Mr. Varastadt Narayan was mopping the floor in the locker room. Mr. Narayan was Armenian. His narrow face and deep-set eyes made me uncomfortable. I'm not sure if he realized that or not, but I was glad that he seldom made eye contact. His teeth seemed large and appeared to be crammed into his gums without any rhyme or reason. As I watched him, his head turned to the side, looking for another spot to mop. I wondered why he was mopping in here. The players would come back from the game tonight covered with mud and grass and mess it up again. His efforts seemed wasted.

The Narayans lived on the same block as Arvi. Arvi knew Mr. Narayan's daughter Shelly. Arvi said when she left her house and walked ahead of him in the morning, she stunk. I asked him once why he didn't wait a few minutes longer before he went to school so she would be way ahead of him. He said his mother pushed him out the door right after Shelly walked by. I joked that, if this was true, why didn't he have Shelly over for a sauna. I suggested he could sweat the smell out of her and then beat her with some cedar branches to sweeten her up.

I looked at myself in the mirror. I was a mess from rescuing Boris. And my shirt was ripped. I thought about Dave's offer to go to his house and get a change of clothes. *Should I take him up on his offer?* I pondered. *Any chance to get to meet Tammy outside of school might be a good deal, no matter who was making the offer. I wouldn't make a very good impression looking dirty with a torn shirt.*

I turned so abruptly that I bumped into Dave. "Okay, let's go to your place. I'll shower there and use your fresh shirt."

Mr. Narayan let us out. We headed to Dave's house.

Dave's house looked fresh. White with dark green trim, it sat in the middle of the block. I thought his dad painted it every year. My father said painting a house every year was a waste of time and money. The purpose of paint was to seal the wood and keep moisture out. Doing that made wood siding last longer. If water got into the wood, seasonal changes turned the moistness to ice which later melted. When this happened over and over, the wood degraded faster and started to rot.

The wood needed to be scraped before being painted. This gave the air a chance to pull the moisture out, which should be allowed for a few days. Otherwise, paint didn't stick or cover. Once the wood was dry, the walls needed to be coated with linseed oil before the primer and paint were applied. That was a lot of work, but, unless the wood was prepared just right, paint was just wasted. And paint wasn't cheap. Dad didn't believe in painting to look good. He painted to protect the wood and the house.

Dave's dad belonged to a church group that dressed up like commanders of ocean boats. His father Patrick was called the Grand Knight. Dave showed me his father's regalia. I liked the naval chapeau. The hat looked like the one President Washington wore in the pictures in school books. Dark blue, it sat sideways on his head with a large feather-like plume. I always thought big hats fell or blew off in fights. As good as they looked, they were a waste. They were more for parades than fighting.

Showering at Dave's didn't take long. I liked the smell of his soap; it wasn't homemade. After my shower, I walked downstairs to where Dave was waiting. He motioned me to follow him to the basement. There weren't as many canned goods shelved there as at my house. In fact, the basement was brighter than ours. It looked like it was used for more than storage. In the back corner was a winemaking area. I noticed gallon apple cider jugs filled with homemade wine.

"Joe, do you want to get a little happy before we head up to the game?" Dave asked.

"Dave..." Happy? That was what he had said. I wondered if Dave had been waiting outside the locker room because he was looking for a drinking buddy. I didn't know why he had picked me or how he even knew I was going to be there.

Dave continued, "It's okay if we drink Dad's homemade wine. He lets me do that all the time. I just can't have the stuff he buys. This is the jug he opened yesterday. Try some."

His logic was flawed, but I took a swig from the jug he offered. The wine tasted sweet. I liked it. I didn't think the Irish made wine. My father had never mentioned Irish wine, just whiskey. Maybe Dad had never tasted Irish wine. Or maybe Dave's dad was different. Either way, we each took a couple of swigs and left Dave's house carrying the open gallon of chokecherry wine.

18   Set Up

We reached the football game with a nearly empty jug. The game was over. We were laughing and singing, acting like friends. I followed Dave from the empty football field and stands to Suzanne Swanson's house. Her parents were gone. Dave and I entertained the thought of maybe acting drunk so we could have an excuse for causing a little ruckus. He wanted to challenge our quarterback Robert to arm wrestle. I thought I'd like to "accidentally" brush Tammy's pom-poms.

All the lights were on inside the house. We heard loud voices. Everyone was celebrating. We must have won our homecoming game! I wasn't able to make out whose voice was whose while we stood outside on the lawn. I walked up closer to the front steps to get inside and see who was there. I thought Dave was ahead of me. I got up to the house. I lost Dave. Where was he? I got dizzy. So dizzy, I couldn't stand. *Phew!* I thought. *This must be what it is like to be drunk. I thought I would enjoy this more – not lose control....*

Everyone's faces seemed out of focus. They swirled around me. Someone started to drag me. My consciousness faded. I couldn't keep track of everything that was happening.

"Take him to the backyard!"

Cold water shot into my face.

"God, that's cold! Stop it! Damn it!" I yelled.

I held my hands up and tried to stop the flow. The grass was slippery. I fell.

I crawled to the door. It was locked. I pounded on the door and yelled, "Dave! Dave!"

No one came. I pounded some more.

"Shit!" I fell over again. I was lying on my back. I kicked my feet against the door. Glass broke. I rolled over.

"Dave! Dave! Where the hell are you?" I yelled again. I tried standing up. I was pushed down.

"Stay down you drunk! You dumb ass Finlander!" shouted one voice.

"You think you can come here and cause trouble?" hollered another.

"You stupid communist!" cursed a third.

My face hurt. How did I hurt my nose? Where was my jacket?

"Joe, over here! Come over here!" a voice called me.

I headed toward the sound, hoping it was Dave. I reached out toward the sound. Something slammed into my stomach, "Aghhhhhhhhhh," I groaned. My mind was spinning.

What's happening? I asked myself. I stepped, tripped, and fell. My pants legs ripped. *Am I bleeding? Shit. What's Tammy going to think? I must look like a Finlander, for sure.*

The bed I was lying on was hard, like a park bench. I didn't have sheets. I heard my father.

"Hän on tehnyt mitään väärää. (He has done nothing wrong.)"

An official-sounding voice answered, "Mr. Koivu, we found your son pedaling a tricycle down the middle of Main Street at 11:00 p.m., one hour after curfew. He was driving down the center of the road. He could be dead."

"Poikani on hyvä poika. (My son is a good boy.)"

"You are lucky, Mr. Koivu, that Mr. Swanson called us. We saved your drunken son's life. Now take him back to the woods where he belongs."

"Hän on tehnyt mitään väärää. (He has done nothing wrong.)"

I stunk. My head hurt. I wondered, *Why is everyone in my bedroom? What's my dad doing standing and talking in my bedroom?*

"Stop crying, Mom!" I heard myself say. The truck door slammed. The vehicle jerked. I rolled onto the floor underneath the dash. I remembered saying two more things, "Where's Dave? Shit."

Mom didn't say much Saturday morning when I woke up. Dad was still home; he hadn't gone into the woods. I guessed Rudolph, our horse, wasn't well, but Rudolph had never been sick before. I was supposed to peel lumber for the pulp mill Saturday morning.

"Dad is outside by the truck waiting for you," Mom said. Her shoulders drooped. She looked weary. "Sheriff McFarland was waiting for Dad last night at the police station. They had a long conversation while you were passed out in the car."

My mouth felt dry, and my tongue felt thick. I managed to say, "What did they talk about?"

She looked up at me. "I overheard some of their conversation. I will tell you what I remember."

Then mother recited the conversation word for word.

"Gustav."

"Hey, Sheriff."

"Your son got into a little bit of a jam tonight."

"Yeah."

"Sorry about that."

"Nothing to be sorry for. We all have done crazy things when we were young and had too much to drink," your dad said.

"Joe is different, Gustav."

"Come on, Robert."

"No, he is different. I have talked with Browersfield about him. I pushed for Joe to be the captain of the baseball team," the sheriff told your dad.

"You what?"

"I discussed with Browersfield how well he works at the park taking care of the beach, handling all the swimmers, even escorting them back to their cabins at night. He cares. I pushed for him to be captain of the baseball team."

"That's considerate of you. But, I'd like to have Joe earn the position on his own."

"Gustav. Take it easy. I've covered for you and Launo and your organizing, remember? I let the both of you get by the Pinkertons. I told them you were working for me; you were my moles."

"I know. I don't shave on a regular basis, but calling me a rodent?"

"I haven't shaved, either. I guess we are a pack."

Mother sighed. "Then they both laughed. The sheriff gave your dad a big hug. I didn't hear what was said after that. When Dad got into the car, he seemed satisfied, almost pleased." Mom shook her head. "That was odd. He said he never trusted McFarland, even though his wife is Finnish."

Dad opened the kitchen door. "Let's go, Joe."

"But isn't Rudolph sick?"

"Let's go, Joe…"

I got into the truck. We took off. I looked into the back of our truck and saw seedlings in wooden crates. We had grown them in the back of the woodshed over the summer.

Dad didn't talk after we left the house. We drove for about thirty minutes before Dad stopped the truck. He got out, took a shovel, grabbed a handful of seedlings, and walked to the edge of the woods. Stepping on the shovel, he forced it into the ground. He pulled back on the shovel's handle, leaving the earth split open. Dad dropped one seedling into the crevasse, pulled the shovel out, and stepped on either side of the little tree, packing her tight so she stood straight up. Dad paced off five feet and inserted another into the ground.

Nothing was said. I assumed I was to do the same.

I walked back to the truck, took the other shovel, grabbed a handful of seedlings, and started another row five feet to the left of where he had started. When we were done, I counted over one hundred little trees that I had planted with my shovel.

It was a nice morning. Fall mornings were cool. They warmed up quickly with hard work and the morning sun rising to its noon peak. Today was even cooler. Flies kept biting through the sweat on my forehead and arms. I swatted at them. I think I killed four. The rest lived to bite holes around my ankles and neck. When we got home, Mother hadn't made lunch. Rudolph was resting in the sun near the sauna. I went to bed without lunch and woke up feeling normal on Sunday.

Monday morning during homeroom the principal called me into his office. He instructed me to stand as he spoke. "Joe, the police told me Mr. Swanson reported you came to his daughter's homecoming party at their house late Friday night. You had been drinking."

"Mr. Browersfield, Dave and I had been at his house and –" I wasn't able to finish. I guessed he didn't want me to say anything.

Mr. Browersfield was focused. "Joe, the police didn't say there was anyone with you. That surprises me, Joe. You have never done anything like this before."

Damn you, Dave, I was thinking. *Friday night was too unbelievable to be an accident. Dave just happened to be in the school. Tammy wanted to see me that night. What kind of a fool had I been? I have to defend myself. I have to stick up for myself.*

"Mr. Browersfield, please listen to my story. I went to the locker room to clean up and met Dave O'Malley there. He suggested –"

"Joe, I am doing the talking. The police said you were drunk, by yourself, and riding a tricycle down the middle of the street. That's all I need to know. I have made my decision. You are no longer the captain of the baseball team or even on the baseball team."

"Sir –"

"There will be no discussion, Joe."

"But –"

"Joe, I took a chance asking the coach to make you the captain. Sheriff McFarland wanted to use you as a role model for the other Finnish boys to show that they also can be a part of the school and the community."

I didn't respond. It was obvious there was nothing I could say to change his mind. I waited for him to finish. He remained silent for a while looking at me. I guessed he wanted this to stick into my thick head.

"Now get to class, Joe!"

My head was full of thoughts. *My senior year! I didn't believe it. Shit! I should tell the principal a few stories about what the non-Finnish players do. That might change his mind. But I think he wanted to take me off the team. Now he had a reason. I'm not telling Dad right away.*

He never came to my games, anyway. So where is Dave? Damn, he set me up! He has his senior letter already, so he didn't need to play in the game. He must have stayed behind until the bonfire was done and pretended Tammy Browersfield was available. Why did he do it? Was it his idea, or did he have help?

"Joe!" Sara's voice broke my self-absorption. She was standing outside Mr. Browersfield's office. "Didn't you notice me?"

Surprised, my mind was blank. I stared at Sara.

"I suppose Tammy was in there, too," Sara sarcastically blurted out.

"Tammy?" I repeated. I was perplexed and had nothing to say.

"I heard she was with you when you got drunk. Damn it, Joe!"

I thought her cheek looked wet.

I looked around. *The hallway was empty, as it should have been. Everyone was in homeroom. Why wasn't Sara?* I wondered. *She would never miss class. Maybe she asked to go to the bathroom. God, had she waited the whole time while I was in the office? How did she find out? Dave's not setting me up again, is he? I don't believe this day. Right now I want to disappear into the woods with my shotgun loaded. I'd shoot every branch off every tree! Then I'd break the gun on a stump. I wanted to say out loud, 'Go back to class, Sara! I am not ready to face you yet.'*

"You are the talk of homeroom this morning, Joe Koivu. Tammy's told everyone she dared you to ride the tricycle down the middle of Main Street Friday night. She said if you did that she'd kiss you."

I couldn't believe what I was hearing. Sara couldn't be right, could she? Tammy and Dave conspired together? I wonder who really called the cops ...

Aloud, I finally responded, "Sara, I don't feel good."

"How do you think I feel, Joe?"

"I'm sorry. Look, I have to go to the bathroom. You need to get back to homeroom."

"Joe, I need some answers," Sara demanded.

"I don't know what to say." I paused, trying to think. After what seemed like an awfully long time with Sara staring at me, I had an idea. "Tell you what. I'll come by the store after we're done with school today. We'll talk then."

I turned and stumbled toward the restroom. I didn't look back to see where Sara went.

Suddenly, I felt paranoid. I hated when that happened. I didn't know who to trust. I didn't want to think of the world in the way my father did … but … last year when I cut my chin sliding into home plate, nothing had been in the school newspaper. I had thrown a shutout that game. When Dave twisted his ankle during a basketball game, he made the news. Dave wasn't that great an athlete. He was only a third string player. He barely scored more than six points in a game.

I don't remember much of the day. I went through the motions of going from class to class. Every period I heard snickers, giggles, and comments. Tammy had the worst comments in English class. After that class my interest in her died. I caught sight of Sara's stony look in the hall after English class and later during lunch. Even Elaine, who was with her, didn't give me a smile. I was glad to escape to shop class in the afternoon and work with my hands. By that time, my classmates were talking about other happenings at school instead of my Friday night drunken activities.

After school, I went to the co-op. The stairway down to the basement was located at the back of the store. I had never been downstairs where Sara worked before. I looked down the stairway. The steps were swept clean, likely Sara's work. When I started down, I smelled the dampness and felt the colder temperature. Walking down those stairs felt like forever. I stopped at the bottom. Her work area was about thirty feet to the right. I saw her sitting by herself at the desk next to a window.

I had hoped talking here would be easier, but now I didn't want to talk with her. I felt like we were both in a cave, a mine shaft, all by ourselves. I felt alone. At Mesaba Park, people were always around, conversations filled the air, and nature surrounded us. Here we were surrounded by boxes, sacks, clothing, tools, and hardware. We seemed to be the two only living beings in the world.

Sara looked up. I didn't feel like saying "Hi." I walked up to her. She sat up straight. We both were silent. In the silence, we needed each other; we had to trust each other. I determined to be as honest as I could.

I decided to speak first.

"Thanks for letting me meet you here, Sara."

"I apologize for this morning at school, Joe. I was upset. When I got home I talked with my mother. She said I shouldn't believe what Tammy said about what had happened Friday night until I talked with you."

My face relaxed. I smiled.

"I want you to tell me what happened, Joe. You don't have to worry that Dad or Mom will interrupt us. I took care of that."

I wasn't good at talking about things. With my mother being ill so much, my father and mother rarely talked. I don't ever remember them talking in order to "work things out." I knew Sara's family talked a lot. They seemed to work out their problems. Uncertain, I told her about meeting Dave in the locker room after the bonfire and how he said that Tammy was interested in seeing me after the game.

"Why would you want to see her, Joe?" Sara asked.

"I sit next to her in English class, and she has complimented me," I answered. "She seems friendly, so I thought I'd like to get to know her."

After I said those words, I thought about what I had just said. I felt those words drop to the basement floor. They didn't even bounce.

"Get to know her? Joe …" Sara stopped. She was still upset.

I thought I better say something to calm her down. "Tammy didn't promise to kiss me if I rode the tricycle down Main Street," I blurted out. "I don't even remember riding that damn tricycle. Sara, I don't know how that night got so screwed up. I am beginning to think just like my father. I think I got set up. I think everything that happened Friday night was planned."

"Are you blaming Dave and saying Tammy lied?"

"Yeah, in a strange sort of a way, I guess I am, Sara. I wanted to go to the game. Dave invited me to clean up at his house. He said he'd loan me a shirt. He brought out his father's wine and offered it to me. I wasn't interested in a drink until he encouraged me. When Dave told me Tammy wanted to see me, I believed him. I thought maybe I could get to know her a little more."

"Even if she liked you, why should that matter? I may not be a cheerleader or the principal's daughter, Joe, but I care about you. We have a good relationship. I don't want to lose you," Sara stated, tears welling up in her eyes.

I was overwhelmed. I hadn't thought my interest in Tammy would hurt Sara. I felt she was beginning to think I didn't like her.

"Sara, I am sorry." I didn't know what else to say. I moved closer to her and opened my arms to hug her. She let me.

Holding her close helped me paint a picture of love. I realized love was a connection between two people that was special, different, and unique. My ideas about Tammy were never close to what Sara and I already had. I needed to tell Sara that. I knew I couldn't explain Friday night, especially since I really didn't remember, but I wanted to tell Sara how I felt. "Sara, I have always liked you. Tammy could never mean as much to me as you do."

"Thanks," Sara choked.

"I don't know how to say it better," I confessed.

"You don't have to," Sara replied, hugging me tightly.

Walking home after seeing Sara, I noticed Dad by himself at the edge of woods, not too far from the house.

19   Confession

"Why are you so quiet, Joe?"

"Nothing, Dad."

"C'mon son, you always have something to say. Something happened in school today?"

"Nothing."

"Got girls on your mind?"

"Dad... "

"I don't want you distracted. You could get hurt, like your Uncle Danny."

"The principal threw me off the baseball team."

"What!"

"Principal Browersfield told me I am no longer captain or even on the baseball team."

"Why?"

"For drinking."

"You mean for riding the tricycle down the middle of Main Street? That doesn't seem fair, does it?"

"No, it doesn't. Mr. Browersfield said I wasn't a good role model for the other Finnish boys." I raised my voice in frustration. "I don't remember riding a tricycle at all and definitely not down the middle of Main Street!"

"Well, that was their story. What happened to that Dave guy, the Irish football and basketball player you were with?"

"I don't know."

"Why don't you know?"

"Dad … You know I don't socialize with those people."

"The non-Finnish?"

"Yes, *the non-Finnish*."

"Sounds like you better start, son. You need some non-Finnish friends."

"Don't start that with me now. I don't want to socialize with people who I feel have hurt my family and friends. Think about it, Dad. Why are you cutting wood for a living? Maybe you should socialize with some non-Finnish people so you can get a job that is easier or pays you more money."

"Joseph."

"I mean it, Dad."

"Joseph."

"You are cutting wood for the same reason I am no longer captain of the baseball team. It has everything to do with who we socialize with. It has everything to do with who we are and who we are connected to. And we are connected to the woods and radical socialists. We are locked out, Dad, locked out!"

I turned my head away from the conversation. I kicked a rock by the side of the road. I couldn't believe my dad wouldn't admit he had lost his job because of his politics. Why didn't he understand? This fit his mental fixation with conspiracy ideas!

"Well, so you know, Mr. Schoolboy, half the city council members in Minneapolis are socialists and so is the mayor. They voted against supporting an American intervention into WWI. The same is true in Milwaukee. And those are some big cities."

I remained silent. I hadn't known that. *Hmm…* I thought. *Maybe Dad was not a depressed, betrayed political refugee. Maybe he was a believer in the impossible. Maybe Dad really believed Marx's dream was right. Maybe all the study sessions and tense political discussions were not the flaying arms of a man drowning, but the claws of a badger gripping the ground slowly and steadily to crawl out of his hole and strike back at the dog, defy the hunt.*

On impulse, I felt prompted to share what Arvi and I had seen at the Bruce Mine shaft. "Something happened when I was hunting with Arvi the other weekend."

"Did you wing him?"

"Ha, ha. A butt full of birdshot wouldn't faze him, Dad."

"You're getting funny now – that's good… I remember when I used to hunt with Arvi's father, Impi…"

"Dad, I don't want to hear about how you two shot Impi's parents' chickens, cleaned them, brought them to his grandparents' house, and cooked them for his grandpa and grandma. His grandma couldn't believe that the grouse you shot were so big and tasted so good – just like chicken."

We smiled at each other. Dad playfully threatened me, "Tell me what's on your mind, Joe, or I'll tell the story again. You wouldn't want that, right?"

"There were two guys near the Bruce Mine the other weekend when Arvi and I were hunting. They wanted us to check and see if their friends were still hunting by the underground shaft. So we did, and they gave us a dollar."

"A dollar? What did you say they wanted you to do?" Gustav questioned.

"Check on if their friends were hunting by the Bruce Mine shaft."

"Then what?"

"They wanted us to report back to them about their friends –"

Dad exploded. "You idiot! You and Arvi could be dead! Those guys weren't hunting. They were the leaders of a group of paid thugs. They wanted you to check to see if their hired gunman had done the deed. If you witnessed them kill anyone and reported back what you had seen, they would have killed you."

I remembered thinking I saw the one guy aim his gun at our backs. I shivered. "I never thought of that."

"That's happened to others who were naively asked to check and came back with the wrong answer. Don't ever do that again!" Dad declared.

Dad had me so scared I told the rest of what had happened. "After we reported back to the guys that we didn't see their friends, I was bothered by the whole situation. So Arvi and I went back to the area they had had us check. It was near the cable car shack. We went inside the shack and noticed the cable car wasn't there. The brake was off. Nobody was around –"

"Did you tell anyone?" Dad interrupted.

"Let me finish, Dad. Arvi and I decided to go over to the Chisholm shop to tell them and see if anyone there knew anything about what had happened in the shaft. We saw Frank Vainionpaa, Toivo Soumi, and their crew arguing with the two guys who had given us the dollar. Then Sheriff McFarland arrived with four of his deputies. There was a fight. We saw McFarland knocked to the ground."

"You're not lying to me, son, are you?"

I rolled his eyes back. My dad persisted, "You heard about the mining accident, right, Joe?"

"Yes. In school. We had to be quiet and pray about it, I mean think about it."

The connection hadn't occurred to me before. I had filed the cable car incident away as another suspicious act by the steel owners. Something seemed to be out of place. *Oh God…* I thought. *What if the two incidents were connected! I hadn't wanted to let Dad know. Now I was beginning to think in conspiratorial patterns. I think the bonfire incident had affected me.*

"Did it occur to you there might be a connection between what you two experienced and the mining accident?"

"Dad, with you everything is connected. Everything is a conspiracy."

"And you think life isn't?"

"No… I mean … I don't know what I mean. Maybe things just are. Some things are broken, just because. Other things are broken by somebody! Does there always have to be someone to blame? Is there always a conspiracy by those with money?"

"Remember my cousins who worked in the copper mines on the Upper Peninsula of Michigan? The Christmas tragedy? Fifty-six children and eighteen women and men were trampled to death. Eight more died later at the hospital. The mining company offered to bury the victims, but the strikers turned them down. Three of my cousins died there."

I knew I had to be quiet. The dam had broken.

"Remember Uncle Danny?"

"You mean your brother who got sliced up in the sawmill?"

"Yes."

Grandpa and Grandma had gone back to Finland because of Danny's accident. I never knew why that was so important. I had wanted them to come back when Mom got sick, but they hadn't.

"Uncle Danny was pushed into the saw blade –"

"Pushed? I don't get it, Dad? What's that have to do with the miners in the mine shaft?"

"I am trying to teach you that things just don't happen, Joe. They may look like they just happen, but –"

My thoughts drifted to Dave. *Did he set me up? Did Dave know all along he was going to get me drunk and then set me up to be arrested?*

"My oldest brother Irv worked for Czar Nicolas IV. None of us knew what he did. We hated the Czar and anyone associated with him. Irv didn't talk much about his work, which made us even more suspicious. The mill where my brother Danny slabbed had the contract to cut wood for the Czar. That lumber was to be used to build his expensive house in the country.

"Nicolas wanted to impress his foreign guests with that expensive home. Irv had certified the wood. He told the Czar it had the right grain and color for the Czar's structure. He ordered five shipments. Typically the Czar over-ordered. He would use leftover wood for formal bonfires behind the palace. Danny assumed there had been too much wood ordered. He was right; there had been. Well, Danny arranged to have half of the third shipment stolen. He figured stealing the wood would help his family. This was better than letting the excess wood be burned in a bonfire.

"For some odd reason, the Czar canceled the last two loads. Irv didn't know this, so neither did Danny. With just three loads sent, losing half of a third shipment became obvious even to the Czar. Irv asked Danny why the third load was short. Danny blamed a small band of gypsies in the area for hijacking half the shipment. He even told the Czar's soldiers where the gypsies were camped.

"When Nicolas was told the gypsies had taken the lumber, he ordered Irv to round them up and execute every one of them. The Czar asked to be notified of the lynching date so he could arrange to be there. Irv jailed all eighteen gypsies and gave the Czar the execution date. The Czar planned to attend. When Nicolas arrived, the hangings began. As the palace soldiers got ready to lynch the last woman, Dalenka Lyubitshka, she cried out to Danny to save her life. Now it isn't unusual for anyone who's being put to death to cry out for mercy, but this gypsy cried out Danny's full name over and over. Something in her emotions connected with the Czar's heart.

"Czar Nicolas IV stopped the last execution to hear what she had to say. He walked down to the staging platform in the town square and talked with Dalenka on the gallows. Her kin were dangling dead next to her, still warm. Dalenka told the Czar she knew Danny's name because her brother Lensar had met with Danny. Together they had arranged the hijacking of the Czar's wood. Danny was standing with them on the gallows. He called Dalenka a liar, pulled out his hand pistol, and shot her on the spot. Nicolas left. He went back to his palace in St. Petersburg. Irv had the gypsies buried in one large grave in the woods.

"When the mill started up the next week, Danny's jacket sleeve got caught on the first slab just starting to head through the mill. Somehow Danny's body swung around in the front of the blade rather than to the side table where the slab falls after the first pass. He was cut up badly but survived. The superstitious in town thought a gypsy curse caused the accident… So did I."

Dad stopped telling his story. The look in his eyes saddened me. Usually I ignored those moments when I found it hard to separate the mixture of grief, despair, and injustice in Dad. I didn't know how to penetrate his mood. The shadows in his soul were the gears of his Marxism grinding out hate for the steel owners. I wondered how long I would have to live and what I would have to endure before I would be able to stop those same cogs from turning inside me. How could I jam them up?

Suddenly, Dad continued his story. "Irv told me the Czar had a secret spy system. His spies told the small band of gypsies who had agreed to buy the stolen lumber the story of Danny's betrayal. Coming to stop the execution, they had run into a storm and stopped to take shelter. That caused them to arrive a day too late. As an act of revenge, they made sure Danny's 'accident' happened the next week."

I hadn't heard that story before. Why hadn't I suspected there were spies and conspiracies back in Finland, too? That's why my father was so good at seeing them here. He had been raised in them. Sometimes I didn't believe the connections and patterns Dad and Launo talked about. Even Niilo got caught up in them, thinking they were real stories instead of exaggerations. On the other hand, what Dave O'Malley had done to me was persuading me to start considering a conspiracy or two in my life.

"Son, nobody deserves to get hurt or murdered. Those gypsies died because of Danny's greed. When Grandpa and Grandma went back to Finland to nurse Danny, your Uncle Farley told them this story. Irv, not Nicolas IV, ordered the spies to tell the story of Danny's betrayal to that small band of gypsies. My brother, your uncle, crippled his own brother Danny for life!"

Phew! I didn't expect a story like that. I knew Irv wasn't a radical Bolshevik. I didn't know what he was. No one ever talked about him. Now I knew why. They were hiding a sad family secret of betrayal by a brother. This made me shiver.

"Grandpa and Grandma will never see you or your brother and sister grow up. They can't even get back to America. That isn't fair. And it wasn't fair for those people to get trampled to death at a Christmas celebration."

This seemed like a long way around for Dad to take to explain something. But maybe that was okay. I learned a bit more about how complicated his life had been growing up. We only had to survive the loss of his job at Oliver Mining. The lumber thing was doing okay. We had food and were warm.

"Something tells me those four miners weren't in a cable car accident. If the cable had snapped, as reported in the newspaper, the cable car's operator would have had a hell of a time getting the car back up in a few hours. He would have asked for help from the Tower Underground Mine that has a special cable rewind machine. The lack of pictures in the paper is also suspicious. Joe, you know the paper loves pictures of train crashes, accidents… But there wasn't a picture of a smashed cable car anywhere. That's because there wasn't a crashed cable car."

My dad's face was red. When he was angry, the veins on his neck got larger. His neck veins were gigantic. He was breathing hard. He held his hand up for me not to say anything. I didn't.

After a couple of deep breaths, he was ready to continue. "I've got to go tell this to my brother Launo. He and the boys said they thought something was brewing."

"So who will die or get hurt when you tell your brother and the IWW gang gets rallied up?"

"Joseph, this is serious business. We're not playing cowboys and Indians here. This is war."

"And who is fighting whom? Can anyone win?"

"You need to get your ass over to those Saturday morning study sessions more often, Joe. We have to be on guard. A lot of people have been hurt or killed. And I think there are going to be more."

Dad cleared his throat. Now he was on the war path. He had seen the enemy pop up its ugly head again. The boys had to find a bopper to bop its disgusting face. My father wouldn't be interested in anything I had to say now. He was on a mission. He started walking away and then stopped like he had forgotten something and had to come back and get it.

"Joe, you are graduating this summer. Have you thought about going to school in Duluth? The People's Labor College is the official IWW College for the United States. Your cousin Niilo is being sent to Russia next year by the college to study at a university in Moscow. Think about it."

This was the first time I had heard of this. Niilo hadn't told me.

Dad continued, "This is a great time to be alive. The revolution is almost complete. Who knows where it will go next? College can prepare you and put you in contact with the next overthrow."

"I'll think about it, Dad."

I said that to please Dad. Until now, I hadn't had any interest in learning more about how this town, the mine owners, and the public schools were conspiring together to strangle the worker, especially us Finnish. I had so many stories in my head it was easy for me to think there were conspiracies everywhere, even if I didn't believe it. But, even if there were dark doings in the backrooms, what could I do?

Common sense told me that once all the ore was dug up and there was nothing left to dig, the mine owners would pick up, go somewhere else, and dig the ore there. So what was all the scheming to overthrow them worth?

It didn't change the evitable.

20   Conspiracy

Crowding together, Gustav, Launo, Nillo, Impi, Mika, and Yrkki stared at the front page of the *Mining News.*

Four Miners Crushed in Cable Car Crash
at the Bruce Mine Shaft

Rescuers found the bodies of four miners who disappeared after a cable snapped and the brakes gave out at the Bruce Mine shaft outside of Chisholm. The four miners were found inside the cab near the shaft entrance where they normally began work. They were identified as: Elder Metsa, Herman Bjorkland, Taisto Rantala, and Helmer Valamaki.

The Oliver Mining Company expressed sympathy to the families. Father James Sustarich from the Holy Family Roman Catholic Church blessed the bodies before burial at the Hibbing City Cemetery. Oliver Mining conducted the burials. Individual funerals were not held.

Mining inspectors arrived from Saint Paul, Minnesota, in response to a request to inspect the accident scene and file a report. Since this is the third accident in the same shaft, the Bruce Mine will be closed until further notice. Other mines in the area will find work for the displaced workers.

Launo slammed the paper onto the table with disgust. "Do you believe that, Gustav?"

"The capitalists killed and buried four men and didn't allow their families to wish them goodbye. Are we surprised? Have they ever acted any differently, Launo?" responded Gustav.

"Damn it! You would think the newspaper is owned by the mining company!" Impi spat on the ground and wiped his chin. "Shit! How did this happen? How did the steel trust know these guys were organizers? I was hoping Eileen's cousin Wayne's stuff about spies and letters and codes was crap."

"Impi, my son Joe told me two guys wanted to check on friends of theirs who had been hunting around the Bruce Mine shaft. They paid Joe and Arvi each a dollar to go to the Bruce location and report back if they saw the friends," Gustav explained.

"What the hell are you talking about, Gustav? My son, Arvi?" Impi demanded.

"Would you listen? A couple of weekends ago, Joe was hunting with your kid by the Kitzville location outside of Chisholm near the Bruce shaft. Joe said these two guys asked the boys to walk back to the Bruce underground entrance and see if those guys' friends were hunting grouse there and then come back and tell them," Gustav repeated.

"Arvi never told me that," Impi asserted.

"That doesn't matter, Impi," Gustav returned.

Gustav watched as Impi shook his head back and forth like he had just been swatted by a cedar branch in a super-hot sauna or maybe more like a cat who had gotten splashed with water. Impi rolled his eyes after the head shaking.

When Impi finished, Gustav continued. "They told Joe and Arvi their hunting group got split up. Both boys went to the shaft to check for the men. They didn't find anybody there. After they reported that back to the guys, the boys got suspicious. They returned to the shack and went inside. Joe claimed the cable car was at the bottom of the shaft and the brake wasn't engaged. Neither Joe nor Arvi had seen those two guys before. One had a mustache."

Impi exploded again. "What the hell! A mustache! That sounds like Armstrong's cousin Thomas! He is the regional director for the Pinkertons."

"Who is Armstrong?" said Mika.

Niilo replied calmly, "The president of Oliver Mining Company. Keep going, Gustav."

Gustav shifted his position and leaned forward. "Joe and Arvi ran over to the Chisholm maintenance shops. I think they wanted to tell somebody about what had happened to them. When they got there, they saw this mustached character beat up Sheriff McFarland."

"Okay, I got the pieces together now," replied Impi. He sat up, looked at the sky, and then glanced back down at the others. "I was there. This clown, I mean Thomas Armstrong, and a group of his Pinkerton mercenaries were walking around the shops, looking in windows, kicking barrels, and acting suspicious. You know me; I got worried, wondering why there were strangers out there. I went to talk to them.

"They started yelling at me about why Rantala and Valamaki weren't at work…something about Americanization paperwork problems … They threatened me that they were going to report those guys. When the Pinkertons asked Frank Vainionpaa about Taisto and Helmer's whereabouts, Frank jumped Thomas …started pounding him. I thought, *Oh my God.* Frank was so pissed he didn't notice the other men with Thomas. You know Frank, just look at him wrong and he punches, and hard, too. He never takes time to think about the odds of winning or losing; he just fights. Then, out of nowhere, McFarland showed up.

"This was the first time I had seen his new scrawny deputy, the Croatian, who looks like a bean pole. I thought something seemed off. I wondered how they knew there was trouble and came so quickly."

"In the 1907 Rainy Lake lumber strike there had been a scuffle between the local law and the Pinkertons," Launo added. "When we talked about it, we realized how odd it was for both groups to show up without one calling the other to say there was trouble. Back then, we began to think maybe they both had come together looking to cause trouble."

"Shit," said Gustav. "The Czar had made it look like his soldiers were acting independent of the town constables, but, if you thought about it, you wondered why both were showing up at the same time. If it had been a war, it would have taken a little time to get reinforcements from another area. You can only travel so fast."

Mika smirked. "I'm with you, Gustav. Their uniforms may look different, but they are all part of the same group, and that is not our group. I probably have told you this before. My dad would watch the infantry come off the trains at the station where he dispatched. He saw many small packages the size of bills being handed out and stuffed into the infantry members' pants' pockets. When Dad stopped at the tavern after work to catch up on the news of the day, he saw the constable's men at the bar with unwrapped packages, just like the wrapped ones the Czar's soldiers had had. They were paying for their malts with the same money. God! The Czar had thought we Finns didn't notice things then, and Armstrong thinks the same today."

"Nothing's changed," said Launo. "The same thing happens now. They are all together in this. Remember the fifteen men who were killed when the underground ceiling collapsed in Soudan? All of them were buried without a funeral, too."

"You're right," said Mika.

"That was about a month before the cable car crashed at the Keewatin, if I remember correctly," commented Yrkki.

"I hope you didn't remember wrongly," joked Mika. Yrkki grabbed Mika around the neck with his right arm and gave him a little squeeze. "You better watch it," continued Mika. "If I pass out, you'll be a part of the conspiracy. Then Impi will scratch your eyes out."

Impi grunted, but his eyes held their twinkle.

Launo added, "If you count the train accident at midnight in Dunwoody Mine this October and the premature explosion underground in Eveleth, that's almost forty men killed in three months. Don't you think that is suspicious?"

"The steel trust is spreading the murder all around. They make it look like accidents," Impi spat out with disgust.

"Hell, there have always been accidents. What's so unusual about that?" Niilo said. "Right, Yrkki?"

"That's why we are organizing to get safer working conditions," Impi interjected.

Niilo's sarcasm thickened their cynicism.

"Safety, my ass," said Yrkki. "No one's figured out that every 'accident' takes out two to three strong unionists, Finnish unionists. Well, we have figured it out. Those pricks in Duluth think if they keep their activities covert and spread all over at several locations, the public won't see the pattern."

"We know it's more than suspicious, and Haywood agrees with us," said Impi. "This time it hurts because four men that we knew died, and each dared to speak up. The powers that be didn't even try to cover these deaths with a distraction."

"Shit! What are we going to do now? Nobody will believe us," said Mika.

"We have to prove them wrong," said Gustav. "Launo, didn't you say you knew some IWW men who are willing to dig up the mass grave? Once we get them dug up, we just need a doctor to look at the bodies and tell us how they died."

"You mean dig up the dead men?" questioned Mika, alarmed.

"Yes! Oliver Mining isn't going to dig the men up; the company buried them for a reason. Their families aren't going to do it, either; they are too scared," answered Gustav.

Yrkki stood up and lit a Camel. He offered Niilo and Mika one. Then he motioned for Launo, Niilo, Impi, and Gustav to come closer. After throwing his match, Yrkki perched his foot on the stump in front of him. Taking a long drag and exhaling, Yrkki spoke. "The 1906 and 1916 strikes failed. Bill Hayward doesn't know if another strike will work. He's down in Chicago trying to solidify and hold the union together. What if our four brothers help us in a way the strikes never did? I don't know how, but I am for digging them up and giving them some protection. If Gustav's and Impi's boys know about the faked accident, it won't be long before more know. You can't trust kids to keep their mouths shut about stuff like this. Sooner or later they blab."

"Watch what you say about my son. I might have to paste you," Impi teased.

"I'll follow with a few more punches," said Gustav with a slight smile, "and a knee to the groin."

Launo cleared his throat and added, "Before we hurt each other too much, let's think about what Yrkki just said. With Unlucky Andy's and Frank's help, I know we can get fifteen to sixteen men together. Let's set a date to dig up the bodies. Tell no one, not even your wives."

"I agree," said Gustav. "Make sure no more than three of you come to the graveyard together."

Mika nodded.

21   Graveyard Discovery

"I'm glad we're in the back corner, Dad. Nobody can see us," Niilo noted.

"Yes, there are quite a few of us," Launo answered, looking around at the group which was huddled together.

"How far under do you think the bodies are?" Gustav asked.

"My guess is four feet," Niilo answered. "You have to bury at least that deep so the winter freeze doesn't cause the coffins to heave and float up."

"Four feet and four bodies," Frank said to Impi. "We are lucky they were even buried."

"Ain't that the truth," Toivo responded.

"The mine owners could have had them shot way back in a mine shaft and then left them there – no funeral, no burial, just darkness and cold," Frank continued.

"Yeah...," Impi sighed.

"Fall is a good time to dig. Dirt has less moisture in the fall, so it's easier to spade. This dryness signals the leaves to turn colors and drop lazily to the ground. Before the hard frost and first freeze, the ground is softer," Niilo commented.

"I kind of figured that, Niilo," Impi huffed.

"When you cover a coffin with dirt, the dirt settles down creating a pocket in the grass so rain collects. If we waited 'til the winter freeze, the frozen dirt could cause coffins to float up. In the spring, water could pool up on a settling grave and offer a breeding site for mosquitoes –" explained Niilo.

Impi interrupted, "Damn it, Niilo, I don't mind a little explanation, but what's all the science talk for? Leave that stuff up to George in the Saturday sessions. This is not the place for it." Impi turned and looked at Launo. "Shit, Launo, you should take your son out of school."

"Niilo gets talkative when he's nervous," Launo explained.

"Impi," Gustav said, smiling, "if you don't quiet down, we'll have you under the soil."

Gustav motioned for the men to gather closely together. "With the bodies somewhere down about four to six feet and four of us guys around each side of the grave, we should be able to find the caskets in less than an hour. This will give us enough time to uncover the coffins, take a look, and then rebury them."

"I've never done this before," Unlucky volunteered, "…never dug a coffin up before."

Gustav reassured Unlucky. "But you've put fence posts in the ground. You've dug basements for houses. Digging is digging."

"You are a miner; I'm not," Yrkki confessed.

Gustav divided the men into four groups and assigned each a side of the mass grave to dig. Gustav, Impi, Launo, and Niilo each led a group. All four groups were within easy eyesight of each other, even in the dark. The four miners being exhumed were buried in a public section purchased by Oliver Mining. The Hibbing cemetery was divided into categories. The largest was Christian with Protestants and Catholics. Catholics included Roman, Russian, and Greek Orthodox. A small Jewish section was fenced off toward the east end. The public section held the family lots and those not identified with a religious identity.

"I think I hit something!" Launo announced.

"I think we did, too…" Gustav said.

Launo whistled softly. "Hey! Everybody over here! Let's start here first."

Gustav, Impi, and Niilo directed their groups toward Launo's. Bent over and holding a short handled broom, Launo stated, "We have one of the coffins uncovered."

Heavy breathing from shoveling thickened the air, and Yrkki sneezed. "Jumala teitä siunatkoon! (God Bless!)"

"Gustav, take a shovel and pry off the top," Launo ordered.

Gustav hesitated. Impi moved over to the open grave and lowered his shovel into the hole, planning to lift the lid. Not knowing what was respectful, he slowly dragged the shovel across the top of the coffin. The steel blade slipped off the top, dropped an inch, and stopped. Impi pushed the shovel handle back to lift the coffin lid. The lid didn't move.

"Step on the shovel harder. They're only nails. Lean into it, Impi!" Launo encouraged.

Gustav joined Impi beside the shovel. Impi gave the blade a firm kick and pressed down hard. The shovel bit into the wood cover snugly. Together, the two men pushed the handle down. At first the cover resisted, but then it moved with a cracking noise and a snap. Both men lost their balance and fell backward.

Launo instructed, "A couple of you guys grab the cover with your hands and pull it back so we can see what's inside."

As two of the men followed instructions, the group tightened their formation, shading the kerosene light from being seen beyond the graveside gathering. The kerosene smell increased. "Niilo, bring your lamp here! Closer, damn it! He won't melt... That looks like Elder Metsa."

No one replied. Impi leaned over to get a closer look. He shook his head and spit.

Gustav ordered, "Lift the casket on this end and pull it up here. Now, Impi, have your men lift with their shovels on the back end. Between both our groups I think we can pull this casket out of the grave."

Impi's group placed their shovels under the opposite end of the coffin and pried upward. Collectively, they easily lifted the coffin onto the grass. Now that the coffin was up and partially open, Launo resumed giving instructions. "Damn, it's dark. We need another lamp! I can hardly see with mine."

Jari leaned over with his. "Will that help?"

"Let's get one more!"

With the glow of three kerosene lamps clustered close to each other, most could see the open coffin. The wood was intact, and no unpleasant smells wafted from it. No one other than Launo acknowledged that he recognized the corpse. Launo was quiet. He stared as if in thought.

Gustav motioned with his hands. "Roll the coffin over, and let's get the corpse out on the ground so that we will be able see who we have." Gustav put his arm on Impi's back. "Impi, get closer in here. Isn't that Elder Metsa?"

Impi paused before he spoke. "I can't see…"

Irritated, Launo pushed a few men back. "Get out of the damn way so Impi can see the body."

Gustav persisted. He asked Impi one more time. "Impi, isn't that Elder Metsa?"

"I'm still having a hard time seeing... The face seems covered with cheese cloth."

"Let me get a closer look, Impi," Gustav suggested. "You're right. Looks like when they put Elder in the coffin, they took his clothes off and wrapped him in some material."

"The body's size and build is Metsa's, but I would feel better about saying it is him if he had some identifiable clothes on and I could see his face," Impi maintained.

"Didn't you ever take a sauna with him? Pull back the cloth. See if he is circumcised," suggested Gustav.

That got a chuckle or two. Tension broke.

Gustav and Niilo remained bent over the body. They were scraping the dirt away from the head with their fingers. They tried to figure out, rather than guess, which body they had dug up. After a short while, Launo lost patience. "Damn it! We've got a head, a body, two arms, and two legs. What more do we need?"

"But something seems whacked, irregular," Gustav said. "Niilo, his arms and the legs are on the body, but doesn't Elder's head look kind of funny?"

"I guess so," Nillo agreed.

"What do you mean, 'I guess so?'" Launo questioned impatiently.

"I don't know what you mean by kind of funny? Is it laughing? Smiling? Spitting at you?" Niilo clarified.

"Let's just say, if you think of a head as a pumpkin, half of the pumpkin is missing," Gustav explained.

"Hold the lamp up, and let me take a closer look," Launo ordered. He leaned close to the body. "Damn it, you're right! It looks like half the pumpkin is missing."

"Shit!"

Gustav looked up at the sky and thought to himself, *How did we get here?*

He noticed how much brighter the stars were with a new moon. Even the North Star seemed easier to find above the end of the Big Dipper without moonlight. As he thought about the night and Metsa's body, he connected the constellation to the night's grave digging. The Big Dipper tonight was an open grave. *Hmmm.* He was standing on the handle looking down into the ladle. The association of the Dipper and Metsa's coffin left a comfortable, almost calm feeling. Gustav pondered this. *If the Big Dipper can point to where north is, maybe these bodies will give some direction to our organizing and grant a final honor to these four brave men.*

A feeling of confidence rose in him. He straightened. "Launo, listen to me. We may not know which body this is, but we know the names of the four men that are buried here: Metsa, Bjorkland, Rantala, and Valamaki. It's got to be one of them. Even if we can't tell one body from another, we may be able to tell how they died. They have a story to tell by their deaths."

"Yeah, that's right," Launo agreed. Pausing for a moment, he gathered his thoughts. Placing his foot on the coffin, he looked around the group. "Let's go back to raising the other three bodies. My group will clear an area here next to this coffin we have opened already to make room for the others. Quick! Let's hurry!"

Gustav, Impi, and NIllo's groups went back to their sides of the mass grave and resumed digging. In less than five minutes, quick exchanges were made.

"Over here! Over here! We found another coffin and have the lid off."

"Do you have a head, a body, two legs, and two arms over there, Gustav?"

"Looks like we have everything, but the head... "

"Is the head smashed?"

"There isn't a head."

"Nope. We don't see a head."

"Check the coffin again."

"No pumpkin . . ."

Launo tallied, "So now we have two bodies, one with no head and one with half a head. Lift the coffin up and out, drag it over here, and roll the body out."

Launo's men ran to help them.

"Impi and Niilo, hurry and get those other two coffins dug up."

After half an hour, they had exhumed the other two bodies and placed all the coffins and bodies next to each other. Holding up kerosene lamps, they illuminated the four corpses on the ground. They set five other kerosene lamps in various locations around the crudely opened wood coffins. A few men lit cigarettes. More men were down on their knees than those standing. Two leaned against trees. From a distance, the assembly resembled a crowd outside a bar after it had closed. No one wanted to go home, and no one knew where to go. Suddenly, one man waved everyone over to one of the coffins.

"What's that piece of metal in there?"

"Where?"

"See, there in the far corner!"

"Let me get that."

"Shit! It's a badge."

"What the ... Launo, come over here. You've got to see what we found."

Launo hurried over to the three men. "Is that the sheriff's? It can't be... It's probably from one of the Feds from the Cities who came up here for the cable car inspection. We need more light to read the words."

Launo called Nillo, Gustav, and Impi together. The rest watched as the four examined the badge and intensely exchanged words. Heads nodded, and the group broke up. Launo walked toward the rest of the group. He stopped by the corpses and looked up. "Now think about this, men. Supposedly, four men were sitting in a cable car, and the cable brake on the spool let loose. Then the car crashed into the bottom of the mine shaft, killing all four. Why would all four bodies have damage only to the heads?"

There was silence. Some feet shuffled. A few coats were pulled closed. Launo continued, "I bet before this cable car crashed into the bottom of the mine shaft, these four men were already dead. I suspect they were shot in the head with shotguns and then put into the cable car. The operator lowered the cable car down to the bottom of the shaft with bodies, not live men, inside."

Short conversations took place between the men. "That's seems right."

"Hmmmm."

"You think so?"

"Niilo, Gustav, Impi, and I believe the reason the coffins were closed at the funeral wasn't because the bodies were mangled from hitting the mine shaft floor at 50 miles an hour. The coffins were closed because these four men were murdered –"

"Shit, Launo, just say it right. They were executed!" Jari picked up one of the shovels and held it like a rifle against Launo's head. Jari pulled his finger back as if there was a trigger. "That's how they did it! No shame. Shotguns were held to their heads, and triggers were pulled. Instant death. There were no screams; there was no defense. Anybody in the area of the shaft who heard the four shots that Sunday would have thought the shots were the sounds of happy hunters on a morning grouse hunt."

Launo stepped back and allowed Gustav to speak. "Since the murders were committed in the morning, nobody would know that the men were dead until at least one or two hours after their shift was done later that evening. If the cable car had really been in a free fall, a cable or two may have snapped, the car would be damaged, and the bodies would have signs of a sudden stop. In other words, more than just their heads would have been busted up. There would have been some broken limbs, arms, maybe even a torn body, but all four bodies had damage only to the heads."

Unlucky added, "Look at those bodies ... May our brothers rest in peace. Everything else is intact except their heads."

"What do we do now?" asked Yrkki.

"Well, I don't think we need a doctor or a mortician," Niilo responded.

"I think we all know how these four brave neighbors died. Somehow we have to get the real story out to the public or at least to their families right away," Launo answered.

Impi cautioned, "If we do that, someone might leak our story to the mining company, and the steel trust will know that we know what really had happened."

"Well, I don't think anyone has believed all that's been said about the accidents that have happened," Unlucky countered. "None of us knows the real story about them. We just know the company has misinformed us."

"We don't have a choice, Andy," replied Yrkki. "Look at how they have shut down every strike we have started."

Launo decided to challenge the men. "We need to do something more dramatic, something that calls attention to what is going on here. The president of our country needs to know. This is something the whole country needs to know."

"How are you going to do that?" asked the man in the back.

"I think we should take time to plan something large and dramatic. We have to tell Haywood. Bill will know what to do," Niilo stated.

The group became quiet. Someone asked, "What are we going to do with the bodies in the meantime?"

"Niilo and I don't want to put them back into the ground right now. If the mining company finds out we have dug the miners up, they may come back and destroy the bodies. Then we'll never be able to prove anything," Gustav cautioned.

"You have a point there," Unlucky Andy said.

"Niilo, Gustav, Impi, and I think our only choice is to keep the bodies," Launo affirmed. "So don't rebury the coffins. Let's fill the grave with dirt. While you guys do that, we'll do some planning on where we can hide the bodies.

"Go back to where you were digging. Check the area for anything we missed. Maybe there is another badge or some piece of clothing. I don't know what you are looking for, just look. Gustav, Niilo, and I will look the bodies over. Leave us a couple of extra lanterns."

The men left. Some were kicking the loose earth. Others were shining the lamps close to the ground, combing for evidence.

Gustav looked at Launo. "Where are you going to hide four dead bodies?"

Launo was hunched down on both arms and knees as if he was tending wood in the fireplace. He seemed to be fascinated by imaginary flickering flames, not a large fire but small fires, ones he could control easily. Gustav decided to catch Launo's attention and refocus him with one more question. "Look at all the forest around this end of the burial grounds. A wild animal may dig them up and finish what Mother Nature hasn't. We don't want that."

"No."

Niilo realized that Gustav was having a problem getting Launo's attention. He placed his hand on his dad's left shoulder. "We will keep the secret between us."

Launo still didn't respond. Niilo and Gustav looked at each other. Launo hadn't moved. Niilo shrugged. Gustav moved closer to Launo. Nothing was said. Niilo broke the quietness, "I was talking to this Jewish rabbi I know."

"What?" Gustav responded.

"Listen to me. The Jewish don't do anything with dead bodies. They bury their dead within twenty-four hours of their passing. They wrap them in cheese cloth."

"God, a dead body starts to stink right away! Rot doesn't take twenty-four hours...," Gustav directed his remarks in Launo's direction. He thought maybe this would engage Launo, but Launo remained preoccupied.

Niilo continued, "Yeah, I know, but the rabbi said they delay the rot by putting the body on ice. The cold temperature slows down the decomposition. It freezes the flesh and all the organs. That's kosher."

"Niilo, we already agreed we did not want to leave them in the woods … so …"

"Gustav, we've had a frost already this fall, and the temperature is getting down to 40°F every night."

Finally, Launo rejoined the conversation. He looked up. "I have an idea. There are no more festivals at Mesaba Park this year. What if we take the bodies there and hide them in the ice sheds? Nobody would think of going out there to find the bodies at this time of year. If we hide the bodies well, they will stay preserved and frozen through the winter and spring and into next summer."

"Hell!" Niilo said, excited his father was ready to talk. "The bodies will last longer than that! Some ice has lasted until the next winter in those sheds. The sheds are in a shady spot and get a cool lake breeze."

"Hey, we're lucky, because they'll be storing extra ice this winter for the grand opening for the park next fall. That will freeze the bodies even more. We have plenty of time to decide how we can use the bodies to create an event that makes the national news. We'll get Rockefeller, yet!"

22   **Fermented Worm Juice**

January

"Joe."

"Huh?"

"Joe."

"Who's here?

"Joe, open the door. It's your father, Joe."

I was surprised. I headed over to the hall's kitchen door and opened it. "Dad, what are you doing here?"

Gustav stepped in, left the door open, and wiped his nose on his jacket sleeve. "Aunt Lillian stopped by and put your brother and sister down for me. Mom was asleep already so I asked Lillian if she would stay. I thought you might want some company tonight."

"Are you staying the night?"

"No, but I hauled a couple hardwood logs and a bottle in on the sled. Dropped the wood by the camp sauna on the way in here; the bottle is outside. I was thinking we could sweat a bit before I leave tonight."

"Thanks." I paused. Wondering why he was really here, I asked, "Why did you stop by tonight? Are you still coming by tomorrow? With Rudolf? For the Winter Ice Bee?"

"I'm not sure what you mean? I am concerned. You haven't been yourself since Principal Browersfield threw you off the baseball team. You don't seem happy. I haven't heard you talk about Sara in a while."

The conversation didn't take hold with me. Noticing that the kitchen door was still open, I shivered, reached past my father, and pushed on the door. It didn't close completely because of the snow-packed doorjamb.

"I'll say it again, Joe. I want to give you some company tonight," Dad repeated.

Still a little leery, I shoved the door again, and this time it shut. We stood still. Dad picked up the conversation, "Joe, what scares you?"

"Isn't that one of your favorite lines, Dad? *What are you afraid of?*"

"Joseph, when was the last time we took a sauna together? I haven't come to your baseball games. I've never spent much time with you. When you were willing to help out with the family when Mom got sick, I was happy. I knew that I could work harder and keep us afloat. I couldn't have done that without your taking care of the house and family. Lillian reminded me tonight of how much you have given . . . She thinks I haven't noticed how much you give. . ."

Nothing was said for a few minutes. I was thinking about what needed to get done by tomorrow. *Dad could have picked a better time to get sentimental. Why tonight, the night before the Winter Ice Bee?* There was prep to get done. First, I had collected the ice cutting saws. I made sure their wooden handles were screwed on tight. Next, I had checked the ice picks. Thankfully, they hadn't needed filing. I didn't have to prep the ice clamps. Alpertti, Atro, and Ilvari were responsible for sharpening those and having them ready for work tomorrow. The saws and picks had seemed sharp. They had cut through my leather mitten choppers earlier when I moved them from the lower storage area. The last large task I had left was the ice chisels.

Maybe something important was about to happen. I suggested, "Why don't you go out and light the sauna? That will give me some time to chisel some test holes in the ice. I like to know its thickness. I also want to mark where we start cutting tomorrow."

"All right. Now, that's my boy!"

We got up, left the kitchen, and headed outside. Dad headed north along the shoreline to the sauna shack, and I headed straight out to the lake with the ice chisel. Made out of iron, an ice chisel was about twelve inches long with a two inch width. It was like a wood chisel. Instead of being held in my hand and hit with a hammer, an ice chisel was used like a spear. In the top of the chisel was a recessed hole where workers had placed a wooden pole. Workers had drilled a hole in the top of the pole. Then they had threaded a long, leather-like strap through the hole and tied it to form a loop. I wrapped the leather strap around my hand to prevent the chisel and attached pole from ending up on the bottom of the lake when it broke through the ice.

Since bean poles were straight and of good wood, I used them in the camp's ice chisels. They had been used over and over again as a structure for the bean plants to climb, which meant they were stout. Before he lost his home, Sara's grandfather had had a stack of them. He had used them in his backyard garden plot and had donated the poles to the Work People's Co-op.

The snow crunched under my boots as I walked onto the lake. This winter had thickened North Star Lake's face with eighteen inches of ice. An ice slab that thick eliminated any room for the fish to swim close to shore on the shallow end. They had to migrate to the eastern edge of Mesaba Park's lake. About ten feet from the far shoreline the lake's bottom dropped off forty feet. This "hole" in the lake bottom held needed oxygen. Bubbling ground water also fed the deep area of the lake and kept the currents circulating. Moving water did not freeze. This was nature's preventive method not to have North Star Lake turn into one large ice cube.

When I had determined the best spot to cut the ice, I marked out the straightest line back to the ice sheds. This set the route on which we would build a plank path to haul the ice. After hauling the ice the next day, we would stack it in rows in the sheds.

I looked at the full moon in the southern hemisphere. Sheets of cumulus clouds crossed over starlight. Each sheet transitioned the gray night into a white circular patch. Like long pieces of rope, alto-cumulus clouds stretched from east to west. Their texture resembled the rag rugs I had seen Grace, Sara's grandmother, weave from old work clothes: warp and wefts, warp and wefts. I saw peacefulness in the wefts of the valleys and the warp of the winter's night sky.

I was alone.

Standing here in the cold staring at the shoreline brought back memories of the past summer with Sara at camp. I had been with Sara more than once after most other campers were asleep. One particular time we were looking out the east window at the moon dog. I was trying to explain to her how moon dogs happened, in my own scientific way, and working hard to impress her. As we looked at the night sky, I kissed her on the cheek. Sara was startled. I guess I had surprised her. I remained quiet. For a few seconds, she stood still, then turned her face to me and said, "Try my lips."

I did – more than once.

This fall I had run my hands underneath her blouse and bra. Her nipples were small and tight like green raspberries. I wanted to harvest those. With all that's happened to me, I wondered if I ever would. Holding her memory, I headed toward the hall.

The smell of smoke from the sauna permeated the air. I looked up and saw the smoke climbing straight upward. The night wind was still. My dad's sled was parked outside the sauna door. He looked out at me. I waved and pointed to the picnic table outside the hall kitchen door still visible in the snow. He nodded his head in understanding, and we met at the table.

"Do you want a drink, Joe?"

"What do you have, Dad?"

"A special brew I have been keeping in the food cellar. Dad made these before he went back to Finland with your grandma. I only have three bottles. This will be the first one I have opened. My plan was to save a bottle for each of my children's weddings."

He wanted to open up Grandpa's brew for just me and him? Now I knew he had to have something on his mind. My father never opened a bottle without a special reason or occasion.

Dad continued, "I don't know if tonight is that special, but Lillian got me thinking – maybe too much." He paused, cleared his throat, and then continued, "I am hoping my being here is special enough. Tonight I am not toasting you for a wedding … I don't know how you and Sara are doing, but I got to thinking that there might not be a wedding toast if I don't drink with you tonight."

I didn't believe I was hearing what I had just heard. My dad was allowing his emotions for me to overrule his family traditions. I did not trust him now. Dad looked in the direction of the sauna. He appeared to be checking the smoke rising up from the sauna shack. Slowly, he turned his head back and looked me in the eyes. A few hairs on the back of my neck tried to stand up, but my scarf held them down. *What was he up to?* I wondered.

"It's only you and me, Joe. This stuff is really good. We won't share it with anyone else. Just you and me. Tonight. Let's get a little crazy."

I didn't know what he was not telling me, but I liked the offer. I couldn't get arrested here or thrown off any athletic team. I responded, "Let's not get our expectations too high tonight, Dad."

I smiled. Dad smiled slightly. We both laughed.

I didn't think I had laughed with my father in a long time. God! I didn't even realize I had missed his belly laugh. Maybe I was wrong. Perhaps he just wanted to be with me.

Dad bent over and lit the end of a branch he had broken off a frozen cedar. He held the flaming branch in his right hand and picked up the bottle in his left. He tilted the bottle's top toward the branch, and the flame licked at the bottle. Grandfather had covered his special brew bottles with bee's wax. The wax slowly melted, and the flame went out. Frustrated, Dad relit the branch. The second flame went out. "Well, I'm not trying for three," he said in disgust.

I agreed. "Three strikes, and you are out - as they say in baseball. Why don't we go inside? Maybe we can find a pair of pliers or a screwdriver and a hammer to pry the top off."

Dad stood up. "Don't bother. I know what to do."

I followed him inside.

"I'll just bust the top off, Joe. Here's when the fun begins."

Moving over to the kitchen stove, he placed the bottle in his right hand, cocked his arm back, and swung hard at the stove's black, iron surface. The neck of the bottle shattered. The largest part bounced off the wall and then ricocheted off the wood pile. He looked at me, and we yelled, "Juoma."

"Good one, Dad."

"How about that, Joe! That was more fun than popping champagne bottles on New Year's Eve. I had to hit the stove just right so the broken glass would wash out of the bottle. Now we smile and pour. We can't cork the bottle again, so we have to get corked," Dad finished.

We laughed.

"I'll get some glass jars. Let's drink!" I added enthusiastically.

"Juoma!"

I found two mason jars. Turning them upside down, I knocked them on the table to get rid of the dust and dead spiders. Then I flipped them right side up and set them down for Dad to fill. He poured generous amounts into each one and emptied the bottle between the two.

"Pohjanmaan kautta! (Bottoms up!)"

"Pohjanmaan kautta! (Bottoms up!)"

Dad set down his empty glass jar. "Phew! This is good. I can feel the heat already. It's the best, son!"

"Why is it so smooth?" I wondered.

"Grandpa distilled this shine five times. Each time he increased the sugar and fermented it longer so that it has stronger fermentation. The alcohol content will kick some ass."

Feeling happy, we grabbed a set of coffee cup saucers, headed outside, and saw who could throw his saucers further. The saucers didn't make a sound as they flew through the air. We had a hard time following them. Stealth saucers! They shattered when they hit a tree. After five flings each, we lost count. Thanks to the full moon, we found twelve unbroken saucers in the snow. Seven were Dad's and five mine.

"What is this shine made from?" I asked.

"Army worms … Grandpa said it is a long process … kotipolttoinen. (home burnt …)"

"He distilled army worms?"

"Yes."

"Juoma!" I exclaimed.

"Worm juice, samisen mate menu (fermented worm juice)," he repeated.

"Let's act like an army!" I suggested.

We marched through the snow, lifting each leg high like goose-stepping Germans. Each of us tried to out step the other. Lifting our legs higher and higher, we marched down to the sauna singing *Juomalaulu*,

"Juon juon minäpoika juon (I drink; I drink; I drink like a boy.)"

"Minä tykkään olla kännissä. (I'd like to be drunk.)"

"Juon juon minäpoika juon. (I drink; I drink; I drink like a boy.)"

"Tahdon heilua hulluna humalassa. (I want to swing from crazy drunk.)"

I was sweating. Whether it was the march or the alcohol, I didn't know. I flashed back to that night in Arvi's sauna. I had never told Dad about it, and I doubted Impi had either. I asked, "Did you know Impi saunas nude with his family?"

"Yes. How do you know?"

"Remember that day last fall when you had a meeting at Taisto Rantala's and I caught a ride home with you after school? I went to Arvi's first. He invited me to sauna."

I watched surprise, anger, and sadness cross his face. "What's wrong, Dad?"

Whatever he was thinking, Dad shook it off and smiled. "Did you do it?"

"I got nervous when I walked in and saw all three naked."

We both laughed. I liked laughing with my dad. Why didn't I remember doing this before?

"What did Impi's wife look like naked now?" Dad asked.

"I couldn't tell. I was more interested in his daughter Irene."

"I remember his wife Eileen. I thought she was Impi the first time I walked into a sauna in Finland. But then I saw him sitting next her."

We both laughed hard. Dad suggested, "Let's roll in the snow!"

"No, no. Wait till we get naked and sweat!"

"I almost forgot!"

"What – You almost forget what?"

"How to get naked!"

Dad and I laughed and laughed.

23   Gruesome Revelation

I had no idea how my dad had gotten home or how I had fallen asleep, but in the morning I found my clothes under my blankets. They were warm and soft, not cold and frozen. Dad must have put them there before he left. My head hurt. I stumbled outside to relieve myself, not bothering to walk to the outhouse.

Sara's Uncle Unlucky and members of Viola's dance band were to arrive that morning when winter ice bee work began. Every year we held a winter ice bee for gathering ice needed for refrigerating food, drinks, and ethnic foods at Mesaba Park. Since the grand opening for the Mesaba Park festival campgrounds was planned for the coming fall, we had to harvest more ice than in the past. We had a full day. I realized that I would have to spend another night at camp just to put the tools away after we finished. I was glad when I heard Viola Turpeinen's band had decided to attend the winter ice bee. That was unusual for them.

Unlucky had told me that the band would have a full schedule performing at all the music festivals and weddings in the coming spring and summer. At that time, band members couldn't volunteer for any work bees because they were too busy. They felt the upcoming fall grand opening was an important event both for the park and the Finnish population so they wanted to contribute. The winter ice bee was the best way for them to do that. Turpeinen would not be there, just his band. With those seven band members plus me, my father, and Unlucky, we had ten men for the ice bee.

I thought back to when I had started storing ice during the camp's winter work bee. We had covered the cut ice with anything we could find: straw, sawdust, leaves, and salt – even dirt. All of these materials had kept the ice insulated and chilled until late summer and early fall. As more Finnish joined the park and became members, the demands for better tasting ice for drinks had increased. Having bits of dirt mixed with the crushed ice had not been appetizing for some campers. We had thought about salt, but it was expensive and left a residual flavor. When the air temperature got to a certain degree, the salt accelerated the melting process. Leaves hadn't been any good, either, since they rotted and left a bad taste. We put a lot of work into picking and sweeping the mushy leaves off the ice. By the process of elimination, we selected sawdust as the insulator of choice. Ground wood didn't decompose, seemed more sanitary, and was reusable from year to year. Hence, we had boxes filled with sawdust ready for this year's ice bee!

The planks we used for the path upon which Rudolph dragged the ice blocks were stacked neatly, six planks high and eight planks wide. As I approached the stack of planks, I noticed the planks were higher off the ground than usual. Normally, the top plank was a little lower than my waist, but this morning it was shoulder-height. Looking down at the bottom of the pile, I saw that the planks were lying on top of wooden boxes. I thought someone had decided to build containers to hold the sawdust. I liked that. It made sense to me. By removing the runway planks, I made the sawdust boxes more accessible for the ice stackers.

We stored the ice in three three-sided framed sheds on the north side of the festival hall. The park's builders had placed the sheds in a small gulley dug into the ground between two low hills. The gulley protected the shed's walls from the sun, and large oak trees extended their branches over both storage sheds. Oaks held their leaves longer so their shade blocked the sun through spring and fall.

Usually, we cut two-foot wide by four-foot long blocks of ice from the lake. The thickness varied each year. Using saws, four men cut ice blocks. With their ice clamps, the loaders pulled the blocks to the ramp. Two men with ice picks called pickers pushed the blocks up the ramp and onto the runway.

My dad had created a system for transporting the ice. He had asked Sara's Grandma Grace to sew a gill net into a large sock shape. The pickers guided the cut blocks along the planks into the net. A rope was attached around the net's opening. That rope wound around pulleys suspended above the shed and the trees along the runway. That way, Rudolph had to walk only ten feet to have the ice blocks slide thirty feet. To make the blocks move the proper distance and not slide off the runway, my dad guided Rudolph by his bit. When Rudolph got to his destination, two to four men removed the ice from the ice sock and stacked it in the sheds.

Unlucky arrived at 7:00 a.m. with seven members of the band. He had decided to leave the truck parked out on Highway 37. That seemed best since they didn't know how deep the snow was on the frontage road and the trail into the park. They didn't want to risk getting their vehicle stuck because they had to play for a dance in Chisholm in the evening. Digging out a stuck truck would have taken time away from what they had come to do – cut ice for the camp.

I heard them approaching the camp through the trail in the woods. Unlucky had split the band members into two groups and guided Yrkki, Alpertti, Atro, and Ilvari in first. They were a comical sight! With busted bindings, broken ski tips, and trousers caked with snow, the guys looked like they had never skied before. Even on the military-issued skis they had brought from Finland, they didn't look like they had fought in the Winter War against Russia.

"I'm glad you weren't on the Winter War front, Yrrki," laughed Unlucky. "You kicked up so much snow, the Russians would have seen you from twelve kilometers away!"

"That's the first time I've been on skis in five years," said Yrrki.

"From the way you were falling, I thought it was your first," joked Alpertti.

"Funny. I felt like a frog with extra-large, webbed toes," said Yrrki.

"I don't care whether you are a frog or a rabbit. My trousers are full of snow from all the commotion you were causing. Some even settled down into my long underwear," chuckled Alpertti as he patted his wool pants.

"After you do some ice chiseling, the snow will melt, and you will look like you wet your pants," Unlucky teased.

"And I'm not sharing my jerky with someone who wets his pants," Atro added with a grin.

"Or with someone who has a wet jerky," joked Unlucky.

Ilvari laughed so hard his skis came out from underneath him. He landed on his back, his skis straight in the air. As I stared at the sight, I thought how funny and odd Ilvari looked. His skis were longer than his height. They reminded me of the rear feet on snowshoe rabbits I had snared. Snowshoes had the longest feet of any animal I had seen, but they were only, at the longest, one-fourth a rabbit's full body length. Seeing long sticks of wood that were taller than Ilarvi strapped to his feet standing straight up in the air was ridiculous.

A half an hour later, Unlucky led in Jari, Nikko, and Mika, the second group. Mika brought a flask to share.

Looking at the guys gathered for the cutting ice bee, I felt proud. They had come without their families and the conveniences that were available in better weather. Back in the kitchen, my father and Unlucky were having an intense conversation. I decided not to wait for them to finish. They had done more winter bees than any of us and didn't need briefing. Since the band was waiting for me to start, I had everyone gather in the dining area.

"Joe," said Yrrki, "I don't know if we should have Ilvari chiseling ice. He could barely stand up on his skis."

"If you don't watch it," answered Ilvari, "I may try standing on your head."

"That is just like you," stated Mika who was pouring shots for everyone. "You'll do anything to attract attention when we play."

"Remember the time you stood on the bar stool and played your accordion?" Yrkki asked.

"No he doesn't," said Nikko. "When he fell and hit his head on the floor, he lost some of his memory."

"He also shook some things loose," added Yrkki. "I hear them rattling around inside his head when he dances." Yrkki put both hands on Ilvari's head and shook it jokingly. "Huh … I can't hear anything now. There must be a lot of snow in there. Here, have another shot. Maybe it will melt faster."

We all laughed.

I stood and walked in front of everyone. That was the third time I had been placed in charge of the winter ice bee. I was lucky! At the campground I was respected. Mr. Browersfield had taken away my position as captain of the baseball team and humiliated me in town, but he couldn't demote me here. The park was a place where I was safe, a place where I was somebody. Even though I was seven years younger than the youngest member of the band, they all were willing to work with me and have me give them work assignments for the day. I knew part of it was because we were all Finnish. And the grand opening of the park was a major event in our community life. I thought about how lucky I was to have a role of responsibility in the preparation for the event.

We decided to go with four cutters, two pickers/loaders, and three stackers. I was a cutter along with Yrkki, Nikko, and Mika. Alpertti and Jari were the pickers/ loaders. Unlucky was a stacker along with Atro and Ilvari. My father guided Rudolph in pulling the ice blocks across the planks from the lake to the shed.

Since a cloudy sky prevented the sun from warming the ice on the lake, the ice stayed firm. Our sawing did not form slush. Yrkki and I had cut ice before so we sawed twice as much as Nikko and Mika. As we sawed, Yrkki and I talked about past bees. In the years we had cut ice, neither of us had fallen into the lake. We didn't fear the temperature of the water if we fell into the lake. We were concerned about becoming panicky when our clothes got wet. That could happen quickly. We knew that we would feel heavy and begin to sink to the bottom of the lake. We also knew that we would have to focus, take our gloves off, and strip off our outer garments. During that time, we were aware that our arms could get heavy and our fingers could freeze. If we fell in, hopefully, good ice pickers would snag us with their picks and pull us out of the lake.

Before sawing the ice, we drilled holes through the lake's surface by hand. Then we inserted a stick into one of the holes to maneuver the ice out of the lake. In the summer, the same stick was used for lifting the ice block out of the ice shed and moving it into the kitchen ice box. Drills were expensive so we had to be careful. The volunteers often dropped drills into the lake, and the drills remained irretrievable until summer.

Alpertti and Jari, our pickers, had some time until we got the first chunks of ice cut. To amuse themselves, they started throwing ice picks like spears. Their play reminded me of the games of stretch Yrkki, me, and others played at summer camps. Stretch was a knife game. The players stood face-to-face with their legs closed tightly and arms at their sides. The one winning the coin toss went first. The winner pulled out his pocket knife, opened the blade, and threw the opened knife as far as he could to the left or right of the other player. If the knife stuck in the ground, the opponent kept his leg opposite the stuck knife in place. Then his opponent stretched his other leg to where the knife was. The point was not to fall over. If he was successful in the stretch, then it was his turn to throw the knife from his stretched position. The first person to fall over lost.

The trick to winning the game was not to throw the knife eight or ten feet on the first throw. A long throw was hard to make stick. If the first throw was about three feet, the opponent had a hard stretch. If he made the stretch, his balance was challenged on his return throw, and he might fall. If he got a throw off, his throw might be a miss. To win, the second throw of the knife had to go one foot beyond the opponent's leg. At that point, the opponent was not able to make the stretch. When I played this game with Arvi on the lawn in front of the junior high school, Principal Paul Anderson had suspended us, not for having knifes, but for throwing them on public property.

"Come here. Hurry! Come here," Ilvari yelled urgently from the ice sheds.

"What's up?" I hollered back.

"Just come here!" Ilvari yelled again.

We all ran over to the ice sheds. Unlucky, Atro, and Ilvari were standing in the back of one of the ice sheds next to what looked like piles of winter clothes.

"What the hell is going on here?" Atro asked.

"Nobody's getting naked, I hope?" said Yrkki.

"If you are, the alcohol's got to be good to get a shine on this early," joked Mika.

Unlucky explained the excitement. "Ilvari opened up the sawdust boxes and found these bodies … I mean these body parts. There's something about them that doesn't seem right."

"None looks like a complete body. The body in one box doesn't have a head," Ilvari added, breathless.

"I'm glad they are frozen. Imagine what they would smell like," laughed Mika.

"Gross," said Atro.

"How long you think they've been here?" asked Mika.

"Gosh, I have no idea," replied Atro.

My dad cleared his throat and then cleared it again. Unlucky turned to Dad. "Gustav, do you want to explain what's going on here?"

Dad didn't answer. He just stood quietly. Everyone stared at him, unwilling to do anything until he spoke.

Rudolph whinnied, and Dad let go of the bit. Rudolph wanted to get loose. Finally, Dad replied, "These are the bodies of the four miners who were killed this past fall in the Bruce Mine shaft."

"How can that be? Weren't they buried in the cemetery?" questioned Ilvari.

"Yes," said my father.

"Who moved them here then? And why?" asked Alpertti.

"I helped put them here," Gustav admitted.

"You did, Dad?" I responded, alarmed.

"Yes."

Everyone was silent. Even Rudolph stopped pawing the snow.

We stared at the frozen carcasses in the ice sheds, absorbing this information.

I wanted to get past the issue. I was more worried about getting enough ice than having bodies stored in the ice sheds. If we were going to get enough ice stored for next year's festivals, we needed to get the blocks cut, stacked, and stored. At this point dead bodies seemed the lesser of the day's problems. "I don't get it, Dad. Why didn't you leave them where they were, in the graveyard?" I asked.

"Launo, Niilo, the IWW group, and I questioned whether the four were murdered. So we dug them up to check and see how they had died … and you're seeing what we saw."

I thought about the stories my dad had told me about the various strikes he had been on, and, in that context, this situation didn't seem that out of line. I had never taken him seriously. Everything seemed to be just his stories. Knowing he helped bring the bodies here made me want to reconsider everything he had told me. I thought about the bodies themselves. I didn't know if corpses had germs or could pass along diseases, but if they could – ouch! Was this why Dad came by last night? He knew this was going to happen. How could he not?

My father continued, "We were going to take the coffins and corpses to a mortician or a doctor to see what exactly had caused their deaths.

After we opened the boxes, we saw each of the men's bodies was intact, but their heads were all damaged. In fact, one head was missing. We never did find it."

As cold as it was, everyone remained still. No one shivered. I thought back to that Saturday morning Arvi and I had gone hunting. Arvi had good instincts. Were these bodies lying in that shaft with the car at the bottom? The thought bothered me, and I came back to the present situation. In a way, I was glad the ten of us were the only ones in the woods with the frozen bodies. I tried to imagine how people would react, especially the children, if the bodies were discovered at a fall festival.

Unlucky broke into my thoughts. "It's one thing to think that the company is out to kill workers who try to organize, and it's another thing to see the evidence that the workers have been murdered."

Rudolph moved his feet up and down as if he was packing snow down and making a path.

"Why store them here at the park?" asked Mika.

Dad replied, "Launo thought if we put the corpses back into their graves, nobody would believe us when we described what we had seen. They would say we were making up stories. We wanted Haywood to see them, too. We know he will know what to do."

Two failed mining strikes, and they were still hanging their hopes on Bill Haywood, I thought.

"Also, we were afraid if the steel trust found out we had dug the bodies up and then reburied them, they might think we know what had happened. Then they might have re-dug the bodies and destroyed the evidence of the murders. Since we didn't want that to happen, we thought we'd hide the bodies here until Bill Haywood could tell us what to do," Dad finished.

I was still thinking about germs. I knew we would never eat a dead animal such as a deer if it had been killed and then was lying around for a couple of weeks, even a couple of days. In fact, my dad had been very strict about eating game as soon as it had been killed. If we couldn't do that, we smoked or dried it out. I was told we did this because of the germs in a dead animal's body.

Nikko never said much. When he did, it was worthwhile. "Now, with the dead bodies here, all the good people who use the park are involved with what you've done. I don't suppose you thought about that."

Unlucky walked over to Nikko, put an arm on Nikko's shoulder, and answered Nikko in a voice loud enough for all to hear. "Nikko. It is easy to get upset with what we have done. I admit I am unsure of how this will turn out. So are Gustav, Launo, Frank, and Niilo. However, I'm not surprised there has been foul play, serious foul play. That is the greater issue. Think of all the times we have suspected foul play but couldn't do anything. Now we have proof. I am glad for that."

Jari added, "I didn't like it when we dug the bodies up. I don't like talking or thinking about it, either. Leave it for Haywood. Let's get back to why we are here, cutting ice. Because of the bodies, let's cut more ice than we had planned. Let's make sure the four men are preserved until justice can be served."

"I agree with Jari," said my dad. "We have a complicated issue here - one we're not going to solve this afternoon."

Unlucky removed his arm from around Nikko, reached into his jacket, and pulled out a metal flask. "Gustav and I don't know what happens next and what Haywood will want to do. I trust we are all agreed that talking this out today isn't what we need to do." He lifted the flask and took a swig. "If you are like me, something like this is difficult to leave unfinished. So I have a suggestion to liven our spirits. I have a flask and so does Mika. We will pass them around as we sing *Finlandia*. After one time through, we'll go back to doing what we came here to do."

Unlucky started singing *Finlandia* as he passed his flask to Gustav who took the first swig. Dad wiped his lips and passed the flask to Yrkki. Mika gave his to Ilvari. Everyone raised their voices in song:

O, Finland, behold, your day is dawning,
The threat of night has been banished away,
And the lack of morning in the brightness sings,
As though the very firmament would sing.
The powers of the night are vanquished by the morning light,
Your day is dawning, O land of birth.
O, rise, Finland, rise up high
Your head, wreathed with great memories.

O, rise, Finland, you showed to the world
That you drove away the slavery,
And that you did not bend under oppression,
Your day has come, O land of birth.

As we sang, I heard how beautiful my dad's voice sounded. I hadn't heard him sing anything but drinking songs. As I thought about it, why would I have heard him sing anything else? We didn't go to church, and, with my mother sick and all, he rarely went to dances and festivals. His tenor voice melted the snow on my head gear. Even Rudolph seemed lighter and worked faster after Dad sang.

I was glad Mr. Browersfield wasn't there. I wouldn't have been allowed to graduate from high school that spring if he had seen those bodies and heard about how they got there.

24   Cover Up

As we sawed more ice, Yrkki talked about hockey with Nikko and Mika. I pretended to listen as my thoughts drifted.

What a year this had been! For the first time in my life the stories of my dad and his friends were coming alive. I didn't doubt anymore that I was set up that night at the football game. Dave's not suiting up for the homecoming game was not a coincidence. He had planned it, likely with others. Tammy and her father could have even been in on it. The complexity of the possibilities made my head spin. I thought I had lost my political innocence the day Little Rob had pounded on the Indian on the sidewalk outside of school. Now frozen dead bodies were in the ice storage sheds at Mesaba Park and Campground. That had been the one place I thought was safe and removed from the bizarre actions and behaviors of the politics I had known.

I began to wonder how much Sara knew. What would she think of not just northern pike in the ice shed but dug-up, frozen human corpses to boot? How much were her mother and father actually steeped in organizing?

I knew her grandpa Mattai had been involved with the 1906 strike. In fact, he had been an organizer with my father. Dad said Mattai was a smart man, a good organizer. Mattai had gone to medical school in Russia as a young man. Something had gone bad for him. That was how he got into the co-op business in Finland before he came here to work in the mines.

Whatever had happened, Mattai had developed a suspicious nature as a result. When he and his wife Grace had built their house, he had set their buildings into an L pattern. The L's long line was created by the outhouse, horse stable, pig pen, and the garage. The chicken coop, cow area, and their house in that order were at the short end of the L. The kitchen was on the back side of the house facing the chicken and cow areas.

In the corner of the kitchen, he positioned two windows and silently watched out both during meals. He sat so that he blocked the back door, preventing unannounced access. He was not concerned about the front door; his family never used it. The window to his left looked into the backyard and his buildings. The other window had a view of his neighbors' lot and the main road. He knew when the mailman or anybody else was coming. He didn't want the Pinkertons or any anti-organizing people to come onto his property without his knowledge.

I shook my head. Being suspicious had become a part of Sara's grandfather's life. My dad had a similar attitude. As I continued working, I wondered if I would become that suspicious, too.

At four o'clock, Dad and Unlucky gathered us inside the meeting hall. A fire was going. I watched Unlucky loosen the top of his jacket to reach for his flask and then remember it was still outside. He decided not to retrieve it at that moment and stayed in the hall.

I looked around the room at everyone. I still felt the pride I had had this morning when everyone arrived and we began the winter ice bee. Dad said he wanted to wrap things up for the day, but I stood to talk. "Thank you all for coming today. I was surprised to find Elder, Herman, Taisto, and Helmer still with us. I am sure my dad wants to say a few things about that. I realized today that the stories I have heard you tell aren't just stories. I have some things to learn."

"You did a good job, Joe," offered Yrkki.

"I'd give a toast, but –" said Mika.

My dad interrupted Mika, "Thanks for helping us and Mesaba Park today. Joe, you did a good job organizing the work."

Alpertti and the rest nodded their heads. Atro gave me a wink and a smile. My dad continued, "What happened today was a surprise for all of us, but I want us to be proud. We have our weapon to win our war with the mine owners. When we leave here today, let's not create surprises for any other people in the community, especially for the families of these murdered men." Dad paused a moment.

Unlucky stood. "I ask that you do not tell anyone about what you learned today, not even Viola. We'll have more time to talk tonight at the dance."

"I am in agreement. Don't tell anyone about what happened here today," added my dad.

"We are in agreement," concluded Yrkki, a spokesperson for the rest. "None of us knows what is going to happen because of these bodies, and we all want the best for our murdered friends."

Unlucky clapped his hands. "Okay, band members, we need to leave and make a lot of people happy tonight at the dance in Chisholm. Gustav and Joe will stay behind and work with the bodies. That way only they will know where the bodies are in the ice sheds, which will make it harder for any of us to leak the location to the steel trust. We don't want the trust finding out what we know."

The band members followed Unlucky out the door.

Dad and I walked to the ice sheds. As Dad had placed the ice blocks in the sheds throughout the day, he had positioned one ice block at the back of one of the sheds on the bottom and left space on top of the block for the bodies. Together we dragged the stiff, awkward, unyielding corpses and shoved them into that space. "Give me a hand here, Joe. There is some more straw over there at the back of the shed."

I helped Dad cover the corpses with straw.

"Get the shovel, Joe. We'll put six inches of snow on top of the bodies."

After we finished shoveling the snow, I offered, "Do you want me to take Rudolph down to the lake and drag up the three remaining ice slabs?"

"Yes."

I moved quickly.

We carefully maneuvered the three slabs on top of the corpses, creating a human ice sandwich. The snow which we had shoveled on top of the straw helped us level the slabs of ice atop the bodies.

When we were finished, we stood back and looked at the three ice sheds. The two with just ice looked the same as the third shed with the frozen corpses. Since the bodies were in the back of the shed, they wouldn't be discovered until the ice slabs in front of them had been used, which would be late summer.

I couldn't think of anything to say. After all, this wasn't a funeral. The men had been dead for months. Dad broke the silence. "This isn't the last of it, Joe. These corpses won't lie silent forever."

"I know."

Dad offered, "Let me help you pick up the tools and put the rest of the stuff away before I take Rudolph home."

I started picking up tools and planks and putting them away. Dad helped me. Since we both knew what needed to be done, we worked without talking.

When we were finished, Dad walked Rudolph back to our place. I stayed behind. I told Dad I'd be home in time to say good night to my little brother and sister before they fell asleep. He said he'd keep the sauna hot until I got home.

I sat on a bench outside the pavilion and watched the sunset. What a day, I thought to myself. I thought about all the events that happened in the woods and no one knew about them. I imagined the trees held memories of those events. After today, they had a few more secrets to keep. How long would they keep their secrets? I didn't know. To whom they told their secrets, I didn't know, either.

I thought about grouse hunting. Arvi and I hunted grouse in the same area we had found grouse the year before. Those grouse were the children of the grouse we had harvested the prior year. They lived in the same part of the woods as their parents who had raised them. They ate the same food, walked the same areas, and roosted at the same time every evening. Was I like the grouse? Was I going to be like my father? Would my life mirror his?

I had no answers, just the silence, which was quieter than I had ever remembered. I got up and began to walk home. I looked at the trees. They looked back. I stared back at them.

I noticed trees were not straight. At best, a tree's trunk was only straight for five to eight inches. Then it had a turn, a jig, or a jag. The branches did not make nice curves, either. The needles of the pines, balsams, and spruce were not all the same shape, color, or size. They were not even all the same color green. They were many shades of green and offered an amazing amount of variety.

I realized that when I walked among the trees I was not just observing. I was connecting and building a relationship with them.

That night I perceived that no matter what happened, where I was going, or why I was there, the woods gave me a feeling of peace.

A tree did not say to me, *Stand straight and tall. Be like me.*

Instead, the tree seemed to whisper, *I like the way you are. Be yourself.*

The forest was about being who I was, not who other people wanted me to be. My life was not about how I was like other people or how I was different from other people. My life was about me. I had started as a seed that would grow up to be the tree I was to be.

When I walked through the woods, sometimes I found a birch tree among some cedar trees. I found hazelnut bushes next to maple trees. No one had planted them that way. No one had planned this arrangement. It had just happened. The fact that a maple tree could grow beside a hazelnut bush was a lesson for people. Even though we were all different, we could live together peacefully in the woods of humanity.

I listened more. I understood I was not listening to what the forest was doing. I was hearing and feeling what the woods believed about me. The forest in all its theater was talking to me. All the interactions of all the actors and actresses of nature said to me,

You are okay.
Be who you are.
You are.

I realized that was why I loved the woods. That night I began to learn the woods liked me; the woods cared for me. The woods had always cared for me, my family, and everyone who walked among the trees. The woods accepted and loved us unconditionally. And maybe because of that unconditional love, I had innately understood I was to love and be loved.

25   Special Audition

May

"It was good to see Arvi walk across the platform Friday night at graduation," said Martin.

"Yep," agreed Impi, looking out the co-op's front window. He was less focused than normal.

Noticing Impi's preoccupation, Martin tried to get his attention. "Come on, Impi, you were taking a nap. I saw your eyes close. You never saw Arvi cross," teased Martin.

Rocking his chair back on its rear legs, Martin leaned back and rested his head against the wall. As he waited for Impi to respond, he looked across the table at Elizabeth and Eileen. They smiled at him, also waiting for a reaction from Impi.

Impi turned toward Martin with a funny smirk on his face and then looked back out the window. Martin smiled. He had gotten a response, but he wanted more. Impi seemed to have something important on his mind.

"Arvi and Joe are sure smart boys," interjected Eileen, wanting to avoid a battle of barbs between Martin and Impi. Those types of exchanges left Eileen and Elizabeth out of the conversation.

"I agree, Eileen," replied Elizabeth. "I am hoping the two can still work at the park this summer. Sara is. I know Joe would like to, but Gustav has his ideas for Joe –"

The four of them were sitting near the front of the store. Martin kept that area of the co-op free of goods. The open area provided room for members who were waiting for a ride. That part of the store also offered shelter from storms and harsh winter weather. Often newspapers were strewn around on the front window ledge for reading. Co-op membership and board meetings were held in that area when the store was closed.

"I've been talking with Launo," Impi interrupted. "I am hoping to get Arvi working with Niilo this summer … Launo is expanding the sawmill –"

"Where was Niilo? I don't remember seeing him there last night during or after the ceremony," asked Martin.

"He wasn't. Launo wouldn't let that happen. To be present at the ceremony would be showing support for Oliver Mining. I wished both of them had been there and Gustav, too. I'm sure they would have been set off by Browersfield's talk about how this area is a melting pot. They would have heckled," Impi answered. "And … I probably would have joined them." His eyes twinkled.

Elizabeth and Eileen didn't say anything. They began a quiet conversation as a diversion from the intense political sentiment that appeared imminent.

"You, Launo, and Gustav don't like the melting pot idea, or the way Browersfield describes it," Martin stated. Impi didn't say anything. Martin suspected Impi was imagining scenarios of what might have taken place.

Impi starred at Martin. "Remember the time we were in Cleveland and saw those furnaces, Martin? All I could think of what a frightening sight the blast furnaces were. All the hot air being forced into the furnace … and for what? To get us all to be the same?"

"A blast furnace also separates the slag from the iron ... and you know who the slag is," Martin replied.

"That's why Launo didn't let Niilo come," said Impi. "I know that's also why Gustav wasn't there, either. They are not interested in being turned into slag or being melted together with Browersfield and the mine owners to form a chunk of steel."

"To think about the melting pot that way, Impi, who'd want to be joined with the steel trust? Even Sara has figured out the new high school was a bribe of some sort…"

When Martin mentioned Sara, Elizabeth dropped her conversation with Eileen and expressed her feelings. "I felt sorry for Joe last night. I went over to where he was sitting by himself and asked him to sit with us. He said he was all right. Then I encouraged Sara to go over and ask him. When she asked, he came over and sat with us. Mattai struck up a conversation with Joe. My dad is so good with him."

"Yeah. And I suppose Mattai gave Joe a cigarette," quipped Impi. Martin rolled his eyes slowly so all could see.

Impi continued, "I have to leave in a few minutes. Gustav invited me to his place. Haywood will be there."

"Well, I am surprised I haven't been invited," said Martin.

"When Gustav asked if you'd be available, I told him tonight was the monthly Co-op Federation's meeting night and you would be looking at costs for the grand opening celebration of Mesaba Park this fall."

"I suppose Gustav had forgotten the Mesaba Co-op Federation meets the last Sunday of the month," quipped Martin.

"I don't think he forgot," said Elizabeth bluntly. She turned and looked for support from Eileen on that point. Eileen was quiet. Realizing Eileen wasn't interested in polarizing the group, Elizabeth placed her hand on Martin's right leg. "Eileen and I will be heading over to the theater now. Jacque and Viola will be there."

"What for?" asked Impi.

"Impi, you know Elizabeth thinks Irene should audition again. Her voice is superb …" Eileen replied firmly, looking at Impi.

"We have discussed why Viola and Jacque are resistant to Irene's getting involved with the theater," Impi stated.

"Let me guess," said Martin. "Could it have something to do with your involvement with Haywood?"

Impi spat and then jested. "I know Jacque and Viola are afraid of the melting pot effect. If they allow a radical like my daughter to become a cast member, they might not remain white Finns. They might melt into red ones."

Martin smiled slightly and continued the joke. "But they may not turn all red, Impi. They could blend together to create pink Finns."

Eileen grinned. Impi stared at her. She leaned closer to her husband. "Don't be so serious, honey. Gustav and Launo together have enough dense thought. You don't need to be as dark."

Just as she finished, the door opened, and Irene shyly stepped into the store. "There you are!" Eileen acknowledged. She motioned to Elizabeth to get up and follow her. They stood, turned, and headed out the co-op's door with Irene in tow.

As the three women stepped onto the sidewalk, they met Matthew Wirtannen. He smiled brightly. "Good evening, ladies," he said and headed into the store. "How are my fellow federation officers?"

"Good to see you," said Martin.

"Same here," echoed Impi.

"Did I see Jacque and Viola standing in the front lobby of the theater?" Matthew wondered.

"Yes, you did. Elizabeth and Eileen are going to see if they can get those two to give Irene, a radical Finnish youth, another audition for the theater," Martin explained.

"Yikes! I thought Jacque and Viola were whitening up the productions?" mused Matthew.

"God damn you!" spat Impi. "I'm glad I'm not staying for the federation meeting. I've had enough of these melting pot ideas."

"Melting pots?"

"Impi is being cynical. He didn't like Browersfield's commencement speech," explained Martin.

"I suppose the principal gave the melting pot Americanization talk again and tried one more time to enlighten the community on how we can become steel-promoting capitalists like him."

"Go to hell," spat Impi.

"I thought that's what I was doing by coming here to meet with you and Martin," joked Wirtannen. "Well, if you were to stay for the meeting, I don't know if you would understand how to put together a budget for the park's grand opening. After all, didn't you waste a lot of money in putting a sauna in your house?"

"It's not 'in' my house," replied Impi. "It's in the breezeway to the garage."

"The breezeway? We don't say hallway anymore? You're starting to sound pretty bourgeois, Impi. Maybe Irene will get a chance to sing in a musical."

"Damn it! I'm leaving."

Using his shoulder, Impi playfully gave Matthew a little shove, shook his hand, and walked to the back of the store. When they heard the back door slam, Matthew sat down next to Martin. They sat quietly for a short while. Through the store's front window they watched townspeople head over to the Lyric Theater.

The town traditionally held a special commencement recognition event the night after graduation. Elizabeth and Martin had encouraged Sara to go. Joe was with her. At least that was where they assumed Sara and Joe were. Impi had forbidden Arvi to attend. Arvi had gone to Niilo's to sauna.

"Impi's not joining us tonight. Haywood's in town. I guess Gustav and Niilo invited Impi but somehow forgot we were having the monthly federation board meeting tonight. They must be a having real red meeting," Martin informed Matthew.

"So Haywood's in town? And Jacque and Viola? What are the odds of that? Am I missing something here, Martin?"

Martin stared pensively at the floor and didn't immediately answer. After a few moments, he turned to Matthew. "I think I am."

"I am sure the Frenchman and the czarist Finn are at the theater for more than an audition for Irene," said Matthew.

"I know," replied Martin. "Elizabeth was talking with me last night about Jacque's plans."

"About what?"

"Jacque and what he's been thinking."

"And?"

"Jacque is nervous about the grand opening celebration for Mesaba Park with Haywood and all the 'red' Finns in town. Jacque's afraid Haywood will demand the theater all weekend to grandstand for the IWW. He is thinking about cancelling all the plays or musicals that weekend –"

"Then he won't be able to sell tickets for his musicals, huh? Is that really what is bothering him? Why doesn't he schedule something for the park? Maybe an outdoor production?"

Martin smiled at Matthew's ironic wit. That's what Martin liked about Matthew. Matthew's slightly twisted humor lightened Martin's mood.

"Jacque can't stand the number of 'radical' Finns attending the theater now, and that number has decreased since he started doing productions in English." Martin smiled. "Think of him in charge of an outdoor production at the park. He wouldn't have a back office to hide in during intermission. I can't imagine him or Viola at Mesaba Park actually rubbing shoulders with some of the Duluth labor college people … out in nature …. having a beer with Haywood or a cigarette with Gustav and Launo... sitting around the bonfire pit telling stories and laughing …"

They both chuckled at the mental pictures those words created. Matthew wondered, "Did you say Launo or Luna?"

"Luna, I like that," said Martin. "It's closer to loony."

"Maybe we should check for a full moon tonight after our meeting is done," suggested Matthew.

"Haywood's coming unannounced is enough for me. I don't need a full moon," Martin responded.

"All we would need to create some real insanity would be for McFarland to show up …"

Matthew's idea broke Martin's worried mood, and he added, "Along with Armstrong's cousin Thomas."

Both wanted to laugh at the craziness of such an event, but they didn't.

26   Construction Diversion

Haywood turned to look out the window. "I thought Impi was coming? Did any of you offer him a ride?"

Whether standing or sitting, Haywood's physical presence attracted attention. Haywood was a head or two taller than Gustav, Launo, and Unlucky as they sat around Gustav's kitchen table. "He'll be here," Gustav replied. "He told me he would."

Haywood changed the subject. "How's the business, Gustav?"

"Launo is planning on having his son Niilo and Impi's son Arvi work with us," replied Gustav.

"I thought they were working with you already," Haywood observed.

"Well, they've helped out, but now they will be with us all the time," Launo smiled.

"Are you paying them?" asked Haywood.

"I'm not sure what you are asking," Gustav responded.

Unlucky turned to Gustav and repeated Haywood's question. "Are you paying them?"

"Well, they share the business with us, Bill. It's a family business," Gustav explained.

Everyone was a little unsure of what Haywood had in mind. They were intimidated. That was the first time they had met with him alone. He never traveled by himself. Typically he had two or three men with him. Usually, Martin met with Haywood. In fact he had slept overnight at Martin's once when a rally had gone on until morning. He got along with Mattai. Mattai was able to relate to Haywood and didn't fear him.

Rather than wait for an answer, Haywood looked at Gustav. "Is Joe going to work with you?"

"He's thinking… Got a couple things he's tossing around. One idea is the labor college in Duluth. He and Arvi went down there a couple of times."

"That's where I would send Joe if he were my son," agreed Haywood. "Joe's smart. He'll get a good education there. I can see him as a labor leader someday."

Gustav nodded. "I mentioned to him the idea of doing what Oscar Corgan has been –"

Haywood interrupted, "Oscar Corgan. Oscar Corgan. I've talked with him, but I don't like his ideas."

Gustav seemed surprised at Haywood's response.

Haywood switched topics. "What is there to think about? Unless you think he can get a job at Oliver Mining… But everyone knows Joe is your son. He's blackballed."

There was a hard knock at the door. Without waiting for a response, Impi opened the door and stepped into the room. He immediately walked over to Haywood and held out his hand. Haywood stood up and gave Impi a big hug and a thump on the back. "Impi, you rascal! Where have you been? You are an hour late. Have a seat. We were just getting started."

Impi took a chair next to Gustav and answered Haywood, "I was at the co-op with Eileen."

"I didn't think the co-op was open on Sunday," Haywood commented. "If you need some cedar boughs for the sauna, just get them in the woods."

"To throw them in the sauna stove? You city folk don't know what a log is," teased Impi.

Gustav and Launo didn't smile. They were interested in Haywood's plan. Life was not about camaraderie with everyone you met. Instead, tasks demanded focus and attention.

"You know the co-op isn't open on Sundays, Haywood. Eileen and I were there with Martin and Elizabeth."

"Why isn't Martin here?" asked Haywood.

"The Co-op Federation has its monthly meeting tonight. They are looking at the budget for the grand opening dedication for Mesaba Park this fall," replied Launo. He paused and looked directly at Haywood. "I didn't invite him."

"I was talking to Impi," Haywood interjected, dismissing Launo. "So why were you and Eileen there if you knew you were to be here and Martin wasn't coming?"

Impi hesitated. Unlucky jabbed Impi in the ribs. Impi cheered his throat. Haywood asked one more time.

"Come on, Impi, let us in on your conversation," Gustav said sarcastically.

"We were waiting for my daughter Irene to arrive," Impi responded. Unlucky could feel Impi's feet tapping on the floor underneath the table. He quickly placed his hand on Impi's legs for a second. Impi stopped his leg movements.

"I didn't think Eileen and Elizabeth got along," observed Launo.

Unlucky wanted to calm Impi down. "Launo is playing with you." Turning to Haywood, he added, "Eileen is the person who discovered the Oliver spying activities. She got us aware that something was going on."

"Her tip helped the IWW be a little more careful with where and when we met for conversations and planning outside of the rallies," complimented Haywood.   "We always suspected they used spies."

Impi was anxious to find out what Haywood had planned for the frozen miners. Knowing Launo and Gustav would wait until Haywood brought up the topic, he decided to initiate the subject. "Haywood, did you find a doctor who will look at the bodies for us?"

Haywood wasn't surprised at Impi's abruptness. He used the question as his cue. "Everyone is here so let me update you. After Gustav let me know about your suspicions of murder, I made contact with an instructor at the Milwaukee School of Medicine. He is willing to look at the bodies."

"I thought the medical college was in Marquette?" asked Impi.

"Have you ever left Minnesota?" responded Haywood. "The Milwaukee School of Medicine is the best in the country. Doctors from all over come there to learn. I'm making arrangements for the four miners to be shipped to Milwaukee before Mesaba Park's grand opening."

Launo smiled. Gustav's face relaxed. Haywood was suggesting the possibility that the dead miners might yet have their say. The group was proud of Haywood.

"I'm hoping that you can help me with a plan for moving the bodies from Mesaba Park to the rail station in Hibbing. I can get as many men as you need –"

Impi blurted, "I don't know if we want to use your men."

"What Impi means is that would raise suspicions. I think we should use our people," clarified Gustav.

"I'll listen to what you've got," Haywood replied.

"We have to do some work to the roof of the pavilion before the park's dedication. I told Martin that I wouldn't be able to let my guys work during the day since we have to keep the business going. Martin was okay with the work being done one evening. Maybe that would be a good time?" Launo offered and looked at Gustav for agreement.

"Help me out here. I am unsure of what you have in mind," said Haywood.

"What the Co-op Federation wants us to do is to reinforce some of the roof joists above the main hall of the pavilion. Last winter we had heavy snow. A few joists cracked, leaving the roof uneven. Nothing leaked. But it's just a matter of time before something does leak or maybe even snap. Martin and Matthew thought the fall dedication would provide a reason for getting it done and maybe a way to find some money for it," Gustav explained.

"I am not sure of how fixing a roof helps us," Haywood wondered.

"When we talked about the project with the federation, I told them this was a big project and I needed a time to do it when there was no one at the camp so I could have my equipment there and not worry about hurting anyone," added Launo.

"You're definitely not a mine owner," jested Haywood.

"Matthew Wirtannen suggested a work bee the first weekend in August. The federation would close the campground to campers," Unlucky informed Haywood.

"That's where we left the planning," finished Gustav.

"The boxes we built for the bodies look like storage cabinets. In fact the band has some like them, not as large, but they are similar. I'll suggest to the band that they come to the work bee in August. While Gustav and Launo work on the roof, I'll have the band members load the miners into the boxes so that we can sneak them out. Since those boxes look like ones the band usually carries, no one will notice," Unlucky explained.

"I like what I am hearing," said Haywood. "We have time to plan the details, but I came today to make sure we agreed on the general plan, first. I do wish Martin had been able to come."

"Well, we thought you would be staying at his place tonight. Then you could discuss what we had planned with him. That's what you usually do, right?" Gustav replied.

"Yes, it is. But I thought Martin was going to be here so I planned on heading to Winnipeg tonight. I am on a tight schedule."

"Winnipeg?" questioned Impi. "What's going on up there?"

Haywood grimaced. "Trompeure' is opening another theater."

Gustav pulled the conversation back to the subject at hand. "I'll inform Martin about scheduling the work bee for the first weekend in August. We'll limit the work bee to those who the federation contacts."

"I'll let Yrkki, Alpertti, Atro, Ilvari, and Mika know. I don't need to let all the band members know we are moving bodies. The six of us can get the work done," Unlucky assured everyone.

"And I have a word of caution for all of you before we leave," added Haywood, remembering a strange package he had received in the mail. "Somehow, I think Viola isn't on our side, and that definitely goes for the sheriff. McFarland, that's his name, right?" Everyone was quiet. "Did I get that right?"

Gustav nodded.

Haywood looked intently around the group. "We'll meet again in September. By then I am sure I will know something more about how those four died. Also, I will have a better idea of what type of demonstration to stage for the Mesaba Park dedication to attract some national attention."

Someone knocked at the back door. "Gustav?" a voice boomed. "Gustav, are you home?"

Haywood looked at Gustav. "Is someone coming I don't know?"

"No," said Gustav. Impi rolled his eyes back. Launo sat stoic. Unlucky got up and went to the door.

"Oh, look," announced Unlucky. "It's the sheriff and his shadow!"

Unlucky pulled the door open. One hinge had loosened, and the door scraped the floor. He held the door steady with his left hand as he shook McFarland's hand with his right. Stephan Steblibovich nodded toward Unlucky as he followed the sheriff into the house.

"That one hinge always is loose. I can't seem to keep it tight against the door jamb," admitted Gustav.

"Drive a small piece of wood into the screw hole," said Unlucky. "Then tighten the screw. It will hold better."

"Gustav has better use for his time than that," interjected Launo. "I'll have Niilo look at the door."

Nobody motioned for the sheriff or the deputy to sit down nor pulled out chairs for them. Haywood remained quiet.

"This has to be a serious meeting," said McFarland. "I don't see any beer on the table."

No one replied.

McFarland continued, "William Haywood. I guess it's good to see you. Nobody told me about a rally or demonstration tomorrow. Sunday's a big day for picnicking and politicking at the park. Are you here to say a few words tomorrow? Am I missing something?"

Unlucky fidgeted.

After tapping his fingers a few times on the table, Launo looked at Haywood and said, "I can't believe the sheriff is planning ahead."

"Tomorrow is not that far away," said Stephan curtly.

"I'm not accustomed to a sheriff dropping by someone's house unannounced. Is this a raid?" wondered Haywood.

"Stephan and I were just on our night rounds through the countryside. We noticed Haywood's car. We thought that was odd," McFarland replied.

"Watch it, Sheriff. Can't I go anywhere, or am I confined to town and the People's Theater? Are you watching out for me?" A smile gently creased Haywood's face.

Unlucky sat down at the table.

Gustav addressed McFarland and Stephan. "We were talking about the grand opening of Mesaba Park in September. Haywood thought it might be nice to have some students from the Duluth labor college participate. We were discussing possibilities for where they could spend the night."

"So the man of the people will be gracing us with his presence at the grand opening," McFarland noted.

"No. I said we were discussing whether or not students from the Duluth labor college will participate in the park's grand opening and dedication," repeated Gustav. "We think it would be good for them to socialize with members of an active Finnish community. We were even thinking of bringing the college band up for a parade down Main Street Sunday morning."

"I had planned on being at the college that weekend for a rally," added Haywood. "Then it occurred to me, why not move the rally up here? There will be good crowds in town and at the park. I love addressing a crowd."

"I just assumed you would be there. And we know, if you're there, I will be there… a little crowd control. That's my job," smiled McFarland.

Haywood's eyes twinkled. Unlucky and Gustav noticed. Gustav wondered, "What else were you thinking, Haywood?"

"Well, a rally is inspirational, and a parade attracts more people. What if we dug up the four brave Finnish miners, put them on a wagon, and paraded them around for everyone to see? If I remember right, they didn't have a proper funeral or burial."

The room got quiet. Stephan's mouth slightly dropped open.

McFarland shook his head. "Haywood, you always have a flair for something grand … digging up the dead …" Stephan started to speak, but the sheriff nudged him. McFarland continued, "You'd really put my people to work with all the commotion that would cause. I think you shouldn't get your hands that dirty, Haywood."

"As you said, Sheriff, a little crowd control is the kind of work you do well," Unlucky noted dryly.

"That's part of being the guardian of the Finnish people…" Launo paused.

"Guardian?" repeated Haywood.

"We haven't had a conversation about that with you, Haywood," explained Gustav.

"The governor put the sheriff on special assignment with the Finnish people," added Unlucky.

"Shortly after the appointment, he got into a scuffle with Armstrong's cousin Thomas," inserted Impi. "He took some hard kicks in the ribs and got a bunch of other bruises."

"I still hurt," replied the sheriff.

"The suffering Messiah," Haywood mumbled under his breath. Unlucky caught the comment and winked at Haywood.

"Now that you know everything is okay, it's time for you and Stephan to get back to your night rounds," advised Gustav.

Gustav stood. Unlucky jumped up and swung the door open. McFarland and Stephan exited into the night. Their departure was silent. After the sheriff and his deputy had driven away, Haywood brought everyone back to the discussion of moving the bodies.

"That was a surprise," said Haywood. "At least McFarland seems uncomplicated. What does he know about the bodies?"

27 Assassination Plot

Late August

Looking around the table at those in attendance, Kenneth Armstrong thought, *I have enjoyed the view from my office above the Lyceum Theater in downtown Duluth for fifteen years, and I have enjoyed my work every day. I love telling people that I have never taken a sick day. Today's meeting might make me sick, though. He took a deep breath. I can't get sick now and go home early. I'm stuck.*

He plunged in and started the meeting. "The last time me met, I traveled north to Lake Vermillion. I look back on that conversation as a time when we began a closer working relationship for the benefit of northern Minnesota. Today I called you here for a meeting so we could focus on the real enemy of our partnership, Bill Haywood.

"John D. Rockefeller asked me to enlist your help in devising a plan to remove Haywood from Rockefeller's operations in Colorado and Minnesota. Mr. Rockefeller is merging his mining interests on the Mesaba Range. He has the railroad and will go public with the new United States Steel Company but only if we stop those IWW Wobblies."

His cousin Thomas took the unifying moment as a platform to throw a barb at Trompeure'. "Jacque, we know Rockefeller's interests. What are yours – besides taking Elizabeth Niemi for a ride?"

Jacque felt forced to reply. "Knock it off, Thomas. You have your ideas but no knowledge about anything."

Finnegan came to Jacque's defense. "Everyone here knows Jacque is working for a group of investors who want to bring cinema to all the theaters currently producing socialist propaganda and cheap musicals."

"And we are all in favor of that transition," Armstrong stated. He tried to get back to the purpose of their gathering. "None of us is interested in the Finnish Utopia or Haywood's ideas. That's why we are here today."

Thomas continued needling Jacque. "We agree, Kenneth, but Jacque would like a personal Utopian encounter with that blonde Finnish bombshell."

Armstrong wondered why he had allowed his cousin to get involved with these meetings. Thomas was a mercenary, interested only in his paycheck. His type was not always the best to have at meetings. Mercenaries thought everyone else should be as focused as they were, but they were intent on their tasks rather than the big picture goal. Thomas accomplished tasks he was given. That made him a real asset.

Since Thomas needed to have an enemy, Armstrong refocused the group on Haywood. "Let's take some time and get agreement on a few things. Unions will get here eventually, even Rockefeller knows this. So the real question is how long they will take to become formalized. When that happens, we will have to make concessions to the workers." Armstrong sensed agreement building. He continued, "Since the time will come when we will need to make concessions, we want to minimize what we will have to give up. That is why removing Bill Haywood as soon as possible will help us. We want him out of the union activities."

"Mr. Haywood has those immigrants thinking too big. He is promoting concessions that will cost us a lot," added Finnegan.

Armstrong felt he was nearing his sweet spot. Thomas now had an enemy, and, if McFarland was paying attention, he would understand who was on which side. Armstrong looked at Finnegan and nodded for him to continue.

"We need to keep the miners focused on long hours and mining accidents. When they negotiate shorter work days, that won't hurt us; we will just have more shifts. We want them to worry about their safety, too. Concessions for safer conditions will be easy to give. Fewer accidents help us. But we don't want them demanding vacation days, medical care, sick days, and who knows what else."

Thomas leaned his head back and commented into the air above him. "Thank you that no one knows how many of those accidents were arranged and how many we have because of those unstable underground mining shafts. You never know when the earth might shift or an aftershock from a blast might bury a few." He allowed a sly smile on his face to spread as he greeted the heavens with his eyes, not realizing the confidentiality he had just broken.

Armstrong took the lead from Thomas's slip. "I like the idea of a lot of accidents, arranged or not, so when we, as the owners, agree to use safer equipment and shorten the working hours, all the workers will see these two concessions as their victory."

Finnegan agreed. "We must work together to resist union formations and any type of worker solidarity as long as we can before we make concessions."

Around the table, short conversations began among those assembled. The sound was positive, one of capitalistic enlightenment. Thomas and Jacque even appeared to have agreed on a point or two. McFarland was the only one who remained quiet. Armstrong hoped that McFarland would play the game with them. His people had informed him that McFarland had a Finnish wife and one son, Robert, Jr. That pleased Armstrong. He was gambling that having only one child would allow McFarland to align with the steel trust. Armstrong planned to find a job for Robert Jr. so that he could take care of his father and mother when they were older. One child's future was easy to ensure. Five or six would not have been. With more children, McFarland's loyalties to his children's future would have held him hostage, and the steel company's wishes would not have been important.

Armstrong continued, "We know there is enough ore in northern Minnesota for us to be in this part of the country one hundred years from now. We have the potential for a real legacy – if we silence Haywood."

"I am for shooting the bastard," blurted Thomas.

No one responded to Thomas's comment. They all understood this was not a session for suggestions. They were here to find out the plan.

Armstrong picked up a table knife, pointed at Duluth's Mayor Samuel, and indicated he talk next. "Many of you know of our situation here in Duluth. The IWW took over the Lutheran church and seminary here and turned it into the IWW official labor college. We are afraid they want to do the same thing in Hibbing. A labor college there along with their theaters and halls would push out more of their propaganda. We want to stop that from happening."

Armstrong punctuated the mayor's words. "I want to assure you that Mayor Samuel's sentiments are shared by Rockefeller's groups. The IWW does not promote a good business climate and a strong economy on local or national levels."

Mayor Samuel continued, "From talking with the mayors in Hibbing and Virginia and our good friend at the table with us, Principal Browersfield, I have learned that the Finnish organizers will be celebrating a grand opening for their park on North Star Lake just outside of Hibbing, and Haywood will be in attendance. In fact, Haywood has already contacted me and asked for some time with me before or after the ceremony to discuss the plight of the miners. Since the labor college here in Duluth has been officially recognized as an IWW school, we believe Haywood will make some sort of announcement connecting Mesaba Park to the college in some way. Perhaps he plans that Mesaba will serve as a second campus for their college in Duluth. We do not want this to occur."

"Thank you, Samuel, for your perspective. The situation creates an urgency for us to focus on Haywood's demise," said Armstrong. "Here is the first part of our plan. I have asked our governor to recognize Robert McFarland as a long-time supporter of Finnish culture. Last fall the governor gave Robert a special assignment to the Finnish people. The governor's award is the next step to publicly aligning Robert with the Finnish. An article reporting this declaration will be published in all the local newspapers of northern Minnesota. The official recognition will take place Sunday during the dedication ceremony of the grand opening of the Mesaba Park Festival and Campgrounds. Mr. Browersfield will be there, and I plan on showing up for the presentation, too.

"As a spokesperson for Finnish culture, Jacque will present the sheriff with a plaque. We are hoping this gesture of goodwill will appeal to Haywood to be present and lead him to see this official recognition as a sign he is winning us over. We know Haywood is looking for some positive newspaper coverage after the failed strikes of aught six and sixteen. In fact, we are expecting him to be on the range the week before Mesaba Park's grand opening. Mayor Samuel has indicated to Haywood that he is willing to have Haywood participate in a worker rally for the dock workers in the Duluth and Superior ports. This will give Haywood some news coverage."

All around the table, participants nodded and murmured. McFarland was quiet.

Mayor Samuel added, "The governor, under guidance and funding from the Citizens' Public Safety Committee, has put together a militia of hired men, law enforcement personnel, and some federal militia. They are tasked with assassinating Haywood and arresting his followers sometime during the grand opening weekend. Am I right, McFarland?"

Samuel didn't look at McFarland.

McFarland replied, "Yes. The Citizens' Public Safety Committee's militia will be in Hibbing the week leading up to and during the weekend of the grand opening of Mesaba Park. Thomas is leading this group."

He stopped and gestured toward Thomas. Armstrong braced for a backlash from Thomas, but his cousin remained quiet. McFarland continued, "Thomas has briefed the militia on three different assassination scenarios for taking Haywood's life during the weekend. Thomas will give you some of the details now."

Thomas tucked in his shirt and stood. He walked over to the windows and looked out. He turned back to the group and focused on them. Armstrong noticed that Thomas seemed to display some professionalism and hoped it was more than just posturing. Armstrong was impressed. He lit another cigarette.

"Haywood will be leading IWW members in a parade Sunday morning down Main Street in Hibbing. In the parade, they will be displaying the bodies of the immigrants who died at the Bruce underground mine shaft accident last fall," Thomas began.

"I am not getting this," Mr. Browersfield interjected. He took his spectacles off and tried cleaning them with his vest.

"Let me give some background information," Armstrong said. "This past fall, the IWW went to the graveyard and dug up the coffins and corpses of the four miners who were killed in the Bruce Mine shaft accident."

"And what?" Mr. Browersfield injected again.

Thomas explained, "They took the bodies and stored the bodies in the ice sheds at the park."

Browersfield shivered. "What kind of barbarians do we have?"

"Actually," Jacque inserted, "Haywood did not trigger the exhumation. We have reason to suspect the Koivus. Gustav, Launo, and Niilo instigated this."

"Damn it! Excuse my French, Jacque. I have always wondered who's been influencing Joseph Koivu. I had high hopes for Joe. I know his father and uncles are political radicals but digging up graves and storing the bodies. Ugh!" Browersfield exclaimed. "Why can't they just behave?"

Armstrong continued, "We assume Haywood will complete his Sunday morning political parade and funeral procession down Hibbing's Main Street before the Sunday service at the park. This will give Robert McFarland time to stop the parade. He will use the Sunday Morning Quiet Ordinance."

"I have talked this over with the mayor of Hibbing," said Samuel, "and Mayor Powers supports this action."

Armstrong nodded. "When McFarland stops the parade, he plans on trying to anger Haywood. He will be briefing his deputies on specific name-calling techniques to intimidate Haywood. While this is taking place on Main Street, Thomas and the militia will be undercover in the crowd. Thomas will also have a group gathered on Third Avenue waiting to move in quickly. They will start a scuffle. Thomas and the boys will let things get out of control. They will shoot off some of their guns – into the air. We are hoping that Haywood will be shot in the confusion. This will be reported in the newspapers as an unfortunate accident with full apologies from the mayor. Right, Thomas?"

"You are correct. If we are not able to get a shot at Haywood during the scuffle, we suspect Haywood will head over to the park immediately. Our second scenario will be to intercept him on the road. Another group of the governor's men will be posted in key areas along the road to Mesaba Park all weekend. If Haywood heads there before Sunday – but we doubt this – the newspapers will feature an article on how Haywood's car left the road and crashed. Haywood will die from multiple injuries. His body will be unrecognizable." Thomas stopped his presentation, waiting for questions. None were asked, so he continued, "The third scenario would take place at Mesaba Park Sunday afternoon."

"Won't that be too late?" Browersfield asked nervously. "I don't know if a public shooting with so many people around is the best way to accomplish your goals."

Armstrong clarified, "The governor believes this to be the best setting. The size of the crowd will be in the thousands. Visitors who are not from the area but supportive of the camp and sympathetic to IWW will be there. Haywood will want to address them. The biggest crowd is expected Sunday afternoon when the presentation of the award to our Sheriff McFarland will take place. Samuel, Browersfield, and Powers will be there. Actually, this will be the first time any of them have been present at a Finnish celebration. Because of all these connections, Haywood will not miss a major chance to gain some converts for the –"

"The I.W.W.," said Thomas, "The Indecisive Worried Workers."

Finnegan tried his acronym, "How about Incompetent Worry Warts?"

Browersfield added, "How about Incapacitated Weak Weasels?"

"Or Indigestion With Worms?" said Mayor Samuel.

Laughter loosened up the group. Jacque and McFarland stood, stretched together, and then sat down again. Waiters brought in pitchers of water, a bowl of ice, and tongs. These were passed around the table. Armstrong waited for everyone to refill, take some sips, and sit back. He cleared his throat and continued.

"The third assassination scenario will be attempted after all of us, except McFarland, have left the ceremony and the grounds. We are hoping this will occur sometime between one and two p.m. The sun is the brightest then and should decrease visibility. When Sheriff Murphy from Duluth sees our vehicles exit the park and head toward Duluth, he will drive into the park with his men."

Mayor Samuel interjected, "I have asked Murphy to conduct a raid on the camp to confiscate the bodies and coffins used in the parade. The accusations will be trespassing, grave robbing, and stealing personal and public property. Sheriff Murphy will lead the raid using local law enforcement. This should create confusion and some crowd hysteria. During the commotion, we hope to arrest most of the Finnish immigrants McFarland has identified as active organizers."

"This is the scenario for the third assassination, right, Robert?" asked Armstrong.

"That's correct, Armstrong," McFarland answered. "However, I will not actively assist in the assassination. I will look surprised when Sheriff Murphy shows up. As the goodwill ambassador for the Finnish, I will pull together the active IWW organizers in one area of the pavilion in order to protect them. That way Sheriff Murphy will know who to arrest.

I will appear to be resisting Sheriff Murphy's arrest of the organizers. Hopefully, I can preserve my identity as a supporter of the Finnish radicals even if Haywood is assassinated."

"We trust the attendees who are more militant about organizing will all be back from the parade when the raid commences. Their names will be checked against the list of names we have been gathering here at our offices," Armstrong stated.

McFarland continued, "As I was saying, hopefully my identification with the Finnish will polarize the crowd. As they take sides during the commotion, we expect Haywood to stir up a fight or agitate the crowd more. He will want to take advantage of the moment and be identified with the Finnish organizers."

"We will stage an assassination under the guise of crowd control during these activities," added Mayor Samuel.

Armstrong nodded. Jacque seemed surprised by the method for this last assassination scenario. He leaned over and began a quiet conversation with Finnegan. Noticing they were removed from the main discussion, Armstrong stood and added, "I want you to know that it is not the removal of Haywood that is our primary goal. The IWW beliefs and methods are insidious. Their ideas are a poison and kill the hard-working spirit of the majority of immigrants who are looking for a better life and grateful for their jobs. We do not want them taking over the camp or opening a labor college closer to our mining and lumber areas. We believe this is their motivation. That is also the reason why we believe the coffins have been stored in the park and will be returned there after the parade in Hibbing. Haywood is making a stand, and we are making ours."

Finnegan softly clapped his hands in applause. Mayor Samuel and Browersfield joined him. Thomas stood and clapped loudly. Armstrong hoped his cousin wouldn't start whistling and cheering. To prevent the success of the meeting from getting derailed with Thomas's zeal, Armstrong moved around the table shaking hands with everyone. He shook Browersfield's hand last, gave him a hug, and then motioned for the principal to give a final word.

Browersfield noted, "The beautiful high school we built in Hibbing was to give the people of Hibbing a taste of American culture and what it means to be American. We want them interested in and able to live a better lifestyle than what they left across the ocean."

Armstrong put his arm around Browersfield. "Thanks for those words and a good thought to end our meeting. I think we need to get more involved with the local school boards and encourage those we work with to do the same. The mine owners are not the only ones who want a better life for all. Our educators align with us in that desire. They believe their primary mission is to educate the immigrants to have intellectual and technical skills so they can move beyond their status as workers and become a part of the greatest nation that has ever been on earth.

"You will each receive a letter detailing the particulars of who will be driving whom and an itinerary for the weekend of the grand opening of Mesaba Park and Campground."

Armstrong dismissed McFarland, Browersfield, Jacque, Finnegan. and Thomas. Samuel and Armstrong headed back to Armstrong's office.

Walking to his car, McFarland wondered what hand of fate had caused his arrival and departure from a meeting where he had premeditated the killing of a man who had done more good for the Finnish radicals than those who wanted him murdered. McFarland wondered how he could unwind the ball of string they had just tied into knots. At a loss for insights or answers, McFarland decided to drive by Mesaba Park on the way home. Gustav would be there working late, setting up for the grand opening day. As McFarland had mentioned to Gustav the day before, he would stop by after the meeting to update him on what had transpired.

28   Double Moon

I walked over to where Joe was helping his father brace the railing around the entrance to the pavilion. As I approached, he lifted his hand in recognition, said something to his father, and then hurried over to me.

"Joe," I said, "let's go down by the beach."

"No problem, Sara. I told Dad you'd be stopping by. He said it would be okay for me to leave when you came. Sheriff McFarland might be stopping by later to discuss the grand opening details with him. He didn't want me here for that."

We sat down just below the pavilion by North Star Lake's shore. I started the conversation. "My father has been talking with Oscar Corgan, the editor for the *Tyomies* newspaper in Superior. Oscar would like to manage the Work People's Co-op Store for my father. Oscar will move his family to Hibbing to do that."

Joe sat up from his slouched position. "Really?" His eyes sparkled. "My dad and Uncle Launo would love that. They think the world of Oscar. I can't wait to tell them!"

I saw the gears of Joe's mind grinding like the crusher breaking up a load of red ore for the smelter in Pittsburgh. I had to watch that I didn't give him too many new ideas in a conversation. If I did, his mind left where we were and followed romantic notions of adventure rather than pursuing romantic rapture with me.

"The Crogans lost their eleven-year-old son Leo last year. They need to get away from their home where they had lived with their son in Superior and get out from under the pressure of producing the paper." I saw a slight wince in the crow's feet on his face. "My dad is thinking of moving to Superior to help out with the newspaper in Oscar's absence. Dad also wants to be closer to Mom."

Joe hadn't come all the way back. I thought he might, since he cared for a younger brother, too. I had noticed this with other boys in high school. They liked adventure. They became more excited about an adventure when it was further away.

"Unbelievable, Sara. Uncle Launo and my father have been talking about going to Karelia, Finland, to fight for socialism with the Communist Party. I thought it was just talk, sauna bullshitting to pass the time, to keep their dreams of a worker's paradise alive. Maybe not."

I thought Joe went even farther than I wanted. His emotional undertones were sounding like he might want to go, too. Perhaps the suspension from baseball last year had gotten to him. I remembered when we had first talked about Finland my first year in high school. Then he hadn't even wanted to pack clothes and supplies to send over to Finland to support the revolution. Mom warned me that men can be unpredictable that way. They were romantic, but their romance was with Minnesota where they had trees to chop, ore to dig, and land to grow food.

The romance train steamed down the tracks leaving a trail of smoke and sparks. I was trying to get him to think about us, the lake, and the times we had had at Mesaba Park, and he was idealizing a mythical Finlandia of Marxian proportions. Meanwhile, I was enjoying pictures in my mind of Joe, tan and tall, watching our children swimming. He held his right hand above his eyebrows, blocking the sun from blinding his view of the youngsters at play. Several times the past year I had imagined Joe looking after our children when we came to the park as a family.

"My Uncle Launo says Finland has no ruling class, rich industrialists, or kings and czars, just people working together for the common good."

"Joe, you sound like you want to go there."

"What?"

"I said you sound like you want to go. I thought you didn't want to leave your mother without someone to care for her. What about your brother and sister?"

"My dad said he'd stay behind if I would go over. I am young and strong. Besides I am tired of being treated like a second class citizen around here. I'll never get a real job here. I'll be a lumberjack all my life like my father."

Joe shocked me with how quickly he switched from some idyllic adventurous notion to the present. I hadn't thought he was fanciful, but perhaps his thinking had changed. I never thought he minded staying in

Hibbing, working and raising a family. He had been so good with helping out when his mother had been ill for so long. Sometimes I had thought he might enjoy being home with his family rather than being with me.

For the first time I feared losing Joe. His excitement about a mythical Finlandia had never before flashed across his face or exploded passionately in our conversations. In that way, he was very different from his father and uncle. In fact, I had been afraid he might not feel as deeply as I did about workers' rights. All he had ever done was complain about how much his father focused on socialism and nothing else. Once Joe had even told me he wished he had been named Marx or Lenin. Then his father might have paid more attention to him.

Something was stirring in Joe tonight. I felt it in the air, like a shiver, a cool breeze blowing through my blouse. I thought I needed to do something and quickly. I didn't want to lose this opportunity to snare our future. I had planned for it a long time.

I moved next to him so my side touched his and placed his hand on my thigh. Then I set my palm on top of his. I prayed he would feel the warmth of my touch, the heat of the home hearth. I waited for him to return from the Russian revolution, march through Finland, and cross the Atlantic back to the United States.

I stared at the lake bottom and noticed that ridges in the sand were already forming. They formed close to the shore first. Water skippers were dancing on the quiet lake surface. In the dusk, they were hard to see because their brown bodies resembled the color of the leaves sitting on the lake's bottom. The sandy-colored skippers were playful. I never saw one by itself. They moved in groups, not tightly organized, but loosely scattered in one area of the beach. They always danced by the shore, never out in the deep water. Nobody ever wrote poems about the skippers. I wondered why. Skippers weren't annoying like mosquitoes or menacing in appearance like dragon flies. I thought a poem describing a dragon fly devouring a mosquito would not have been attractive, but anything written about skippers would have to be cute.

"Joe, remember when we talked about having our own family?" Joe was still mentally out in the deep waters.

"Did you know that the poem *Kalevala* was written in Karelia, Sara?"

"Joe."

"Oscar said for four hundred dollars a whole family and their belongings can travel to Finland on the Swedish America boat lines."

Joe was still skipping on the water. He wasn't near the shore. He was with his father, Uncle Launo, his cousin Niilo, and the Bolsheviks.

"I do not understand why you want to go to Finland all of a sudden."

"I don't know if I know why, Sara. I think, with all that has happened, I am questioning what I really want. I am realizing the difficulties of living in an area where I mainly associate with my relatives."

"Joe, you talk to me and lots of people at the park."

"I know, Sara, but we can't live at the park all our lives. Somehow, we have to try to understand these people who live around here with us."

Now he was philosophizing. Puberty was one major change in his life. I remembered the first time he had put his arm around me. We had been in the dining hall. I was caught off guard, and I liked it. Then after ten minutes he moved his arm away for no obvious reason. At the nightly bonfire while we sang a song, he pulled me close and sniffed my hair. I watched him as he stared at my breasts. He was unaware that I was watching. I liked his attention.

"Well, that's not going to happen if you go to Finland."

"My dad thinks I should go to the labor college in Duluth or to Karelia. He says that this type of revolution doesn't happen every day. It's history in the making! I need to do everything I can to make the most of this time."

"Everything is history, Joe. Having a family you love and trust is good history, too."

"I know, but I think I owe it to my father to go. I have three uncles there. My mother will never be able to go back. Maybe I can see her family for her."

"But that's your parents' families, Joe. I am talking about making something new, a new family. You and I will decide where to live and how to raise our children. We will start a new generation during this time of change."

Joe turned his head away. I had thought tonight was going to be different. I had hoped our last night at camp would be romantic. I had planned this for three weeks, making sure there were no distractions or chores. I wanted the two of us alone by the lake. Now I didn't know what to say or how to act. Somehow I had to get Joe's thoughts back to us and our future.

"Joe, you and I have good health. We are smart. We can get plenty of work at the co-op, Mesaba Park, or lumbering. Maybe we can start our own business."

"How do you know we can make it, Sara? Look at your parents. They don't know where they want to live. Look at mine. My mother's ill, and my dad is blacklisted. Do you think we can do better?"

I pushed hard against his side, and he let me. I held his hand with my palm atop like a water skipper on the lake's surface. My fingers tapped on the back of his. I imagined my fingers to be the legs of a pond hopper. Lightly, they pushed his tanned skin. I placed my hand on his back and let a water jumper travel softly up and down. His shoulder blades were lily pads, large, smooth, and round. I thought about going under his shirt and touching him. Then I thought about drifting down to his trouser line – the shoreline.

"Elaine has talked to me about Jewish history –"

"Now, what? Sara, you know I am not religious and not Jewish –"

Well! He came back in a hurry from Europe!

"Jewish people aren't a nation. They used to have a piece of land, a claim like a country, where their Jewish heritage began. Now they all grow up in different countries. They marry and sometimes go to other areas. They are like gypsies, roaming all over the world. Joe, we have a country we are from and one we are living in. I love my mom and dad, uncles, aunts, and cousins. Don't you want to have our families nearby? We are meant to care for each other, love each other, and miss each other. Let's unite our families by staying here, by making it work."

There, I said it all, maybe too much.

"Sara, I dislike everything my father has told me about life and how it works. He always seems angry, afraid … he sees conspiracies in anything that happens."

"My father never talks about conspiracies."

"I know there must be good conspiracies, but all I have been told about are bad ones. I have spent so much time hating the world he lives in that I don't know what world I live in. I don't even know if there are families who stay together for a lifetime. I don't know what I do believe!"

"I am not sure what you mean, Joe."

"Sara, I only have questions. I wish I had more answers. I know the opposite of socialism is capitalism. As much as I hate all the discussions on capitalism and who is a true communist or not, I don't know what type of a socialist I am. When I threw a good game with ball control, I felt proud. My performance mattered. Because of me and my pitching, our team won. I don't think individuals and what they do matter in our political world where both sides are groups, larger then teams, huge in proportions, as large as night and day. Individuals are not important in the political world."

The water jumpers dissipated as the sun set. Maybe they were cold-blooded like reptiles. They chilled after sunset. I noticed our reflections in the water and didn't remember ever seeing our reflections together anywhere. I liked what I saw. Joe was handsome. I was very lucky. Seeing us reflected in the water reassured me we were right for each other. I felt it the same way I felt my mother's emotions when she sang. I wondered what it would be like to see a reflection of the two of us kissing. I thought I would look at the window in the door of my cabin tonight when Joe dropped me off. Maybe I could get him to stay for a moment and catch a glimpse of his goodnight kiss.

"I know I'm not a capitalist the way my father talks about them. And I know there is a difference between me and the other boys at high school. I guess I could use the words class or class struggle like my father does, but I don't know what I believe about the life I live and see every day. Your saying you love me and let's have a family seems too easy. This simplicity confuses me more."

All the water skippers had vanished. The sunset's colors painted the lake's surface.

"Joe, I am not pressuring you to marry me. You graduated from high school last spring, and I have a year left. This has me thinking. I would like to get married not long after I graduate."

"Sara, I don't know if I can even make a decision like that. How can you talk about it so effortlessly?"

"Joe, I love you."

"How can you know you love me if you haven't fought for it? Shouldn't there be a struggle to gain love just as there is struggle to gain workers' rights?"

"I'm afraid you're sounding like your father. There doesn't have to be bloodshed and conflict.

"Sometimes things are true, just true. That's the way it is. There is no hoopla, conflict, or engagement .... Oops!"

Joe smiled, "Gotcha!"

"Oh, Joe…" He was back. He smiled. Humor made Joe's face come alive and shine.

"Doesn't the sky look romantic tonight? I love the way the moonlight dances off the lake's surface. It looks like fairies throwing diamonds as they dance," I said.

"Remember the moon dog last summer?" Joe reminisced.

"Yes, that was the first time you kissed me."

"Did I?"

We both laughed.

"You just did it again."

"Sara, I haven't forgotten that kiss, and I won't forget the kiss I'm about to give you." Joe leaned in and gave me a long kiss. He looked into my eyes. "When a guy remembers a kiss as long as I have, that means something."

"I am not sure what you mean?"

"I love you, Sara."

"Joe…"

"I mean it. I want to kiss you for a long time."

"So you don't want me to tell you to stop, Joe?"

Joe smiled. "But not here on the beach. Let's row out to the sandbar about mid-lake."

"There are no sandbars on this lake, Joe."

"I know, Sara, but I was on one earlier today. My father said the lake springs have shifted from the mine blasts."

"Isn't the sand wet?" I asked him.

"Sara, I could feel heat waves radiating up through the grasses when I rowed over earlier tonight. We'll be warm."

"You better not be lying to me, Joseph Niilo Koivu."

"You know I never lie."

"Yeah, that's only true when you're with your parents or in school. And now you have graduated…"

"Sara!"

"Do you have any blankets, Joe?"

"Yeah, I've got the ones some kids left in the boat."

After Joseph helped me into the flat-bottomed rowboat, I grabbed an oar and pushed against the sandy shore bottom to help us head out into the lake. Joe jumped into the lake and pushed hard on the aft end. As he did, the boat broke from the sand and drifted free. Joe jumped back in and landed so hard that the boat waddled back and forth. Sometimes I wondered if he had stones in his shoes.

Joe grabbed the oars. After a few minutes of Joe's rowing, the boat hit the sandbar. We stopped. Joe pointed to the north shore.

"Sara! The moon's reflection on the lake tonight is a double!"

"I have never seen a double! Show me."

"Look, over by the other side. See the reflection just below the tree line?"

"Yes."

"Now follow my finger with your eyes as I trace a line back to the boat."

"I see it Joe; I see the double!"

A double was the second reflection of the full moon on the lake's surface. When the fall night sky was free of clouds, the rising full moon was reflected on the horizon and then again about two hundred yards away from the first reflection. This second reflection was not as bright. On a calm lake surface, it appeared for about thirty minutes. I whispered to myself, "How lucky I am! I have seen the northern lights, and now I am seeing a double moon!"

Joe steadied the boat as I stepped out. We walked to where the sandbar was the highest above the lake's surface. I looked up and stared at Joe's face. His pupils invited the dark night to surround and cover us. Like refreshing pools, his eyes settled my soul. I sensed our connections in the touch of my head on his shoulder, his hand on my waist, and our slow, steady breathing.

I was reminded of watching my parents Elizabeth and Martin dance. I loved seeing them together. Mom and Dad moved slowly and gracefully – palm to palm, chest with chest, hips against hips. They seemed to hold their love between their bodies – invisible, curled, and settled. When I was anxious at night, Mom had taught me to place my palms over my heart. As I slowly breathed in and out, I quieted. Resting my hands on my chest created a safe feeling. I imagined myself in front of a fire with friends warming my hands after a long winter walk in the woods.

Seeing Dad and Mom dance created those same peaceful feelings inside me. As I had watched them, I had imagined soft wavy auras outlining their bodies. They had shimmered like the heat waves I had seen rising up from the blacktop roads in the summer when we drove to Duluth. I had painted an image of a soft white-yellow flame flickering between their chests. I had thought of them as a candle in the window at night, a round fairy light floating across the yard, a will - o'- the - wisp skipping in and out of the night air.

Mom had told me I was the result of a summer's night full of festival dancing. She and Dad had made love until the sun started to rise in the morning. Making love had never been absent from my parents' lives. They had never been ashamed of showing affection for each other in public. I think that was why people liked Mom in the plays and musicals in which she sang and acted. She exuded love.

I was hoping Joe and I would also have an enduring closeness. I had always thought that was how I could make life better. That was my mission, my path to walk, no matter where I ended up or lived. If there was a life after this one and a God, I imagined God's love dancing with Joe and me like my parents danced with each other.

Joe opened the larger wool quilt and spread it on the ground. "Let's put one blanket on the ground and use the others to keep us warm."

"Hey! What fell out?" I asked.

He held one up. "The kids made these candles today. They must have forgotten to take them when they left the boat."

I smiled. "Look, Joe, the candle's upside down. Here, let's make sure the side with the designs is up. There. Now I like that... What would you do if you didn't have me?"

"Sara, light the candle."

As I lit the candle, the flame had two reflections on the lake's surface!

"Joe! Look! I made a double!"

Joe placed one blanket over me and wrapped himself in the other. We sat. The double candle reflection had shimmered away. I realized we had been quiet for a while. That was not like us, but I didn't mind. I was peaceful.

"I don't want to lose you, Sara," Joe said in a soft voice.

I sensed his earnestness. I paused before responding and let his words seep into our souls. I knew there was more on his mind, more he wanted to say. I thought back to the last time we had talked and waited for more. I felt him give me a gentle squeeze. "I want things to turn out for us, Joe. I want everything to be perfect. I don't want anything messy. You won't lose me; I'll make sure –"

Joe had gotten to the heart of his feelings sooner than I had expected. Mother said guys could be very unpredictable when it came to talking about what they felt and how much they liked you. Joseph's tone was strong, but all the Koivus communicated strength in their words. They made people feel protected, guarded – like nothing could ever happen. Joe interrupted, "If things don't turn out right, we'll know what to do."

"I know our love is strong," I reassured him. Now Joe was here with me. He was in touch with what he was feeling.

He rubbed my back. His hands were stiff like scrub brushes on the floor. He didn't bend his elbows. He moved fast. Reaching around and placing my hands on his, I gently slowed his movements. Suddenly, I released my grip and rolled over on my back, a little away from him. Joe was puzzled. Tightening his eyebrows, he whispered, "You really don't need to worry... I don't think I was serious about going to Finland and helping the Bolsheviks."

I had thought he had been serious, but I liked that Joe was romantic and saying the right things. Joe had changed so much this past year. I hugged him. "When we go back home from summer camp, I will miss you."

I took my eyes off him and focused on the stars above. His warm hands slid under my sweater. I felt the heat of Joe's breath. He dropped a kiss on the top of my head. I heard him smell my hair. I whispered softly, "Breathe deep, Joseph. Breathe deep; breathe slowly. Taste my love, I pray. You belong with me, Joe. I desire to be with you; we can't wait."

We breathed in deeply. The autumn night held our breath. Our breath emerged, hanging, swirling, and dancing. The air's frozen impurities dropped to the ground. A bright star fell. Silently, shoreline trees, camp bushes, and marsh grasses began their nocturnal night watch, singing lullabies in ancient tongues. Musky smells covered us, and heavy quilts of sewn winter jackets cut into squares pressed us to the ground.

The earth lay still as our bodies met. We both initiated; we both explored. We chased pain away, entered our centers, and then curled up like we'd just warmed our bodies by the fire – content. No one heard our breathing; no one smelled pine oil in the air.

We had begun our life together.

29   Revelation

Gustav saw the headlights of a car as it headed toward the camp. The headlights looked like those on Gustav's truck, two miniature harvest moons, cheddar-colored. *That must be the sheriff,* Gustav thought. He had mentioned he might stop by after his meeting in Duluth.

Gustav was reminded of how things looked different at night. He thought about a dog's eyes at night. They looked like red stars in a bonfire's light, just like a wolf's. Conversations were also different at night, sometimes stumbling into interactions that weren't intended or expected.

"Hey, Sheriff! How was Duluth?" Gustav greeted the sheriff as he exited the car.

"That's what I want to talk to you about. This will be hard for me," McFarland replied. "I'm in over my head, Gustav."

"Well, this is not the first time. I remember the time –"

McFarland interrupted, "I can't joke tonight. My head's driving me crazy. All the way from Duluth I couldn't shut it down… They wanna kill Haywood."

"Haywood?" Gustav repeated.

Sheriff McFarland looked at the ground. He kept quiet. Gustav walked closer. "They want to kill Haywood? Who are they?" Gustav asked.

"Armstrong. He says Rockefeller ordered Haywood's assassination."

Gustav shrugged. "I don't find that hard to believe, Sheriff."

"I know. You and I have even tossed the idea around that they might slow the organizing this way, but I never thought it would really happen. I never thought I would be a part of it," McFarland confessed.

"Slow down, Robert. You are a part of it …. You are going to shoot Haywood?"

"I am supposed to be a part of the plan to kill Haywood sometime during the weekend of the grand opening of Mesaba Park. Three assassination scenarios are planned."

Instinctively, Gustav offered, "Just say no."

"I didn't want to say no at the meeting with everybody there." McFarland paused as if to gather his thoughts. "And then I got to thinking about what you had said about digging up those four miners and having Haywood use them in some way to help with the organizing…" McFarland paused again.

"I never told you I dug up anything," Gustav stated, steely-voiced.

After a few seconds, Robert looked directly into Gustav's eyes. "Gustav, how did Armstrong know? I don't even know any details."

Gustav turned and looked away.

"Gustav, whether you or your brother Launo dug up those men doesn't matter now. But somehow Armstrong thinks you did it. This is fueling the plans to kill Haywood. Browersfield couldn't believe anyone would dig up dead bodies. When he was told it was you … Oh! You should have seen his face…. Where the hell did Armstrong get his information…?"

Gustav didn't look at McFarland when he answered. He talked slowly and pronounced each word carefully. "One day this summer I was in the co-op listening to Viola talk to Martin about the Finnish Civil War. Viola said some Red Finns had dug up townspeople who had been slaughtered by a group of White Finns outside of Karelia in the northern forests. He said digging up the bodies so everyone could see them gained sympathy for the Red Finns."

McFarland's interrogating experience came into play, and he didn't reply. He knew that silence provoked more talk, especially when feelings of fault or guilt existed.

After several minutes, Gustav broke the silence. "I was so interested in the incident I got excited. I asked Viola what he thought of the idea of digging up the miners in the cemetery here."

McFarland looked at Gustav in disbelief. He let Gustav continue.

"Then I asked Viola if he thought using the bodies of the dead miners here might generate more momentum for unionizing…"

Gustav realized his supposition to Viola could have been taken as truth. What had made him think Viola was even a little supportive of organizing, let alone digging up dead Red Finns?

McFarland's face turned from disbelief to disgust. Gustav had become so enamored with Haywood and what he might do with the dead miners that Gustav wasn't seeing a possible Armstrong conspiracy. McFarland decided to get Gustav to look beyond Haywood's eventual plans for the four dead miners. He wanted Gustav to see a possible information leak in Hibbing.

"Why even talk with Viola about such a wild idea?" McFarland questioned.

"I was just making a suggestion," Gustav confessed.

"What did you do that for? Shit. From what I know, all of Viola's family are White Finns. None are sympathetic toward the IWW and especially Haywood. You know that. His relatives in Finland probably even approved the slaughter in that town."

"You're right," Gustav replied. "I doubt if Viola's kin even thought twice about the mass murder in Finland."

"Why would Viola bring up such a topic, anyway, Gustav?"

"I hadn't –" Gustav stuttered.

McFarland cut Gustav off. "That's right, you hadn't even thought about what Viola might have really been doing … Maybe he was trying to get Martin to let him in on the IWW and Haywood."

"I never thought of Viola as sneaky. If he was, wouldn't he have been nosing around our Saturday morning meetings or befriending George Ivanovich… but he hasn't made any sneaky moves," Gustav noted.

"That's my point. He hasn't. So maybe there is another explanation, a bigger conspiracy. Maybe Armstrong was using Viola to verify what he had heard about the dead miners. With that information, Armstrong could have the support of Rockefeller in doing something to Haywood. Maybe there was and is a bigger conspiracy."

Gustav mulled over McFarland's ideas. His group had joked about Viola and Jacque, but he had not seriously considered the two were pawns being played by Armstrong.

"Viola must have told Jacque about what you said. Maybe he told Armstrong," suggested McFarland.

"Sounds like a bunch of dominoes collapsing on the table top," Gustav concluded. Both took deep breaths of the cool fall night air.

"I came here tonight to let you know Armstrong knows that the bodies were dug up, and I am involved in an assassination plan to eliminate Haywood. And I don't know what to do. I am still hoping you have some ideas."

"Right now my head is full of too many thoughts. I do know Haywood is coming to the dedication of Mesaba Park in a couple of weeks. I am hoping whatever he decides to do will break the hold of the steel trust here. I don't know where you stand. I hope it isn't in the way, McFarland."

"Gustav –"

Gustav's confusion turned to anger. "McFarland, are you going to help Armstrong shed blood?"

"I don't want to ask too many questions, but I think there's more going on than what you've told me about those dead miners. You know when push comes to shove, I have always backed you and your IWW doings –"

"Before I lose what little trust I have in you, Robert, my advice is for you to shut up and leave right now before I call you something worse than an asshole –"

"Hey, you wait a minute. I came here tonight to confide in you, and now you are treating me like some greedy mine owner – you son of a bitch! I was hoping for something more than that, Gustav…"

"If you want something more, here it is, bastard. You know in every situation there is one pin, gear, one key person who holds the whole machine together. He may not even be the big man … take care of that person."

Both men glared at each other.

Gustav threw up his hands in disgust. "Just do what you've got to do, McFarland. I wasn't at your business meeting with Armstrong. And I never want to be at one. Now get the hell out here. Leave!" Gustav turned away from McFarland and headed toward the pavilion.

Full of uncertainty, McFarland spun on his heel and headed back to his car.

Gustav grabbed the railing around the entrance to the pavilion and pulled it as hard as he could. It didn't move. Then he bent over, clasped his hands together, turned his right shoulder, and rammed it into the railing.

He could hear McFarland drive down the entrance road back to County Road 37.

"Gustav!" Martin yelled.

Gustav stood up quickly. He brushed off his shirt.

"Martin?" Gustav replied.

"Who just drove down the road?" Martin asked.

"McFarland."

"McFarland? Hmm... What's he doing here so late? Usually he patrols on the east side of town at this time of night."

Gustav was quiet.

"Anything I need to know about?" queried Martin.

Gustav didn't answer.

"This is not like you, Gustav. You always have something to say after McFarland visits."

Gustav picked up his hammer and the can of nails he had been using. "The sheriff just came from Duluth."

"Duluth?" Martin echoed.

"Yeah."

"What was he doing there?" Martin wondered.

"We need to talk."

"I have time," Martin replied.

"Let's get a cup of coffee in the kitchen."

"I've had too much today. Let's go over to the bonfire pit. I noticed some good chairs there, and the sky is clear tonight. We can talk under the stars," Martin suggested.

"I'll be there in a few minutes. I want to put the rest of the tools away."

When Martin arrived at the bonfire pit, he didn't know how long this conversation would take so he placed a few logs near the edge of the stone fire ring where they would be sitting. He lit them.

He and Gustav seldom had a conversation alone. In fact, both of them were seldom alone. Martin's responsibilities with the store, the co-op federation, and the theater kept him busy. Gustav had his lumbering business, organizing activities, and demanding involvement with the IWW.

Martin's thoughts wandered to the four frozen bodies that had been in the camp's ice shed. He was glad Gustav and Launo had removed them the other weekend when they redid the roof on the pavilion. The idea of those four men frozen in the ice shed at the park was a little gruesome but not as gruesome as cold-blooded murder. Martin had a hard time imagining how anyone could place a shotgun against another person's head, pull the trigger, and not feel remorse. To have executed four men that way, faked their deaths as an accident, and buried them without a funeral was barbaric. Martin had just been on the phone earlier that morning discussing Haywood's and the IWW's involvement and activities during the park's dedication. He needed to review those with Gustav and thought this might be a good time.

"Hey, Martin."

"Grab a chair."

They both sat and looked at the fire. Martin cleared his throat. "I'll start. I talked with Haywood this morning."

"That's who McFarland and I were talking about," said Gustav.

"Was Haywood in Duluth?" wondered Martin.

"No."

"That's what I thought. Maybe you had better go first then," replied Martin.

"McFarland has let me in on Oliver Mining's activities when he thought it was appropriate."

"He has told you more than has told me," Martin acknowledged.

"Well, he was down in Duluth today at a meeting with Armstrong and some others. Apparently there's a plan to assassinate Haywood the weekend of the grand opening."

"Doesn't surprise me," said Martin. "In fact, that is what Haywood and I were discussing this morning."

"He knows about the plot?" Gustav exclaimed.

"Haywood had gotten information that the sheriff from Duluth was bringing some men up for the grand opening. Haywood didn't think it was because the band from the labor college was going to be here… even though the band is known to get a little rowdy at times and agitate those listening."

"McFarland and his deputies have always been able to handle them," Gustav noted. "The sheriff from Duluth has never needed to back up Robert before."

"Who's backing whom up here is not the issue. Bill has decided not to be at the park Sunday morning of the dedication."

"Hmm. He must take the assassination seriously. We'll have the largest crowd ever! I can imagine people rallying behind Haywood as he stumps."

"And… he is also going to have a mock funeral procession Saturday morning. He wants you, Launo, and Niilo to carry the flags," Martin added.

Gustav didn't respond to what Martin said but returned to McFarland's news. "McFarland said the sheriff from Duluth was coming with a posse on Sunday to help with the assassination."

"Help who?"

"I'm not sure…"

"You don't think McFarland is a part of the plot, do you?"

"I never told you this, Martin, but when we dug Taisto and the boys up, we found McFarland's badge in Helmer's coffin."

"What would it be doing there, Gustav?"

"Hell if I know. Look, I got it right here." Gustav placed the badge into Martin's left hand.

"Well, I'll be damned. I don't know what to make of this." Martin turned the badge over, looked at the back side, and then flipped it back and stared at the front side again. He held it for a while. Then he placed it in his right hand and tapped it against the arm of his chair. Neither said anything.

"It doesn't make sense, Gustav. McFarland wouldn't place his badge in the coffin." He tapped the badge some more. "It wouldn't have fallen off. And if it had, someone would have noticed… especially Stephan. He has an eye for detail." He tapped the badge some more. "This just doesn't add up."

"Damn!" exclaimed Gustav. "You hear that car, Martin? Is that McFarland coming back? Sounds like the car is moving pretty fast. I wonder what is on his mind now?" They heard the car stop, and the door open and slam shut.

"Gustav!" McFarland yelled. "Gustav!" he yelled louder.

After Gustav did not respond, McFarland continued, "I know you're here. Your truck has not moved. Damn it! I'll find you."

McFarland walked briskly toward the light in the bonfire pit. As he neared, Gustav and Martin heard heavy breathing.

"McFarland. This is Martin. I'm over here by the bonfire."

McFarland stopped. His eyes narrowed. Martin? Why was he here?

Martin waited until the sheriff moved closer. Then Martin stood and held out his right hand. McFarland reached out as if to shake Martin's hand and then brushed it aside. The badge Martin still held flew out of his hand and clunked as it bounced off one of the rocks that ringed the pit.

McFarland paused and looked in the direction of the sound. "What was that?"

"That's what I want to know," replied Martin.

McFarland stepped toward the sound, bent over, and felt around. His hand found the badge, clutched it, and brought it up. "Feels like a badge."

"How about like your badge," sneered Gustav.

"You shut your mouth. I drove back here because of you and what you said."

"Take a deep breath and calm down," advised Martin. "Grab a chair, and let's talk."

"I talked enough with Gustav already."

"Then what are you doing back here?" asked Martin.

"Your conscience got a hold of you?" wondered Gustav.

"The plans Armstrong has, the way Thomas disrespects me, the idea Haywood might be murdered … Shit … I have lots on my mind."

"Forget what's on your mind for a moment. Is that is your badge, Sheriff?" questioned Martin. "Gustav found it in Helmer's coffin."

"What?!"

"You heard me. I want an explanation."

"I don't know what you're talking about."

"How did it get in the coffin?" Martin wondered.

Gustav walked over to the sheriff. "When we dug up those four coffins, we found your badge in one of them. How did it get there?"

"Hell if I know. I was never near those bodies," McFarland denied.

"How did the badge get in the coffin then?" Gustav demanded.

McFarland stepped over to the firelight, leaned down, and tilted the badge until it caught the light. He looked closely at the metal stampings. "Damn it. This is my badge." He looked up at Gustav and Martin. "What the hell is going on here?"

"The badge causing you trouble?" Martin asked. "I want an explanation, Robert – excuse me – Sheriff McFarland."

Robert looked around the bonfire pit. There were no more logs to feed the fire. He got up to get some wood.

"Do you ever remember losing or giving your badge away?" questioned Martin.

The walk for the wood gave McFarland time to think. As he neared the fire pit with an armload, he replied, "Not until now." He turned to

Gustav. "Remember the scuffle at the maintenance shops in Chisholm last fall?"

"You mean when my son Joe and Impi's kid got involved with that Thomas character –"

"What's that have to with the coffins in the graveyard?" asked Martin.

McFarland answered Gustav, ignoring Martin. "Yes. That scuffle was preplanned by Armstrong,"

"Armstrong?" quizzed Gustav.

"Armstrong wanted me and my department to be seen as pro-Finnish, especially with my special assignment by the governor as a friend of the Finnish. So he staged a little stunt to make me look good. I went along with the idea. I figured everybody won."

Martin listened intently.

"Thomas took it too seriously. He and his thugs really hurt me. My deputies had to carry me back to the car."

"Do you think Thomas meant to hurt you?" questioned Gustav.

"Yes," replied McFarland. "After I left you earlier, I realized that was the case. That's why I came back."

"Robert, you know Thomas was acting as an organizing-buster during the lumber strikes and then moved on to the mines. He hasn't changed. He gets paid well to do what he does," said Martin.

"Remember, his cousin is Armstrong," added Gustav, trying to help the sheriff tie the pieces together. It was like throwing more wood on a fire. The right-sized pieces with seasoned dryness made a fire blaze immediately.

"Come on, McFarland …" urged Martin. "Think about what has happened over the past fifteen years."

In the firelight, Gustav and Martin watched Robert's changing facial expressions reflect the gears whirling in his head. His investigative thought processes had sprung to life and were aligning all the possible scenarios. Scenes fluttered. Some weren't related; others were doubles, even triples. They flew by, mixing and matching with the pile of facts and observations he had made. His mind was a one-armed bandit at the casino looking for three cherries. McFarland's eyes flashed. The story was forming; an explanation was emerging.

"Wait a minute! I remember not being able to find my badge shortly after the scuffle. When I got back to the station, I took my shirt off to change into a clean one for the evening patrols. I asked Stephan if he had seen my badge when they put me into the car. He said no. I told him I couldn't find it. He was concerned about the beating I had just taken... and who the hell all those men were with Thomas. He had not noticed my badge was missing."

"So Thomas took your badge from you," guessed Gustav. He looked at Martin.

"I can't think of any other person who would have planted it in the coffin," concluded McFarland.

Gustav repeated what he said moments earlier. "So Thomas took the badge from you and then set you up."

Robert pointed his finger Gustav, cocked his finger back, and aimed. His lips formed the word "Bang!" Gustav had hit the bull's eye.

McFarland began to pace around the fire pit. His mind started on the next chapter of the story. "Since Thomas always follows Armstrong's orders, Armstrong must have instructed Thomas to hurt me during the scuffle in Chisholm."

McFarland moved faster around the fire. Martin and Gustav watched and listened.

Suddenly, he stopped. "Damn it!"

Just as suddenly, he returned to circling. "He probably would have murdered me right then and there if I hadn't had several of my men with me."

"That's right. Neither Thomas nor Armstrong are interested in promoting you as a friend of the Finnish; they are just using you for what they really want," inserted Gustav.

"Shit!" exclaimed McFarland.

"But he didn't finish you off," added Martin. "You were and are still of use to him and Armstrong. The person they have wanted all along is Haywood."

"So now they think they have my loyalty. They're hoping I'll help them assassinate Haywood during the Mesaba Park dedication weekend."

"And if they accomplish their goal –" prompted Martin.

"Once they accomplish their goal, I am no longer needed."

"Correct," agreed Martin.

"At that time," clarified Gustav, "you no longer serve their needs. You will have helped them catch the largest northern pike that exists in the radical labor movement lake right now. They can throw you out of their fishing boat and let you sink to the bottom of the lake."

"Just like they blew the heads off our four brothers," Martin finished.

McFarland stopped pacing. "Their heads were blown off?" This information made him pause. He glanced at Gustav. "That is what you didn't tell me. They were executed. Aghhh…"

He looked from Gustav to Martin. "I'm next. They won't need me anymore."

Gustav imitated Robert's earlier gesture. He pointed his finger at McFarland, cocked his thumb back, and fired. His lips formed the word "Bang!"

McFarland began to pace again. Martin and Gustav watched patiently. They looked at each other and silently agreed to give the sheriff all the time he needed. A few minutes later, McFarland stopped in front of them. "I wonder why they are having Sheriff Murphy show up with some of his officers for Sunday dedication."

"Sheriff Murphy?" questioned Gustav.

"Yes," replied McFarland. "If I am no longer needed after Haywood is assassinated, it might be to their advantage to remove me … maybe that weekend. Why keep me around? Especially when I am connected to everyone … you, Armstrong, Rockefeller, the mayors, and even Browersfield… With Haywood gone, my special assignment to the Finnish is completed."

"Before you overthink your role," said Martin, "think about who's been holding the powers that be together."

"I am not sure what you mean?" McFarland wondered.

Gustav stood and walked over to McFarland. "Who was working against the lumber organizing? Who has been working against the mine organizing? Who is leading the assassination attempts on Haywood?"

"Thomas."

"That's right."

McFarland repeated, "Thomas."

Now all three of them were standing. They cast one large shadow against the trees outside the bonfire pit.

"Thomas has been the key person all along, hasn't he, Robert?" Gustav concluded.

"Yes, he has," said McFarland resolutely. "Yes, he has."

Martin suggested, "When you meet with mine owners, mayors, and the others like them, you can easily be led to think they are the –"

"Damn it!" interrupted McFarland. "Damn it! I should have known. Thomas! He's everywhere. And he never has a good thing to say to me."

"Or any of us," added Martin.

"That son of a bitch," yelled McFarland. He stomped his foot. "Thomas, Toivo Soumi should have castrated you when he had the chance in Alango!"

Gustav's and Martin's eyes twinkled a bit when they recalled the story that had been told so many times since it happened. They watched McFarland. He wasn't laughing.

"Robert," Gustav said.

"I'm done talking," said McFarland. "I am done being played a fool!" He headed to his car. There was something about the way McFarland said "fool" that bothered Martin. He had seen the sheriff angry before, but Martin sensed a determination in McFarland that did not need to be punctuated with swearing.

Like a train loaded with ore headed down the tracks, nothing was stopping the sheriff. He got into his car and started it. Before he drove off, Martin and Gustav heard McFarland holler, "I am going to kill you, Thomas. I am going to blow your damn head off!"

30   Coffin Procession

"The parade you see today is not a parade. It is a procession, a funeral procession. Four brave miners were murdered last fall and put in the ground by the Oliver Mining Company: *Elder Metsa, Herman Bjorkland, Taisto Rantala, and Helmer Valamaki.* As their brothers and sisters, we were not given a proper chance to grieve these four brave men. Today we will," Bill Haywood pronounced.

Haywood's loud voice early in the morning attracted local residents and visitors. People lined up, talked quietly, and watched. Informal parades by the IWW were common. Usually, they had political slogans on banners. However, this was different. This was a funeral procession of four horse-drawn carriages carrying coffins without the religious paraphernalia. This was something no one had seen before. A wave of expectation ran through the crowd that the procession would not make it to the end of Main Street. Curiosity was at its peak.

Seizing the moment, Bill shouted, "These four men were not given separate funerals. Their families were not allowed to attend their burials. Oliver Mining buried them without any family members present." Bill paused, cleared his throat, and continued, "I am here today to tell you those four were murdered. Their heads were blown off by hired thugs using shotguns!"

Bill's statements sparked a variety of comments. Surprised and angry responses rippled among the watchers and bystanders. Rumors had circulated that the four miners had been murdered, but none of the newspapers had noted or even hinted at any explanation other than an accident. Even the *Tyomies* newspaper had been quiet. A few little bouts of pushing and shoving began. With this commotion, more people gathered and moved closer to the street, lining up on both sides.

Haywood stepped back to the procession and stood tall between the second and third horse-drawn coffin carriages. Gustav, Launo, and Niilo were standing at attention ahead of the first carriage. Each one held a flag: United States of America, State of Minnesota, and Communist Party. Between the first and second coffins and third and fourth were groups of four men dressed in black coats, hats, and ties. They did not wave or smile. Each looked straight ahead and not at the eyes of those watching from the sidewalks and store windows. After a short gap, a group of twenty-five women and children dressed in black were at the end of the procession, sobbing and crying. One older child was pulling a young baby in a wagon.

Bill explained the particulars of the first memorial activity. "After the band strikes up the funeral cadence, we will solemnly proceed four blocks to Fifth Avenue where the procession will stop. One by one, I will shout out the names of the murdered miners symbolized by the coffins. I will bow my head, place my right hand on my heart, and wait for the shotgun salute after each name. Eight shotguns will be used for the gun salute, two for each man. They are reminders of the shotguns that shattered each of these men's heads under orders from the Oliver Mining Company. Let's begin."

The People's Labor College marching band from Duluth led the procession. The blue uniforms with gold trim were striking. The band struck up the cadence. The procession headed toward Fifth Avenue.

The townspeople trusted the reality of the drama they were observing. They had no reason to disbelieve. The tribute to the miners had originally been scheduled for Sunday morning before the dedication service at Mesaba Park. At the last minute, Bill Haywood had changed the time. Instead of Sunday morning, the procession began about nine Saturday morning. That explained why more people were downtown milling about than usual.

Why was Joe late in meeting me? I was hoping to watch the procession with him.

"Sara!"

I turned and saw Joe walking my way.

"Joe," I replied.

Joe appeared a little agitated. He had sweat on his brow.

"Are you ready for the procession?" I asked. I reached out for his hand. He didn't notice. He was preoccupied.

"As I came up Fifth Avenue, I noticed people gathered at the livery and stopped to see what was going on. They were looking at a horse. Then I saw this man there. He had a mustache. He looked familiar."

I stretched out my hand. "I don't understand. Lots of men have mustaches. Look around."

"No. It's not the mustache that makes this man special. This is the man I told you about that Arvi and I met in the woods hunting last fall. He and his friend started the fight down at the machine sheds in Chisholm."

"Did his voice sound like you remembered?" I asked.

"No. There was a sheriff there...not McFarland. So I was nervous. And there were some other men armed with handguns. I wondered what they were doing there since the procession was downtown. I know people are here from out of town for the grand opening of Mesaba Park –"

I cut Joe off. "When Dad opened the store this morning, a sheriff and three men came in. They wanted some rope and a few other things. I didn't think much of it. I thought maybe they were from out of town and needed some camping supplies. Then Dad called me over and introduced me to the sheriff. He was from Duluth. He knows Jacque –"

Still following his own train of thought, Joe interrupted me. "There was a boy about ten with them. He had one of those hats, those fancy hats, the type that have a snap in front ..." He looked down the street, searching for the boy.

I wanted to get Joe's attention, but I knew that was difficult when he was wrapped up in an incident. I thought I would try to help him understand what he had just seen on Fifth Avenue. "I didn't see a boy at the store this morning, just –"

Joe didn't allow me to finish. He was still trying to figure out what he had observed. "The boy seemed intent on what the mustached guy was telling him, like he was being given directions. They were looking at the horse's hindquarters, like there was something wrong... No one else was paying attention. The rest of them were looking at the head and mane."

"Joe, after Dad introduced me to the men, Grandpa Mattai pulled me aside to the back of the store. He said all of the men were from Duluth. One of them was Thomas –"

Joe cut me off again. "That makes sense, Sara. That's why I didn't recognize any of them! I didn't think they were from around here. I'd never seen most of them before…except for that one guy, the guy with a mustache. He's the one Arvi and I met in the woods."

I leaned close to Joe's ear and whispered, "One of the men with the sheriff was Thomas Armstrong, Armstrong's cousin."

Joe drew away like a bolt of lightning had just shot through his body. "You mean the Armstrong that owns all Oliver Mining?"

"Yes," I confirmed. "Thomas has a mustache…"

I watched the phrase "…has a mustache," bounce around Joe's thoughts. I loved watching Joe's mind work. In less than a minute, I knew his brain would make the connections to see the bigger picture.

Suddenly, we seemed alone. Despite the commotion happening all around us, our focus was only on who Thomas was, what he did, and how he had used Joe and Arvi at the incident at the Bruce Mine shaft.

Joe frowned. The muscles around his mouth drew taut. "That's it, Sara. The mustached man at the livery was Thomas. He's the one we had met in the woods. The way he was talking to the boy and looking at him was the same way he talked with Arvi and me in the woods last fall… slow, steady, almost kind – but manipulative."

"Grandpa used those same words to describe Thomas."

Joe remembered Thomas's words in the woods. "'I hope we see you boys again. You are real nice kids, real nice kids.' That's what Thomas said to us. He called us nice kids because we had helped him do his nasty deed, not because he liked us."

"Grandpa said Thomas led the strike breakers in 1906. Thomas identified Grandpa as an organizer, blacklisted him, and got him fired." Sara hesitated and then added, "He got Unlucky fired, too, along with your father and uncle."

"When did Mattai –"

"Shhh! The band has stopped and so has the procession."

The funeral cadence stopped. In a booming voice, Haywood

announced, "We will now have a gun salute. I will shout out the name of each of the murdered miners one by one. After each name, I will bow my head, place my right hand on my heart, and wait for the shotgun salute."

With military-like readiness, two IWW men moved beside each coffin. They removed the red flags with sickles from the pine box coffins Niilo had crafted. They folded and handed the flags to the widows and fatherless children at the end of the procession. Then they opened the lids of the coffins. Each coffin contained two double-barrel twelve gauge loaded shotguns and shells. Each man took a shotgun, raised it to his shoulder, pointed it in the air, unclicked the safety, and waited for Haywood to call out the miners' names.

"Elder Metsa!"

Two shotguns fired simultaneously.

"Herman Bjorkland!"

Two more shotguns fired.

"Taisto Rantala!"

The third pair of shotguns fired simultaneously.

"Helmer Valamaki!"

The final two shotguns fired simultaneously. The memorial salute ended.

We watched as the IWW gun-salute team lowered their shotguns, cracked them open, and took out the spent shells. Bill Haywood walked over to each of the men and collected the shells into a cigar box. Then he walked to the end of the procession where the widows and their children were waiting.

After he had let each child take a shell from the box, he solemnly walked back to the center of the coffins and spoke to the crowd. "Please shout after me, Dignity for the Dead!"

The crowd responded, "Dignity for the Dead!"

Bill hugged each of the widows. After her hug, Fiina Metsa took her folded flag and placed it in her son's hands. Charles Metsa turned and gently tucked it under the head of his baby brother Marc who was cradled in his sister Sharon's arms. Marc's head lay on the yellow sickle. Charles then took his and his brother's empty shell in each hand, held them up in the air, and walked over to Haywood. Bill held his palm open and smiled at Charles. Charles laid the two shells into Bill's palm. Bill kissed each one, placed both in the breast pocket of his suit coat, and patted his heart.

Each of the other children walked over to the coffins and one-by-one handed an empty shell to the IWW member standing at attention in front of the coffin of the child's parent. With tears trickling down their cheeks, they walked back to their mothers who embraced them.

Hecklers screamed, "Cockamamie Communists! Bloody Bolsheviks! Stinky Finlanders! You should leave and go back where you came from! You are making fools of yourselves and us! No one was murdered!"

Bill Haywood did not respond. He waited until the hecklers subsided, and all was silent. Raising his voice, Haywood extended an invitation. "Thanks for honoring our fallen by participating in the gun salute. Please, stay with us if you believe." Bill paused and looked around at all those gathered. Then he continued, "We will walk four more blocks and then stop for a short time of silence. After that, we will turn and walk north to the graveyard. There we will grieve for our lost friends, spouses, leaders, and comrades. Please join us."

The People's Labor College marching band struck up a funeral cadence again and proceeded the final four blocks down Main Street. Niilo, his father Launo, and Gustav followed with the flags. Behind them towering over the three was Bill Haywood. Bill walked four slow deliberate steps, stopped, and bowed his head. He repeated this routine over and over. In single file, the four carriages carrying the coffins followed slowly behind.

One of the butchers from the market walked out, stood still, and bowed his head as the coffins rolled by. A young boy selling newspapers stopped barking until the group passed, and then he resumed his cry. After two blocks, everything had quieted downtown.

After four blocks, as the procession began to make the turn and head north to the graveyard, Robert McFarland and two deputies stepped into the street in front of the People's Labor College marching band. The band stopped.

I tugged at Joe's shirt. "Joe, what's McFarland doing? I thought Haywood and McFarland were friends. I have never seen the sheriff bother Haywood when he spoke at the theater. They always joked with each other."

"Yeah, well, my dad has questioned Sheriff McFarland's loyalties," Joe answered as he removed my hand from his shirt.

"McFarland wasn't in the store this morning with that sheriff from Duluth or Thomas, Joe," I replied.

Joe didn't say a word.

We watched as McFarland waited for Haywood to approach him. When he did, McFarland asked for a permit. Haywood responded, "You didn't investigate how Taisto, Helmer, Elder, and Herman died. Why are you interrupting our grieving for them?"

"They were buried a year ago," McFarland answered. "Everyone could grieve then."

"They weren't buried," Haywood sneered. "They were covered with dirt so no one would know how they died."

"What are you talking about?"

Suddenly, a young boy from the side of the street ran over to find out what was going on. Using his nightstick, McFarland blocked the boy. A woman from the area where the boy had run out yelled, "Don't you dare hit my nephew! Help! That officer hit my nephew! He's bleeding! He's bleeding! You damn son of a bitch! I'll scratch your eyes out!"

McFarland turned away from the boy and moved toward her.

Unexpectantly, a horse came galloping north on Fifth Avenue. A ten-year-old boy was running behind the old mare, hitting the mare with a switch. A large dog was right behind him, barking. The horse caught its hoof in a manhole cover, stumbled to the ground, and tipped the third coffin over. When the coffin crashed against the street, a box of shells exploded. Startled, the horse tried to stand up and fell again. She screamed in pain. The two men closest to the mare grabbed her halter. Avoiding her flailing hooves, they managed to help her stand up. The other horses started to whinny and snort. Gustav, Launo, and Niilo steadied them.

The mare looked around in response. The dog barked at her, and they both ran off down the street with the boy in hot pursuit.

Bill directed the women and children toward the sidewalk and formed them into a tight group. Then he ordered the IWW gun salute men to form a line in front of them.

He walked over to the sheriff and stood beside him. McFarland commanded, "Haywood, get your men and coffins off the street and head back to where you are staying. I'm going to clear the whole Main Street and call off the parade."

"What will you do if we continue?" Haywood sneered.

"Just south of us on Fifth Avenue is a militia of thirteen armed men led by Duluth Sheriff Murphy. They are authorized by the governor to arrest you and take you to jail," McFarland replied.

"They'll take me, anyway," responded Haywood. "In fact, they probably had my arrest planned even if the procession hadn't been disrupted. And later they will probably be waiting in the woods to shoot me in the back when I ride down the road to Mesaba Park's dedication."

"Mr. Haywood, I have no time to talk. I'm stopping your parade and sending everyone home."

McFarland raised the megaphone and ordered the crowd to disperse. His deputies waded into the crowd and helped the older folk and children. They cleared the immediate block of all parade watchers and those in the procession.

As the crowd scattered, Thomas was revealed. He stood alone, scowling. He gestured to McFarland to come over, and McFarland complied.

Thomas stepped so close to McFarland that their noses seemed to be touching. "You messed up again, McFarland ... letting the horse get away. Hell, how was I supposed to create any commotion during that scene so Haywood could be shot?"

"Where did the horse come from, Thomas? A horse wasn't in the original plan. But what do you care of plans? You do whatever the hell you want… If Armstrong wasn't your cousin, I'd kill you right now! I wouldn't care who saw! In fact I'd invite everyone to join me!" McFarland turned and walked away from Thomas. Suddenly, he stopped, spun around, and asked, "Where's Murphy? Still down on Fifth? Or did you make another decision there, too, to suit your insanity?"

"Why the hell would I have Murphy and the rest positioned there?" Thomas answered. "I knew you would mess up. I sent him and the men to set up the ambush along County Road 37… Hopefully they'll get a shot at Haywood as he drives over to Mesaba Park. I'm headed over there next. First, I wanted to tell you that you screwed up again. You can't get anything right!"

"Consider it done. Now get your ass out of here! I hope you can find your way through the woods without me, you bastard."

Haywood had planned all along to head to Milwaukee the evening before the dedication. He intended to use the bodies, which were already in Milwaukee, in a parade there mid-week. To provide a cover for the Wisconsin demonstration, the IWW had started rumors indicating he would be at Mesaba Park on Sunday. He thought he could get out of town without being arrested if he left Saturday night rather than after the grand opening dedication on Sunday.

Joe pointed to McFarland and Thomas. "Look, Sara, there's the mustached man. That's him! That is Thomas. He used that boy like he had used Arvi and me… I wonder if that boy got paid a dollar to chase the horse into the procession."

Joe was fixated on Thomas, but I was overwhelmed with everything. Watching the procession and the ruckus was breathtaking. I didn't know if I had heard everything, but what I did hear and see was more than I had ever thought could happen. I didn't feel excited like when I watched my mother sing or the night Ian and I sneaked over to the Lyric Theater. This was an eerie feeling. I also felt happy. I was proud of Joe's dad, uncle, and cousin. Watching them march while holding the flags felt courageous to me, not in a patriotic way but in a righteous way. I wanted to let him know that down deep his family made me feel good, the same type of feeling I had when I listened to my mother sing.

I wanted to help Joe and thought to distract him. "What did you think of your father and uncle and cousin with Haywood and the procession?"

Joe persisted, "Thomas used that boy. That boy had no idea there was a funeral procession. He thought he was just chasing a horse down the street for a dollar. Just like Arvi and I didn't realize we were checking to see if the miners were dead and underground. We thought we were looking for guys who were lost from a hunting party…for a dollar."

"Joe. Things happen."

"Sara, things don't just happen. I didn't just happen to get drunk and arrested homecoming night. Your grandfather and Unlucky didn't just happen to lose their jobs. Oliver Mining didn't just build us a new school out of goodwill. Those four miners didn't just have an accident."

"Joe –"

"I never wanted to think like my father. I never wanted to believe that people with more money and power will plan and think of ways to use people like us for their gain, not our gain. I'd like to think life is like the forest. The forest has no planning or strategies …"

I had never seen Joe this agitated before. In fact, I had never seen anyone as agitated as Joe was at that moment. My armpits were wet. I was worried. Bits and pieces of the stories Joe had been told by his father and uncle, what we had seen today, and the little Grandpa Mattai had told me rushed through my mind. I had a feeling of foreboding.

"Damn!" Joe yelled. "Damn!" I saw frenzy cloud Joe's face. He began talking faster. "I'm getting sick of everyone using everyone… And I am sick of Thomas…" Joe turned and looked down the avenue from where the horse had come. His face tightened. "He probably blew the heads off those four miners!"

Someone brushed against me, and I stumbled. When I regained my balance, I didn't see Joe. I was in the midst of townspeople leaving the procession.

Fear overwhelmed me. I pushed past two people near me, struggling to get a glimpse of Joe. I caught sight of his shirt briefly and then got stuck behind three more people. They didn't budge. Desperate, I hopped up and down to see better. Joe was not too far ahead of me; I could still reach him. I found an opening and dashed around those people blocking me, frantic to reach Joe and calm him down. "Joe! Joe!" I screamed.

I didn't see Joe anywhere.

31   Woods Murder

I was still mad. I had never conceived of a person as deceitful as Thomas. My chest tightened at the thought of having been used by him a year earlier. Feelings of betrayal mixed with my anger. I hoped a walk along County Road 37 through the woods to Mesaba Park would distract me.

On my way, I stopped at home and picked up my shotgun, thinking to hunt some grouse. Even with my shotgun in hand, I was so absorbed in my anger I forgot to look for grouse. I kicked the rotted stump of a birch tree and watched it crumble. Then I swung the stock of my shotgun and knocked off more of the dead wood. Rotted birch trees were orange on the inside. Often large black carpenter ants gathered around the punky orange section to feast. I swatted a group swarming the trunk, and they flew into the high grass. As I watched them scatter, I heard voices. Looking up, I saw a group of about thirteen men ahead of me walk briskly from the county road a short distance into the woods. Their voices were loud, and they didn't seem alert to their surroundings. They definitely weren't hunting. They startled a covey of five to seven grouse into flight and didn't seem to notice. They just kept moving.

A few of them broke away and started to run. I saw what looked like a wolf running ahead of them. The wolf didn't seem scrawny enough to be wild. As I watched it run, the colors appeared to be more like a long-haired German shepherd, almost like Kaveri. Were they following it? *Didn't they know the difference between a German shepherd and a wolf,* I wondered. I tried to identify someone in the group, but no one looked familiar.

In order to get a closer look, I decided to take a path at a forty-five degree angle toward them. After checking my gun's safety, I jogged. The man who was leading the main group waved his group forward without him. After leaning his shotgun on a nearby maple tree, he stopped to urinate. I turned sharply to my left and approached him. He looked familiar. I moved closer just as he zipped up his fly. He lifted his head, and we locked eyes. It was Thomas. He was wearing the same clothes he had worn at the livery that morning. His words resonated in my brain, "I hope we see you boys again; you are real nice kids, real nice kids."

"Hey!" I shouted.

"Who are you, boy?"

"One of the real nice kids, real nice kids."

"What are you talking about?"

"Remember the dollar you gave me and my friend?"

"Dollar?"

"I didn't think you would remember, but I do. Did that boy this morning get a dollar, too?"

"What the hell are you talking about, boy?"

"Is that what you pay nice kids who do your dirty work? Remember grouse hunting at the Bruce Mine shaft last fall?"

"I don't know what you mean. I don't hunt grouse. Never will."

"I am one of those boys you hired as spies so you could know those miners were dead!"

Without flinching, Thomas denied my accusation. "I don't know what you mean, kid."

His use of the word "kid" threw more wood crates and boxes on the bonfire raging inside me.

"You'll never know what I mean."

I clicked the safety off on my shotgun.

"Put your safety on. You don't know who you're dealing with, idiot."

Either he couldn't remember the incident, or he was lying right to my face. Both stirred an anger I hadn't felt before. Hate and betrayal swirled together into a tornado of intense feeling.

I looked at Thomas and felt taken over by a powerful realization. A bonfire had ignited in my soul, and its raging flames quickly grew out of control. The effigy of capitalism sitting atop the bonfire exploded in flames, and deep waves of anger swirled inside of me. Thomas became a representation of all that was wrong in my life: my family's struggling for survival, the school's being loyal to the mine companies, the community's picking on the Finnish, and those with power and money manipulating all of us.

I spoke louder than I had addressed anyone in my life. "I probably don't."

I lifted the shotgun and pointed the barrel into Thomas's face.

Thomas rejected the action. "Damn it! Put down that gun, you stupid Finlander!"

"So you remember who I am…

"What are you talking about? I mean you smell and stink like a stupid Finlander!"

"Is that what your friends said to Valamaki, Bjorkland, Rantala, and Helmer before they blew chunks of their heads off? 'You stupid Finlander! You stink and smell!'"

Thomas stood defiant. He showed no indication of fear.

"That's right; you wouldn't have known their names. They were just Finlanders to you."

"What is your name, boy?"

"Finlander."

"Finlander? Is that a joke?"

"No. A smelly, stinking Finlander is who I am."

"Then, damn it, put that gun down, you stinky, smelly Finlander."

"It's Mr. Finlander, sir.

"Don't get smart with me, Mr. Pinhead Finlander."

"Pinhead? Or did you mean pisshead? Would you like to leave a chunk of your skull on the forest floor to match the ones in the mine shaft?"

"I told you, Finlander boy, to put that gun down!"

"Or what?"

"This is the last time I'm telling you, you red devil!"

"Or what?"

"Or I will kick you in your damn nuts, Finlander. Then when you fall to the ground clutching your crotch, I will stomp out any brains you have in that smart ass head of yours. After that I will use my bare hands to scoop them up and smear them all over those white birches behind where you are standing."

"So the white birches become red birches?"

"Yes, you're right, damn red birches. Commie trees!"

While the fury swirled and I held my shotgun to Thomas's head, I heard someone shouting, "Thomas! Thomas! Where are you?"

I pulled back the trigger on each barrel of the shotgun, one by one, click, click. They locked into place, click, click. I steadied the barrels at Thomas's head. He realized I was dangerous. He commanded, "You won't get away with this! The people I am with will hear the shots and come running over here. They will kill you before you can reload."

Despite my angry adrenalin rush, I kept the gun steady. "Should we find out how fast they can get here, Thomas? Should we time how long it takes me to reload? Oh, but you won't know how long that is 'cause you'll be dead."

"You bastard! You dumb son of a bitch! You'll never get away with this."

"Get on your knees, Thomas Armstrong."

"You get on your knees, Finlander!"

"Remember, I have the gun. You get on your knees, Thomas. This is the last time I'll ask you."

Glaring at me, Thomas knelt. I felt the bonfire inside me cool. I was able to focus on him and thought a few words were in order.

"Now it is my turn, Mr. Thomas. My father lost his job at Oliver Mining because he wanted to be like you. He wanted to have a job that would not take more than he gave. Metsa, Valamaki, Bjorkland, and Rantala wanted to live long enough to raise their children, maybe see their grandchildren. They hoped to work long enough and organize hard enough to bring about shorter hours and safer conditions… just in case their children would be working in the mine someday.

"Maybe you don't remember who those four men were in the cable car gondola, but in a minute you will be meeting them. Make sure you apologize to all four and ask for their forgiveness."

Pow! A shotgun blasted. The left side of Thomas's head shattered, splattering blood, bone, and brains all over my clothes.

"What the …!"

"Joe! Get the hell out of here! Nobody needs to see you here with us."

"McFarland! Did you just shoot him?"

"Run, Joe! You don't have much time… Just get out of here… run as fast as you can!"

I heeded McFarland's command and started running through the woods. I didn't know where I was going. I kept thinking the county road can't be that far away. I'd have to cross it soon. Thoughts ran through my head, *How did this happen! Why did he say 'us'? I only had seen McFarland.*

My elbow hit a tree, and my shotgun flew out of my hand. The safety was off, and the triggers were cocked. When the gun's stock hit the ground, the impact caused both barrels to fire. Two loud blasts pierced the air. Careening away from me, the gun slammed into a large birch. I kept running.

Seeing the county road ahead of me, I jumped face down into the ditch alongside the road. The stagnant rain water felt cold… It stank… and tasted like swamp slue. My heart pounded louder than my thoughts. My lungs gasped for air. I tried to catch deep breaths and calm my mind … Robert McFarland – What the hell was going on? Stagnant green water soaked into my shirt and pants. I lay there. Resting my head on my arms, I hoped to cool down.

I imagined myself in the woods sitting against a huge pine with sap smells in the air. Some were sweet, some perfume-ish. Warm sun relaxed my feet; shade cooled my head. I suppose I didn't need to know more. Some things don't have to be connected. Conspiracies don't have to be everywhere and in everything.

"Joe, keep your head down and don't move."

I felt a boot's sole slowly press down on the middle of my back. I moved my right arm forward so I could push up and see who it was. The voice was soft and low. It spoke again. "Joe, don't move."

The boot gave a little harder push down to my back. "Stay in the ditch and don't move until you hear someone say your first and last name."

I moved my arm back to my side. The pressure left my back. I wanted to look, but, after everything that had happened, I thought it would be smart to lie and wait. The voice seemed trustworthy, soothing. The person's voice was so soft that I couldn't figure out whose voice it was. After about an hour had passed, I heard the voice again. "Joseph Koivu, you can get out now."

I crawled to my knees and pushed myself up. There was Dad.

"There's no time for questions, Joe. Follow me and pretend nothing's wrong."

Pretend nothing's wrong? I think I just witnessed Sheriff McFarland kill Thomas. I am completely soaked with green slue. Now I am supposed to walk casually and pretend nothing's wrong. I'm beginning to think nothing was ever right.

Dad had Rudolph saddled. He pointed to the saddle. I hopped up on Rudolph, and Dad slapped the horse's flank three times quickly. That was the signal he used on Rudolph at the end of the day when he wanted Rudolph to head home.

As Rudolph trotted toward home, I looked back at the ditch. I saw Dad, McFarland, Launo, and Niilo huddled. McFarland looked like he was giving directions or explaining something. By the way his was using his hands, I thought the words he was using were important. Nobody even questioned what McFarland was saying. Unlucky Andy pulled up in his truck. They all jumped on the back and hung their feet over the edge of the truck bed. The truck headed toward Hibbing.

When I got home, Mattai was there with Kaveri. Both were at the kitchen table. Kaveri was panting. I didn't hear my brother or sister making noises or playing, and Mom wasn't anywhere.

With a sparkle deep in his eyes, Mattai greeted me, "Hey, Joe."

"What are you doing here, Mattai?"

"Your dad asked me to stop by."

"Where are Hannah and Tommy and Mom?"

"They are still at the co-op, Joseph."

"The co-op? They're still in town?"

"Sara was pretty shook up when you disappeared after the procession ended on Main Street. She came over to the co-op sobbing. She was worried about you."

"She knew I was going to go grouse hunting. Besides Thomas is –"

Mattai interrupted me. "Listen to me, Joseph. You were angry, very angry at the procession. She told me how upset you were ….with Thomas. I trusted Sara's judgment."

"Thomas is dead … Mattai. ..What the hell was that all about in the woods? Shit!" I was still standing. I wanted to kick something.

"I know what happened in the woods. I am here to tell you more," Mattai said in a firm voice.

His response slowed me for a moment. I looked at Mattai and then glanced down at Kaveri. Kaveri's message container that hung around his neck was pulled apart. Crumpled in Mattai's right hand was some paper.

Sara had told me stories about how Mattai had used the dog to pass messages to her parents before Mattai and her grandmother came to live with her family. He had also sent messages via Kaveri to his friends when they were at the park. Now that Mattai and Grace were living with the Niemis above the co-op, I thought those games were over.

I looked at Mattai again. All his white hair, the scholar-like glasses… I took a deep breath, pulled a kitchen chair over, and sat down next to Kaveri. As I reached to pet him, I accidentally knocked the makeshift shotgun shell message holder to the ground. I picked it up and smelled the inside. No spent gun powder… There shouldn't have been ….

I was still shaking from the shooting. Blood from Thomas and green ditch slime clung to me. My head was spinning. Mattai leaned over and placed his hand on my leg, which felt comforting. The crumpled paper in his hand fell to the kitchen floor. The handwriting on the paper looked like Martin's.

"No sooner had Sara come over to me upset and crying than McFarland came over cussing up a blue streak, upset over how Thomas had broken up Haywood's procession. He wanted to shoot Thomas right then and there."

"Why did he wait?"

Mattai squeezed my knee. "I asked Andy to get your dad, uncle, and Niilo. When they reached the co-op, Sara told them how angry you were and how you connected Thomas to Armstrong and Oliver Mining."

I interrupted Mattai, "Niilo knew I was going to go grouse hunting 'cause I asked him to come with me after Arvi said he couldn't go."

"Niilo told us that. What you didn't know was that Thomas, Sheriff Murphy, and the rest of the crew were in the woods following the county road to the park. We were worried what might happen if you and that group accidently ran into each other."

"Well we did. Damn. My head hurts. What were all of them doing in the woods along the county road?"

"They were waiting for Haywood to drive by so they could murder him."

Thomas and his men were going to murder Haywood? What is going on here? I groaned. Now my heart hurt.

Mattai continued, "We decided the guys better track you down before you ran into the assassination attempt. With your house being so close to where they were planning to murder Haywood, Gustav had the rest of your family wait at the co-op with Sara and Elizabeth."

"Didn't they know Haywood had taken the train to Milwaukee?"

"They didn't even know Haywood was going to have the procession this morning until they stopped by the co-op to buy some supplies. They were on their way to set up ambushes for Haywood for tomorrow morning."

I trusted what Mattai was telling me was true, but it smacked of too many conspiracies for me.

"Andy drove the five of us and Kaveri as fast as he could. He dropped McFarland off first. Then he took a back trail here to drop the rest of us off. Gustav had me stay here to wait for you. He grabbed Rudolph and headed through the woods along with your uncle and Niilo to look for you. Andy stayed with his truck and drove around trying to spot you from the road and trails."

Now my manic mind began to think of the combinations and possibilities of those people being in the woods at the same time, all with different missions.

"I wanted Martin to be aware of what was happening. If Sheriff Murphy and any of those men showed up at the park and you hadn't been found yet, I wanted Martin to delay them. That's why I have Kaveri with me."

"So that was Kaveri I saw running through the woods!"

Mattai chuckled.

"Kaveri the wolf," I whispered softly as I scratched Kaveri behind his ear. We both smiled at Kaveri for a moment.

"Fortunately, McFarland did locate you and Thomas. Thinking something might happen between the two of you, he did what he did."

"So he was trying to protect me?"

Mattai didn't say anything right away. And I didn't feel like talking or thinking anymore. We sat in silence. I was certain Mattai heard the gears in my mind twirling away, unable to stop. I was dazed from the shooting and finding out Haywood could have been murdered, too. I was sure there were more things Mattai wanted to tell me.

Trying to pull myself together, I focused on being home. I smelled the smoke from the sauna stove. I heard Rudolf whinny outside. I thought I heard a few grouse drumming. I smelled Kaveri's dampness. I looked at the empty kitchen table and then outside into the yard and the woods. I wondered if the forest would ever place its arms around me and embrace me again in its green quilt.

32   Ambush

8 p.m. Saturday

McFarland looked up from cleaning his shotgun and saw Armstrong standing ominously in front of his desk. "Who shot Thomas?"

Caught off guard, McFarland carefully laid his gun down, buying some time for his reply. "Hello, Armstrong. You are in town early. I didn't expect you until morning."

Armstrong leaned over the desk. "Answer my question. Who shot Thomas?" he repeated with the same commanding tone.

McFarland locked eyes with Armstrong. "I don't know."

"You don't know?" Armstrong reiterated, his voice rising. "Why aren't you finding out instead of sitting here cleaning your gun?"

McFarland had to think quickly. "Well, I have my suspicions."

"What are they?"

"I think Thomas's ambush was part of a plan by Haywood."

Armstrong straightened. "Haywood! Really? His ability to sway a crowd has been a thorn in my side, but I never thought he had the balls to shoot someone."

"I didn't say that Haywood shot Thomas. I said it was part of his plan."

Armstrong stepped away from McFarland's desk, turned, and looked over at the jail cells. They were empty. "Then why isn't he in jail? Where is Haywood?"

"He's gone."

"Gone!? Where?"

"Near as I can figure, he left on the train today."

"I thought he came for the dedication."

"So did I. His leaving leads me to believe he got out of town before we could arrest him for Thomas's murder." McFarland glanced away, acting nervous.

Accustomed to watching small changes in people's body language, Armstrong picked up on McFarland's nervous tension. "There's more. What?"

Slowly, McFarland met Armstrong's glare. "I wonder what else is part of Haywood's plan."

"Such as?"

"Such as snipers strategically-placed to ambush your party."

Suddenly, Armstrong's anger changed to fear. He sat down on a hard chair and drew a deep breath. "How many snipers? Where will they be?"

"I don't know. I am just concerned about it. After they've successfully killed Thomas, they may be bold enough to attack you and your party, too. Perhaps at the dedication when you are up on the platform … a public execution… I'm not sure."

"How are you going to protect me?"

"That's what I was thinking about when you walked in."

Armstrong's managerial instincts took over. "I'm not taking the risk of attending the dedication. Without Haywood around, our presence doesn't matter anyway. We'll return to Duluth."

"What about the men you brought with you?"

"I'll post them around our hotel rooms tonight. I'll take most of them back with us in the morning as a protective detail to watch for an ambush. You can keep a few to disrupt the celebration. I'll have them report to you in the morning."

Without further comment, Armstrong got up and walked out of McFarland's office.

McFarland let out a long breath. That was close. He had not figured out an explanation for Thomas's death when Armstrong walked in. He was relieved the idea of blaming Haywood had popped into his mind. That answered who had killed Thomas and planted fear in Armstrong, prompting him not to attend the dedication. McFarland smiled. Both problems were solved by the specter of Haywood.

Gustav and Martin had been right. Armstrong's not even mentioning the award ceremony indicated McFarland's status with Oliver Mining. He wasn't important to anyone in the Oliver offices in Duluth or the governor's office in St Paul. Shit! More than ever, McFarland was convinced the mine owners were only interested in the amount of ore they could get out of the ground and down to the boats in Duluth. All the politicians cared about were their public faces.

4:30 a.m. Sunday

McFarland was awakened by a pounding on the front door.

Next to him in bed, Marian woke up. "Who is that?" she mumbled, half-asleep.

"No one I'm expecting," McFarland responded. "I'll check. Go back to sleep."

He pulled on a shirt and pants and thrust his bare feet into a pair of shoes. Then he reached into the stand by the bed, slipped out a handgun, and stuffed a handful of bullets into his shirt pocket.

As he stepped out of the bedroom, McFarland noticed his son standing down the hall. With quick strides, McFarland approached his son. "Go back in your room, close the door, and don't come out," McFarland commanded. "I don't know what this is about. Stay in your room."

Robert Jr. turned and followed his dad's orders.

The pounding on the door continued. McFarland hugged the wall, descending the stairs without turning on a light. At the bottom of the stairs, he noiselessly walked through the kitchen and out the back door. He continued his quiet progression outside around the house to the front. Loading two bullets into his handgun, he walked up behind the pounding guy. "What do you want?"

The guy stopped pounding, turned, and noticed the gun pointed at him. McFarland clicked off the safety. "What is so important that you are pounding on my door, waking my family and the neighbors at this hour?"

"Mr. Armstrong sent me to get you. He wants to talk with you."

"I'll see him before he leaves this morning," McFarland growled.

"He's leaving as soon as he talks to you. He wants to get out of town while it's still dark. He wants to see you right now."

Realizing that a summons from Armstrong was not to be ignored, McFarland got into the guy's car and was escorted to Armstrong's hotel room. Armstrong was impatiently waiting for McFarland. Armstrong launched into his directive without greeting. "I want those Finns intimidated. Send them a message that nobody gets away with killing my men. Let them know that the entire Finnish community will suffer the consequences for such an action. I don't want any more ambushes or threats of them.

"I'm getting out of town before daybreak. I am leaving six men to help you today. Johnson, Murphy's deputy from Duluth, will be reporting back to me on today's events. Thomas never trusted you. I don't necessarily share his view, but our plans have been disrupted. I want backup to assure that our plans are carried out. Johnson is here to make certain events go as planned." Armstrong made his last statement slowly and threateningly. "I expect a spectacle at the park. Do you understand McFarland? A spectacle... one I'll read about in the newspapers on Monday."

Without giving McFarland a chance to respond, Armstrong walked out of the room, heading to his waiting sedan and leaving McFarland alone. McFarland bristled at Armstrong's treatment of him as a Finlander instead of a valued member of Armstrong's entourage. He realized now was not the time to express his anger. He was treading a fine line between Armstrong and the miners. He had to create intimidation without hurting anyone, and the tactics had to look good to Johnson.

7 a.m. Sunday

The six men, Murphy's Deputy Johnson, and the extra men McFarland had deputized waited by the bridge over the Esquagama River on Highway 37 within a mile of Mesaba Park.

"I heard Thomas was ambushed in the woods yesterday afternoon," said one of the six.

"That's right," replied Johnson.

"What happened?"

"Thomas and McFarland were guiding the men from the governor's citizens' committee militia with Sheriff Murphy along 37 to Mesaba Park, watching for Haywood. Someone in the group saw a wolf. A few of the men got excited and started to chase the animal. I wasn't with them. I was in Thomas's group. He waved us ahead and stopped to relieve himself. McFarland hung back and waited nearby to make sure Thomas could find us.

"We heard a shotgun blast. The wolf chasers thought the animal they were chasing was shot. They cheered. When they realized the shot came from behind them, they ran back to the rest of us to find out what had happened. Then we heard two more shots. McFarland started yelling. When we found the sheriff, he was standing near Thomas whose head was shattered, bleeding all over...

"We saw a farmer driving by in a truck and stopped him. McFarland asked the fella if he knew where the railroad crossing was for the p.m. passenger train. He said yes. McFarland told the guy that we needed him to help us get Thomas's body to the train. We loaded it on the truck and went to the crossing where McFarland flagged down the train.

"McFarland said Thomas was hauled down to the big city. He was in Duluth last night for medical care."

"I heard he didn't make it," another inserted.

"That's why we are all here instead of at the park. We're supposed to wait here for Sheriff McFarland. He'll let us know what to do."

Like the hands of children grabbing penny candy in a store, the follow-up comments were quick.

"Who shot Thomas?"

"Damn. I never liked coming up here to mining country."

"No one knows."

"It's like the Wild West here – no rules."

"That's right. Anything can happen. And does."

The deputy from Duluth added, "When McFarland went back and found Thomas, no one else was there. Thomas's shotgun was lying on the ground nearby. He grabbed it and began looking around for evidence. He found another shotgun not too far from Thomas. Both shells had been recently fired. McFarland said the gun powder smell was fresh. He thought it was the gun that was used on Thomas. McFarland said he –"

One of McFarland's men interrupted. "I'll tell yeah, if anybody can find the murderer, McFarland can. I have known him for years. He's the best. He knows the woods back here and all the trails."

The deputy continued, "Apparently, McFarland caught sight of a Finnish guy running fast through the brush back by the swamp. The sheriff shot at him, but the Commie was out of range. That's all we know right now. We have to focus on our raid on the Mesaba Park dedication. Let's wait for direction. Take some time for a smoke, stretch, and relax but don't go far. Be within the sound of my voice."

9:00 a.m. Sunday

Stephan Steblibovich appeared with four more men. "I am Sheriff McFarland's Lieutenant Deputy Stephan Steblibovich."

The men nodded recognition and whispered.

Stephan continued, "Haywood caught us off guard yesterday by holding the procession a day early. That's why some of you were in town instead of in the woods setting up what was going to be this morning's ambush. After the ruckus with the horse in town, Thomas had you head along County Road 37 toward Mesaba Park watching for Haywood to drive by. Then Thomas was shot."

Stephan paused before delivering the next news. "Haywood left yesterday and won't be at the park today."

"Haywood left yesterday? I thought we were to …"

Someone sneered, "The dedication should have been a funeral service for Haywood."

"No nasty comments," admonished Stephan.

"You still didn't answer my question. What about Haywood?"

"Haywood won't be at the park today. We also have learned there will be more people than expected at the church service. We had intended to create a distraction as a cover for Haywood's assassination. Now –" Stephan stopped when he saw McFarland heading toward them.

Everyone turned to watch McFarland approaching. He moved slowly, wiping his forehead as he walked. When he reached the group, he looked around at each man. "Morning."

The group murmured soft greetings in response.

McFarland cleared his throat. "I'm sorry to report Thomas was pronounced dead when he arrived at the Duluth hospital yesterday. Because of his ambush, I am concerned the IWW may try to take down another steel person or town official at the dedication today. For that reason, Mr. Armstrong and his party returned to Duluth early this morning."

"Sorry about Thomas," Stephan said.

Others mumbled their surprise and condolences. The sheriff waited for the murmuring to stop. "The award ceremony scheduled for noon has been cancelled. However, our raid continues. We are going to disrupt this morning's dedication ceremony. We will let them know ambushes are not tolerated."

He paused and let his comment ripple among the men.

"We are breaking into two groups," McFarland instructed. "Stephan will take the larger group. You will take time to search the cars. Look for any evidence of IWW activities: guns, explosives, anything that we can tie to illegal activity for arrests. This sweep should take about thirty minutes. At the end of your search, fire eight to shots into the air. My group will be inside the hall. Your shots will be the signal for us to wrap up what we are doing and head outside.

"Both of our groups will meet outside and walk out of the park together. On the way out, Stephan will direct some of you to shoot out tires on certain cars as we head across the festival grounds and through the woods. A truck will be parked by the river's bridge on Highway 37. Those of you going back to Duluth will get in the back of the truck. The driver will take you to the Hibbing rail station where you will catch the train back to Duluth."

No one had questions. Preliminary checks were made on the shotguns. Some of the men hid ammunition and a few handguns in holsters running through their belts. McFarland and Stephan split the men into two groups. All of them headed through the woods toward Mesaba Park.

33 Dedication Disruption

Members of Viola Turpeinen's band played songs as people waited inside and outside the hall. When they started *Les Internationalle*, Reverend Karl walked up to the front stage. The band orchestrated a quick closing. He began, "Thank you for attending this Sunday morning's dedication of Mesaba Park. I am Reverend Karl Levanieman. I am a Finnish immigrant first, a Lutheran pastor second, and always a believer in this beautiful park and its mission to serve the solidarity of the miners and lumbermen of this area."

Reverend Karl bowed his head toward the crowd. He continued, "I realize many of you do not go to church and some of you are antagonistic to Christianity,

"Die Religion ... ist das Opium des Volke. (Religion is the opiate of the masses.)

"Mutta olen teidat kaikki tervetulleiksi! (But, I welcome all of you!)"

The audience gave a warm applause for the humor. Sitting next to my dad Martin, I grinned at their response.

Reverend Karl Levanieman looked at the gathering and smiled. The hall seemed to be a great place for a service. I could see the trees outside. From some parts of the hall, the lake was visible. With all the windows propped open, I felt the breeze from the lake. Hitchhiking on the lake air were smells of the camp kitchen's morning fare: fried potatoes, bacon, grilled sausage, coffee, eggs, and fresh bread. At his Lutheran church, Karl always made sure the doors to the church's basement were closed during the service. Otherwise, the smell of lunch from its kitchen wafted through the congregation and caused cognitive disorientations to those listening to his sermons.

The crowd was larger than expected. The size was due to the award ceremony for Sheriff McFarland that was scheduled to follow Uncle Karl's dedication sermon and ceremony. The cancellation of the ceremony had not yet been announced. Reverend Karl had been told Sheriff McFarland would interrupt the dedication service around 11:30 a.m. Karl's sermon was to be just about complete before the sheriff stopped him.

Trusting rapport had been established, Reverend Karl continued, "The Finnish are neither the first nor the last group to be oppressed. In fact, history is full of stories of one nation oppressing another nation. The Bible has those stories, too. The Bible tells us about the oppression of one particular group of people, the Jewish race.

"I will begin with my first portion of scripture for today. It is found in Exodus 3: 1-10. I believe you remember this story.

"Moses was amazed because the bush was engulfed in flames, but it didn't burn up. God called to him from the bush, 'Moses, Moses!'

"'Here I am,' Moses answered.

"'Do not come any closer. Take off your sandals, for you are on holy ground,' God commanded.

"Let us reflect on what the words 'Holy Ground' may mean.

"Was the dirt under Moses's sandals more holy than other dirt in the area?

"Was the ground where the bush grew more fertile than the ground you and I walk on every day? Or the earth we farm?

"How about the earth out of which we dig the iron ore?

"Can dirt from the Holy Lands be more holy than the dirt here in Mesaba Park or in Finland?

"Isn't dirt, dirt?

"I am going to guess we all agree dirt is dirt. So why does this passage call the dirt around the burning bush 'holy'?

"I believe what made the ground holy in this story was that God talked with Moses there. Their conversation made that spot of earth special or holy.

"If Moses had been in a boat and talked with God, underneath the boat would have been Holy Water. That is a joke for any of our Eastern European brothers and sisters who are Catholic and here with us this morning." Karl smiled and paused again for a few more chuckles.

He didn't get many, but I sensed the crowd was relaxed and ready to hear my uncle's main point.

Karl continued, "This particular conversation resulted in Moses's ability to believe the Jewish people would no longer be dominated by another nation. They would finally have a country of their own, a place to call their own.

"Moses's conversation with God created Holy Ground. On that Holy Ground we find the hope we need for the times we live in here and around Mesaba Park. Many of us feel the domination of Oliver Mining and have had our lives changed by the company. We want safer working conditions. We have led and participated in strikes and want to be paid with money we can use in our co-ops rather than those puppet stores of Oliver Mining.

"I believe our struggles here on the Iron Range can be described as God described the Jewish people in Exodus. The Bible says God was sad because he had '... seen the misery... heard their cries ... I am aware of their suffering... I have come to rescue them ...'

"Moses saw how the Egyptians used his kinfolk to build huge buildings and pyramids for their leaders and kings. We have all seen the houses the steel owners and Armstrong live in because our labor.

"Moses felt the despair of his people because they were pushed around by the ruling Egyptian class. Do I need to remind you of the many ways this has happened to us? We had to move our homes so Oliver Mining could dig more ore.

"Moses detested the monuments the Jews built for the Pharaohs, the monuments Jewish families would never enjoy or inhabit. How many houses could have been built with the money that was used to build our beautiful high school?"

My family didn't go to church, so I didn't get to see Uncle Karl preach, but if church was like Uncle Karl's delivery that day, I wanted to go. I thought religion was about God and being good so we could go to heaven after we died. Heaven was like ice cream for dessert; you had to wait for it. And you couldn't have the ice cream if you didn't clean your plate. My uncle's message sounded like there was help in this life. Elaine said her rabbi didn't talk about life after death. He directed the congregation to make this life a better one. If that was what God was about, then my family was religious. My mother sang to people, and they felt good. Sometimes they fell in love. My dad ran the Work People's Co-op Store so people could make their lives easier and have things they needed.

Joe drew his strength from the story of King Arthur's roundtable. In Arthurian legend, every knight sat around a roundtable with no throne or special chair for the king. All were equal comrades. Every knight was equal to the knight at his left and right. King Richard the Lion-Hearted even sat with the knights at a roundtable.

The flour we used in the camp kitchen, King Arthur Flour, supported Joe's roundtable idea. King Arthur Flour was America's oldest flour company, founded in Boston in 1790. When I grabbed a sack of flour, I thought of the roundtable and how it was a form of socialism, a red flour company. Two other red items we had in the kitchen were Red Star Yeast and Red Star Coffee.

Joseph believed this medieval idea fit better with defining Holy Ground. Joe saw us as brothers and sisters striving together. We all focused on rightness. We all had to set strategies to achieve our ideals of social equality. There was nothing magical about living. Nobody was going to come and rescue us, not even God. Each of us had to determine to live without the help of burning-bush experiences. Life was the process of making decisions to do what we believed was right.

I believed elements other than choice were at play as we lived our lives. My life was a result of more than my decisions. Our lives were interconnected in ways we didn't see or understand.

Uncle Karl continued, "Let's take a lesson from this Bible story this morning. When we feel the capitalists are taking everything we have or when we are denied the right to work, we need to remember there will be deliverance. We will have deliverance from wickedness. Mark my words. There will be a time when we will be allowed to organize. There will be a time when we will form unions.

"I pray for all of you here today and all those who will come to Mesaba Park in the future that we will all have the chance to hear the voice of the burning bush saying to each of us that we are on Holy Ground in this beautiful Mesaba Park and Campground. I also pray everyone who comes here will hear the voice of the burning bush calling them to build relationships in communities with like-minded people.

"In our community here at Mesaba Park, I pray this Holy Ground will heighten the significance of our relationships, despite the extreme material wealth of those who oppress us and their unwillingness to share the profit they have gained because of our labor.

"I declare the grand opening of Mesaba Park as a co-operative endeavor by brothers and sisters joined together on our Holy Ground!"

Applause started in the front and swept like a wave to the back of the hall. My uncle seemed surprised. People didn't applaud in church. He looked around. He bowed. There was more applause. He bowed a second time. When he raised his head from his second bow, he noticed heads had slowly turned away. They were looking toward the back. In front of the main entrance to the pavilion a short line of several men stood with Sheriff McFarland. At McFarland's signal, the men fanned out, half down each of the outside aisles.

My uncle straightened up. He addressed the sheriff. "Sheriff McFarland, is there a problem?"

"Yes, Pastor, we have counted over seventy-five cars on the campgrounds."

"Thank you for the information, Sheriff. With that many cars, I will expect a nice offering this morning. Perhaps I will be able to finally finance a vacation in Finland."

There wasn't any laughter. Many were unsure of what was happening. I knew I was. I moved closer to my father. He put his arm around me.

"Pastor –"

"You can call me the Reverend Karl Levanieman. I am a pastor of the Finnish Lutheran Congregation."

"Then, Reverend Levanieman, do you know the ordinance for the number of vehicles at a church service is limited to fifty?"

"Yes, I do."

"There are least twenty-five cars over the limit in the lot."

"Yes, and there are even more since you arrived."

The people slowed the pace of fanning themselves. I even saw one or two smiles. Uncle Karl's poise was magnificent this morning.

"Reverend, this is a violation of the city ordinance."

"Sir, we are not in the city."

Over half the attendees seemed more confident now. Uncle Karl's firmness and attempt at humor was working. It softened the sheriff's forcefulness. Dad squeezed my hand.

Sheriff McFarland moved forward. Pushing aside the overflow of people in the middle aisle, he walked up to Uncle Karl. This squelched the smiles.

Many of the men present had been intimidated in the underground mine shafts by Pinkertons and stalked in the company stores by union busters. Most of these harassed miners had not shared those experiences with their families. They just kept the incidents between themselves. They didn't want their children scared. Now the intimidation they had kept from their families seemed about to break out into the open.

McFarland continued, "We want twenty-five cars removed from the park."

"There appears to be a misunderstanding about geography," Karl replied and stepped off the platform. He walked around the sheriff, blocking the congregation's line of sight on McFarland. "I am going to continue with the scheduled hymn on the program. After we finish singing, I am going to distribute communion. I know communion was not planned, so you are free to leave at that time. If you care to stay, please feel free to participate or just watch. I promise this will be a short activity."

Much to the surprise of everyone, Sheriff McFarland turned and walked to the back of the hall. Just as McFarland reached the doorway, we heard a shot outside. The congregation gasped and glanced nervously at the sheriff's men. The sheriff motioned to his men not to move.

Four more shots rang out.

Uncle Karl walked over to the piano player and whispered. Heikala signaled to the members of the band to play *Finlandia* softly in the background. Karl directed the ushers to pass plates around the crowd. Each plate had a loaf of bread torn into pieces.

We heard three more shots. At each shot, the crowd flinched.

When the shots ceased, Sheriff McFarland opened the doors, motioned his men out, and closed the doors.

The crowd then looked at Uncle Karl. He directed, "Please take a piece of bread. When the plate comes by, hold it in your hand and think about a time when you were helped by someone. I will pause a while for us to take some bread and reflect." Uncle Karl closed his eyes and looked thoughtful.

After a while, he opened his eyes. "If that person who helped you is here this morning, go over and thank him or her with a hug or handshake. If you cannot reach the person because of the large crowd, look at him or her and wave. Take your time. Ignore your thoughts about what might be going on outside. Focus on each other. Be thankful. We don't need to hurry. This is a time for us to build our community."

Uncle Karl walked down from the platform and over to an older lady who had worked at Mesaba Park since the land was purchased. He hugged her; she cried. Uncle Karl held her for a while. Her tears flowed. Then he shook the hands of her husband and said something to both. The man laid his head on Uncle Karl's shoulder. Karl gave him a strong embrace and kissed them both on their foreheads. That set the example for the rest.

I was amazed. All the hugging and shaking hands awakened something in the crowd. I watched the people's reactions. When I saw Grandpa Mattai and Grandma Grace, I went over to them. Grace had tears in her eyes. She squeezed me tight. Grandpa was hugging Unlucky. They both stopped and hugged me. That felt good.

People moved back to their original pews and chairs. My cousin Karla gave me a squeeze as she passed.

Five loud shots rang out.

Uncle Karl raised his eyes toward the pavilion's ceiling and prayed, "Thank you, Lord, for your death on the cross and your resurrection from the dead. We remember this during our taking of communion." After a pause he continued in his strong voice, "Please give the communion bread to a person next to you. When you receive the bread broken for you, chew and swallow."

Wine was passed up and down the rows. Everyone sipped.

In the background, the members of Viola Turpeinen's band continued to play *Finlandia*. When everyone finished the wine, Uncle Karl motioned for everyone to stand. They stood. He led them in the lyrics of *Finlandia*:

O, Finland, behold, your day is dawning,
The threat of night has been banished away,
And the lack of morning in the brightness sings,
As though the very firmament would sing.
The powers of the night are vanquished by the morning light,
Your day is dawning, O land of birth.
O, rise, Finland, rise up high
Your head, wreathed with great memories.
O, rise, Finland, you showed to the world
That you drove away the slavery,
And that you did not bend under oppression,
Your day has come, O land of birth.

Uncle Karl dismissed everyone with these instructions, "Before we go outside, I want you to take some time to find peace and calmness inside yourselves and each other.

"We don't know why the sheriff and his men visited us this morning, and we don't know how many others were outside. We also don't know what has happened since the sheriff and his men left our service. And we don't know if these men have left the campgrounds.

"When you leave, stay together in groups. If you see anything amiss, stay calm. I ask you not to leave the park. I will make sure messengers are sent around the park to inform all of you as to what the rest of the day holds.

"Would the board members of the federation join me by the doors to shake the hands of the congregation? Once everyone has left, the board will meet with me by the bonfire pit and go over the plans for the rest of the day."

Along with the other board members, Dad rose and walked to the doors.

As the west entrance doors were opened, I held my breath. I imagined everyone else was doing the same. For those first few seconds, no one moved. My sister Hannah squeezed my hand so tightly that my fingers started to go numb. "I have to go potty," Hannah whispered. I tried to smile. To stay calm in front of Hannah and Tommy, I hummed Finlandia's last stanza.

O, rise, Finland, you showed to the world
That you drove away the slavery,
And that you did not bend under oppression,
Your day has come, O land of birth.

The three of us and Mom were the first in line to exit the hall. As I stepped out, I looked up. The sky was a bright blue, the same color we had seen over the lake from inside the hall. I didn't know why I thought it might have been a different color. No one was talking near us, but I heard a conversation or two behind us. I craned my head around to see the length of the line. My grandparents were in back of the hall by the inside doors to the kitchen area. I didn't see Unlucky and my cousin Karla. Hanging onto Hannah with my left hand and Tommy with my right, I pushed ahead of Mom and got outside so that I could take Hannah to the outhouse.

I glanced to the left and noticed that Dad had left the building. I wondered why he had not stayed to shake hands. He was standing with Unlucky, Impi, and Toivo. They were blocking our view of the car and didn't move toward me or Mom. I saw the front bumper behind them, shining in the sun. But something wasn't right ... The car seemed to be parked at a funny angle like when Dad had run over a large branch. I dropped my gaze to the ground below the car. Dad and Unlucky's coats were on the ground in front of the car. They appeared to have just slid off the hood. Broken fingers of glass reached out from underneath both their jackets and stretched across the grass toward me.

Oh, my God, I thought. *The windshield of our car is broken! Is a tire flat, too?*

"I have to go to the bathroom real bad," Hannah whispered urgently. I began humming the hymn again. I steered her and Tommy to the right, away from Dad and our car, toward the outhouses. As we approached, I noticed the air there smelled funny. It wasn't the waste. It wasn't the fire embers. It was more sulferish - like the smell of fireworks wafting in the wind on the Fourth of July. *Discharged shotgun shells!* I thought. *That's what I smell!*

Something didn't seem right. Concerned about Hannah and Tommy's safety, I stopped moving toward the outhouses. I glanced to my left. I saw Mom talking to Dad and Unlucky. Continuing to turn my head, I noticed a large group of people outside the hall. Everyone seemed uncertain about what to do. Nobody was moving. I looked back toward the outhouses.

"Varoom!" A loud explosion splintered the women's outhouse and sent shards of wood flying in all directions.

The force of the blast pushed me backward, and I fell to the ground. Tommy and Hannah dropped on top of me, screaming. Blood from Hannah's face dripped on me. "Mommy! Mommy!" Hannah cried.

I felt her small heart race as she lay on me. Tommy seemed shocked after the first scream. He was quiet. I rolled over, gathered Hannah and Tommy in my arms, and covered them for their protection. Before I could wipe my face or theirs, Unlucky yelled, "Vaara! Vaara! On the ground. Everybody on the ground! Vaara! Vaara!"

I covered Hannah and Tommy's faces. When I looked up, I caught sight of Unlucky whisking Mom and others back inside the hall. Fixated on us, Mom was not cooperating. She was moving backward slowly. Dad hurried over to her and whispered in her ear. Evidently, what he said was effective because Mom reluctantly turned and followed the others into the hall. Dad and Impi nudged in the stragglers and closed the doors.

"Pow!"

There was a second explosion. The men's outhouse exploded. I felt the ground tremble.

"Vaara! Vaara!" Unlucky yelled. Hannah and Tommy were crying. Their fear increased mine. Hannah tried to squirm away. I held her tight, and her wriggling increased.

Joe, Mom, Dad! Where are you? screamed my heart. I tried to calm myself. My mind swirled.

"Sara, Sara!" Joe called. I didn't move. I didn't see him. His voice sounded outside the hall but not in front. Then I felt Joe crawl next to me. "Sara, I'm here. God, where did the blood come from?"

I turned. Joe's face was next to mine. I felt his breath on my face. My terrified feeling was reflected in his eyes. "Hannah is hurt. I'm scared."

Joe placed his arm over us. His steady breathing calmed me. I remembered how Kaveri calmed me when I used to snuggle next to him on Grandma's kitchen floor.

Expecting another explosion, I tensed. Things happen in threes flashed through my mind.

Suddenly, Dad was leaning over us. "Sara, are you hurt?"

"No, Dad, but Hannah…," I whispered shakily. "Something hit her when the outhouse exploded. She's got blood on her face. I don't think it's bad, though."

"Andy and I forced your mother back through the hall to the kitchen with the promise that I would get you kids. Joe, help Sara up."

Joe stood and, with this arm around my waist, pulled me up like a rag doll. As soon as I was off Hannah, Dad picked her up. She was crying. "How's my little girl?" Dad soothed her as he gently touched the wound on her forehead, "Rakastan sinua kallista aikaani yksi, Rakastan sinua. (Love you my precious one) Kallista aikaani yksi."

Hannah smiled weakly and laid her head on Dad's shoulder. Joe bent down and picked up Tommy. Some of Hannah's blood was on him, too. Dad noticed. Joe tried wiping the blood. When it wiped cleanly, Joe directed to Dad, "Han on satu. (He isn't hurt.)"

"Kiitaa siita, etta Taivaan isa. (Thank our father in heaven)," Dad replied. "Follow me to the hall."

My knees felt weak. I swayed. With Tommy in his left arm, Joe put his right arm around me. "C'mon, Sara. Let's go to the hall. Your mom's there."

I can't remember how we got inside.

Mom had not waited in the kitchen. As Dad opened the hall door, she was right there. Seeing the blood on Hannah, Tommy, and me, she stiffened and gasped. Before she could say anything, Dad handed Hannah to her. "Mother, Tässä on arvokasta. Hän on hieman hidastetta ylitettäessä. (Here is our precious one. She has a little bump)," he began, downplaying Hannah's wound to calm Hannah and Mom. "You'll want to take her to the kitchen, clean her up, and give her a cookie. Hän on rohkea prinsessa. (She's a brave princess.)"

Mom instantly mirrored Dad's calm. "Yes, sweetheart, let's clean you up and find a cookie. Joe, bring Sara and Tommy along. Sara looks like she needs to sit down."

"Once you get Sara and Tommy settled in the kitchen, come back and go outside with me," Dad instructed Joe.

In the kitchen, Joe gently helped me sit down and handed Tommy to me. He seemed reluctant to leave. "Go with Dad. I'm okay," I assured him.

"I'll be back as soon as I can," Joe replied, concern evident on his face. After one long look, he left the room and went back outside with Dad.

McFarland had run from the parking lot to the hall. His deputies were with him. He had watched our procession and was concerned. "Everyone all right?" he asked Martin.

"My Hannah's hurt. Sara's pretty shook up. Tommy seems okay."

Hearing Hannah was injured, McFarland grimaced. "Damn! How bad?"

"She'll be okay," Martin responded. Then he added, "Joe helped me get them all inside to Elizabeth."

"Joe," McFarland said, "you go with my deputies. Help them scour the brush and trees along the bottom of the hill by the outhouses. See if you can find out what caused the explosions."

Joe and the deputies spread across the bottom of the hill, searching.

McFarland stayed back with Martin and Toivo. "Damn it, Martin. This has gotten out of control. I didn't expect your car to be vandalized. And, shit, I didn't want anything to happen to your kids."

"We've got to do something here, McFarland –"

"I feel like such a fool. I shouldn't have trusted that bastard Thomas … now Johnson seems to be the same. Damn, Martin, there isn't a one in that bunch who cares who they hurt."

"I wish they all had been taking a dump when those houses blew!" Toivo exclaimed. "I'd even have helped clean up the mess! Then I'd have thrown their leftovers in the bonfire pit and burned them to ashes."

"Hannah…"McFarland sighed. He turned resolute. His chin stiffened. His stance quickened. He appeared taller than Martin or Toivo.

The three looked toward where the outhouses had been standing. Joe and one of Robert's deputies were pushing over the only side that was still standing. Crack! It snapped, bounced off a Norway pine, and rolled over a congested group of hazelnut bushes. Surprisingly, the wood slab then bounced back, tossed by two men.

They yelled, "Take that, you Commies! Damn Bolshevik lovers! Why don't you go to Russia?"

Then they took off running up the hill toward the bonfire area.

Standing by Martin and McFarland, Toivo yelled back, "You bastards! Sin Bitchstes!"

He rumbled in the direction of what was left of the outhouses and stared at the two men as they climbed the hill, cussing them out at the top of his lungs.

McFarland ran to stand by Toivo. Pointing his pistol harmlessly upward, McFarland commanded, "Stop, or I'll shoot!"

The men kept climbing. McFarland shot twice. Toivo was looking for a rock to throw. Joe bellowed, "Dad! Uncle Launo! Niilo! Arvi! Where are you? We need your help! Get those guys!"

Launo, Niilo, Arvi, and Gustav appeared at the top of the hill. Niilo leapt downward, throwing his body in front of both men. The three rolled backward and came to a halt near Toivo. Toivo swung at the first man to stand up and knocked him down. When the second stood, Toivo punched him, too, swinging wildly. Niilo kicked at the first downed man. Meanwhile, Arvi had slid down the hill to help and arrived just as Nillo kicked the second guy. McFarland and his men surrounded the five.

The front doors of the hall opened. Stephan Steblibovich and Deputy Johnson came out followed by five others in uniform. No one else exited. Steblibovich and Johnson had directed the rest of the crowd out the back of the hall to the beach area. From there they easily accessed the campgrounds and cabins, where most of them were staying.

"Victor! Howard!" Deputy Johnson shouted. "What the hell is going on here?"

Hurrying over to the downed men, the deputy and his men helped Victor and Howard up. By then, Gustav and Launo had descended the hill and joined the group. Arvi gave Niilo a congratulatory punch in the arm. McFarland said something to the four and gave Nillo a slap on the behind. Arvi walked over to his dad Impi. Gustav, Launo, and NIilo headed back up the hill, nervous about the presence of Deputy Johnson. Joe saw his opportunity to return to Sara. While everyone was distracted, he slipped around the hall to the beachside door of the kitchen.

"We sure blew them to hell!" said Victor.

Howard smiled. "We used their own dynamite. Mr. Armstrong will be proud of us!"

"Knock it off," said Johnson. "I'll ask the questions."

The deputy looked toward McFarland. Toivo was waving his hands. "Sheriff, those two bastards were with Thomas when they jumped you at the Chisholm maintenance sheds last fall. I'd recognize them anywhere."

"Damn, you're right, Toivo! Victor, you're the one who pulled me to the ground," McFarland growled.

"Dad, those are the two guys Joe and I saw in Chisholm beating up the sheriff!" Arvi exclaimed.

"You bastards," screamed Toivo. He lunged at both, but Steblibovich grabbed Tiovo and held him back.

"What's that fat-assed Finlander talking about, Sheriff?" asked Johnson.

"Don't play stupid with me," barked McFarland, glaring back.

"Tell that stinking Finlander he had no business smacking my men," growled Deputy Johnson. "We make the arrests, not him!"

"These aren't even your men. They are Thomas's misfits," retorted McFarland.

"One thing at a time here, McFarland," said Johnson.

"Don't give me that one thing at a time bit, Johnson. Maybe you didn't notice little Hannah's bloody face…"

"Hannah? What are you talking about?"

"I didn't think you'd know a little girl was injured from the blast. Just like you're going to tell me you didn't know your two men blew up those outhouses. You'll probably blame it on some Finlanders…"

"Everybody is a Finlander here, McFarland," Johnson returned. "In fact, I am beginning to think you are one in disguise."

"You imposter of justice," McFarland responded. "You don't know the first thing about –"

"Just do your job, you half-Finlander," Johnson said, cutting off McFarland's remarks. "Sheriff, I want to know why this fat guy was harassing my men. And where is that younger fellow that was here? What happened to him?"

"You know damn well what happened here. Your two sons of bitches blew up those outhouses," Toivo snarled. "You better take them back to Duluth right now and hide them up Armstrong's butt or I'll –"

McFarland jabbed his elbow into Toivo's ribs. Martin leaned over and said something to Toivo.

In hopes of getting McFarland and Johnson to tone down and cooperate, Martin stepped closer to the two men. "Let's move away from this area. I don't know if more explosives have been set. I want to get some men over here to check. When they are certain the area is safe, they can clean it up a bit before this afternoon's ceremony."

Victor glared at Martin. "You're not in charge here, Finlander. You don't tell the deputy of the Duluth police force what he does or doesn't do."

"And you don't talk to the president of the Co-op's Federation like that," ordered McFarland.

Johnson grabbed Victor's arm and pulled him aside. "Keep your mouth shut, Victor. Don't you understand what you did? You and Howard blew up those outhouses right here in front of everyone. Some little girl got hurt. Now you let me handle this, or I'll let McFarland throw you in his jail."

Victor flashed an angry look at Johnson. "Well, you chickenshit deputy. Whose side are you on? I'm going to tell Armstrong what a wuss you are!"

"You'll have to crawl out of his asshole first to do that," inserted Toivo.

Victor clenched his fists and shoved them into Toivo's face. Then he kicked a rock that bounced toward McFarland and veered left. The sheriff looked at the rock a moment. "Go ahead and get the men you need for clean up," advised McFarland.

Martin nodded and motioned to Impi, Arvi, and Andy to follow him.

As the men walked away, McFarland turned to Johnson. "Get these two out of my jurisdiction right now, or they will be in my jail. Take the rest of your men, too, and leave town immediately."

Without a reply, Johnson did as McFarland instructed, herding the grumbling men out of the park and back to Duluth.

When the beachside door to the kitchen opened, I looked up. Joe entered. He immediately locked eyes with me and quickly strode over. "How are you doing?" he asked.

"Better," I replied. "Listening to Mom sing while she takes care of Hannah has calmed me." I searched his face. "What happened outside? I heard more shots."

"We found the guys who blew up the outhouses. They were hiding at the bottom of the hill. They tried to get away by running up the hill to the bonfire pit. The sheriff shot into the air to get them to stop."

"Did they?"

"No. Dad, Uncle Launo, Niilo, and Arvi were at the top of the hill. Niilo leapt for them, and they all rolled down the hill to Toivo. The two of them took care of the guys until the sheriff could get there. Arvi helped, too." Joe squeezed my hand. "They won't set any more explosives around the park."

Joe sat down beside me. "I was afraid today," he admitted.

"Afraid?" I repeated.

"Not of the explosions."

"Then what?"

Joe didn't immediately respond.

Mom had finished washing Hannah and was drying her with a towel. Mom still played peek-a-boo. She rubbed Hannah's face, stopped, threw the towel on my sister's head, had it sit there for a moment, pulled it off, and said, "Boo."

Hannah giggled. Mom dried her again and repeated the peek-a-boo.

Joe broke his silence. "I was afraid you had died today."

"I thought I smelled something funny before the explosion, but I wasn't expecting it. When I heard the loud bangs, I didn't know what was happening," I admitted.

"Before you came out of the hall, my dad, uncle, cousin, Arvi, and I were watching those two guys place the sticks of dynamite in the outhouses. We wanted to wait until they had everything set up, and then we were going to head down the hill and nab them," Joe explained.

"Why didn't you?"

"The shooting distracted us. We went to see what that was all about. When we got back, you were out of the hall and headed to the outhouses. Hannah and Tommy were with you. Rather than yell a warning, Dad said, 'Joe, run down and stop Sara, right now!' He thought I had time to do that. He didn't think those guys would blow up the outhouses until everybody was out of the hall so they could scare the most people. They must have gotten spooked or something. I was halfway down the hill when the first outhouse exploded. I slipped and rolled. When I got up, you were down on the ground. I got scared. I thought you were hurt. I was up and running again when the second one blew. I thought you had been blown to death!" Joe shivered.

He looked down, trying to hide his emotions. I placed my hand on his chin and gently tilted his head up. Joe didn't resist. His blue eyes shone bright wet with tears. He grasped my other hand. I felt the warmth of his face. I looked into his eyes. "I thought I had lost you, Sara," Joe whispered. "Then I saw the blood, and I could hardly breathe. I don't want to lose you, Sara."

"I don't want to lose, you, either, Joe," I murmured before I leaned forward and gave him a long kiss.

34   Aftermath

"Hey, Sheriff, over here … by the bonfire pit! We are having a little awards ceremony for you!" Impi jested, waving his arm.

"When would you like us to give you your award?" quipped Unlucky Andy.

Everyone watched McFarland approach. Robert wasn't moving fast. His gait was as steady as the look on his face. A slight smile warmed his face, yet his dark hazel eyes were cautious. Stephan walked next to him. Arriving at the gathering, they both sat down, McFarland next to Martin and Stephan near Unlucky Andy. McFarland's face brightened. He smiled. "I do prefer receiving the award from you guys rather than from those who turned tail and ran."

"So where are they?" Impi asked. "Did Toivo chase them back to Duluth?"

Impi snickered. Everyone turned and looked at McFarland, waiting for his response.

"I am sure they are near Duluth by now," answered McFarland.

"And may I say, God grant them speed… great speed!" added Reverend Karl. His joke prompted a few laughs.

Rather than laugh, McFarland placed his hand on Martin's knee. "Once again, I'm sorry about what happened to Hannah." McFarland sighed. "I am glad she's all right… just a little scratched, right?"

"She'll be fine. Hannah's a brave one," Martin replied. "But I was shook up a bit, especially since the explosions occurred after I had seen what had happened to my car. At that moment the danger Armstrong presents to me and my family hit home."

McFarland patted Martin's knee reassuringly.

"Maybe you should hire Toivo to be your bodyguard!" joked Impi. "Toivo may have a huge ass, but he's quick and strong."

"Pardon my bluntness, McFarland," inserted Reverend Karl. "I don't mean to minimize what happened to Hannah, Martin, but what was all that mischief outside the hall this morning before the outhouses blew? You had mentioned to me you were going to interrupt the service. But destroy outhouses? Mess up cars?"

Unlucky Andy attempted to deflect the blame Karl seemed to be directing toward McFarland. "Did you detain those two crazy guys … Victor and Howard?"

Before McFarland could answer, Matthew Wirtannen interjected, "Did you see the damaged cars out there by the road when you and Stephan came in?"

Neither McFarland nor Stephan answered. Matthew persisted, "I'll ask again. Coming into camp, did you see some of the cars out by the road? I saw three damaged cars –"

Directing his comments to McFarland, Reverend Karl interrupted, "I bet that's the result of the gunshots we heard after you left the dedication service."

Matthew finished his observations. "I didn't recognize any of the cars. They must have been out-of-towners."

"Did any of you walk around the grounds after the service to see what had happened?" asked Stephan pointedly.

No one responded.

Reverend Karl placated the deputy, "I asked the board members at the dedication service to meet around the bonfire pit after we had dismissed everyone. I don't think anyone took time for exploring. Besides, word got around that Hannah may have been seriously hurt. That raised the anxiety level even higher. People weren't interested in poking around and being surprised by an explosion."

Matthew ignored Karl's mention of the anxiety levels at the park. He still wanted his questions answered. He looked squarely at McFarland and made his demand again. "What about the tires shot on the three cars on the road near the parking lot? And the broken windows?"

"The damage is not as bad as it seems," snapped McFarland. "Seven cars total were damaged at the park. And five of the cars were ones Gustav and his brother Launo had brought from his lumber camp last night."

"Launo? Gustav?" questioned Matthew, his briskness increasing. "How are they involved?"

"Excuse me," stated Martin. "I want us to focus on why we're here. Our reason is not to point fingers or figure out who had screwed up this morning." Martin looked around at the group. He wasn't smiling. "As leaders we have a responsibility to all the people here today to let them know we're a community working together for the common good. We won't be bullied."

"I did not intend to be so intense. I apologize," murmured Matthew.

McFarland nodded his head in acceptance of Matthew's apology. Stephan gave a quick smile. Impi turned and spat on the ground behind the log where he was sitting.

Martin continued, "I want to thank McFarland for acting quickly after the outhouse explosions."

Martin paused to make sure he had everyone's attention. Then he stood and walked around the bonfire pit. Everyone watched him. "First I thought Karl's instruction to meet here was odd. I don't think I've been at the bonfire pit during the day…It didn't seem right … Just like you, I'm here in the evenings, having great conversations and telling stories from the day – wonderful stories – stories that make me feel good about what we believe in and what we do."

He stopped and let that thought settle. Then Martin resumed walking and continued, "I want that to be the experience tonight when I sit around this bonfire pit and tell stories from today. So I ask you to join me in rethinking today and what we do. That way, tonight we will tell stories around the bonfire which keep us bold and promote the common good."

Having returned to where he had been sitting before his speech, Martin sat back down.

"I'm in," said Unlucky Andy.

Everyone agreed.

"I suggest that we proceed with the awards ceremony. In fact, I think we should present our own award to McFarland," stated Reverend Karl.

"That would mean a lot to me," replied McFarland.

"I agree with that idea," concurred Martin.

McFarland smiled.

"Karl and I can plan the particulars needed for the presentation," directed Martin. "While we do that, Robert, why don't you, Impi, and Stephan check on which cars need repairs?"

Robert McFarland nodded. "I think that's a good idea. We can figure out whose cars have been damaged without asking everyone and stirring things up."

"Since there are only a few, I think those owners would appreciate your meeting with them one-on-one and letting them know what had happened to their cars. They are all at their cabins now and easy to reach," offered Martin.

"Can we get them some help with the repairs?" wondered Matthew.

"Gary Maki is here," said Unlucky Andy. "He has worked with me on some of the farms in the area. He's done some work for Gustav and Launo, too. Maybe he would do the repairs and just charge for the parts, not the labor."

"Gary. He's a good man," volunteered Impi, "and a good mechanic. I know where to find him."

"Impi," suggested McFarland, "how about if you, Stephan, and me go talk with him first. Let's find a way for him to do some fixing right here at the park."

"I think that's a possibility. And a show of solidarity. Thanks!" praised Martin. "Gary regularly comes to the co-op. I am impressed with him. I know he'll help out."

"Before we came, I saw Gustav, Launo and the rest of the group going into the kitchen," said Unlucky Andy. "On your way to talk to Gary, let them know what you're doing. They may have some ideas or want to help out."

"Impi, ask Arvi to help, too. He's learned a little bit about mechanics working with for the Koivus this summer. Include him, too," suggested Martin.

Impi nodded. "Let's go!" he urged and walked away from the fire pit.

Impi led the way, and McFarland and Stephan followed him down the hill to the hall. Matthew turned to Martin. "While you and Karl work on the ceremony, I would like to walk around the park grounds and let everyone know what's happening the rest of the day."

"Yes, you and Andy tell all the campers and others who came this morning what is planned for the rest of the day. Assure them there will be no more intimidation by Oliver Mining," directed Martin.

"Are we sticking to the original program?" asked Unlucky Andy.

"I see no need to change anything," Reverend Karl answered.

"Neither do I," agreed Martin. "If anyone asks, make it clear Hannah's not dying or dead."

"I wonder if having Elizabeth with us might bring reassurance that the rest of the day will be peaceful," proposed Unlucky Andy. "Most people know her from the theaters here and in Duluth."

"I am sure Elizabeth would be glad to help," Martin responded. "I'll make sure Mattai and Grace take care of Hannah, Tommy, and Sara."

"As I think about it, I know my sister would love to sing a song for everyone this afternoon," added Reverend Karl.

"Why don't the four us go talk with her," said Martin. "On the way, we can review the order of events. That will help Andy and Matthew put together what they will share with all those gathered for the day."

As the four stood up to leave, Joe appeared. He walked over to Martin. "Mr. Niemi, I want to talk with you."

"Can we wait till later?"

"I want to do it now."

35   Unexpected Announcement

"Sheriff Robert McFarland!"

Standing to the right of my father and in front of the microphone, McFarland looked an inch taller than my father. I watched him look out at the people gathered. He appeared proud and satisfied. He was older than my dad but not as old as Mattai. He had been sheriff more than eighteen years, longer than I had been alive.

Applause sprinkled across the hall, a splash one place, a pitter-patter in another. Like a refreshing shower, the clapping continued about three minutes and then stopped.

"Matthew Wirtannen and Reverend Karl Levanieman please join Sheriff McFarland and me on the platform. Please bring the Mesaba Range Co-op Federation recognition award with you," requested Dad.

As he followed Matthew up on to the platform, my Uncle Karl carried the award. Matthew stopped just to the right of McFarland. Uncle Karl halted to the right of Matthew. The four stood waiting for the flash from the *Tyomies's* camera. After the flash, my dad reached over, lifted up the microphone stand, and placed it in front of Matthew.

"As Chairman of the Mesaba Range Co-op Federation, the Federation acknowledges your support of the Finnish peoples of Minnesota," Matthew pronounced and stepped back, allowing Uncle Karl to place the award in the sheriff's hands. I recognized it as the model of the Park Grandpa Mattai had been creating in the workshop in the rear of the co-op. While it wasn't fancy or even painted, I thought it was cute. They waited through another camera flash.

Then Dad stepped over to the microphone. "I personally want to thank Sheriff McFarland for his friendship over the years. I know we weren't always in agreement, but I always respected our sheriff as fair." He looked at McFarland and extended his hand.

McFarland shook Dad's hand. Uncle Karl showed his approval by clapping. Applause from the crowd followed. During the applause, the sheriff, Uncle Karl, and Matthew walked off the platform.

As I watched them leave, I felt nervous. Joe moved closer to me. He didn't seem nervous. Dad announced, "Joe Koivu approached me this morning to ask if he and my daughter Sara could have five minutes to make a special announcement. I agreed. I'd like for Joe and Sara to come up on the platform."

Dad turned and looked at Joe and me standing near the front right of the platform. Dad smiled, put his mouth close to the microphone, and whispered loud enough for everyone to hear him tease us, "Now's not the time to be shy."

"Let's go," Joe said, taking my hand. I loved the strong decisiveness I heard in Joe's tone.

I gave his hand a slow, firm squeeze. "I love you, Joe." I felt secure. I knew nothing would ever happen to us.

We walked to the center of the pavilion. Joe paused and smiled at Dad. Then we continued to the steps on the platform's side. Once atop, we walked to my dad, turned, and looked out at the people gathered. I thought about how my mother must feel adored on stage. What a feeling! What a sight!

Joe's mother Irene sat on a bench in the front row. I had never seen her in a dress before. She hadn't had an occasion to wear one, especially since she'd been sick. She was adorable; her dress had long sleeves in a light blue color. Irene's fair skin glowed. Her light blond hair was pulled back and held in place by a carved wooden broach from her mother. She looked beautiful. I saw the same energy and pride that must have captured Gustav's heart.

I had red maple leaves and pussy willows in my yellow hair. The gold thread braiding on my linen blouse swirled Nordic-like patterns across my chest. A full length earth-brown cheesecloth-textured skirt brought the fullness of mother earth from the soles of my feet to my waist. I thought of myself as an autumn princess announcing her engagement to her community.

Gustav led Irene onto the platform, supporting each of her steps. Full of emotion, his brown eyes danced. When Joe and his dad embraced, I got goose bumps. Then Joe held both his mother's hands as he lightly kissed her on the cheek. Applause erupted. I even heard a whistle or two. Apparently, the show of emotion ignited something because the applause grew. People started to stand up; the volume inside the hall increased.

I watched as the heads of those gathered turned to the left of Joe and me. My mother had walked onto the platform. She stood there shining like Saint Lucia. The wreath of flowers in her hair radiated love up through the stems to the blossoms crowning her headpiece and out to the people. Her smile widened slowly; everyone was on their feet. I expected her to sing! She stopped to the left of my father and took his hand in hers.

"Boom, boom," Dad tapped the microphone again. "Boom, boom." He stepped back and motioned for Joe and me to come to the microphone. We did. Joe's palms were sweaty. He leaned too close, and his lips touched the metal screen. His head popped back quickly. "Ouch!"

Laughter broke out. Dad stepped up, adjusted the microphone, and whispered in Joe's ear. Joe cleared his throat. "Good afternoon. I am Joseph Koivu, and this is Sara Niemi. You may recognize us as the life guard and the kitchen help – I mean cook ..." Joe stalled. He looked at me. I winked. Joe continued, "Today is the grand opening dedication for Mesaba Park Festival and Campgrounds. Sara and I welcome you."

Now Joe appeared to be nervous. I hadn't ever seen Joe this nervous.

"Sara and I have an announcement to make." The cheering started before he said anything. People started to stand. Arvi and Mika were jumping up and down. They began chanting, "Kiss her! Kiss her!"

I think I even remember a little stomping to the chant. Andy had the drummer in the band do a drum roll. Then Karla came to the front, took the extra drumsticks, and began hitting the cymbals. Everyone clapped, yelled, and whooped more! I remembered disengaging my hand from Joe's, slipping my hand down his wrist, placing his hand on my heart, and crying. They knew what we were going to say; we had said it already by being on the platform together. Or maybe we said it already in the ways we had acted together all the summers working at the park... whatever... Dad shook Joe's hand. Mother put her arms around me. She held me tight. Gustav shook Dad's hand. Irene came over and hugged me. Then she turned to my mother and embraced her. Hannah and Tommy walked over and gave Joe and me the flowers they had picked. Jon and Becky, Joe's brother and sister, did the same.

My father yelled into the microphone, "They are marrying one year from today right here at Mesaba Park!"

I felt my toes tingle. The tingle traveled up my leg and throughout my body. I imagined myself pushing apart a farmer's barbwire fence to open up a passage through which I passed. The grass-covered cow trail led me down to the lake. I pushed aside the tall grasses in front of me and stepped onto the sandy beach. The smell of lake water filled my soul. I stripped off and laid my clothes on the grass. I stepped onto the wood steps nailed on the top side of a large maple tree lying on the shore with its head in the lake. I took five steps and stopped.

Looking down into the water I saw minnow schools. They moved across the lake's floor in crowds. Clouds reflected off the lake's surface. The sun warmed my nakedness. I heard the ducks swimming to my left and frogs croaking on my right. I jumped straight up and landed on the tree top. It bent into the lake, and then bounced back up into the air. I leapt with its motion. Folding my body like a pocket knife, I straightened out and stretched my fingers. They pierced the lake's surface. I found silence under the water. A light tingling in my ear signaled the dive was perfect. Pushing off the lake's sandy bottom, I exploded back up to the lake's surface. I leveled off and floated silently on my back, nipples in the air.

I was the swimmer. The diving board was Joe. The lake was our love.

Joe and I walked off the platform. Our families followed, except for Dad.

We met Oscar Corgan as he came up the steps. He congratulated us and then walked over to my father. They shook hands. Dad introduced Oscar. Oscar held his typed speech in both his hands as he waited for the applause to subside. Once it did, he began. "As Martin said, I am Oscar Corgan. For the past ten years I have lived with my family in Superior, Wisconsin, and managed the *Tyomies* newspaper and Society. Many of you support our paper. I thank you. I have just moved to Virginia, Minnesota, to direct the Work People's Co-op store. Most importantly, I represent the Karelian Technical Aid Agency (KTAA).

"The KTAA is looking for all kinds of skilled workers: miners, loggers, fishermen, machinists, mechanics, carpenters, and plumbers to come to Karelia, Finland. Karelia is like northern Minnesota; it has forests and lakes rich with pine and birch. Our comrades will build the new world there. No ruling class, no rich industrialists, or kings and czars will tell us what to do there. We will just be workers working together for the common good. Our communist comrades invite you to join them. You can be pioneers all over again. You will live in log cabins with no electricity and work hard from morning until night building the Utopia we could not build here in Minnesota.

"For four hundred dollars, the Karelian Technical Aid Agency will arrange your travel, take care of immigration, and ship your tools, supplies, and families. I am asking you to join this great immigration of Canadian and American Finns to participate in building the brand new country of the Soviet Union. Help create a new land where workers will rule, where there will be no unemployment, and no exploitation. Everyone will be comrades. This is history! Let's make it together!"

I noticed Joe had leaned forward and was taking in Oscar's every word. We had just very publicly become engaged. A sick feeling started in the pit of my stomach and slowly spread throughout my body. I felt cold and shaky. What did Oscar's words mean for our future? Did Joe want to go to Finland? Would I be following him there?

Author Stephen Ivancic volunteers at the Minnesota History Center in St. Paul, Minnesota, and posed next to the *then now wow* exhibit there.

Stephen Ivancic

My grandfather worked in the underground mines on the Mesaba Iron Range in northern Minnesota. My father worked for the railroad which transported the mined and processed ore to the docks in Duluth. As a young man, I was employed by United States Steel in their Minnesota ore operations. The foreman on my first midnight shift in the open pit mining operation at Mt. Iron had been a co-worker with Grandfather many years before. From these sources came stories of earlier days when the miners organized into unions. When I worked on my doctorate focusing on the evolution of technical colleges in Minnesota, I collected more stories of organizing among articles on the growth of industrial training and vocational education. My imagination forged a fictitious story of a young Finnish couple growing up in the middle of the radical politics of unionization.